EVERYMAN, I will go with thee

and be thy guide,

In thy most need to go by thy side

SIR WALTER SCOTT

Born at Edinburgh in 1771. Called to the
Bar, 1792; Sheriff-Depute of Selkirkshire,
1799; a Principal Clerk of Session, 1806.
Moved to Abbotsford in 1812, and died
there on 21st September 1832. Created a
baronet in 1820.

SIR WALTER SCOTT

The Talisman

PREFACE AND GLOSSARY BY
W. M. PARKER

DENT: LONDON, MELBOURNE AND TORONTO
EVERYMAN'S LIBRARY
DUTTON: NEW YORK

© Introduction, J. M. Dent & Sons Ltd, 1956

All rights reserved
Printed in Great Britain
by
Biddles Ltd, Guildford, Surrey
for
J. M. DENT & SONS LTD
Aldine House · 33 Welbeck Street · London W1
This edition was first published in
Everyman's Library in 1906
Last reprinted 1980

Published in the U.S.A. by arrangement
with J. M. Dent & Sons Ltd

No 144   Hardback ISBN 0 460 00144 2
No 1144   Paperback ISBN 0 460 01144 8

PREFACE

THE theme of the crusades attracted Scott at intervals throughout his literary career. In 1817 he touched on it in his essay on 'Chivalry' where, remarking that many illustrations might be quoted 'to show the nature of the zeal which was supposed to actuate a Christian knight,' he observed that it was needless to ransack works of fiction for that purpose. 'The real history of the crusades, founded on the spirit of chivalry, and on the restless and intolerant zeal which was blended by the churchmen with this military establishment, are an authentic and fatal proof of the same facts.'[1] Then, towards the end of his life, Scott reverted to a crusading subject for one of his two last novels, *Count Robert of Paris*.

Scott's greater imaginative treatment of the theme, however, was produced in the intervening years when the financial disaster was impending and more or less foreseen. Early in 1825 he was working on *Tales of the Crusaders*. The first of them was *The Betrothed*, which, Lockhart declares, 'found no favour' with Scott's critical printer, James Ballantyne. Roused by this disappointment, Scott wrote *The Talisman*, Ballantyne's satisfaction with which increased as the MS. poured in upon him so that on its completion he pronounced it a masterpiece. While Scott was composing the romance, John Carne, the Cornish travel writer, stayed at Abbotsford, and from him, who had recently been in the Holy Land, Scott received vivid impressions of the scenery near the Dead Sea and Engedi.

The title, *Tales of the Crusaders*, Scott tells us in his Introduction to *The Betrothed*, was determined by the advice of friends rather than by the author's own taste, although 'he saw plainly enough the interest which might be excited by the very name of the Crusades, but he was conscious at the same time that that interest was of a character which it might be more easy to create than to satisfy.' *The Tales*, in four volumes, appeared in the middle of June 1825, and were well received. Since their initial publication, they have been

[1] Supplement to the fourth, fifth, and sixth editions of the *Encyclopaedia Britannica*, vol. iii (1824), p. 118.

translated into French (1825), German (1825), Spanish (1826), Italian (1825 and 1829), Portuguese (1835), Finnish (1880), and Irish Gaelic (1936). Of several *Talisman* stage versions one (1825) was supplied with incidental music by Bishop. There have also been operas, based on the novel, by Giovanni Pacini (1829), Adolphe Adam (1844), and Michael W. Balfe, revised by Macfarren (1874). A favourite book with the young, numerous school editions of *The Talisman* have always been in evidence.

The locality of the tale is Syria; the period 1191-2. The action happens in the desert near the Dead Sea, and in the Crusaders' camp between Jean d'Acre and Ascalon. The plot concerns the Crusade led by Richard Cœur de Lion to the Holy Land and with the adventures of a poor but doughty Scots crusader, known as Sir Kenneth or the Knight of the Leopard, but who is really the Prince Royal of Scotland. The talisman, from which the novel takes its name, is the amulet by which Richard's noble enemy, Saladin, disguised as a physician, cures Richard of sickness. There is a love romance between Sir Kenneth and his kinswoman, Lady Edith Plantagenet. Disguised as a poor knight, the Scots prince is sentenced to death for leaving his post, and chooses to be executed rather than break a vow by disclosing his rank. But his honour is redeemed by his heroic dog, Roswal;[1] he is rescued by Saladin's entreaties; and, having saved the king's life, he obtains his own pardon. Eventually he and Edith marry. The talisman incident has an historical basis in the amulet which was procured by Sir Simon Lockhart of Lee, who, accompanying Lord Douglas on his journey to the Holy Land with the heart of King Robert the Bruce, brought back the talisman to his estate of Lee in Lanarkshire. It continued to have miraculous healing powers, and was thereafter known as the Lee Penny. It is now in the possession of Major Simon Foster Macdonald Lockhart of Lee, the head of that branch of the Lockhart family.[2]

From the time of its first publication *The Talisman* has afforded ground for diverse views among the critics as to the use that can be justifiably made of historical facts in fiction.

---

[1] Scott's staghound Maida was the original of Roswal, the only dog in the Waverley Novels that plays an important part with the exception of Bevis in *Woodstock*.

[2] For a recent account of the Lee Penny see *Curses, Lucks and Talismans* by J. G. Lockhart (1938), pp. 119-29.

First in the field was Charles Mills, who, in *The History of Chivalry*, took Scott to task for his remark that 'the historians substituted the widowed Queen of Naples, sister of Richard, for the bride, and Saladin's brother for the bridegroom' instead of the imaginary Edith and Saladin himself. 'They appear to be ignorant of the existence of Edith of Plantagenet.' 'But,' Mills continued, '"the historians" are correct. . . . The novelist has not supported his assertion by a single historical testimony: and we may defy him to produce a tittle of evidence on his side. . . . If he seriously designed to unite the province of the historian with that of the novelist, he has chosen a very unlucky expedient for his own reputation.'[1] To this Scott made two rejoinders. On 1st November 1825 he wrote to Mills, explaining the difference between the use of actual sources and the literary device of inventing fictional sources for fictional material. And again, in the 1832 Introduction to the novel, Scott replied that Mills 'was not, it may be presumed, aware that romantic fiction naturally includes the power of such invention, which is indeed one of the requisites of the art.'

While the *Edinburgh Magazine* extolled the novel's incidents, characters, diction, and costume, it objected that 'in *The Talisman* there is too little Orientalism for our taste; and what we have is frequently bad.' The *New Monthly Magazine* commented: 'The age of the Crusaders is at once too vast and too visionary to be subjected to that process by which he [Scott] has given reality and present life to distant periods.' After pronouncing that *The Talisman* was as wild as Ariosto,[2] and that Richard was the only good character, the democratic journal, the *Examiner*, asserted that 'even the vulgar begin to yawn at melodrama and processions, turbans and helmets, caftans and coat-armour.' The criticism in the *London Magazine* found Scott's bores worse than ever and deplored the tedious descriptions of clothes and furniture, 'apparently culled from the antiquaries.'

But it remained for the *Quarterly Review* critic to discuss more fully the vexed question of historical fact and fiction. After noting the prevalent prejudice against the historical novel, he stated his own views. 'We are no advocates for the falsification of historical fact, the distortion of character, or the reversion or inversion of events; but we are altogether blind

[1] Vol. i, Preface, pp. xviii–xix.
[2] A good comparison would also be between the treatment of the crusades in *The Talisman* and in Tasso's *Jerusalem Delivered*.

to the evils of embellishing an historical outline with graceful and not improbable fiction, taking advantage of the doubtful points of history, and giving them the colouring most expedient for the fable, or conducive to the cause of truth and morals.' He commended *The Talisman* for surpassing grandeur and effect. 'The story is constructed with the skill of a consummate artist. The incipient poet and novelist might learn from this the proper use of traditionary lore and historical knowledge.'[1]

As a fact, in *The Talisman* Scott attempted 'to avoid settings and characters that might challenge comparison with the better informed Orientalists among his colleagues.' In a tale of the past such as this imagination may quite legitimately come to the aid of fact. John Buchan maintained that an historical novel is one which aims to reconstruct the life and recapture the atmosphere of an age other than that of the writer. Jonathan Nield's definition, on the other hand, was that 'a novel is rendered historical by the introduction of dates, personages, or events, to which indentification can be readily given.' In the present work Scott formed his own judgment as to facts, and kept scrupulously faithful to the *spirit* of the period. This he did despite an occasional anachronism. Verdicts on his performance have differed. Taine censured him for selecting from history only what suited him and for not concerning himself with 'the sensuality and brutality of the Middle Ages or with the epicureanism of the Renaissance.' Prescott thought that by his attention to costume and character Scott raised his novels to historic importance without injuring their interest as works of art. Nassau Senior rated *The Talisman* high because as Scott receded into the remote past his imagination supplied the lack of exact historical material.

It was unnecessary that Scott should visit the East for topographical purposes. He relied on Carne's retailed impressions and on his own reading to create the appropriate atmosphere.[2] And it was to this triumph of imagination that Whitwell Elwin drew attention in his article on 'Sacred Geography' in the *Quarterly Review*, praising 'the extraordinary

---

[1] 'Historical Romance,' *Quarterly Review*, March 1827, p. 530. Sir John Murray has informed me that the reviewer was J. A. Heraud, the poet and dramatist.
[2] Scott succeeded with convincing reproductions of Swiss landscape in *Anne of Geierstein* and of Constantinople in *Count Robert of Paris* although he never visited either Switzerland or Turkey.

insight into the minute lights and shades of the oriental character as depicted in Saladin.'[1] An even more valuable tribute came from Sir George Adam Smith, the eminent historical geographer of the Holy Land. 'Of his [Scott's] geography little need be said' was his comment on the landscape treatment. 'This is as true as the topographical resources at his disposal enabled him to make it. . . . The local colours and the atmosphere are genuine, and on the whole the sense of distances. . . . Scott's portrait of the King is an accurate as well as a living one, attested by contemporary chroniclers, whether Christian or Arab like Beha-el-din, the biographer of Saladin.'[2]

The historical value of *The Talisman* depends chiefly on the characters of King Richard and Saladin, both commended by most readers. Incidentally, Scott has given a more favourable interpretation of Richard than that limned by Gibbon, who thought him the possessor of 'brutal and ferocious valour.' In his treatment of religious sects Scott was often detached, and that attitude is as apparent here in his representation of the Mohammedans as it was in his depiction of the Covenanters in *Old Mortality*. Indeed, *The Talisman* is probably the first, or among the first, of English novels to praise Mohammedans. If some readers find passages in *The Talisman* as arid as the Syrian desert itself, they cannot but respond to such memorable pictures as the lonely coast of the Dead Sea; the scene where Berengaria woos Richard to relenting; the detection of the traitor by the dog; and the rather uncivil loyalty of Tom of the Gills.

After Scott's death in 1832, the MS. of *The Talisman* was bought at a sale in November 1833, by his publisher, Robert Cadell, who died in 1849. It was sold at Christie's on 9th July 1868, but, perhaps by private treaty with the trustees, it passed into the hands of Cadell's son-in-law, the Rev. John Lander, rector of Donnington, Herefordshire. Ultimately the MS. was acquired by Count Vladimir Petrovich Orloff Davidoff, for whom it was bought by Thomson & Bonar, Russian merchants in Old Bond Street. It is possible that Lander may have purchased the MS. at the firm's request on behalf of the count, whose interest in the novel was due to the fact that in

---

[1] *Quarterly Review*, March 1854, pp. 367–8.
[2] In his oration on Scott at the Edinburgh Sir Walter Scott Club Dinner on 28th November 1930. Mrs Maxwell-Scott of Abbotsford, in her Preface to *The Talisman* (1907), indicates that the description of the chapel in the romance was taken from that of Roslin, Midlothian.

1835 he had visited the Holy Land, doubtless urged thereto from reading Scott's romance. How the MS. eventually reached the State Historical Museum at Moscow has never been clearly defined, but it was discovered there in 1933 by Professor L. I. Ponomareff, then director of archives. When Davidoff (who had received the LL.D. degree from his Alma Mater, Edinburgh University) returned to this country in 1872 he met Scott's great-granddaughter, Mrs Maxwell-Scott. He died in 1882.

W. M. PARKER.

1956.

SELECT BIBLIOGRAPHY

POETICAL WORKS. Editions are very numerous but none are definitive. The best available is published by the Oxford University Press.

Separate major works: *The Lay of the Last Minstrel*, 1805; *Marmion*, 1808; *The Lady of the Lake*, 1810; *The Vision of Don Roderick*, 1811; *Rokeby*, 1813; *The Bridal of Triermain*, 1813; *The Lord of the Isles*, 1815; *The Field of Waterloo*, 1815; *Harold the Dauntless*, 1817.

NOVELS AND TALES. Collected edition: Dryburgh Edition, 25 vols, 1892–1894; Everyman's Library, 25 vols, 1906, etc.; Oxford edition, 24 vols, 1914, etc., and many other editions.

Separate works: *Waverley*, 1814; *Guy Mannering*, 1815; *The Antiquary*, 1816; *Tales of My Landlord* (first series, *The Black Dwarf* and *Old Mortality*), 1816; *Rob Roy*, 1818 [1817]; *Tales of My Landlord* (second series, *The Heart of Mid-Lothian*), 1818; *Tales of My Landlord* (third series, *The Bride of Lammermoor* and *A Legend of Montrose*), 1819; *Ivanhoe*, 1820 [1819]; *The Monastery*, 1820; *The Abbot*. 1820; *Kenilworth*, 1821; *The Pirate*, 1822 [1821]; *The Fortunes of Nigel*, 1822; *Peveril of the Peak*, 1822 [1823]; *Quentin Durward*, 1823; *St Ronan's Well*, 1824 [1823]; *Redgauntlet*, 1824; *Tales of the Crusaders* (*The Betrothed* and *The Talisman*), 1825; *Woodstock*, 1826; *Chronicles of the Canongate* (first series, *The Highland Widow*, *The Two Drovers*, and *The Surgeon's Daughter*), 1827; *My Aunt Margaret's Mirror*, *The Tapestried Chamber*, and *The Laird's Jock* (in *The Keepsake*), 1829 [1828]; *Chronicles of the Canongate* (second series, *St Valentine's Day*; or *The Fair Maid of Perth*), 1828; *Anne of Geierstein*, 1829; *Tales of My Landlord* (fourth series, *Count Robert of Paris*, and *Castle Dangerous*), 1832 [1831].

MISCELLANEOUS PROSE WORKS. The only collected edition is: *The Miscellaneous Prose Works* [edited by J. G. Lockhart], 28 vols, 1834–6.

Separate works: *Paul's Letters to His Kinsfolk*, 1816; *Description of the Regalia of Scotland*, 1819; *The Visionary*, 1819; *Provincial Antiquities of Scotland*, 1826 [1819–26]; *A Letter* (and *A Second* and *Third*) *to the Editor of the Edinburgh Weekly Journal, from Malachi Malagrowther*, 3 pts, 1826; *The Life of Napoleon Buonaparte*, 9 vols, 1827; *Tales of a Grandfather* (four series, 1828–31); *Religious Discourses by a Layman*, 1828; *The History of Scotland* (in Lardner's *Cabinet Cyclopaedia*), 1830 [1829–30]; *Letters on*

Demonology and Witchcraft, 1830; *Private Letters of the Seventeenth Century* (first published 1948).

Scott also contributed many articles to the *Edinburgh Review, Quarterly Review, Edinburgh Annual Register, Blackwood's Edinburgh Magazine*, and *Foreign Quarterly Review*. Full details of these are given in *New C.B.E.L.* See below, under Bibliography. His essays in the *Encyclopaedia Britannica* have been issued in various editions as *Essays on Chivalry, Romance and the Drama*.

EDITED WORKS. Scott edited numerous works, the chief being: *Minstrelsy of the Scottish Border*, 2 vols, 1802, 2nd ed. 3 vols, 1803, and later editions (re-ed. T. Henderson, 1902); *Sir Tristrem*, 1804; *Works of John Dryden*, 18 vols, 1808, 2nd ed., 1821; Somers's *Tracts*, 13 vols, 1809–15; *Works of Jonathan Swift*, 19 vols, 1814, 2nd ed., 1824; *Ballantyne's Novelist's Library*, 10 vols, 1821–4 (the memoirs later issued as *Lives of the Novelists*, including Everyman's Library, 1910, etc.).

LETTERS. Edited by Sir Herbert Grierson, 12 vols, 1932–7.

JOURNAL. Edited by W. E. K. Anderson, 1972.

BIOGRAPHY. J. G. Lockhart, *Memoirs of the Life of Sir Walter Scott*, 7 vols, 1837–8; 2nd ed., 10 vols, 1839; abridged by Lockhart as *Narrative of the Life of Sir Walter Scott*, 2 vols, 1948 (available in many editions, including Everyman's Library, 1906, etc.); *Memoirs of Sir Walter Scott*, ed. by A. W. Pollard, 5 vols, 1900 (Lockhart's 1839 text with additions from the 1848 *Narrative*); G. Saintsbury, *Sir Walter Scott*, 1897; John Buchan, *Sir Walter Scott*, 1932, etc.; Dame Una Pope-Hennessy, *The Laird of Abbotsford*, 1932; Sir Herbert Grierson, *Sir Walter Scott*, 1938; Hesketh Pearson, *Walter Scott*, 1954; Carola Oman, *The Wizard of the North*, 1973.

BIBLIOGRAPHY. J. P. Anderson, *Bibliography* (in C. D. Yonge's *Life of Sir Walter Scott*, 1888); Greville Worthington, *A Bibliography of the Waverley Novels*, 1931; W. Ruff, *A Bibliography of the Poetical Works of Sir Walter Scott, 1796–1832* (Edinburgh Bibliographical Society, 1937–8); J. C. Corson, *A Bibliography of Sir Walter Scott, 1797–1940*, 1943, repr. 1968 (critical works only); J. C. Corson, 'Sir Walter Scott' (in the *New Cambridge Bibliography of English Literature*), 1969.

INTRODUCTION

THE "Betrothed" did not greatly please one or two friends, who thought that it did not well correspond to the general title of "The Crusaders." They urged, therefore, that, without direct allusion to the manners of the Eastern tribes, and to the romantic conflicts of the period, the title of a "Tale of the Crusaders" would resemble the play-bill, which is said to have announced the tragedy of Hamlet, the character of the Prince of Denmark being left out. On the other hand, I felt the difficulty of giving a vivid picture of a part of the world with which I was almost totally unacquainted, unless by early recollections of the Arabian Nights' Entertainments ; and not only did I labour under the incapacity of ignorance, in which, as far as regards Eastern manners, I was as thickly wrapped as an Egyptian in his fog ; but my contemporaries were, many of them, as much enlightened upon the subject as if they had been inhabitants of the favoured land of Goshen. The love of travelling had pervaded all ranks, and carried the subjects of Britain into all quarters of the world. Greece, so attractive by its remains of art, by its struggles for freedom against a Mahommedan tyrant, by its very name, where every fountain had its classical legend ;— Palestine, endeared to the imagination by yet more sacred remembrances, had been of late surveyed by British eyes, and described by recent travellers. Had I, therefore, attempted the difficult task of substituting manners of my own invention, instead of the genuine costume of the East, almost every traveller I met, who had extended his route beyond what was anciently called "The Grand Tour," had acquired a right, by ocular inspection, to chastise me for my presumption. Every member of the Travellers' Club, who could pretend to have thrown his shoe over Edom, was, by having done so, constituted my lawful critic and corrector. It occurred, therefore, that where the author of Anastasius, as well as he of Hadji Baba, had described the manners and vices of the Eastern nations, not only with fidelity, but with the humour of Le Sage and the ludicrous power of Fielding himself, one who was a perfect stranger to the subject must necessarily produce an unfavourable contrast. The Poet Laureate also, in the charming tale of "Thalaba," had shown how extensive might be the researches of a person of acquirements and talent, by dint of investigation alone, into the ancient doctrines, history, and manners of the Eastern countries, in which we are probably to look for the cradle of mankind ; Moore, in his " Lalla Rookh," had successfully trod the same path ; in which, too, Byron, joining ocular experience to extensive reading, had written some of his most attractive poems. In a word, the Eastern themes had been already so successfully handled by those who were acknowledged to be masters of their craft, that I was diffident of making the attempt.

These were powerful objections, nor did they lose force when they became the subject of anxious reflection, although they did not finally prevail. The arguments on the other side were, that though I had no hope of rivalling the contemporaries whom I have mentioned, yet it occurred to me as possible to acquit myself of the task I was engaged in, without entering into competition with them.

The period relating more immediately to the Crusades, which I at last fixed upon, was that at which the warlike character of Richard I., wild and generous, a pattern of chivalry, with all its extravagant virtues, and its no less absurd errors, was opposed to that of Saladin, in which the Christian and English monarch showed all the cruelty and violence of an Eastern Sultan ; and Saladin, on the other hand, displayed the deep policy and prudence of a European sovereign, whilst each contended which should excel the other in the knightly qualities of bravery and generosity. This singular contrast afforded, as the author conceived, materials for a work of fiction, possessing peculiar interest. One of the inferior characters introduced was a supposed relation of Richard Cœur de Lion ; a violation of the truth of history, which gave offence to Mr. Mills, the author of the History of Chivalry and the Crusades, who was not, it may be presumed, aware that romantic fiction naturally includes the power of such invention, which is indeed one of the requisites of the art.

Prince David of Scotland, who was actually in the host, and was the hero of some very romantic adventures on his way home, was also pressed into my service, and constitutes one of my *dramatis personæ*.

It is true I had already brought upon the field him of the Lion Heart. But it was in a more private capacity than he was here to be exhibited in the Talisman ; then as a disguised knight, now in the avowed character of a conquering monarch ; so that I doubted not a name so dear to Englishmen as that of King Richard I. might contribute to their amusement for more than once.

I had access to all which antiquity believed, whether of reality or fable, on the subject of that magnificent warrior, who was the proudest boast of Europe and their chivalry, and with whose dreadful name the Saracens, according to a historian of their own country, were wont to rebuke their startled horses. "Do you think," said they, "that King Richard is on the track, that you stray so wildly from it!" The most curious register of the history of King Richard is an ancient romance, translated originally from the Norman; and at first certainly having a pretence to be termed a work of chivalry, but latterly becoming stuffed with the most astonishing and monstrous fables. There is perhaps no metrical romance upon record, where, along with curious and genuine history, are mingled more absurd and exaggerated incidents. We have placed in the Appendix to this Introduction, the passage of the romance in which Richard figures as an Ogre, or literal cannibal.—(Appendix, p. 6.)

A principal incident in the story, is that from which the title is derived. Of all people who ever lived, the Persians were perhaps most remarkable for their unshaken credulity in amulets, spells, periapts, and similar charms, framed, it was said, under the influence of particular planets, and bestowing high medical powers, as well as the means of advancing men's fortunes in various manners. A story of this kind, relating to a Crusader of eminence, is often told in the west of Scotland, and the relic alluded to is still in existence, and even yet held in veneration.

Sir Simon Lockhart of Lee and Cartland made a considerable figure in the reigns of Robert the Bruce and of his son David. He was one of the chief of that band of Scottish chivalry, who accompanied James, the Good Lord Douglas, on his expedition to the Holy Land, with the heart of King Robert Bruce. Douglas, impatient to get at the Saracens, entered into war with those of Spain, and was killed there. Lockhart proceeded to the Holy Land with such Scottish knights as had escaped the fate of their leader, and assisted for some time in the wars against the Saracens.

The following adventure is said by tradition to have befallen him:—

He made prisoner in battle an Emir of considerable wealth and consequence. The aged mother of the captive came to the Christian camp, to redeem her son from his state of captivity. Lockhart is said to have fixed the price at which his prisoner should ransom himself; and the lady, pulling out a large embroidered purse, proceeded to tell down the ransom, like a mother who pays little respect to gold in comparison of her son's liberty. In this operation, a pebble inserted in a coin, some say of the Lower Empire, fell out of the purse, and the Saracen matron testified so much haste to recover it, as gave the Scottish knight a high idea of its value, when compared with gold or silver. "I will not consent," he said, "to grant your son's liberty, unless that amulet be added to his ransom." The lady not only consented to this, but explained to Sir Simon Lockhart the mode in which the Talisman was to be used, and the uses to which it might be put. The water in which it was dipt operated as a styptic, as a febrifuge, and possessed several other properties as a medical talisman.

Sir Simon Lockhart, after much experience of the wonders which it wrought, brought it to his own country, and left it to his heirs, by whom, and by Clydesdale in general, it was, and is still, distinguished by the name of the Lee-penny, from the name of his native seat of Lee.

The most remarkable part of its history, perhaps, was, that it so especially escaped condemnation when the Church of Scotland chose to impeach many other cures which savoured of the miraculous, as occasioned by sorcery, and censured the appeal to them, "excepting only that to the amulet, called the Lee-penny, to which it had pleased God to annex certain healing virtues which the Church did not presume to condemn." It still, as has been said, exists, and its powers are sometimes resorted to. Of late, they have been chiefly restricted to the cure of persons bitten by mad dogs ; and as the illness in such cases frequently arises from imagination, there can be no reason for doubting that water which has been poured on the Lee-penny furnishes a congenial cure.

Such is the tradition concerning the Talisman, which the author has taken the liberty to vary in applying it to his own purposes.

Considerable liberties have also been taken with the truth of history, both with respect to Conrade of Montserrat's life, as well as his death. That Conrade, however, was reckoned the enemy of Richard, is agreed both in history and romance. The general opinion of the terms upon which they stood, may be guessed from the proposal of the Saracens, that the Marquis of Montserrat should be invested with certain parts of Syria, which they were to yield to the Christians. Richard, according to the romance which bears his name, "could no longer repress his fury. The Marquis, he said, was a traitor, who had robbed the Knights Hospitallers of sixty thousand pounds, the present of his father, Henry; that he was a renegade, whose treachery had occasioned the loss of Acre; and he concluded by a solemn oath, that he would cause him to be drawn to pieces by wild horses if he should ever venture to pollute the Christian camp by his presence. Philip attempted to intercede in favour of the Marquis, and throwing down his glove, offered to become a pledge for his fidelity to the Christians; but his offer was rejected, and he was obliged to give way to Richard's impetuosity."—*History of Chivalry*.

Conrade of Montserrat makes a considerable figure in those wars, and was at length put to death by one of the followers of the Scheik, or Old Man of the Mountain; nor did Richard remain free of the suspicion of having instigated his death.

It may be said, in general, that most of the incidents introduced in the following tale are fictitious; and that reality, where it exists, is only retained in the characters of the piece.

1st July, 1832.

APPENDIX TO INTRODUCTION

WHILE warring in the Holy Land, Richard was seized with an ague.

The best leeches of the camp were unable to effect the cure of the king's disease; but the prayers of the army were more successful. He became convalescent, and the first symptom of his recovery was a violent longing for pork. But pork was not likely to be plentiful in a country whose inhabitants had an abhorrence for swine's flesh; and

> ——— "though his men should be hanged,
> They ne might, in that countrèy,
> For gold, ne silver, ne no monèy,
> No pork find, take, ne get,
> That King Richard might aught of eat.
> An old knight with Richard biding,
> When he heard of that tiding,
> That the kingis wants were swyche,
> To the steward he spake privyliche—
> 'Our lord the king sore is sick, I wis,
> After porck he alonged is;
> Ye may none find to selle;
> No man be hardy him so to telle!
> If he did he might die.
> Now behoves to done as I shall say,
> Tho' he wete nought of that.
> Take a Saracen, young and fat;
> In haste let the thief be slain,
> Opened, and his skin off flayn;
> And sodden full hastily,
> With powder and with spicery,
> And with saffron of good colòur,
> When the king feels thereof savòur,
> Out of ague if he be went,
> He shall have thereto good talènt,
> When ne has a good taste,
> And eaten well a good repast,
> And supped of the *brewis* a sup,
> Slept after and swet a drop,
> Through Goddis help and my counsail,
> Soon he shall be fresh and hail.'
> The sooth to say, at wordes few,
> Slain and sodden was the heathen shrew.
> Before the king it was forth brought:
> Quod his men, 'Lord, we have pork sought;

Eates and sups of the brewis *soote*,
Thorough grace of God it shall be your boot.'
Before King Richard carff a knight,
He ate faster than he carve might.
The king ate the flesh and *gnew* the bones,
And drank well after for the nonce.
And when he had eaten enough,
His folk hem turned away, and *lough*.
He lay still and drew in his arm ;
His chamberlain him wrapped warm.
He lay and slept, and swet a stound,
And became whole and sound.
King Richard clad him and arose,
And walked abouten in the close."

An attack of the Saracens was repelled by Richard in person, the consequence of which is told in the following lines :—

" When King Richard had rested a whyle,
A knight his arms 'gan unlace,
Him to comfort and solàce.
Him was brought a sop in wine.
'The head of that ilke swine,
That I of ate !' (the cook he bade,)
'For feeble I am, and faint and mad.
Of mine evil now I am fear ;
Serve me therewith at my soupere !'
Quod the cook, 'That head I ne have.'
Then said the king, 'So God me save,
But I see the head of that swine,
For sooth, thou shalt lesen thine !'
The cook saw none other might be ;
He fet the head and let him see.
He fell on knees, and made a cry—
'Lo, here the head ! my Lord, mercy !'"

The cook had certainly some reason to fear that his master would be struck with horror at the recollection of the dreadful banquet to which he owed his recovery, but his fears were soon dissipated.

" The swarte *vis* when the king seeth,
His black beard and white teeth,
How his lippes grinned wide,
'What devil is this?' the king cried,
And gan to laugh as he were wode.
'What ! is Saracen's flesh thus good?
That, never erst I nought wist !
By God's death and his uprist,
Shall we never die for default,
While we may in any assault

> Slee Saracens, the flesh may take,
> And seethen and roasten and do hem bake,
> [And] Gnawen her flesh to the bones !
> Now I have it proved once,
> For hunger ere I be wo,
> I and my folk shall eat mo !'"

The besieged now offered to surrender, upon conditions of safety to the inhabitants ; while all the public treasure, military machines, and arms were delivered to the victors, together with the further ransom of one hundred thousand bezants. After this capitulation the following extraordinary scene took place. We shall give it in the words of the humorous and amiable George Ellis, the collector and the editor of these Romances.

"Though the garrison had faithfully performed the other articles of their contract, they were unable to restore the cross, which was not in their possession, and were therefore treated by the Christians with great cruelty. Daily reports of their sufferings were carried to Saladin ; and as many of them were persons of the highest distinction, that monarch, at the solicitation of their friends, dispatched an embassy to King Richard with magnificent presents, which he offered for the ransom of the captives. The ambassadors were persons the most respectable from their age, their rank, and their eloquence. They delivered their message in terms of the utmost humility, and, without arraigning the justice of the conqueror in his severe treatment of their countrymen, only solicited a period to that severity, laying at his feet the treasures with which they were intrusted, and pledging themselves and their master for the payment of any further sums which he might demand as the price of mercy.

> "King Richard spake with wordes mild,
> ' The gold to take, God me shield !
> Among you *partes* every charge.
> I brought in shippes and in barge,
> More gold and silver with me,
> Than has your lord, and swilke three.
> To his treasure have I no need !
> But for my love I you bid,
> To meat with me that ye dwell ;
> And afterward I shall you tell.
> Thorough counsel I shall you answer,
> What *bode* ye shall to your lord bear.'

"The invitation was gratefully accepted. Richard, in the meantime, gave secret orders to his marshal that he should repair to the prison, select a certain number of the most distinguished captives, and, after carefully noting their names on a roll of parchment, cause their heads to be instantly struck off; that these heads should be delivered to the cook with instructions to clear away the hair, and, after boiling them in a caldron, to distribute them on several platters, one to each guest, observing to fasten on the forehead of each the piece of parchment expressing the name and family of the victim.

> " 'An hot head bring me beforn,
> As I were well apayed withall,
> Eat thereof fast I shall;
> As it were a tender chick,
> To see how the others will like.'

"This horrible order was punctually executed. At noon the guests were summoned to wash by the music of the waits; the King took his seat, attended by the principal officers of his court, at the high table, and the rest of the company were marshalled at a long table below him. On the cloth were placed portions of salt at the usual distances, but neither bread, wine, nor water. The ambassadors, rather surprised at this omission, but still free from apprehension, awaited in silence the arrival of the dinner, which was announced by the sound of pipes, trumpets, and tabours; and beheld, with horror and dismay, the unnatural banquet introduced by the steward and his officers. Yet their sentiments of disgust and abhorrence, and even their fears, were for a time suspended by their curiosity. Their eyes were fixed on the King, who, without the slightest change of countenance, swallowed the morsels as fast as they could be supplied by the knight who carved them.

> " Every man then poked other;
> They said, ' This is the devil's brother,
> That slays our men, and thus hem eats!'

"Their attention was then involuntarily fixed on the smoking heads before them; they traced in the swollen and distorted features the resemblance of a friend or near relation, and received from the fatal scroll which accompanied each dish the sad assurance that this resemblance was not imaginary. They sat in torpid silence, anticipating their own fate in that of their countrymen, while their ferocious entertainer, with fury in his eyes, but with courtesy on his lips, insulted them by frequent invitations to merriment. At length this first course was removed, and its place supplied by venison, cranes, and other dainties, accompanied by the richest wines. The King then apologized to them for what

had passed, which he attributed to his ignorance of their taste ;
and assured them of his religious respect for their character as
ambassadors, and of his readiness to grant them a safe-conduct
for their return. This boon was all that they now wished to
claim ; and

> " King Richard spake to an old man,
> ' Wendes home to your Soudan !
> His melancholy that ye abate ;
> And sayes that ye came too late.
> Too slowly was your time y-guessed ;
> Ere ye came, the flesh was dressed,
> That men shoulden serve with me,
> Thus at noon, and my meynie.
> Say him, it shall him nought avail,
> Though he for-bar us our vitail,
> Bread, wine, fish, flesh, salmon and conger ;
> Of us none shall die with hunger,
> While we may wenden to fight,
> And slay the Saracens downright,
> Wash the flesh, and roast the head.
> With *oo* Saracen I may well feed
> Well a nine or a ten
> Of my good Christian men.
> King Richard shall warrant,
> There is no flesh so nourissant
> Unto an Englishman,
> Partridge, plover, heron, ne swan,
> Cow ne ox, sheep ne swine,
> As the head of a Sarazyn.
> There he is fat, and thereto tender,
> And my men be lean and slender.
> While any Saracen quick be,
> L vand now in this Syrie,
> For meat will we nothing care,
> Abouten fast we shall fare,
> And every day we shall eat
> All so many as we may get.
> To England will we nought gon,
> Till they be eaten every one.' "
>
> ELLIS's *Specimens of Early English
> Metrical Romances*, vol. ii. p. 236.

The reader may be curious to know owing to what circumstances so extraordinary an invention as that which imputed
cannibalism to the King of England should have found its way
into his history. Mr. James, to whom we owe so much that is
curious, seems to have traced the origin of this extraordinary
rumour.

" With the army of the cross also was a multitude of men," the
same author declares, "who made it a profession to be without

money: they walked barefoot, carried no arms, and even preceded the beasts of burden in their march, living upon roots and herbs, and presenting a spectacle both disgusting and pitiable.

"A Norman, who, according to all accounts, was of noble birth, but who, having lost his horse, continued to follow as a foot soldier, took the strange resolution of putting himself at the head of this race of vagabonds, who willingly received him as their king. Amongst the Saracens these men became well known under the name of *Thafurs*, (which Guibert translates *Trudentes*,) and were beheld with great horror, from the general persuasion that they fed on the dead bodies of their enemies, a report which was occasionally justified, and which the king of the Thafurs took care to encourage. This respectable monarch was frequently in the habit of stopping his followers, one by one, in a narrow defile, and of causing them to be searched carefully, lest the possession of the least sum of money should render them unworthy of the name of his subjects. If even two sous were found upon any one, he was instantly expelled the society of his tribe, the king bidding him contemptuously buy arms and fight.

"This troop, so far from being cumbersome to the army, was infinitely serviceable, carrying burdens, bringing in forage, provisions, and tribute; working the machines in the sieges, and, above all, spreading consternation among the Turks, who feared death from the lances of the knights less than that further consummation they heard of under the teeth of the Thafurs."[1]

It is easy to conceive, that an ignorant minstrel, finding the taste and ferocity of the Thafurs commemorated in the historical accounts of the Holy Wars, has ascribed their practices and propensities to the monarch of England, whose ferocity was considered as an object of exaggeration as legitimate as his valour.

[1] James's *History of Chivalry*, p. 178.

THE TALISMAN

CHAPTER I

————They, too, retired
To the wilderness, but 'twas with arms.
Paradise Regained.

THE burning sun of Syria had not yet attained its highest point in the horizon, when a knight of the Red-cross, who had left his distant northern home, and joined the host of the Crusaders in Palestine, was pacing slowly along the sandy deserts which lie in the vicinity of the Dead Sea, or, as it is called, the Lake Asphaltites, where the waves of the Jordan pour themselves into an inland sea, from which there is no discharge of waters.

The warlike pilgrim had toiled among cliffs and precipices during the earlier part of the morning; more lately, issuing from those rocky and dangerous defiles, he had entered upon that great plain, where the accursed cities provoked, in ancient days, the direct and dreadful vengeance of the Omnipotent.

The toil, the thirst, the dangers of the way, were forgotten, as the traveller recalled the fearful catastrophe, which had converted into an arid and dismal wilderness the fair and fertile valley of Siddim, once well watered, even as the Garden of the Lord, now a parched and blighted waste, condemned to eternal sterility.

Crossing himself, as he viewed the dark mass of rolling waters, in colour as in quality unlike those of every other lake, the traveller shuddered as he remembered, that beneath these sluggish waves lay the once proud cities of the plain, whose grave was dug by the thunder of the heavens, or the eruption of subterraneous fire, and whose remains were hid, even by that sea which holds no living fish in its bosom, bears no skiff on its surface, and, as if its own dreadful bed were the only fit receptacle for its sullen waters, sends not, like other lakes, a tribute to the ocean. The whole land around, as in the days of Moses, was "brimstone and salt; it is not sown, nor beareth, nor any grass groweth thereon;" the land as well as the lake might be termed dead, as producing nothing having resemblance to vegetation, and even the very air was entirely devoid of its ordinary winged inhabitants, deterred probably by the odour of bitumen and sulphur, which the burning sun exhaled from the waters of the lake, in steaming clouds, frequently assuming the appearance of waterspouts. Masses of the slimy and sulphureous substance called naphtha, which floated idly on the sluggish and sullen waves, supplied those rolling clouds with new vapours, and afforded awful testimony to the truth of the Mosaic history.

Upon this scene of desolation the sun shone with almost intolerable splendour, and all living nature seemed to have hidden itself from the rays, excepting the solitary figure which moved through the flitting sand at a foot's pace, and appeared the sole breathing thing on the wide surface of the plain. The dress of the rider, and the accoutrements of his horse, were peculiarly unfit for the traveller in such a country. A coat of linked mail, with long sleeves, plated gauntlets, and a steel breastplate, had not been esteemed a sufficient weight of armour; there was also his triangular shield suspended round his neck, and his barred helmet of steel, over which he had a hood and collar of mail, which was drawn around the warrior's shoulders and throat, and filled up the vacancy between the hauberk and the head-piece. His lower limbs were sheathed, like his body, in flexible mail, securing the legs and thighs, while the feet rested in plated shoes, which corresponded with the gauntlets. A long, broad, straight-shaped, double-edged falchion, with a handle formed like a cross, corresponded with a stout poniard on the other side. The knight also bore, secured to his saddle, with one end resting on his stirrup, the long steel-headed lance, his own proper weapon, which, as he rode, projected backwards, and displayed its little pennoncelle, to dally with the faint breeze, or drop in the dead calm. To this cumbrous equipment must be added a surcoat of embroidered cloth, much frayed and worn, which was thus far useful, that it excluded the burning rays of the sun from the armour, which they would otherwise have rendered intolerable to the wearer. The surcoat bore, in several places, the arms of the owner, although much defaced. These seemed to be a couchant leopard, with the motto, "I sleep—wake me not." An outline of the same device might be traced on his shield, though many a blow had almost effaced the painting. The flat top of his cumbrous cylindrical helmet was unadorned with any crest. In retaining their own unwieldy defensive armour, the northern Crusaders seemed to set at defiance the nature of the climate and country to which they had come to war.

The accoutrements of the horse were scarcely less massive and unwieldy than those of the rider. The animal had a heavy saddle plated with steel, uniting in front with a species of breastplate, and behind with defensive armour made to cover the loins. Then there was a steel axe, or hammer, called a mace-of-arms, and which hung to the saddlebow; the reins were secured by chain-work, and the front-stall of the bridle was a steel plate, with apertures for the eyes and nostrils, having in the midst a short sharp pike, projecting from the forehead of the horse like the horn of the fabulous unicorn.

But habit had made the endurance of this load of panoply a second nature, both to the knight and his gallant charger. Numbers, indeed, of the Western warriors who hurried to Palestine, died ere they became inured to the burning climate; but there were others to whom that climate became innocent and even friendly, and among this fortunate number was the solitary horseman who now traversed the border of the Dead Sea.

Nature, which cast his limbs in a mould of uncommon strength, fitted to wear his linked hauberk with as much ease as if the meshes had been formed of cobwebs, had endowed him with a constitution as strong as his limbs, and which bade defiance to almost all changes of climate, as well as to fatigue and privations of every kind. His disposition seemed, in some degree, to partake of the qualities of his bodily frame; and as the one possessed great strength and endurance, united with the power of violent exertion, the other, under a calm and undisturbed semblance, had much of the fiery and enthusiastic love of glory which constituted the principal attribute of the renowned Norman line, and had rendered them sovereigns in every corner of Europe where they had drawn their adventurous swords.

It was not, however, to all the race that fortune proposed such tempting rewards; and those obtained by the solitary knight during two years' campaign in Palestine, had been only temporal fame, and, as he was taught to believe, spiritual privileges. Meantime, his slender stock of money had melted away, the rather that he did not pursue any of the ordinary modes by which the followers of the Crusade condescended to recruit their diminished resources, at the expense of the people of Palestine; he exacted no gifts from the wretched natives for sparing their possessions when engaged in warfare with the Saracens, and he had not availed himself of any opportunity of enriching himself by the ransom of prisoners of consequence. The small train which had followed him from his native country had been gradually diminished, as the means of maintaining them disappeared, and his only remaining squire was at present on a sick-bed, and unable to attend his master, who travelled, as we have seen, singly and alone. This was of little consequence to the Crusader, who was accustomed to consider his good sword as his safest escort, and devout thoughts as his best companion.

Nature had, however, her demands for refreshment and repose, even on the iron frame and patient disposition of the Knight of the Sleeping Leopard; and at noon, when the Dead Sea lay at some distance on his right, he joyfully hailed the sight of two or three palm-trees, which arose beside the well which was assigned for his mid-day station. His good horse, too, which had plodded forward with the steady endurance of his master, now lifted his head, expanded his nostrils, and quickened his pace, as if he snuffed afar off the living waters, which marked the place of repose and refreshment. But labour and danger were doomed to intervene ere the horse or horseman reached the desired spot.

As the Knight of the Couchant Leopard continued to fix his eyes attentively on the yet distant cluster of palm-trees, it seemed to him as if some object was moving among them. The distant form separated itself from the trees, which partly hid its motions, and advanced towards the knight with a speed which soon showed a mounted horseman, whom his turban, long spear, and green caftan floating in the wind, on his nearer approach, showed to be a Saracen cavalier. "In the desert," saith an Eastern proverb, "no man meets a friend." The Crusader was totally indifferent whether the infidel, who now approached on his gallant barb, as if borne on the wings of an eagle, came as friend or foe—perhaps, as a vowed champion of the Cross, he might rather have preferred the latter. He disengaged his lance from his saddle, seized it with the right hand, placed it in rest with its point half elevated, gathered up the reins in the left, waked his horse's mettle with the spur, and prepared to encounter the stranger, with the calm self-confidence belonging to the victor in many contests.

The Saracen came on at the speedy gallop of an Arab horseman, managing his steed more by his limbs, and the inflection of his body, than by any use of the reins, which hung loose in his left hand; so that he was enabled to wield the light round buckler of the skin of the rhinoceros, ornamented with silver loops, which he wore on his arm, swinging it as if he meant to oppose its slender circle to the formidable thrust of the Western lance. His own long spear was not couched or levelled like that of his antagonist, but grasped by the middle with his right hand, and brandished at arm's length above his head. As the cavalier approached his enemy at full career, he seemed to expect that the Knight of the Leopard should put his horse to the gallop to encounter him. But the Christian knight, well acquainted with the customs of Eastern warriors, did not mean to exhaust his good horse by any unnecessary exertion; and, on the contrary, made a dead halt, confident that, if the enemy advanced to the actual shock, his own weight, and that of his powerful charger, would give him sufficient advantage, without the additional momentum of rapid motion. Equally sensible and apprehensive of such a probable result, the Saracen cavalier, when he had approached towards the Christian within twice the length of his lance, wheeled his steed to the left with inimitable dexterity, and rode twice round his antagonist, who, turning without quitting his ground, and presenting his front constantly to his enemy, frustrated his attempts to attack him on an unguarded point; so that the Saracen, wheeling his horse, was fain to retreat to the distance of an hundred yards. A second time, like a hawk attacking a heron, the heathen renewed the charge, and a second time was fain to retreat without coming to a close struggle. A third time he approached in the same manner, when the Christian knight, desirous to terminate this elusory warfare, in which he might at length have been worn out by the activity of his foeman, suddenly seized the mace which hung at his saddlebow, and, with a strong hand and un-erring aim, hurled it against the head of the Emir, for such and not less his enemy appeared. The Saracen was just aware of the formidable missile in time to interpose his light buckler betwixt the mace and his head; but the violence of the blow forced the buckler down on his turban, and though that defence also contributed to deaden its violence, the Saracen was beaten from his horse. Ere the Christian could avail himself of this mishap, his nimble foeman sprung from the ground, and, calling on his steed, which instantly returned to his side, he leaped into his seat without touching the stirrup, and regained all the advantage of which the Knight of the Leopard hoped to deprive him. But the latter had in the meanwhile recovered his mace, and the Eastern cavalier, who remembered the strength and dexterity with which his antagonist had aimed it, seemed to keep cautiously out of reach of that weapon, of which he had so lately felt the force, while he showed his purpose of waging a distant warfare with missile weapons of his own. Planting his long spear in the sand at a distance from the scene of combat, he strung, with great address, a short bow, which he carried at his back, and putting his horse to the gallop, once more described two or three circles of a wider extent than formerly, in the course of which he discharged six arrows at the Christian with such unerring skill, that the goodness of his harness alone saved him from being wounded in as many places. The seventh shaft apparently found a less perfect part of the armour, and the Christian dropped heavily from his horse. But what was the surprise of the Saracen, when, dismounting to examine the condition of his prostrate enemy, he found himself suddenly within the grasp of the European, who had had recourse to this artifice to bring his enemy within his reach! Even in this deadly grapple, the Saracen was saved by his agility and presence of mind. He unloosed the sword-belt, in which the Knight of the Leopard had fixed his hold, and, thus eluding his fatal grasp, mounted his horse, which seemed to watch his motions with the intelligence of a human being, and again rode off. But in the last encounter the Saracen had lost his sword and his quiver of arrows, both of which were attached to the girdle, which he was obliged to abandon. He had also lost his turban in the struggle. These disadvantages seemed to incline the Moslem to a truce: he approached the Christian with his right hand extended, but no longer in a menacing attitude.

"There is truce betwixt our nations," he said, in the lingua franca commonly used for the purpose of communication with the Crusaders; "wherefore should there be war betwixt thee and me?—Let there be peace betwixt us."

"I am well contented," answered he of the Couchant Leopard; "but what security dost thou offer that thou wilt observe the truce?"

"The word of a follower of the Prophet was never broken," answered the Emir. "It is thou, brave Nazarene, from whom

I should demand security, did I not know that treason seldom dwells with courage."

The Crusader felt that the confidence of the Moslem made him ashamed of his own doubts.

"By the cross of my sword," he said, laying his hand on the weapon as he spoke, "I will be true companion to thee, Saracen, while our fortune wills that we remain in company together."

"By Mahommed, Prophet of God, and by Allah, God of the Prophet," replied his late foeman, "there is not treachery in my heart towards thee. And now wend we to yonder fountain, for the hour of rest is at hand, and the stream had hardly touched my lip when I was called to battle by thy approach."

The Knight of the Couchant Leopard yielded a ready and courteous assent; and the late foes, without an angry look, or gesture of doubt, rode side by side to the little cluster of palm-trees.

CHAPTER II

TIMES of danger have always, and in a peculiar degree, their seasons of good-will and of security; and this was particularly so in the ancient feudal ages, in which, as the manners of the period had assigned war to be the chief and most worthy occupation of mankind, the intervals of peace, or rather of truce, were highly relished by those warriors to whom they were seldom granted, and endeared by the very circumstances which rendered them transitory. It is not worth while preserving any permanent enmity against a foe, whom a champion has fought with to-day, and may again stand in bloody opposition to on the next morning. The time and situation afforded so much room for the ebullition of violent passions, that men, unless when peculiarly opposed to each other, or provoked by the recollection of private and individual wrongs, cheerfully enjoyed in each other's society the brief intervals of pacific intercourse which a warlike life admitted.

The distinction of religions, nay, the fanatical zeal which animated the followers of the Cross and of the Crescent against each other, was much softened by a feeling so natural to generous combatants, and especially cherished by the spirit of chivalry. This last strong impulse had extended itself gradually from the Christians to their mortal enemies the Saracens, both of Spain and of Palestine. The latter were indeed no longer the fanatical savages, who had burst from the centre of Arabian deserts, with the sabre in one hand and the Koran in the other, to inflict death or the faith of Mahommed, or at the best slavery and tribute, upon all who dared to oppose the belief of the Prophet of Mecca. These alternatives, indeed, had been offered to the unwarlike Greeks and Syrians; but in contending with the Western Christians, animated by a zeal as fiery as their own, and possessed of an unconquerable courage, address and success in arms, the Saracens gradually caught a part of their manners, and especially of those chivalrous observances which were so well calculated to charm the minds of a proud and conquering people. They had their tournaments and games of chivalry; they had even their knights, or some rank analogous; and, above all, the Saracens observed their plighted faith with an accuracy which might sometimes put to shame those who owned a better religion. Their truces, whether national or betwixt individuals, were faithfully observed; and thus it was, that war, in itself perhaps the greatest of evils, yet gave occasion for display of good faith, generosity, clemency, and even kindly affections, which less frequently occur in more tranquil periods, where the passions of men, experiencing wrongs, or entertaining quarrels which cannot be brought to instant decision, are apt to smoulder for a length of time in the bosoms of those who are so unhappy as to be their prey.

It was under the influence of these milder feelings, which soften the horrors of warfare, that the Christian and Saracen, who had so lately done their best for each other's mutual destruction, rode at a slow pace towards the fountain of palm-trees, to which the Knight of the Couchant Leopard had been tending, when interrupted in mid-passage by his fleet and dangerous adversary. Each was wrapped for some time in his own reflections, and took breath after an encounter which had threatened to be fatal to one or both; and their good horses seemed no less to enjoy the interval of repose. That of the Saracen, however, though he had been forced into much the more violent and extended sphere of motion, appeared to have suffered less from fatigue than the charger of the European knight. The sweat hung still clammy on the limbs of the last, when those of the noble Arab were completely dried by the interval of tranquil exercise, all saving the foam-flakes which were still visible on his bridle and housings. The loose soil on which he trode so much augmented the distress of the Christian's horse, heavily loaded by his own armour and the weight of his rider, that the latter jumped from his saddle, and led his charger along the deep dust of the loamy soil, which was burnt in the sun into a substance more impalpable than the finest sand, and thus gave the faithful horse refreshment at the expense of his own additional toil ; for, iron-sheathed as he was, he sunk over the mailed shoes at every step which he placed on a surface so light and unresisting.

"You are right," said the Saracen ; and it was the first word that either had spoken since their truce was concluded,— "your strong horse deserves your care; but what do you in the desert with an animal, which sinks over the fetlock at every step, as if he would plant each foot deep as the root of a date-tree ? "

"Thou speakest rightly, Saracen," said the Christian knight, not delighted at the tone with which the infidel criticised his favourite steed, — "rightly, according to thy knowledge and observation. But my good horse hath ere now borne me, in mine own land, over as wide a lake as thou seest yonder spread out behind us, yet not wet one hair above his hoof."

The Saracen looked at him with as much surprise as his manners permitted him to testify, which was only expressed by a slight approach to a disdainful smile, that hardly curled perceptibly the broad thick moustache which enveloped his upper lip.

"It is justly spoken," he said, instantly composing himself to his usual serene gravity,—"list to a Frank, and hear a fable."

"Thou art not courteous, misbeliever," replied the Crusader, "to doubt the word of a dubbed knight ; and were it not that thou speakest in ignorance, and not in malice, our truce had its ending ere it is well begun. Thinkest thou I tell thee an untruth when I say, that I, one of five hundred horsemen, armed in complete mail, have ridden—ay, and ridden for miles, upon water as solid as the crystal, and ten times less brittle ? "

"What wouldst thou tell me ? " answered the Moslem ; "yonder inland sea thou dost point at is peculiar in this, that, by the especial curse of God, it suffereth nothing to sink in its waves, but wafts them away, and casts them on its margin ; but neither the Dead Sea, nor any of the seven oceans which environ the earth, will endure on their surface the pressure of a horse's foot, more than the Red Sea endured to sustain the advance of Pharaoh and his host."

"You speak truth after your knowledge, Saracen," said the

Christian knight; "and yet, trust me, I fable not, according to mine. Heat, in this climate, converts the soil into something almost as unstable as water; and in my land cold often converts the water itself into a substance as hard as rock. Let us speak of this no longer; for the thoughts of the calm, clear, blue refulgence of a winter's lake, glimmering to stars and moonbeam, aggravate the horrors of this fiery desert, where, methinks, the very air which we breathe is like the vapour of a fiery furnace seven times heated."

The Saracen looked on him with some attention, as if to discover in what sense he was to understand words, which, to him, must have appeared either to contain something of mystery, or of imposition. At length he seemed determined in what manner to receive the language of his new companion.

"You are," he said, "of a nation that loves to laugh, and you make sport with yourselves, and with others, by telling what is impossible, and reporting what never chanced. Thou art one of the knights of France, who hold it for glee and pastime to *gab*,[1] as they term it, of exploits that are beyond human power. I were wrong to challenge, for the time, the privilege of thy speech, since boasting is more natural to thee than truth."

"I am not of their land, neither of their fashion," said the knight, "which is, as thou well sayest, to *gab* of that which they dare not undertake, or undertaking cannot perfect. But in this I have imitated their folly, brave Saracen, that in talking to thee of what thou canst not comprehend, I have, even in speaking most simple truth, fully incurred the character of a braggart in thy eyes; so, I pray you, let my words pass."

They had now arrived at the knot of palm-trees, and the fountain which welled out from beneath their shade in sparkling profusion.

We have spoken of a moment of truce in the midst of war; and this, a spot of beauty in the midst of a sterile desert, was scarce less dear to the imagination. It was a scene which, perhaps, would elsewhere have deserved little notice; but as the single speck, in a boundless horizon, which promised the refreshment of shade and living water, these blessings, held

---

[1] *Gaber.* This French word signified a sort of sport much used among the French chivalry, which consisted in vying with each other in making the most romantic gasconades. The verb and the meaning are retained in Scottish.

cheap where they are common, rendered the fountain and its neighbourhood a little paradise. Some generous or charitable hand, ere yet the evil days of Palestine began, had walled in and arched over the fountain, to preserve it from being absorbed in the earth, or choked by the flitting clouds of dust with which the least breath of wind covered the desert. The arch was now broken, and partly ruinous; but it still so far projected over, and covered in the fountain, that it excluded the sun in a great measure from its waters, which, hardly touched by a straggling beam, while all around was blazing, lay in a steady repose, alike delightful to the eye and the imagination. Stealing from under the arch, they were first received in a marble basin, much defaced indeed, but still cheering the eye, by showing that the place was anciently considered as a station, that the hand of man had been there, and that man's accommodation had been in some measure attended to. The thirsty and weary traveller was reminded by these signs that others had suffered similar difficulties, reposed in the same spot, and, doubtless, found their way in safety to a more fertile country. Again, the scarce visible current which escaped from the basin, served to nourish the few trees which surrounded the fountain, and where it sunk into the ground and disappeared, its refreshing presence was acknowledged by a carpet of velvet verdure.

In this delightful spot the two warriors halted, and each, after his own fashion, proceeded to relieve his horse from saddle, bit, and rein, and permitted the animals to drink at the basin, ere they refreshed themselves from the fountain head, which arose under the vault. They then suffered the steeds to go loose, confident that their interest, as well as their domesticated habits, would prevent their straying from the pure water and fresh grass.

Christian and Saracen next sat down together on the turf, and produced each the small allowance of store which they carried for their own refreshment. Yet, ere they severally proceeded to their scanty meal, they eyed each other with that curiosity which the close and doubtful conflict in which they had been so lately engaged was calculated to inspire. Each was desirous to measure the strength, and form some estimate of the character, of an adversary so formidable; and each was compelled to acknowledge that, had he fallen in the conflict, it had been by a noble hand.

The champions formed a striking contrast to each other in

person and features, and might have formed no inaccurate representatives of their different nations. The Frank seemed a powerful man, built after the ancient Gothic cast of form, with light brown hair, which, on the removal of his helmet, was seen to curl thick and profusely over his head. His features had acquired, from the hot climate, a hue much darker than those parts of his neck which were less frequently exposed to view, or than was warranted by his full and well-opened blue eye, the colour of his hair, and of the moustaches which thickly shaded his upper lip, while his chin was carefully divested of beard, after the Norman fashion. His nose was Grecian and well formed; his mouth rather large in proportion, but filled with well-set, strong, and beautifully white teeth; his head small, and set upon the neck with much grace. His age could not exceed thirty, but, if the effects of toil and climate were allowed for, might be three or four years under that period. His form was tall, powerful, and athletic, like that of a man whose strength might, in later life, become unwieldy, but which was hitherto united with lightness and activity. His hands, when he withdrew the mailed gloves, were long, fair, and well-proportioned; the wrist-bones peculiarly large and strong; and the arms remarkably well-shaped and brawny. A military hardihood, and careless frankness of expression, characterized his language and his motions; and his voice had the tone of one more accustomed to command than to obey, and who was in the habit of expressing his sentiments aloud and boldly, whenever he was called upon to announce them.

The Saracen Emir formed a marked and striking contrast with the Western Crusader. His stature was indeed above the middle size, but he was at least three inches shorter than the European, whose size approached the gigantic. His slender limbs, and long spare hands and arms, though well-proportioned to his person, and suited to the style of his countenance, did not at first aspect promise the display of vigour and elasticity which the Emir had lately exhibited. But, on looking more closely, his limbs, where exposed to view, seemed divested of all that was fleshy or cumbersome; so that nothing being left but bone, brawn, and sinew, it was a frame fitted for exertion and fatigue, far beyond that of a bulky champion, whose strength and size are counterbalanced by weight, and who is exhausted by his own exertions. The countenance of the Saracen naturally bore a general national resemblance to the Eastern tribe from whom he descended, and was as unlike as possible to the exaggerated terms in which the minstrels of the day were wont to represent the infidel champions, and the fabulous description which a sister art still presents as the Saracen's Head upon signposts. His features were small, well-formed, and delicate, though deeply embrowned by the Eastern sun, and terminated by a flowing and curled black beard, which seemed trimmed with peculiar care. The nose was straight and regular, the eyes keen, deep-set, black, and glowing, and his teeth equalled in beauty the ivory of his deserts. The person and proportions of the Saracen, in short, stretched on the turf near to his powerful antagonist, might have been compared to his sheeny and crescent-formed sabre, with its narrow and light, but bright and keen Damascus blade, contrasted with the long and ponderous Gothic war-sword, which was flung unbuckled on the same sod. The Emir was in the very flower of his age, and might perhaps have been termed eminently beautiful, but for the narrowness of his forehead, and something of too much thinness and sharpness of feature, or at least what might have seemed such in a European estimate of beauty.

The manners of the Eastern warrior were grave, graceful, and decorous; indicating, however, in some particulars the habitual restraint which men of warm and choleric tempers often set as a guard upon their native impetuosity of disposition, and at the same time a sense of his own dignity, which seemed to impose a certain formality of behaviour in him who entertained it.

This haughty feeling of superiority was perhaps equally entertained by his new European acquaintance, but the effect was different; and the same feeling, which dictated to the Christian knight a bold, blunt, and somewhat careless bearing, as one too conscious of his own importance to be anxious about the opinions of others, appeared to prescribe to the Saracen a style of courtesy more studiously and formally observant of ceremony. Both were courteous; but the courtesy of the Christian seemed to flow rather from a good-humoured sense of what was due to others; that of the Moslem, from a high feeling of what was to be expected from himself.

The provision which each had made for his refreshment was simple, but the meal of the Saracen was abstemious. A handful of dates, and a morsel of coarse barley-bread, sufficed to relieve the hunger of the latter, whose education had habituated him to the fare of the desert, although, since their Syrian conquests, the Arabian simplicity of life frequently gave place to the most unbounded profusion of luxury. A few draughts from the lovely fountain by which they reposed completed his meal. That of the Christian, though coarse, was more genial. Dried hog's flesh, the abomination of the Moslemah, was the chief part of his repast; and his drink, derived from a leathern bottle, contained something better than pure element. He fed with more display of appetite, and drank with more appearance of satisfaction, than the Saracen judged it becoming to show in the performance of a mere bodily function; and, doubtless, the secret contempt which each entertained for the other, as the follower of a false religion, was considerably increased by the marked difference of their diet and manners. But each had found the weight of his opponent's arm, and the mutual respect which the bold struggle had created, was sufficient to subdue other and inferior considerations. Yet the Saracen could not help remarking the circumstances which displeased him in the Christian's conduct and manners; and, after he had witnessed for some time in silence the keen appetite which protracted the knight's banquet long after his own was concluded, he thus addressed him :—

"Valiant Nazarene, is it fitting that one who can fight like a man should feed like a dog or a wolf? Even a misbelieving Jew would shudder at the food which you seem to eat, with as much relish as if it were fruit from the trees of Paradise."

"Valiant Saracen," answered the Christian, looking up with some surprise at the accusation thus unexpectedly brought, "know thou that I exercise my Christian freedom, in using that which is forbidden to the Jews, being, as they esteem themselves, under the bondage of the old law of Moses. We, Saracen, be it known to thee, have a better warrant for what we do—Ave Maria! be we thankful." And, as if in defiance of his companion's scruples, he concluded a short Latin grace with a long draught from the leathern bottle.

"That, too, you call a part of your liberty," said the Saracen; "and as you feed like the brutes, so you degrade yourself to the bestial conditions, by drinking a poisonous liquor which even they refuse!"

"Know, foolish Saracen," replied the Christian, without hesitation, "that thou blasphemest the gifts of God, even with the blasphemy of thy father Ishmael. The juice of the grape is given to him that will use it wisely, as that which cheers the heart of man after toil, refreshes him in sickness, and comforts him in sorrow. He who so enjoyeth it may thank God for his wine-cup as for his daily bread; and he who abuseth the gift of Heaven is not a greater fool in his intoxication than thou in thine abstinence."

The keen eye of the Saracen kindled at this sarcasm, and his hand sought the hilt of his poniard. It was but a momentary thought, however, and died away in the recollection of the powerful champion with whom he had to deal, and the desperate grapple, the impression of which still throbbed in his limbs and veins; and he contented himself with pursuing the contest in colloquy, as more convenient for the time.

"Thy words," he said, "O Nazarene, might create anger, did not thy ignorance raise compassion. Seest thou not, O thou more blind than any who asks alms at the door of the Mosque, that the liberty thou dost boast of is restrained even in that which is dearest to man's happiness, and to his household; and that that law, if thou dost practise it, binds thee in marriage to one single mate, be she sick or healthy, be she fruitful or barren, bring she comfort and joy, or clamour and strife, to thy table and to thy bed? This, Nazarene, I do indeed call slavery; whereas, to the faithful, hath the Prophet assigned upon earth the patriarchal privileges of Abraham our father, and of Solomon, the wisest of mankind, having given us here a succession of beauty at our pleasure, and beyond the grave the black-eyed houris of Paradise."

"Now, by His name that I most reverence in Heaven," said the Christian, "and by hers whom I most worship on earth, thou art but a blinded and a bewildered infidel!—That diamond signet, which thou wearest on thy finger, thou holdest it, doubtless, as of inestimable value?"

"Balsora and Bagdad cannot show the like," replied the Saracen; "but what avails it to our purpose?"

"Much," replied the Frank, "as thou shalt thyself confess. Take my war-axe, and dash the stone into twenty shivers;— would each fragment be as valuable as the original gem, or would they, all collected, bear the tenth part of its estimation?"

"That is a child's question," answered the Saracen; "the fragments of such a stone would not equal the entire jewel in the degree of hundreds to one."

"Saracen," replied the Christian warrior, "the love which a true knight binds on one only, fair and faithful, is the gem entire; the affection thou flingest among thy enslaved wives, and half-wedded slaves, is worthless, comparatively, as the sparkling shivers of the broken diamond."

"Now, by the Holy Caaba," said the Emir, "thou art a madman, who hugs his chain of iron as if it were of gold!—Look more closely. This ring of mine would lose half its beauty were not the signet encircled and enchased with these lesser brilliants, which grace it and set it off. The central diamond is man, firm and entire, his value depending on himself alone; and this circle of lesser jewels are women, borrowing his lustre, which he deals out to them as best suits his pleasure or his convenience. Take the central stone from the signet, and the diamond itself remains as valuable as ever, while the lesser gems are comparatively of little value. And this is the true reading of thy parable; for what sayeth the poet Mansour: 'It is the favour of man which giveth beauty and comeliness to woman, as the stream glitters no longer when the sun ceaseth to shine.'"

"Saracen," replied the Crusader, "thou speakest like one who never saw a woman worthy the affection of a soldier. Believe me, couldst thou look upon those of Europe, to whom, after Heaven, we of the order of knighthood vow fealty and devotion, thou wouldst loathe for ever the poor sensual slaves who form thy harem. The beauty of our fair ones gives point to our spears, and edge to our swords; their words are our law; and as soon will a lamp shed lustre when unkindled, as a knight distinguish himself by feats of arms, having no mistress of his affection."

"I have heard of this frenzy among the warriors of the West," said the Emir, "and have ever accounted it one of the accompanying symptoms of that insanity, which brings you hither to obtain possession of an empty sepulchre. But yet, methinks, so highly have the Franks whom I have met with extolled the beauty of their women, I could be well contented to behold with mine own eyes those charms which can transform such brave warriors into the tools of their pleasure."

"Brave Saracen," said the knight, "if I were not on a pilgrimage to the Holy Sepulchre, it should be my pride to conduct you, on assurance of safety, to the camp of Richard of England, than whom none knows better how to do honour to a noble foe; and though I be poor a..d unattended, yet have I interest to secure for thee, or any such as thou seemest, not safety only, but respect and esteem. There shouldst thou see several of the fairest beauties of France and Britain form a small circle, the brilliancy of which exceeds ten thousand-fold the lustre of mines of diamonds such as thine."

"Now, by the corner-stone of the Caaba!" said the Saracen, "I will accept thy invitation as freely as it is given, if thou wilt postpone thy present intent; and, credit me, brave Nazarene, it were better for thyself to turn back thy horse's head towards the camp of thy people, for, to travel towards Jerusalem without a passport, is but a wilful casting away of thy life."

"I have a pass," answered the knight, producing a parchment, "under Saladin's hand and signet."

The Saracen bent his head to the dust as he recognised the seal and handwriting of the renowned Soldan of Egypt and Syria; and having kissed the paper with profound respect, he pressed it to his forehead, then returned it to the Christian, saying, "Rash Frank, thou hast sinned against thine own blood and mine, for not showing this to me when we met."

"You came with levelled spear," said the knight; "had a troop of Saracens so assailed me, it might have stood with my honour to have shown the Soldan's pass, but never to one man."

"And yet one man," said the Saracen, haughtily, "was enough to interrupt your journey."

"True, brave Moslem," replied the Christian; "but there are few such as thou art. Such falcons fly not in flocks, or, if they do, they pounce not in numbers upon one."

"Thou dost us but justice," said the Saracen, evidently gratified by the compliment, as he had been touched by the implied scorn of the European's previous boast; "from us thou shouldst have had no wrong; but well was it for me that I failed to slay thee, with the safeguard of the king of kings upon thy person. Certain it were that the cord or the sabre had justly avenged such guilt."

"I am glad to hear that its influence shall be availing to me," said the knight; "for I have heard that the road is infested with robber-tribes, who regard nothing in comparison of an opportunity of plunder."

"The truth has been told to thee, brave Christian," said the Saracen; "but I swear to thee, by the turban of the Prophet, that shouldst thou miscarry in any haunt of such villains, I will myself undertake thy revenge with five thousand horse; I will slay every male of them, and send their women into such distant captivity, that the name of their tribe shall never again be heard within five hundred miles of Damascus. I will sow with salt the foundations of their village, and there shall never live thing dwell there, even from that time forward."

"I had rather the trouble which you design for yourself, were in revenge of some other more important person than of me, noble Emir," replied the knight; "but my vow is recorded in Heaven, for good or for evil, and I must be indebted to you for pointing me out the way to my resting-place for this evening."

"That," said the Saracen, "must be under the black covering of my father's tent."

"This night," answered the Christian, "I must pass in prayer and penitence with a holy man, Theodorick of Engaddi, who dwells amongst these wilds, and spends his life in the service of God."

"I will at least see you safe thither," said the Saracen.

"That would be pleasant convoy for me," said the Christian, "yet might endanger the future security of the good father; for the cruel hand of your people has been red with the blood of the servants of the Lord, and therefore do we come hither in plate and mail, with sword and lance, to open the road to the Holy Sepulchre, and protect the chosen saints and anchorites who yet dwell in this land of promise and of miracle."

"Nazarene," said the Moslem, "in this the Greeks and Syrians have much belied us, seeing we do but after the word of Abubeker Alwakel, the successor of the Prophet, and, after him, the first commander of true believers. 'Go forth,' he said, 'Yezed Ben Sophian,' when he sent that renowned general to take Syria from the infidels, 'quit yourselves like men in battle, but slay neither the aged, the infirm, the women, nor the children. Waste not the land, neither destroy corn and fruit-trees, they are the gifts of Allah. Keep faith when you have made any covenant, even if it be to your own harm. If ye find holy men labouring with their hands, and serving God in the desert, hurt them not, neither destroy their dwellings. But when you find them with shaven crowns, they are of the synagogue of Satan! smite with the sabre, slay, cease not till they become believers or tributaries.' As the Caliph, companion of the Prophet, hath told us, so have we done, and those whom our justice has smitten are but the priests of Satan. But unto the good men who, without stirring up nation against nation, worship sincerely in the faith of Issa Ben Mariam, we are a shadow and a shield; and such being he whom you seek, even though the light of the Prophet hath not reached him, from me he will only have love, favour, and regard."

"The anchorite whom I would now visit," said the warlike pilgrim, "is, I have heard, no priest; but were he of that anointed and sacred order, I would prove with my good lance, against paynim and infidel——"

"Let us not defy each other, brother," interrupted the Saracen; "we shall find, either of us, enough of Franks or of Moslemah on whom to exercise both sword and lance. This Theodorick is protected both by Turk and Arab; and, though one of strange conditions at intervals, yet, on the whole, he bears himself so well as the follower of his own prophet, that he merits the protection of him who was sent——"

"Now, by Our Lady, Saracen," exclaimed the Christian, "if thou darest name in the same breath the camel-driver of Mecca with——"

An electrical shock of passion thrilled through the form of the Emir; but it was only momentary, and the calmness of his reply had both dignity and reason in it, when he said, "Slander not him whom thou knowest not; the rather that we venerate the founder of thy religion, while we condemn the doctrine which your priests have spun from it. I will myself guide thee to the cavern of the hermit, which, methinks, without my help, thou wouldst find it a hard matter to reach. And, on the way, let us leave to mollahs and to monks, to dispute about the divinity of our faith, and speak on themes which belong to youthful warriors,—upon battles, upon beautiful women, upon sharp swords, and upon bright armour."

CHAPTER III

THE warriors arose from their place of brief rest and simple refreshment, and courteously aided each other while they carefully replaced and adjusted the harness, from which they had relieved for the time their trusty steeds. Each seemed familiar with an employment, which at that time was a part of necessary, and, indeed, of indispensable duty. Each also seemed to possess, as far as the difference betwixt the animal and rational species admitted, the confidence and affection of the horse, which was the constant companion of his travels and his warfare. With the Saracen, this familiar intimacy was a part of his early habits; for, in the tents of the Eastern military tribes, the horse of the soldier ranks next to, and almost equal in importance with, his wife and his family; and, with the European warrior, circumstances, and indeed necessity, rendered his war-horse scarcely less than his brother-in-arms. The steeds, therefore, suffered themselves quietly to be taken from their food and liberty, and neighed and snuffled fondly around their masters, while they were adjusting their accoutrements for farther travel and additional toil. And each warrior, as he prosecuted his own task, or assisted with courtesy his companion, looked with observant curiosity at the equipments of his fellow-traveller, and noted particularly what struck him as peculiar in the fashion in which he arranged his riding accoutrements.

Ere they remounted to resume their journey, the Christian knight again moistened his lips, and dipt his hands in the living fountain, and said to his Pagan associate of the journey —" I would I knew the name of this delicious fountain, that I might hold it in my grateful remembrance; for never did water slake more deliciously a more oppressive thirst than I have this day experienced."

"It is called in the Arabic language," answered the Saracen, "by a name which signifies the Diamond of the Desert."

"And well is it so named," replied the Christian. "My native valley hath a thousand springs, but not to one of them shall I attach hereafter such precious recollection as to this solitary fount, which bestows its liquid treasures where they are not only delightful, but nearly indispensable."

"You say truth," said the Saracen; "for the curse is still on yonder sea of death, and neither man nor beast drinks of its waves, nor of the river which feeds without filling it, until this inhospitable desert be passed."

They mounted, and pursued their journey across the sandy waste. The ardour of noon was now past, and a light breeze somewhat alleviated the terrors of the desert, though not without bearing on its wings an impalpable dust, which the Saracen little heeded, though his heavily-armed companion felt it as such an annoyance, that he hung his iron casque at his saddle-bow, and substituted the light riding-cap, termed in the language of the time a *mortier*, from its resemblance in shape to an ordinary mortar. They rode together for some time in silence, the Saracen performing the part of director and guide of the journey, which he did by observing minute marks and bearings of the distant rocks, to a ridge of which they were gradually approaching. For a little time he seemed absorbed in the task, as a pilot when navigating a vessel through a difficult channel; but they had not proceeded half a league when he seemed secure of his route, and disposed, with more frankness than was usual to his nation, to enter into conversation.

"You have asked the name," he said, "of a mute fountain, which hath the semblance, but not the reality, of a living thing. Let me be pardoned to ask the name of the companion with whom I have this day encountered, both in danger and in repose, and which I cannot fancy unknown, even here among the deserts of Palestine?"

"It is not yet worth publishing," said the Christian. "Know, however, that among the soldiers of the Cross I am called Kenneth—Kenneth of the Couching Leopard; at home I have other titles; but they would sound harsh in an Eastern ear. Brave Saracen, let me ask which of the tribes of Arabia claims your descent, and by what name you are known?"

"Sir Kenneth," said the Moslem, "I joy that your name is such as my lips can easily utter. For me, I am no Arab, yet derive my descent from a line neither less wild nor less warlike. Know, Sir Knight of the Leopard, that I am Sheerkohf, the Lion of the Mountain, and that Kurdistan, from which I derive my descent, holds no family more noble than that of Seljook."

"I have heard," answered the Christian, "that your great Soldan claims his blood from the same source?"

"Thanks to the Prophet, that hath so far honoured our mountains, as to send from their bosom him whose word is victory," answered the Paynim. "I am but as a worm before the King of Egypt and Syria, and yet in my own land something my name may avail.—Stranger, with how many men didst thou come on this warfare?"

"By my faith," said Sir Kenneth, "with aid of friends and kinsmen, I was hardly pinched to furnish forth ten well-appointed lances, with maybe some fifty more men, archers and varlets included. Some have deserted my unlucky pennon—some have fallen in battle—several have died of disease—and one trusty armour-bearer, for whose life I am now doing my pilgrimage, lies on the bed of sickness."

"Christian," said Sheerkohf, "here I have five arrows in my quiver, each feathered from the wing of an eagle. When I send one of them to my tents, a thousand warriors mount on horseback—when I send another, an equal force will arise—

for the five, I can command five thousand men; and if I send my bow, ten thousand mounted riders will shake the desert. And with thy fifty followers thou hast come to invade a land, in which I am one of the meanest!"

"Now, by the rood, Saracen," retorted the Western warrior, "thou shouldst know, ere thou vauntest thyself, that one steel glove can crush a whole handful of hornets."

"Ay, but it must first enclose them within its grasp," said the Saracen, with a smile which might have endangered their new alliance, had he not changed the subject by adding, "And is bravery so much esteemed amongst the Christian princes, that thou, thus void of means and of men, canst offer, as thou didst of late, to be my protector and security in the camp of thy brethren?"

"Know, Saracen," said the Christian, "since such is thy style, that the name of a knight, and the blood of a gentleman, entitle him to place himself on the same rank with sovereigns even of the first degree, in so far as regards all but regal authority and dominion. Were Richard of England himself to wound the honour of a knight as poor as I am, he could not, by the law of chivalry, deny him the combat."

"Methinks I should like to look upon so strange a scene," said the Emir, "in which a leathern belt and a pair of spurs put the poorest on a level with the most powerful."

"You must add free blood and a fearless heart," said the Christian; "then, perhaps, you will not have spoken untruly of the dignity of knighthood."

"And mix you as boldly amongst the females of your chiefs and leaders?" asked the Saracen.

"God forbid," said the Knight of the Leopard, "that the poorest knight in Christendom should not be free, in all honourable service, to devote his hand and sword, the fame of his actions, and the fixed devotion of his heart, to the fairest princess who ever wore coronet on her brow!"

"But a little while since," said the Saracen, "and you described love as the highest treasure of the heart—thine hath undoubtedly been high and nobly bestowed?"

"Stranger," answered the Christian, blushing deeply as he spoke, "we tell not rashly where it is we have bestowed our choicest treasures; it is enough for thee to know, that, as thou sayest, my love is highly and nobly bestowed—most highly—most nobly; but if thou wouldst hear of love and broken lances, venture thyself, as thou sayest, to the camp of the

Crusaders, and thou wilt find exercise for thine ears, and, if thou wilt, for thy hands too."

The Eastern warrior, raising himself in his stirrups, and shaking aloft his lance, replied, "Hardly, I fear, shall I find one with a crossed shoulder, who will exchange with me the cast of the jerrid."

"I will not promise for that," replied the knight, "though there be in the camp certain Spaniards, who have right good skill in your Eastern game of hurling the javelin."

"Dogs, and sons of dogs!" ejaculated the Saracen; "what have these Spaniards to do to come hither to combat the true believers, who, in their own land, are their lords and task-masters? with them I would mix in no warlike pastime."

"Let not the knights of Leon or Asturias hear you speak thus of them," said the Knight of the Leopard; "but," added he, smiling at the recollection of the morning's combat, "if, instead of a reed, you were inclined to stand the cast of a battle-axe, there are enough of Western warriors who would gratify your longing."

"By the beard of my father, sir," said the Saracen, with an approach to laughter, "the game is too rough for mere sport—I will never shun them in battle, but my head" (pressing his hand to his brow) "will not, for a while, permit me to seek them in sport."

"I would you saw the axe of King Richard," answered the Western warrior, "to which that which hangs at my saddlebow weighs but as a feather."

"We hear much of that island sovereign," said the Saracen; "art thou one of his subjects?"

"One of his followers I am, for this expedition," answered the knight, "and honoured in the service; but not born his subject, although a native of the island in which he reigns."

"How mean you?" said the Eastern soldier; "have you then two kings in one poor island?"

"As thou sayest," said the Scot, for such was Sir Kenneth by birth,—"It is even so; and yet, although the inhabitants of the two extremities of that island are engaged in frequent war, the country can, as thou seest, furnish forth such a body of men-at-arms, as may go far to shake the unholy hold which your master hath laid on the cities of Zion."

"By the beard of Saladin, Nazarene, but that it is a thought-less and boyish folly, I could laugh at the simplicity of your great Sultan, who comes hither to make conquests of deserts and rocks, and dispute the possession of them with those who have tenfold numbers at command, while he leaves a part of his narrow islet, in which he was born a sovereign, to the dominion of another sceptre than his. Surely, Sir Kenneth, you and the other good men of your country should have submitted yourselves to the dominion of this King Richard, ere you left your native land, divided against itself, to set forth on this expedition?"

Hasty and fierce was Kenneth's answer. "No, by the bright light of Heaven! If the King of England had not set forth to the Crusade till he was sovereign of Scotland, the Crescent might, for me, and all true-hearted Scots, glimmer for ever on the walls of Zion."

Thus far he had proceeded, when, suddenly recollecting himself, he muttered, "*Mea culpa! mea culpa!* what have I, a soldier of the Cross, to do with recollection of war betwixt Christian nations!"

The rapid expression of feeling, corrected by the dictates of duty, did not escape the Moslem, who, if he did not entirely understand all which it conveyed, saw enough to convince him with the assurance, that Christians, as well as Moslemah, had private feelings of personal pique, and national quarrels, which were not entirely reconcilable. But the Saracens were a race, polished, perhaps, to the utmost extent which their religion permitted, and particularly capable of entertaining high ideas of courtesy and politeness; and such sentiments prevented his taking any notice of the inconsistency of Sir Kenneth's feelings, in the opposite characters of a Scot and a Crusader.

Meanwhile, as they advanced, the scene began to change around them. They were now turning to the eastward, and had reached the range of steep and barren hills, which binds in that quarter the naked plain, and varies the surface of the country, without changing its sterile character. Sharp, rocky eminences began to arise around them, and, in a short time, deep declivities and ascents, both formidable in height and difficult from the narrowness of the path, offered to the travellers obstacles of a different kind from those with which they had recently contended. Dark caverns and chasms amongst the rocks, those grottoes so often alluded to in Scripture, yawned fearfully on either side as they proceeded, and the Scottish knight was informed by the Emir that these were often the refuge of beasts of prey, or of men still more ferocious, who, driven to desperation by the constant war and, the oppression exercised by the soldiery, as well of the Cross as of the Crescent, had become robbers, and spared neither rank nor religion, neither sex nor age, in their depredations.

The Scottish knight listened with indifference to the accounts of ravages committed by wild beasts or wicked men, secure as he felt himself in his own valour and personal strength ; but he was struck with mysterious dread, when he recollected that he was now in the awful wilderness of the forty days' fast, and the scene of the actual personal temptation, wherewith the Evil Principle was permitted to assail the Son of Man. He withdrew his attention gradually from the light and worldly conversation of the infidel warrior beside him, and, however acceptable his gay and gallant bravery would have rendered him as a companion elsewhere, Sir Kenneth felt as if, in those wildernesses—the waste and dry places—in which the foul spirits were wont to wander when expelled the mortals whose forms they possessed, a barefooted friar would have been a better associate than the gay but unbelieving Paynim.

These feelings embarrassed him ; the rather that the Saracen's spirits appeared to rise with the journey, and because the farther he penetrated into the gloomy recesses of the mountains, the lighter became his conversation, and when he found that unanswered, the louder grew his song. Sir Kenneth knew enough of the Eastern languages to be assured that he chanted sonnets of love, containing all the glowing praises of beauty, in which the Oriental poets are so fond of luxuriating, and which, therefore, were peculiarly unfitted for a serious or devotional strain of thought, the feeling best becoming the Wilderness of the Temptation. With inconsistency enough, the Saracen also sung lays in praise of wine, the liquid ruby of the Persian poets, and his gaiety at length became so unsuitable to the Christian knight's contrary train of sentiments, as, but for the promise of amity which they had exchanged, would most likely have made Sir Kenneth take measures to change his note. As it was, the Crusader felt as if he had by his side some gay licentious fiend, who endeavoured to ensnare his soul, and endanger his immortal salvation, by inspiring loose thoughts of earthly pleasure, and thus polluting his devotion, at a time when his faith as a Christian, and his vow as a pilgrim, called on him for a serious and penitential state of mind. He was thus greatly perplexed, and undecided how to act ; and it was in a tone of hasty displeasure, that, at length breaking silence, he interrupted the lay of the celebrated

Rudpiki, in which he prefers the mole on his mistress's bosom to all the wealth of Bokhara and Samarcand.

"Saracen," said the Crusader, sternly, "blinded as thou art, and plunged amidst the errors of a false law, thou shouldst yet comprehend that there are some places more holy than others, and that there are some scenes also, in which the Evil One hath more than ordinary power over sinful mortals. I will not tell thee for what awful reason this place—these rocks—these caverns with their gloomy arches, leading as it were to the central abyss—are held an especial haunt of Satan and his angels. It is enough, that I have been long warned to beware of this place by wise and holy men, to whom the qualities of the unholy region are well known. Wherefore, Saracen, forbear thy foolish and ill-timed levity, and turn thy thoughts to things more suited to the spot; although, alas, for thee! thy best prayers are but as blasphemy and sin."

The Saracen listened with some surprise, and then replied, with good-humour and gaiety, only so far repressed as courtesy required, "Good Sir Kenneth, methinks you deal unequally by your companion, or else ceremony is but indifferently taught amongst your Western tribes. I took no offence when I saw you gorge hog's flesh and drink wine, and permitted you to enjoy a treat which you called your Christian liberty, only pitying in my heart your foul pastimes. Wherefore, then, shouldst thou take scandal because I cheer, to the best of my power, a gloomy road with a cheerful verse? What saith the poet, 'Song is like the dews of Heaven on the bosom of the desert; it cools the path of the traveller.'"

"Friend Saracen," said the Christian, "I blame not the love of minstrelsy and of the *gai science;* albeit we yield unto it even too much room in our thoughts, when they should be bent on better things. But prayers and holy psalms are better fitting than lays of love, or of wine-cups, when men walk in this Valley of the Shadow of Death, full of fiends and demons, whom the prayers of holy men have driven forth from the haunts of humanity to wander amidst scenes as accursed as themselves."

"Speak not thus of the Genii, Christian," answered the Saracen, "for know, thou speakest to one whose line and nation drew their origin from the immortal race, which your sect fear and blaspheme."

"I well thought," answered the Crusader, "that your blinded race had their descent from the foul fiend, without whose aid you would never have been able to maintain this blessed land of Palestine against so many valiant soldiers of God. I speak not thus of thee in particular, Saracen, but generally of thy people and religion. Strange is it to me, however, not that you should have the descent from the Evil One, but that you should boast of it."

"From whom should the bravest boast of descending, saving from him that is bravest?" said the Saracen; "from whom should the proudest trace their line so well as from the Dark Spirit, which would rather fall headlong by force, than bend the knee by his will? Eblis may be hated, stranger, but he must be feared; and such as Eblis are his descendants of Kurdistan."

Tales of magic and of necromancy were the learning of the period, and Sir Kenneth heard his companion's confession of diabolical descent without any disbelief, and without much wonder; yet not without a secret shudder at finding himself in this fearful place, in the company of one who avouched himself to belong to such a lineage. Naturally unsusceptible, however, of fear, he crossed himself, and stoutly demanded of the Saracen an account of the pedigree which he had boasted. The latter readily complied.

"Know, brave stranger," he said, "that when the cruel Zohauk, one of the descendants of Giamschid, held the throne of Persia, he formed a league with the powers of darkness, amidst the secret vaults of Istakhar, vaults which the hands of the elementary spirits had hewn out of the living rock, long before Adam himself had an existence. Here he fed, with daily oblations of human blood, two devouring serpents, which had become, according to the poets, a part of himself, and to sustain whom he levied a tax of daily human sacrifices, till the exhausted patience of his subjects caused some to raise up the scimitar of resistance, like the valiant Blacksmith, and the victorious Feridoun, by whom the tyrant was at length dethroned, and imprisoned for ever in the dismal caverns of the mountain Damavend. But ere that deliverance had taken place, and whilst the power of the bloodthirsty tyrant was at its height, the band of ravening slaves, whom he had sent forth to purvey victims for his daily sacrifice, brought to the vaults of the palace of Istakhar seven sisters so beautiful, that they seemed seven houris. These seven maidens were the daughters of a sage, who had no treasures save those beauties and his own wisdom. The last was not sufficient to foresee this misfortune; the former seemed ineffectual to prevent it. The eldest exceeded not her twentieth year, the youngest had scarce attained her thirteenth; and so like were they to each other that they could not have been distinguished but for the difference of height, in which they gradually rose in easy gradation above each other, like the ascent which leads to the gates of Paradise. So lovely were these seven sisters when they stood in the darksome vault, disrobed of all clothing saving a cymar of white silk, that their charms moved the hearts of those who were not mortal. Thunder muttered, the earth shook, the wall of the vault was rent, and at the chasm entered one dressed like a hunter, with bow and shafts, and followed by six others, his brethren. They were tall men, and though dark, yet comely to behold, but their eyes had more the glare of those of the dead, than the light which lives under the eyelids of the living. 'Zeineb,' said the leader of the band—and as he spoke he took the eldest sister by the hand, and his voice was soft, low, and melancholy—' I am Cothrob, king of the subterranean world, and supreme chief of Ginnistan. I and my brethren are of those who, created out of the pure elementary fire, disdained, even at the command of Omnipotence, to do homage to a clod of earth, because it was called Man. Thou mayst have heard of us as cruel, unrelenting, and persecuting. It is false. We are by nature kind and generous, only vengeful when insulted, only cruel when affronted. We are true to those who trust us; and we have heard the invocations of thy father, the sage Mithrasp, who wisely worships not alone the Origin of Good, but that which is called the Source of Evil. You and your sisters are on the eve of death; but let each give to us one hair from your fair tresses, in token of fealty, and we will carry you many miles from hence to a place of safety, where you may bid defiance to Zohauk and his ministers.' The fear of instant death, saith the poet, is like the rod of the prophet Haroun, which devoured all other rods, when transformed into snakes before King Pharaoh; and the daughters of the Persian sage were less apt than others to be afraid of the addresses of a spirit. They gave the tribute which Cothrob demanded, and in an instant the sisters were transported to an enchanted castle on the mountains of Tugrut, in Kurdistan, and were never again seen by mortal eye. But in process of time seven youths, distinguished in the war and in the chase, appeared in the environs of the castle of the demons. They were darker, taller, fiercer, and more resolute than any of the scattered inhabitants of the valleys of Kurdistan; and they took to themselves wives, and became fathers of the seven tribes of the Kurdmans, whose valour is known throughout the universe."

The Christian knight heard with wonder the wild tale, of which Kurdistan still possesses the traces, and, after a moment's thought, replied,—"Verily, Sir Knight, you have spoken well; your genealogy may be dreaded and hated, but it cannot be contemned. Neither do I any longer wonder at your obstinacy in a false faith, since, doubtless, it is part of the fiendish disposition which hath descended from your ancestors, those infernal huntsmen, as you have described them, to love falsehood rather than truth; and I no longer marvel that your spirits become high and exalted, and vent themselves in verse and in tunes, when you approach to the places encumbered by the haunting of evil spirits, which must excite in you that joyous feeling which others experience when approaching the land of their human ancestry."

"By my father's beard, I think thou hast the right," said the Saracen, rather amused than offended by the freedom with which the Christian had uttered his reflections; "for, though the Prophet (blessed be his name!) hath sown amongst us the seed of a better faith than our ancestors learned in the ghostly halls of Tugrut, yet we are not willing, like other Moslemah, to pass hasty doom on the lofty and powerful elementary spirits from whom we claim our origin. These Genii, according to our belief and hope, are not altogether reprobate, but are still in the way of probation, and may hereafter be punished or rewarded. Leave we this to the mollahs and the imaums. Enough that with us the reverence for these spirits is not altogether effaced by what we have learned from the Koran, and that many of us still sing, in memorial of our fathers' more ancient faith, such verses as these."

So saying, he proceeded to chant verses, very ancient in the language and structure, which some have thought derive their source from the worshippers of Arimanes, the Evil Principle.

AHRIMAN

Dark Ahriman, whom Irak still
Holds origin of woe and ill!
  When, bending at thy shrine,
We view the world with troubled eye
Where see we 'neath the extended sky,
  An empire matching thine!

If the Benigner Power can yield
A fountain in the desert field,
    Where weary pilgrims drink ;
Thine are the waves that lash the rock,
Thine the tornado's deadly shock,
    Where countless navies sink !

Or if He bid the soil dispense
Balsams to cheer the sinking sense,
    How few can they deliver
From lingering pains, or pang intense,
Red Fever, spotted Pestilence,
    The arrows of thy quiver !

Chief in Man's bosom sits thy sway,
And frequent, while in words we pray
    Before another throne,
Whate'er of specious form be there,
The secret meaning of the prayer
    Is, Ahriman, thine own.

Say, hast thou feeling, sense, and form,
Thunder thy voice, thy garments storm,
    As Eastern Magi say ;
With sentient soul of hate and wrath,
And wings to sweep thy deadly path,
    And fangs to tear thy prey ?

Or art thou mix'd in Nature's source,
An ever-operating force,
    Converting good to ill ;
An evil principle innate,
Contending with our better fate,
    And oh ! victorious still ?

Howe'er it be, dispute is vain,
On all without thou hold'st thy reign,
    Nor less on all within ;
Each mortal passion's fierce career,
Love, hate, ambition, joy, and fear,
    Thou goadest into sin.

Whene'er a sunny gleam appears,
To brighten up our vale of tears,
    Thou art not distant far ;
'Mid such brief solace of our lives,
Thou whett'st our very banquet-knives
    To tools of death and war.

Thus, from the moment of our birth,
Long as we linger on the earth,
    Thou rul'st the fate of men ;

Thine are the pangs of life's last hour,
And—who dare answer ?—is thy power,
Dark Spirit ! ended THEN ![1]

These verses may perhaps have been the not unnatural
effusion of some half-enlightened philosopher, who, in the
fabled deity, Arimanes, saw but the prevalence of moral and
physical evil; but in the ears of Sir Kenneth of the Leopard,
they had a different effect, and, sung as they were by one who
had just boasted himself a descendant of demons, sounded
very like an address of worship to the Arch-fiend himself. He
weighed within himself, whether, on hearing such blasphemy
in the very desert where Satan had stood rebuked for demanding homage, taking an abrupt leave of the Saracen was
sufficient to testify his abhorrence; or whether he was not
rather constrained by his vow as a Crusader, to defy the
infidel to combat on the spot, and leave him food for the
beasts of the wilderness, when his attention was suddenly
caught by an unexpected apparition.

The light was now verging low, yet served the knight still to
discern that they two were no longer alone in the forest, but
were closely watched by a figure of great height and very thin,
which skipped over rocks and bushes with so much agility, as,
added to the wild and hirsute appearance of the individual,
reminded him of the fauns and silvans, whose images he had
seen in the ancient temples of Rome. As the single-hearted
Scotchman had never for a moment doubted these gods of the
ancient Gentiles to be actually devils, so he now hesitated not
to believe that the blasphemous hymn of the Saracen had
raised up an infernal spirit.

"But what recks it!" said stout Sir Kenneth to himself;
"down with the fiend and his worshippers!"

He did not, however, think it necessary to give the same

[1] The worthy and learned clergyman, by whom this species of hymn has
been translated, desires, that, for fear of misconception, we should warn
the reader to recollect, that it is composed by a heathen, to whom the real
causes of moral and physical evil are unknown, and who views their
predominance in the system of the universe, as all must view that appalling
fact, who have not the benefit of the Christian Revelation. On our own
part, we beg to add, that we understand the style of the translator is more
paraphrastic than can be approved by those who are acquainted with the
singularly curious original. The translator seems to have despaired of
rendering into English verse the flights of Oriental poetry ; and possibly,
like many learned and ingenious men, finding it impossible to discover the
sense of the original, he may have tacitly substituted his own.

warning of defiance to two enemies, as he would unquestionably have afforded to one. His hand was upon his mace, and perhaps the unwary Saracen would have been paid for his Persian poetry, by having his brains dashed out on the spot, without any reason assigned for it; but the Scottish knight was spared from committing what would have been a sore blot in his shield of arms. The apparition, on which his eyes had been fixed for some time, had at first appeared to dog their path by concealing itself behind rocks and shrubs, using those advantages of the ground with great address, and surmounting its irregularities with surprising agility. At length, just as the Saracen paused in his song, the figure, which was that of a tall man clothed in goat-skins, sprung into the midst of the path, and seized a rein of the Saracen's bridle in either hand, confronting thus and bearing back the noble horse, which, unable to endure the manner in which this sudden assailant pressed the long-armed bit and the severe curb, which, according to the Eastern fashion, was a solid ring of iron, reared upright, and finally fell backwards on his master, who, however, avoided the peril of the fall, by lightly throwing himself to one side.

The assailant then shifted his grasp from the bridle of the horse to the throat of the rider, flung himself above the struggling Saracen, and, despite of his youth and activity, kept him undermost, wreathing his long arms above those of his prisoner, who called out angrily, and yet half-laughing at the same time—"Hamako—fool—unloose me—this passes thy privilege—unloose me, or I will use my dagger."

"Thy dagger, infidel dog!" said the figure in the goat-skins; "hold it in thy gripe if thou canst!" and in an instant he wrenched the Saracen's weapon out of its owner's hand, and brandished it over his head.

"Help, Nazarene!" cried Sheerkohf, now seriously alarmed; "help, or the Hamako will slay me."

"Slay thee!" replied the dweller of the desert; "and well hast thou merited death, for singing thy blasphemous hymns, not only to the praise of thy false prophet, who is the foul fiend's harbinger, but to that of the Author of Evil himself."

The Christian knight had hitherto looked on as one stupified, so strangely had this rencontre contradicted, in its progress and event, all that he had previously conjectured. He felt, however, at length, that it touched his honour to interfere in behalf of his discomfited companion ; and therefore addressed himself to the victorious figure in the goat-skins.

"Whosoe'er thou art," he said, "and whether of good or of evil, know that I am sworn for the time to be true companion to the Saracen whom thou holdest under thee; therefore, I pray thee to let him arise, else I will do battle with thee in his behalf."

"And a proper quarrel it were," answered the Hamako, "for a Crusader to do battle in—for the sake of an unbaptized dog to combat one of his own holy faith ! Art thou come forth to the wilderness to fight for the Crescent against the Cross ? A goodly soldier of God art thou, to listen to those who sing the praises of Satan !"

Yet, while he spoke thus, he arose himself, and, suffering the Saracen to arise also, returned him his cangiar, or poniard.

"Thou seest to what a point of peril thy presumption hath brought thee," continued he of the goat-skins, now addressing Sheerkohf, "and by what weak means thy practised skill and boasted agility can be foiled, when such is Heaven's pleasure. Wherefore, beware, O Ilderim ! for know that, were there not a twinkle in the star of thy nativity which promises for thee something that is good and gracious in Heaven's good time, we two had not parted till I had torn asunder the throat which so lately trilled forth blasphemies."

"Hamako," said the Saracen, without any appearance of resenting the violent language, and yet more violent assault, to which he had been subjected, "I pray thee, good Hamako, to beware how thou dost again urge thy privilege over far ; for though, as a good Moslem, I respect those whom Heaven hath deprived of ordinary reason, in order to endow them with the spirit of prophecy, yet I like not other men's hands on the bridle of my horse, neither upon my own person. Speak, therefore, what thou wilt, secure of any resentment from me ; but gather so much sense as to apprehend, that if thou shalt again proffer me any violence, I will strike thy shagged head from thy meagre shoulders.—And to thee, friend Kenneth," he added, as he remounted his steed, "I must needs say, that, in a companion through the desert, I love friendly deeds better than fair words. Of the last thou hast given me enough ; but it had been better to have aided me more speedily in my struggle with this Hamako, who had well-nigh taken my life in his frenzy."

"By my faith," said the knight, "I did somewhat fail—was somewhat tardy in rendering thee instant help; but the strangeness of the assailant, the suddenness of the scene—it was as if thy wild and wicked lay had raised the devil among us—and such was my confusion, that two or three minutes elapsed ere I could take to my weapon."

"Thou art but a cold and considerate friend," said the Saracen; "and, had the Hamako been one grain more frantic, thy companion had been slain by thy side, to thy eternal dishonour, without thy stirring a finger in his aid, although thou satest by, mounted, and in arms."

"By my word, Saracen," said the Christian, "if thou wilt have it in plain terms, I thought that strange figure was the devil; and being of thy lineage, I knew not what family secret you might be communicating to each other, as you lay lovingly rolling together on the sand."

"Thy gibe is no answer, brother Kenneth," said the Saracen; "for know, that had my assailant been in very deed the Prince of Darkness, thou wert bound not the less to enter into combat with him in thy comrade's behalf. Know, also, that whatever there may be of foul or of fiendish about the Hamako, belongs more to your lineage than to mine; this Hamako being, in truth, the anchorite whom thou art come hither to visit."

"This!" said Sir Kenneth, looking at the athletic yet wasted figure before him,—"this!—thou mockest, Saracen—this cannot be the venerable Theodorick!"

"Ask himself, if thou wilt not believe me," answered Sheerkohf; and ere the words had left his mouth, the hermit gave evidence in his own behalf.

"I am Theodorick of Engaddi," he said—"I am the walker of the desert—I am friend of the Cross, and flail of all infidels, heretics, and devil-worshippers. Avoid ye, avoid ye!—Down with Mahound, Termagaunt, and all their adherents!"—So saying, he pulled from under his shaggy garment a sort of flail, or jointed club, bound with iron, which he brandished round his head with singular dexterity.

"Thou seest thy saint," said the Saracen, laughing for the first time at the unmitigated astonishment with which Sir Kenneth looked on the wild gestures, and heard the wayward muttering of Theodorick, who, after swinging his flail in every direction, apparently quite reckless whether it encountered the head of either of his companions, finally showed his own strength, and the soundness of the weapon, by striking into fragments a large stone which lay near him.

"This is a madman," said Sir Kenneth.

"Not the worse saint," returned the Moslem, speaking according to the well-known Eastern belief, that madmen are under the influence of immediate inspiration. "Know, Christian, that when one eye is extinguished, the other becomes more keen—when one hand is cut off, the other becomes more powerful; so, when our reason in human things is disturbed or destroyed, our view heavenward becomes more acute and perfect."

Here the voice of the Saracen was drowned in that of the hermit, who began to hollo aloud in a wild chanting tone,—"I am Theodorick of Engaddi—I am the torch-brand of the desert —I am the flail of the infidels!—The lion and the leopard shall be my comrades, and draw nigh to my cell for shelter; neither shall the goat be afraid of their fangs. I am the torch and the lantern. Kyrie Eleison!"

He closed his song by a short race, and ended that again by three forward bounds, which would have done him great credit in a gymnastic academy, but became his character of hermit so indifferently, that the Scottish knight was altogether confounded and bewildered.

The Saracen seemed to understand him better. "You see," he said, "that he expects us to follow him to his cell, which, indeed, is our only place of refuge for the night. You are the leopard, from the portrait on your shield; I am the lion, as my name imports; and, by the goat, alluding to his garb of goat-skins, he means himself. We must keep him in sight, however, for he is as fleet as a dromedary."

In fact, the task was a difficult one, for, though the reverend guide stopped from time to time, and waved his hand, as if to encourage them to come on, yet, well acquainted with all the winding dells and passes of the desert, and gifted with uncommon activity, which, perhaps, an unsettled state of mind kept in constant exercise, he led the knights through chasms, and along footpaths, where even the light-armed Saracen, with his well-trained barb, was in considerable risk, and where the iron-sheathed European, and his over-burdened horse, found themselves in such imminent peril, as the rider would gladly have exchanged for the dangers of a general action. Glad he was when, at length, after this wild race, he beheld the holy man who had led it standing in front of a cavern, with a large torch in hand, composed of a piece of wood dipt in bitumen, which cast a broad and flickering light, and emitted a strong sulphurous smell.

Undeterred by the stifling vapour, the knight threw himself from his horse and entered the cavern, which afforded small appearance of accommodation. The cell was divided into two parts, in the outward of which were an altar of stone, and a crucifix made of reeds; this served the anchorite for his chapel. On one side of this outward cave the Christian knight, though not without scruple, arising from religious reverence to the objects around, fastened up his horse, and arranged him for the night, in imitation of the Saracen, who gave him to understand that such was the custom of the place. The hermit, meanwhile, was busied putting his inner apartment in order to receive his guests, and there they soon joined him. At the bottom of the outer cave, a small aperture, closed with a door of rough plank, led into the sleeping apartment of the hermit, which was more commodious. The floor had been brought to a rough level by the labour of the inhabitant, and then strewed with white sand, which he daily sprinkled with water from a small fountain which bubbled out of the rock in one corner, affording, in that stifling climate, refreshment alike to the ear and the taste. Mattresses, wrought of twisted flags, lay by the side of the cell; the sides, like the floor, had been roughly brought to shape, and several herbs and flowers were hung around them. Two waxen torches, which the hermit lighted, gave a cheerful air to the place, which was rendered agreeable by its fragrance and coolness.

There were implements of labour in one corner of the apartment, in the other was a niche for a rude statue of the Virgin. A table and two chairs showed that they must be the handiwork of the anchorite, being different in their form from Oriental accommodations. The former was covered, not only with reeds and pulse, but also with dried flesh, which Theodorick assiduously placed in such arrangement as should invite the appetite of his guests. This appearance of courtesy, though mute; and expressed by gesture only, seemed to Sir Kenneth something entirely irreconcilable with his former wild and violent demeanour. The movements of the hermit were now become composed, and apparently it was only a sense of religious humiliation which prevented his features, emaciated as they were by his austere mode of life, from being majestic and noble. He trode his cell as one who seemed born to rule over men, but who had abdicated his empire to become the servant of Heaven. Still, it must be allowed that his gigantic size, the length of his unshaven locks and beard, and the fire of a deep-set and wild eye, were rather attributes of a soldier than of a recluse.

Even the Saracen seemed to regard the anchorite with some veneration, while he was thus employed, and he whispered in a low tone to Sir Kenneth, "The Hamako is now in his better mind, but he will not speak until we have eaten—such is his vow."

It was in silence, accordingly, that Theodorick motioned to the Scot to take his place on one of the low chairs, while Sheerkohf placed himself, after the custom of his nation, upon a cushion of mats. The hermit then held up both hands, as if blessing the refreshment which he had placed before his guests, and they proceeded to eat in silence as profound as his own. To the Saracen this gravity was natural, and the Christian imitated his taciturnity, while he employed his thoughts on the singularity of his own situation, and the contrast betwixt the wild, furious gesticulations, loud cries, and fierce actions of Theodorick, when they first met him, and the demure, solemn, decorous assiduity with which he now performed the duties of hospitality.

When their meal was ended, the hermit, who had not himself eaten a morsel, removed the fragments from the table, and placing before the Saracen a pitcher of sherbet, assigned to the Scot a flask of wine.

"Drink," he said, "my children,"—they were the first words he had spoken,—"the gifts of God are to be enjoyed when the Giver is remembered."

Having said this, he retired to the outward cell, probably for performance of his devotions, and left his guests together in the inner apartment; when Sir Kenneth endeavoured, by various questions, to draw from Sheerkohf what that Emir knew concerning his host. He was interested by more than mere curiosity in these enquiries. Difficult as it was to reconcile the outrageous demeanour of the recluse at his first appearance, to his present humble and placid behaviour, it seemed yet more impossible to think it consistent with the high consideration in which, according to what Sir Kenneth had learned, this hermit was held by the most enlightened divines of the Christian world. Theodorick, the hermit of Engaddi, had, in that character, been the correspondent of popes and councils, to whom his letters, full of eloquent fervour, had described the miseries imposed by the unbelievers upon the Latin Christians in the Holy Land, in colours scarce inferior to those employed at the Council of Clermont by the Hermit Peter, when he preached the first Crusade. To find, in a person so reverend, and so much revered, the frantic gestures of a mad fakir, induced the Christian knight to pause ere he could resolve to communicate to him certain important matters, which he had in charge from some of the leaders of the Crusade.

It had been a main object of Sir Kenneth's pilgrimage, attempted by a route so unusual, to make such communications; but what he had that night seen induced him to pause and reflect ere he proceeded to the execution of his commission. From the Emir he could not extract much information, but the general tenor was as follows:—That, as he had heard, the hermit had been once a brave and valiant soldier, wise in council, and fortunate in battle, which last he could easily believe from the great strength and agility which he had often seen him display;—that he had appeared at Jerusalem in the character not of a pilgrim, but in that of one who had devoted himself to dwell for the remainder of his life in the Holy Land. Shortly afterwards he fixed his residence amid the scenes of desolation where they now found him, respected by the Latins for his austere devotion, and by the Turks and Arabs on account of the symptoms of insanity which he displayed, and which they ascribed to inspiration. It was from them he had the name of Hamako, which expresses such a character in the Turkish language, Sheerkohf himself seemed at a loss how to rank their host. He had been, he said, a wise man, and could often for many hours together speak lessons of virtue or wisdom, without the slightest appearance of inaccuracy. At other times he was wild and violent, but never before had he seen him so mischievously disposed as he had that day appeared to be. His rage was chiefly provoked by any affront to his religion; and there was a story of some wandering Arabs, who had insulted his worship and defaced his altar, and whom he had on that account attacked and slain with the short flail, which he carried with him in lieu of all other weapons. This incident had made a great noise, and it was as much the fear of the hermit's iron flail, as regard for his character as a Hamako, which caused the roving tribes to respect his dwelling and his chapel. His fame had spread so far, that Saladin had issued particular orders that he should be spared and protected. He himself, and other Moslem lords of rank, had visited the cell more than once, partly from curiosity, partly that they expected from a man so learned as the Christian Hamako, some insight into the secrets of futurity. "He had," continued the Saracen, "a rashid, or observatory, of great height, contrived to view the heavenly bodies, and particularly the planetary system, by whose movements and influences, as both Christian and Moslem believed, the course of human events was regulated, and might be predicted."

This was the substance of the Emir Sheerkohf's information, and it left Sir Kenneth in doubt whether the character of insanity arose from the occasional excessive fervour of the hermit's zeal, or whether it was not altogether fictitious, and assumed for the sake of the immunities which it afforded. Yet it seemed that the infidels had carried their complaisance towards him to an uncommon length, considering the fanaticism of the followers of Mohammed, in the midst of whom he was living, though the professed enemy of their faith. He thought also there was more intimacy of acquaintance betwixt the hermit and the Saracen, than the words of the latter had induced him to anticipate; and it had not escaped him, that the former had called the latter by a name different from that which he himself had assumed. All these considerations authorized caution, if not suspicion. He determined to observe his host closely, and not to be over hasty in communicating with him on the important charge intrusted to him.

"Beware, Saracen," he said; "methinks our host's imagination wanders as well on the subject of names as upon other matters. Thy name is Sheerkohf, and he called thee but now by another."

"My name, when in the tent of my father," replied the Kurdman, "was Ilderim, and by this I am still distinguished by many. In the field, and to soldiers, I am known as the Lion of the Mountain, being the name my good sword hath won for me.—But hush, the Hamako comes. It is to warn us to rest. I know his custom—none must watch him at his vigils."

The anchorite accordingly entered, and folding his arms on his bosom as he stood before them, said with a solemn voice—"Blessed be His name, who hath appointed the quiet night to follow the busy day, and the calm sleep to refrehs the wearied limbs, and to compose the troubled spirit!"

Both warriors replied "Amen!" and, arising from the table,

prepared to betake themselves to the couches, which their host indicated by waving his hand, as, making a reverence to each, he again withdrew from the apartment.

The Knight of the Leopard then disarmed himself of his heavy panoply, his Saracen companion kindly assisting him to undo his buckler and clasps, until he remained in the close dress of chamois leather, which knights and men-at-arms used to wear under their harness. The Saracen, if he had admired the strength of his adversary when sheathed in steel, was now no less struck with the accuracy of proportion displayed in his nervous and well-compacted figure. The knight, on the other hand, as, in exchange of courtesy, he assisted the Saracen to disrobe himself of his upper garments, that he might sleep with more convenience, was on his side at a loss to conceive how such slender proportions, and slimness of figure, could be reconciled with the vigour he had displayed in personal contest.

Each warrior prayed ere he addressed himself to his place of rest. The Moslem turned towards his *kebla*, the point to which the prayer of each follower of the Prophet was to be addressed, and murmured his heathen orisons, while the Christian, withdrawing from the contamination of the infidel's neighbourhood, placed his huge cross-handled sword upright, and kneeling before it as the sign of salvation, told his rosary with a devotion which was enhanced by the recollection of the scenes through which he had passed, and the dangers from which he had been rescued in the course of the day. Both warriors, worn by toil and travel, were soon fast asleep, each on his separate pallet.

CHAPTER IV

KENNETH, the Scot, was uncertain how long his senses had been lost in profound repose, when he was roused to recollection by a sense of oppression on his chest, which at first suggested a flitting dream of struggling with a powerful opponent, and at length recalled him fully to his senses. He was about to demand who was there, when, opening his eyes, he beheld the figure of the anchorite, wild and savage-looking as we have described him, standing by his bedside, and pressing his right hand upon his breast, while he held a small silver lamp in the other.

"Be silent," said the hermit, as the prostrate knight looked up in surprise; "I have that to say to you which yonder infidel must not hear."

These words he spoke in the French language, and not in the lingua franca, or compound of Eastern and European dialects, which had hitherto been used amongst them.

"Arise," he continued, "put on thy mantle. Speak not, but tread lightly, and follow me."

Sir Kenneth arose, and took his sword.

"It needs not," answered the anchorite, in a whisper; "we are going where spiritual arms avail much, and fleshly weapons are but as the reed and the decayed gourd."

The knight deposited his sword by the bedside as before, and, armed only with his dagger, from which, in this perilous country, he never parted, prepared to attend his mysterious host.

The hermit then moved slowly forwards, and was followed by the knight, still under some uncertainty whether the dark form which glided on before to show him the path, was not, in fact, the creation of a disturbed dream. They passed, like shadows, into the outer apartment, without disturbing the paynim Emir, who lay still buried in repose. Before the cross and altar, in the outward room, a lamp was still burning, a missal was displayed, and on the floor lay a discipline, or penitential scourge of small cord and wire, the lashes of which were stained with recent blood, a token, no doubt, of the severe penance of the recluse. Here Theodorick kneeled down, and pointed to the knight to take his place beside him upon the sharp flints, which seemed placed for the purpose of rendering the posture of reverential devotion as uneasy as possible; he read many prayers of the Catholic Church, and chanted, in a low but earnest voice, three of the penitential psalms. These last he intermixed with sighs and tears, and convulsive throbs, which bore witness how deeply he felt the divine poetry which he recited. The Scottish knight assisted with profound sincerity at these acts of devotion, his opinions of his host beginning, in the meantime, to be so much changed, that he doubted whether, from the severity of his penance, and the ardour of his prayers, he ought not to regard him as a saint; and when they arose from the ground, he stood with reverence before him, as a pupil before an honoured master. The hermit was, on his side, silent and abstracted for the space of a few minutes.

"Look into yonder recess, my son," he said, pointing to the farther corner of the cell; "there thou wilt find a veil—bring it hither."

The knight obeyed; and, in a small aperture cut out of the wall, and secured with a door of wicker, he found the veil enquired for. When he brought it to the light, he discovered that it was torn, and soiled in some places with some dark substance. The anchorite looked at it with a deep but smothered emotion, and ere he could speak to the Scottish knight, was compelled to vent his feelings in a convulsive groan.

"Thou art now about to look upon the richest treasure that the earth possesses," he at length said; "woe is me, that my eyes are unworthy to be lifted towards it! Alas! I am but the vile and despised sign, which points out to the wearied traveller a harbour of rest and security, but must itself remain for ever without doors. In vain have I fled to the very depths of the rocks, and the very bosom of the thirsty desert. Mine enemy hath found me—even he whom I have denied has pursued me to my fortresses!"

He paused again for a moment, and, turning to the Scottish knight, said, in a firmer tone of voice, "You bring me a greeting from Richard of England?"

"I come from the Council of Christian Princes," said the knight; "but the King of England being indisposed, I am not honoured with his Majesty's commands."

"Your token?" demanded the recluse.

Sir Kenneth hesitated—former suspicions, and the marks of insanity which the hermit had formerly exhibited, rushed suddenly on his thoughts; but how suspect a man whose manners were so saintly? "My password," he said at length, "is this—Kings begged of a beggar."

"It is right," said the hermit, while he paused; "I know you well; but the sentinel upon his post—and mine is an important one—challenges friend as well as foe."

He then moved forward with the lamp, leading the way into the room which they had left. The Saracen lay on his couch, still fast asleep. The hermit paused by his side and looked down on him.

"He sleeps," he said, "in darkness, and must not be awakened."

The attitude of the Emir did indeed convey the idea of profound repose. One arm, flung across his body, as he lay with his face half turned to the wall, concealed, with its loose and long sleeve, the greater part of his face; but the high forehead was yet visible. Its nerves, which during his waking hours were so uncommonly active, were now motionless, as if the face had been composed of dark marble, and his long silken eyelashes closed over his piercing and hawk-like eyes. The open and relaxed hand, and the deep, regular, and soft breathing, gave all tokens of the most profound repose. The slumberer formed a singular group along with the tall forms of the hermit in his shaggy dress of goat-skins, bearing the lamp, and the knight in his close leathern coat; the former with an austere expression of ascetic gloom, the latter with anxious curiosity deeply impressed on his manly features.

"He sleeps soundly," said the hermit, in the same low tone as before, and repeating the words, though he had changed the meaning from that which is literal to a metaphorical sense —"He sleeps in darkness, but there shall be for him a day-spring.—O, Ilderim, thy waking thoughts are yet as vain and wild as those which are wheeling their giddy dance through thy sleeping brain; but the trumpet shall be heard, and the dream shall be dissolved."

So saying, and making the knight a sign to follow him, the hermit went towards the altar, and, passing behind it, pressed a spring, which, opening without noise, showed a small iron door wrought in the side of the cavern, so as to be almost imperceptible, unless upon the most severe scrutiny. The hermit, ere he ventured fully to open the door, dropt some oil on the hinges, which the lamp supplied. A small staircase, hewn in the rock, was discovered, when the iron door was at length completely opened.

"Take the veil which I hold," said the hermit, in a melancholy tone, "and blind mine eyes; for I may not look on the treasure which thou art presently to behold, without sin and presumption."

Without reply, the knight hastily muffled the recluse's head in the veil, and the latter began to ascend the staircase as one too much accustomed to the way to require the use of light, while at the same time he held the lamp to the Scot, who followed him for many steps up the narrow ascent. At length they rested in a small vault of irregular form, in one nook of which the staircase terminated, while in another corner a corresponding stair was seen to continue the ascent. In a third angle was a Gothic door, very rudely ornamented with the usual attributes of clustered columns and carving, and defended by a wicket, strongly guarded with iron, and studded with large nails. To this last point the hermit directed his steps, which seemed to falter as he approached it.

"Put off thy shoes," he said to his attendant; "the ground on which thou standest is holy. Banish from thy innermost heart each profane and carnal thought, for to harbour such while in this place were a deadly impiety."

The knight laid aside his shoes as he was commanded, and the hermit stood in the meanwhile as if communing with his soul in secret prayer, and when he again moved, commanded the knight to knock at the wicket three times. He did so. The door opened spontaneously, at least Sir Kenneth beheld no one, and his senses were at once assailed by a stream of the purest light, and by a strong and almost oppressive sense of the richest perfumes. He stepped two or three paces back, and it was the space of a minute ere he recovered the dazzling and overpowering effects of the sudden change from darkness to light.

When he entered the apartment in which this brilliant lustre was displayed, he perceived that the light proceeded from a combination of silver lamps, fed with purest oil, and sending forth the richest odours, hanging by silver chains from the roof of a small Gothic chapel, hewn, like most part of the hermit's singular mansion, out of the sound and solid rock. But, whereas, in every other place which Sir Kenneth had seen, the labour employed upon the rock had been of the simplest and coarsest description, it had in this chapel employed the invention and the chisels of the most able architects. The groined roofs rose from six columns on each side, carved with the rarest skill; and the manner in which the crossings of the concave arches were bound together, as it were, with appropriate ornaments, were all in the finest tone of the architecture, and of the age. Corresponding to the line of pillars, there were on each side six richly wrought niches, each of which contained the image of one of the twelve apostles.

At the upper and eastern end of the chapel stood the altar, behind which a very rich curtain of Persian silk, embroidered deeply with gold, covered a recess, containing, unquestionably, some image or relic of no ordinary sanctity, in honour of whom this singular place of worship had been erected, Under the persuasion that this must be the case, the knight advanced to the shrine, and kneeling down before it, repeated his devotions with fervency, during which his attention was disturbed by the curtain being suddenly raised, or rather pulled aside, how or by whom he saw not; but in the niche which was thus disclosed, he beheld a cabinet of silver and ebony, with a double folding door, the whole formed into the miniature resemblance of a Gothic church.

As he gazed with anxious curiosity on the shrine, the two folding doors also flew open, discovering a large piece of wood, on which were blazoned the words, VERA CRUX, at the same time a choir of female voices sung GLORIA PATRI. The instant the strain had ceased, the shrine was closed, and the curtain again drawn, and the knight who knelt at the altar might now continue his devotions undisturbed, in honour of the holy relic which had just been disclosed to his view. He did this under the profound impression of one who had witnessed, with his own eyes, an awful evidence of the truth of his religion, and it was some time ere, concluding his orisons, he arose, and ventured to look around him for the hermit, who had guided him to this sacred and mysterious spot. He beheld him, his head still muffled in the veil, which he had himself wrapped around it, couching, like a rated hound, upon the threshold of the chapel; but apparently without venturing to cross it; the holiest reverence, the most penitential remorse, was expressed by his posture, which seemed that of a man borne down and crushed to the earth by the burden of his inward feelings. It seemed to the Scot that only the sense of the deepest penitence, remorse, and humiliation could have thus prostrated a frame so strong, and a spirit so fiery.

He approached him as if to speak, but the recluse anticipated his purpose, murmuring in stifled tones, from beneath the fold in which his head was muffled, and which sounded like a voice proceeding from the cerements of a corpse,—" Abide, abide—happy thou that mayst—the vision is not yet ended."—So saying, he reared himself from the ground, drew back from the threshold on which he had hitherto lain prostrate, and closed the door of the chapel, which, secured by a spring bolt within, the snap of which resounded through the place, appeared so much like a part of the living rock from which the cavern was hewn, that Kenneth could hardly discern where the aperture had been. He was now alone in the lighted chapel, which contained the relic to which he had lately rendered his homage, without other arms than his dagger, or other companion than his pious thoughts and dauntless courage.

Uncertain what was next to happen, but resolved to abide the course of events, Sir Kenneth paced the solitary chapel, till about the time of the earliest cock-crowing. At this dead season, when night and morning met together, he heard, but from what quarter he could not discover, the sound of such a small silver bell as is rung at the elevation of the host, in the ceremony, or sacrifice, as it has been called, of the mass. The hour and the place rendered the sound fearfully solemn, and, bold as he was, the knight withdrew himself into the farther nook of the chapel, at the end opposite to the altar, in order to observe, without interruption, the consequences of this unexpected signal.

He did not wait long ere the silken curtain was again withdrawn, and the relic again presented to his view. As he sunk reverentially on his knee, he heard the sound of the lauds, or earliest office of the Catholic Church, sung by female voices, which united together in the performance as they had done in the former service. The knight was soon aware that the voices were no longer stationary in the distance, but approached the chapel and became louder, when a door, imperceptible when closed, like that by which he had himself entered, opened on the other side of the vault, and gave the tones of the choir more room to swell along the ribbed arches of the roof.

The knight fixed his eyes on the opening with breathless anxiety, and, continuing to kneel in the attitude of devotion which the place and scene required, expected the consequence of these preparations. A procession appeared about to issue from the door. First, four beautiful boys, whose arms, neck, and legs were bare, showing the bronze complexion of the East, and contrasting with the snow-white tunics which they wore, entered the chapel by two and two. The first pair bore censers, which they swung from side to side, adding double fragrance to the odours with which the chapel already was impregnated. The second pair scattered flowers.

After these followed, in due and majestic order, the females who composed the choir; six, who, from their black scapularies, and black veils over their white garments, appeared to be professed nuns of the order of Mount Carmel; and as many whose veils, being white, argued them to be novices, or occasional inhabitants in the cloister, who were not as yet bound to it by vows. The former held in their hands large rosaries, while the younger and lighter figures who followed, carried each a chaplet of red and white roses. They moved in procession around the chapel, without appearing to take the slightest notice of Kenneth, although passing so near him that their robes almost touched him; while they continued to sing, the knight doubted not that he was in one of those cloisters where the noble Christian maidens had formerly openly devoted themselves to the services of the Church. Most of them had been suppressed since the Mahometans had reconquered Palestine, but many purchasing connivance by presents, or receiving it from the clemency or contempt of the victors, still continued to observe in private the ritual to which their vows had consecrated them. Yet, though Kenneth knew this to be the case, the solemnity of the place and hour, the surprise at the sudden appearance of these votaresses, and the visionary manner in which they moved past him, had such influence on his imagination, that he could scarce conceive that the fair procession which he beheld was formed of creatures of this world, so much did they resemble a choir of supernatural beings, rendering homage to the universal object of adoration.

Such was the knight's first idea, as the procession passed him, scarce moving, save just sufficiently to continue their progress; so that, seen by the shadowy and religious light which the lamps shed through the clouds of incense which darkened the apartment, they appeared rather to glide than to walk.

But as a second time, in surrounding the chapel, they passed the spot on which he kneeled, one of the white-stoled maidens, as she glided by him, detached from the chaplet which she carried a rose-bud, which dropped from her fingers, perhaps unconsciously, on the foot of Sir Kenneth. The knight started as if a dart had suddenly struck his person; for, when the mind is wound up to a high pitch of feeling and expectation, the slightest incident, if unexpected, gives fire to the train which imagination has already laid. But he suppressed his emotion, recollecting how easily an incident so indifferent might have happened, and that it was only the uniform monotony of the movement of the choristers which made the incident in the slightest degree remarkable.

Still, while the procession, for the third time, surrounded the chapel, the thoughts and the eyes of Kenneth followed exclusively the one among the novices who had dropped the rose-bud. Her step, her face, her form, were so completely assimilated to the rest of the choristers, that it was impossible

to perceive the least marks of individuality, and yet Kenneth's
heart throbbed like a bird that would burst from its cage, as
if to assure him, by its sympathetic suggestions, that the female
who held the right file on the second rank of the novices, was
dearer to him, not only than all the rest that were present, but
than the whole sex besides. The romantic passion of love, as
it was cherished, and indeed enjoined, by the rules of chivalry,
associated well with the no less romantic feelings of devotion ;
and they might be said much more to enhance than to
counteract each other. It was, therefore, with a glow of
expectation, that had something even of a religious character,
that Sir Kenneth, his sensations thrilling from his heart to the
ends of his fingers, expected some second sign of the presence
of one, who, he strongly fancied, had already bestowed on him
the first. Short as the space was during which the procession
again completed a third perambulation of the chapel, it seemed
an eternity to Kenneth. At length the form, which he had
watched with such devoted attention, drew nigh ; there was
no difference betwixt that shrouded figure and the others,
with whom it moved in concert and in unison, until, just as
she passed for the third time the kneeling Crusader, a part
of a little and well-proportioned hand, so beautifully formed
as to give the highest idea of the perfect proportions of the
form to which it belonged, stole through the folds of the
gauze, like a moonbeam through the fleecy cloud of a summer
night, and again a rose-bud lay at the feet of the Knight of
the Leopard.

This second intimation could not be accidental—it could
not be fortuitous, the resemblance of that half-seen, but
beautiful female hand, with one which his lips had once
touched, and, while they touched it, had internally sworn
allegiance to the lovely owner. Had further proof been
wanting, there was the glimmer of that matchless ruby ring on
that snow-white finger, whose invaluable worth Kenneth would
yet have prized less than the slightest sign which that finger
could have made—and veiled, too, as she was, he might see,
by chance or by favour, a stray curl of the dark tresses, each
hair of which was dearer to him a hundred times than a
chain of massive gold. It was the lady of his love ! But that
she should be here—in the savage and sequestered desert—
among vestals who rendered themselves habitants of wilds and
of caverns, that they might perform in secret those Christian
rites which they dared not assist in openly—that this should

be so—in truth and in reality—seemed too incredible; it must be a dream—a delusive trance of the imagination. While these thoughts passed through the mind of Kenneth, the same passage, by which the procession had entered the chapel, received them on their return. The young sacristans, the sable nuns, vanished successively through the open door; at length she from whom he had received this double intimation passed also—yet, in passing, turned her head, slightly indeed, but perceptibly, towards the place where he remained fixed as an image. He marked the last wave of her veil—it was gone —and a darkness sunk upon his soul, scarce less palpable than that which almost immediately enveloped his external sense; for the last chorister had no sooner crossed the threshold of the door, than it shut with a loud sound, and at the same instant the voices of the choir were silent, the lights of the chapel were at once extinguished, and Sir Kenneth remained solitary, and in total darkness. But to Kenneth, solitude and darkness, and the uncertainty of his mysterious situation, were as nothing—he thought not of them—cared not for them— cared for nought in the world save the flitting vision which had just glided past him, and the tokens of her favour which she had bestowed. To grope on the floor for the buds which she had dropped—to press them to his lips—to his bosom—now alternately, now together—to rivet his lips to the cold stones on which, as near as he could judge, she had so lately stept— to play all the extravagances which strong affection suggests and vindicates to those who yield themselves up to it, were but the tokens of passionate love, common to all ages. But it was peculiar to the times of chivalry, that in his wildest rapture the knight imagined of no attempt to follow or to trace the object of such romantic attachment; that he thought of her as of a deity, who, having deigned to show herself for an instant to her devoted worshipper, had again returned to the darkness of her sanctuary—or as an influential planet, which, having darted in some auspicious minute one favourable ray, wrapped itself again in its veil of mist. The motions of the lady of his love were to him those of a superior being, who was to move without watch or control, rejoice him by her appearance, or depress him by her absence, animate him by her kindness, or drive him to despair by her cruelty—all at her own free-will, and without other importunity or remonstrance than that expressed by the most devoted services of the heart and sword of the champion, whose sole object in life was to fulfil her commands, and, by the splendour of his own achievements, to exalt her fame.

Such were the rules of chivalry, and of the love which was its ruling principle. But Sir Kenneth's attachment was rendered romantic by other and still more peculiar circumstances. He had never even heard the sound of his lady's voice, though he had often beheld her beauty with rapture. She moved in a circle, which his rank of knighthood permitted him indeed to approach, but not to mingle with; and highly as he stood distinguished for warlike skill and enterprise, still the poor Scottish soldier was compelled to worship his divinity at a distance almost as great as divides the Persian from the sun which he adores. But when was the pride of woman too lofty to overlook the passionate devotion of a lover, however inferior in degree? Her eye had been on him in the tournament, her ear had heard his praises in the report of the battles which were daily fought; and while count, duke, and lord contended for her grace, it flowed, unwillingly perhaps at first, or even unconsciously, towards the poor Knight of the Leopard, who, to support his rank, had little besides his sword. When she looked, and when she listened, the lady saw and heard enough to encourage her in her partiality, which had at first crept on her unawares. If a knight's personal beauty was praised, even the most prudish dames of the military court of England would make an exception in favour of the Scottish Kenneth; and it oftentimes happened, that notwithstanding the very considerable largesses which princes and peers bestowed on the minstrels, an impartial spirit of independence would seize the poet, and the harp was swept to the heroism of one who had neither palfreys nor garments to bestow in guerdon of his applause.

The moments when she listened to the praises of her lover became gradually more and more dear to the high-born Edith, relieving the flattery with which her ear was weary, and presenting to her a subject of secret contemplation, more worthy, as he seemed by general report, than those who surpassed him in rank and in the gifts of fortune. As her attention became constantly, though cautiously, fixed on Sir Kenneth, she grew more and more convinced of his personal devotion to herself, and more and more certain in her mind, that in Kenneth of Scotland she beheld the fated knight doomed to share with her through weal and woe—and the prospect looked gloomy and dangerous—the passionate attachment to which the poets of the age ascribed such universal dominion, and which its manners and morals placed nearly on the same rank with devotion itself.

Let us not disguise the truth from our readers. When Edith became aware of the state of her own sentiments, chivalrous as were her sentiments, becoming a maiden not distant from the throne of England, gratified as her pride must have been with the mute though unceasing homage rendered to her by the knight whom she had distinguished, there were moments when the feelings of the woman, loving and beloved, murmured against the restraints of state and form by which she was surrounded, and when she almost blamed the timidity of her lover, who seemed resolved not to infringe them. The etiquette, to use a modern phrase, of birth and rank, had drawn around her a magical circle, beyond which Sir Kenneth might indeed bow and gaze, but within which he could no more pass than an evoked spirit can transgress the boundaries prescribed by the rod of a powerful enchanter. The thought involuntarily pressed on her, that she herself must venture, were it but the point of her fairy foot, beyond the prescribed boundary, if she ever hoped to give a lover, so reserved and bashful, an opportunity of so slight a favour as but to salute her shoe-tie. There was an example, the noted precedent of the "King's daughter of Hungary," who thus generously encouraged the "squire of low degree"; and Edith, though of kingly blood, was no king's daughter, any more than her lover was of low degree; fortune had put no such extreme barrier in obstacle to their affections. Something, however, within the maiden's bosom—that modest pride, which throws fetters even on love itself—forbade her, notwithstanding the superiority of her condition, to make those advances, which in every case delicacy assigns to the other sex; above all, Sir Kenneth was a knight so gentle and honourable, so highly accomplished— as her imagination at least suggested, together with the strictest feelings of what was due to himself and to her—that, however constrained her attitude might be while receiving his adorations, like the image of some deity, who is neither supposed to feel nor to reply to the homage of its votaries, still the idol feared that to step prematurely from her pedestal, would be to degrade herself in the eyes of her devoted worshipper.

Yet the devout adorer of an actual idol can even discover signs of approbation in the rigid and immovable features of a marble image, and it is no wonder that something, which could be as favourably interpreted, glanced from the bright eye of the lovely Edith, whose beauty, indeed, consisted rather more in that very power of expression, than on absolute regularity of contour, or brilliancy of complexion. Some light marks of distinction had escaped from her, notwithstanding her own jealous vigilance, else how could Sir Kenneth have so readily, and so undoubtingly, recognised the lovely hand, of which scarce two fingers were visible from under the veil, or how could he have rested so thoroughly assured that two flowers, successively dropt on the spot, were intended as a recognition on the part of his lady-love? By what train of observation—by what secret signs, looks, or gestures — by what instinctive free-masonry of love, this degree of intelligence came to subsist between Edith and her lover, we cannot attempt to trace; for we are old, and such slight vestiges of affection, quickly discovered by younger eyes, defy the power of ours. Enough, that such affection did subsist between parties who had never even spoken to one another, though, on the side of Edith, it was checked by a deep sense of the difficulties and dangers which must necessarily attend the further progress of their attachment, and upon that of the knight by a thousand doubts and fears, lest he had over-estimated the slight tokens of the lady's notice, varied, as they necessarily were, by long intervals of apparent coldness, during which, either the fear of exciting the observation of others, and thus drawing danger upon her lover, or that of sinking in his esteem by seeming too willing to be won, made her behave with indifference, and as if unobservant of his presence.

This narrative, tedious perhaps, but which the story renders necessary, may serve to explain the state of intelligence, if it deserves so strong a name, betwixt the lovers, when Edith's unexpected appearance in the chapel produced so powerful an effect on the feelings of her knight.

CHAPTER V

> Their necromantic forms in vain
> Haunt us on the tented plain;
> We bid these spectre shapes avaunt
> Ashtaroth and Termagaunt.
> WARTON.

THE most profound silence, the deepest darkness, continued to brood for more than an hour over the chapel in which we left the Knight of the Leopard still kneeling, alternately expressing thanks to Heaven, and gratitude to his lady, for the boon which had been vouchsafed to him. His own safety, his own destiny, for which he was at all times little anxious, had not now the weight of a grain of dust in his reflections. He was in the neighbourhood of Lady Edith, he had received tokens of her grace, he was in a place hallowed by relics of the most awful sanctity. A Christian soldier, a devoted lover, could fear nothing, think of nothing, but his duty to Heaven, and his devoir to his lady.

At the lapse of the space of time which we have noticed, a shrill whistle, like that with which a falconer calls his hawk, was heard to ring sharply through the vaulted chapel. It was a sound ill suited to the place, and reminded Sir Kenneth how necessary it was he should be upon his guard. He started from his knee, and laid his hand upon his poniard. A creaking sound, as of a screw or pulleys, succeeded, and a light streaming upwards, as from an opening in the floor, showed that a trap-door had been raised or depressed. In less than a minute, a long skinny arm, partly naked, partly clothed in a sleeve of red samite, arose out of the aperture, holding a lamp as high as it could stretch upwards, and the figure to which the arm belonged ascended step by step to the level of the chapel floor. The form and face of the being who thus presented himself, were those of a frightful dwarf, with a large head, a cap fantastically adorned with three peacock feathers, a dress of red samite, the richness of which rendered his ugliness more conspicuous, distinguished by gold bracelets and armlets, and a white silk sash, in which he wore a gold-hilted dagger. This singular figure had in his left hand a kind of broom. So soon as he had stepped from the aperture through which he arose, he stood still, and, as if to show himself more distinctly, moved the lamp which he held slowly over his face and person, successively illuminating his wild and fantastic features, and his misshapen but nervous limbs. Though disproportioned in person, the dwarf was not so distorted as to argue any want of strength or activity. While Sir Kenneth gazed on this disagreeable object, the popular creed occurred to his remembrance, concerning the gnomes, or earthly spirits, which make their abode in the caverns of the earth; and so much did this figure correspond with ideas he had formed of their appearance, that he looked on it with disgust, mingled not indeed with fear, but that sort of awe which the presence of a supernatural creature may infuse into the most steady bosom.

The dwarf again whistled, and summoned from beneath a companion. This second figure ascended in the same manner as the first; but it was a female arm, in this second instance, which upheld the lamp from the subterranean vault out of which these presentments arose, and it was a female form, much resembling the first in shape and proportions, which slowly emerged from the floor. Her dress was also of red samite, fantastically cut and flounced, as if she had been dressed for some exhibition of mimes or jugglers; and with the same minuteness which her predecessor had exhibited, she passed the lamp over her face and person, which seemed to rival the male's in ugliness. But with all this most unfavourable exterior, there was one trait in the features of both which argued alertness and intelligence in the most uncommon degree. This arose from the brilliancy of their eyes, which, deep set beneath black and shaggy brows, gleamed with a lustre, which, like that in the eye of the toad, seemed to make some amends for the extreme ugliness of countenance and person.

Sir Kenneth remained as if spell-bound, while this unlovely pair, moving round the chapel close to each other, appeared to perform the duty of sweeping it, like menials; but, as they used only one hand, the floor was not much benefited by the exercise, which they plied with such oddity of gestures and manner, as befitted their bizarre and fantastic appearance. When they approached near to the knight, in the course of their occupation, they ceased to use their brooms, and placing themselves side by side, directly opposite to Sir Kenneth, they again slowly shifted the lights which they held, so as to allow him distinctly to survey features which were not rendered more agreeable by being brought nearer, and to observe the extreme quickness and keenness with which their black and glittering eyes flashed back the light of the lamps. They then turned the gleam of both lights upon the knight, and having accurately surveyed him, turned their faces to each other, and set up a loud yelling laugh, which resounded in his ears. The sound was so ghastly that Sir Kenneth started at hearing it, and hastily demanded, in the name of God, who they were who profaned that holy place with such antic gestures and elritch exclamations.

"I am the dwarf Nectabanus," said the abortion-seeming

male, in a voice corresponding to his figure, and resembling the voice of the night-crow more than any sound which is heard by daylight.

"And I am Guenevra, his lady and his love," replied the female, in tones which, being shriller, were yet wilder than those of her companion.

"Wherefore are you here?" again demanded the knight, scarcely yet assured that it was human beings which he saw before him.

"I am," replied the male dwarf, with much assumed gravity and dignity, "the twelfth Imaum—I am Mahommed Mohadi, the guide and the conductor of the faithful. An hundred horses stand ready saddled for me and my train at the Holy City, and as many at the City of Refuge. I am he who shall bear witness, and this is one of my houris."

"Thou liest!" answered the female, interrupting her companion, in tones yet shriller than his own; "I am none of thy houris, and thou art no such infidel trash as the Mahommed of whom thou speakest. May my curse rest upon his coffin!— I tell thee, thou ass of Issachar, thou art King Arthur of Britain, whom the fairies stole away from the field of Avalon; and I am Dame Guenevra, famed for her beauty."

"But, in truth, noble sir," said the male, "we are distressed princes, dwelling under the wing of King Guy of Jerusalem, until he was driven out from his own nest by the foul infidels— Heaven's bolts consume them!"

"Hush," said a voice from the side upon which the knight had entered—"Hush, fools, and begone; your ministry is ended."

The dwarfs had no sooner heard the command, than, gibbering in discordant whispers to each other, they blew out their lights at once, and left the knight in utter darkness, which, when the pattering of their retiring feet had died away, was soon accompanied by its fittest companion, total silence.

The knight felt the departure of these unfortunate creatures a relief. He could not, from their language, manners, and appearance, doubt that they belonged to the degraded class of beings whom deformity of person, and weakness of intellect, recommended to the painful situation of appendages to great families, where their personal appearance and imbecility were food for merriment to the household. Superior in no respect to the ideas and manners of his time, the Scottish knight might, at another period, have been much amused by the mummery of these poor effigies of humanity; but now, their appearance, gesticulations, and language, broke the train of deep and solemn feeling with which he was impressed, and he rejoiced in the disappearance of the unhappy objects.

A few minutes after they had retired, the door at which he had entered opened slowly, and, remaining ajar, discovered a faint light arising from a lantern placed upon the threshold. Its doubtful and wavering gleam showed a dark form reclined beside the entrance, but without its precincts, which, on approaching it more nearly, he recognised to be the hermit, couching in the same humble posture in which he had at first laid himself down, and which, doubtless, he had retained during the whole time of his guest's continuing in the chapel.

"All is over," said the hermit, as he heard the knight approaching, "and the most wretched of earthly sinners, with him who should think himself most honoured and most happy among the race of humanity, must retire from this place. Take the light, and guide me down the descent, for I may not uncover my eyes until I am far from this hallowed spot."

The Scottish knight obeyed in silence, for a solemn and yet ecstatic sense of what he had seen had silenced even the eager workings of curiosity. He led the way with considerable accuracy through the various secret passages and stairs by which they had ascended, until at length they found themselves in the outward cell of the hermit's cavern.

"The condemned criminal is restored to his dungeon, reprieved from one miserable day to another, until his awful Judge shall at length appoint the well-deserved sentence to be carried into execution."

As the hermit spoke these words, he laid aside the veil with which his eyes had been bound, and looked at it with a suppressed and hollow sigh. No sooner had he restored it to the crypt from which he had caused the Scot to bring it, than he said hastily and sternly to his companion,—"Begone, begone—to rest, to rest. You may sleep—you can sleep—I neither can, nor may."

Respecting the profound agitation with which this was spoken, the knight retired into the inner cell; but, casting back his eye as he left the exterior grotto, he beheld the anchorite stripping his shoulders with frantic haste, of their shaggy mantle, and ere he could shut the frail door which separated the two compartments of the cavern, he heard the clang of the scourge, and the groans of the penitent under his self-inflicted penance. A cold shudder came over the knight as he reflected what could be the foulness of the sin, what the depth of the remorse, which, apparently, such severe penance could neither cleanse nor assuage. He told his beads devoutly, and flung himself on his rude couch, after a glance at the still sleeping Moslem, and, wearied by the various scenes of the day and the night, soon slept as sound as infancy. Upon his awaking in the morning, he held certain conferences with the hermit upon matters of importance, and the result of their intercourse induced him to remain for two days longer in the grotto. He was regular, as became a pilgrim, in his devotional exercises, but was not again admitted to the chapel in which he had seen such wonders.

CHAPTER VI

Now change the scene—and let the trumpets sound,
For we must rouse the lion from his lair.
Old Play.

THE scene must change, as our programme has announced, from the mountain wilderness of Jordan to the camp of King Richard of England, then stationed betwixt Jean d'Acre and Ascalon; and containing that army with which he of the Lion Heart had promised himself a triumphant march to Jerusalem, and in which he would probably have succeeded, if not hindered by the jealousies of the Christian princes engaged in the same enterprise, and the offence taken by them at the uncurbed haughtiness of the English monarch, and Richard's unveiled contempt for his brother sovereigns, who, his equals in rank, were yet far his inferiors in courage, hardihood, and military talents. Such discords, and particularly those betwixt Richard and Philip of France, created disputes and obstacles which impeded every active measure proposed by the heroic though impetuous Richard, while the ranks of the Crusaders were daily thinned, not only by the desertion of individuals, but of entire bands, headed by their respective feudal leaders, who withdrew from a contest in which they had ceased to hope for success.

The effects of the climate became, as usual, fatal to soldiers from the north, and the more so, that the dissolute license of the Crusaders, forming a singular contrast to the principles and

purpose of their taking up arms, rendered them more easy
victims to the insalubrious influence of burning heat and
chilling dews. To these discouraging causes of loss was to
be added the sword of the enemy. Saladin, than whom no
greater name is recorded in Eastern history, had learnt, to his
fatal experience, that his light-armed followers were little able
to meet in close encounter with the iron-clad Franks, and had
been taught, at the same time, to apprehend and dread the
adventurous character of his antagonist Richard. But if his
armies were more than once routed with great slaughter, his
numbers gave the Saracen the advantage in those lighter
skirmishes, of which many were inevitable.

As the army of his assailants decreased, the enterprises of
the Sultan became more numerous and more bold in this
species of petty warfare. The camp of the Crusaders was
surrounded, and almost besieged by clouds of light cavalry,
resembling swarms of wasps, easily crushed when they are
once grasped, but furnished with wings to elude superior
strength, and stings to inflict harm and mischief. There was
perpetual warfare of posts and foragers, in which many valuable
lives were lost, without any corresponding object being
gained; convoys were intercepted, and communications were
cut off. The Crusaders had to purchase the means of
sustaining life by life itself; and water, like that of the well of
Bethlehem, longed for by King David, one of its ancient
monarchs, was then, as before, only obtained by the expenditure
of blood.

These evils were, in a great measure, counterbalanced by
the stern resolution and restless activity of King Richard,
who, with some of his best knights, was ever on horseback,
ready to repair to any point where danger occurred, and often
not only bringing unexpected succour to the Christians, but
discomfiting the infidels when they seemed most secure of
victory. But even the iron frame of Cœur de Lion could not
support, without injury, the alternations of the unwholesome
climate, joined to ceaseless exertions of body and mind. He
became afflicted with one of those slow and wasting fevers
peculiar to Asia, and, in despite of his great strength, and still
greater courage, grew first unfit to mount on horseback, and
then unable to attend the councils of war, which were, from
time to time, held by the Crusaders. It was difficult to say
whether this state of personal inactivity was rendered more
galling or more endurable to the English monarch, by the

resolution of the council to engage in a truce of thirty days with the Sultan Saladin; for, on the one hand, if he was incensed at the delay which this interposed to the progress of the great enterprise, he was, on the other, somewhat consoled by knowing that others were not acquiring laurels, while he remained inactive upon a sick-bed.

That, however, which Cœur de Lion could least excuse, was the general inactivity which prevailed in the camp of the Crusaders, so soon as his illness assumed a serious aspect; and the reports which he extracted from his unwilling attendants gave him to understand, that the hopes of the host had abated in proportion to his illness, and that the interval of truce was employed, not in recruiting their numbers, reanimating their courage, fostering their spirit of conquest, and preparing for a speedy and determined advance upon the Holy City, which was the object of their expedition, but in securing the camp occupied by their diminished followers, with trenches, palisades, and other fortifications, as if preparing rather to repel an attack from a powerful enemy so soon as hostilities should recommence, than to assume the proud character of conquerors and asssilants.

The English king chafed under these reports, like the imprisoned lion viewing his prey from the iron barriers of his cage. Naturally rash and impetuous, the irritability of his temper preyed on itself. He was dreaded by his attendants, and even the medical assistants feared to assume the necessary authority, which a physician, to do justice to his patient, must needs exercise over him. One faithful baron, who, perhaps from the congenial nature of his disposition, was devoutly attached to the King's person, dared alone to come between the dragon and his wrath, and quietly, but firmly, maintained a control which no other dared assume over the dangerous invalid, and which Thomas de Multon only exercised because he esteemed his sovereign's life and honour more than he did the degree of favour which he might lose, or even the risk which he might incur, in nursing a patient so intractable, and whose displeasure was so perilous.

Sir Thomas was the Lord of Gilsland, in Cumberland, and, in an age when surnames and titles were not distinctly attached, as now, to the individuals who bore them, he was called by the Normans the Lord de Vaux, and in English, by the Saxons, who clung to their native language, and were proud of the share of Saxon blood in this renowned warrior's veins, he was termed Thomas, or, more familiarly, Tom of the Gills, or Narrow Valleys, from which his extensive domains derived their well-known appellation.

This chief had been exercised in almost all the wars, whether waged betwixt England and Scotland, or amongst the various domestic factions which then tore the former country asunder, and in all had been distinguished, as well from his military conduct as his personal prowess. He was, in other respects, a rude soldier, blunt and careless in his bearing, and taciturn, nay, almost sullen, in his habits of society, and seeming, at least, to disclaim all knowledge of policy and of courtly art. There were men, however, who pretended to look deeply into character, who asserted that the Lord de Vaux was not less shrewd and aspiring, than he was blunt and bold, and who thought that, while he assimilated himself to the King's own character of blunt hardihood, it was, in some degree at least, with an eye to establish his favour, and to gratify his own hopes of deep-laid ambition. But no one cared to thwart his schemes, if such he had, by rivalling him in the dangerous occupation of daily attendance on the sick-bed of a patient, whose disease was pronounced infectious, and more especially when it was remembered that the patient was Cœur de Lion, suffering under all the furious impatience of a soldier withheld from battle, and a sovereign sequestered from authority; and the common soldiers, at least in the English army, were generally of opinion that De Vaux attended on the King, like comrade upon comrade, in the honest and disinterested frankness of military friendship, contracted between the partakers of daily dangers.

It was on the decline of a Syrian day that Richard lay on his couch of sickness, loathing it as much in mind as his illness made it irksome to his body. His bright blue eye, which at all times shone with uncommon keenness and splendour, had its vivacity augmented by fever and mental impatience, and glanced from among his curled and unshorn locks of yellow hair, as fitfully and as vividly as the last gleams of the sun shoot through the clouds of an approaching thunderstorm, which still, however, are gilded by its beams. His manly features showed the progress of wasting illness, and his beard, neglected and untrimmed, had overgrown both lips and chin. Casting himself from side to side, now clutching towards him the coverings, which at the next moment he flung as impatiently from him, his tossed couch and impatient gestures showed at once the energy and the reckless impatience of a disposition, whose natural sphere was that of the most active exertion.

Beside his couch stood Thomas de Vaux, in face, attitude, and manner, the strongest possible contrast to the suffering monarch. His stature approached the gigantic, and his hair in thickness might have resembled that of Samson, though only after the Israelitish champion's locks had passed under the shears of the Philistines, for those of De Vaux were cut short, that they might be enclosed under his helmet. The light of his broad, large hazel eye, resembled that of the autumn morn, and it was only perturbed for a moment, when from time to time it was attracted by Richard's vehement marks of agitation and restlessness. His features, though massive like his person, might have been handsome before they were defaced with scars; his upper lip, after the fashion of the Normans, was covered with thick moustaches, which grew so long and luxuriantly as to mingle with his hair, and, like his hair, were dark brown, slightly brindled with grey. His frame seemed of that kind which most readily defies both toil and climate, for he was thin-flanked, broad-chested, long-armed, deep-breathed, and strong-limbed. He had not laid aside his buff-coat, which displayed the cross cut on the shoulder, for more than three nights, enjoying but such momentary repose as the warder of a sick monarch's couch might by snatches indulge. This baron rarely changed his posture, except to administer to Richard the medicine or refreshments, which none of his less favoured attendants could persuade the impatient monarch to take; and there was something affecting in the kindly, yet awkward manner, in which he discharged offices so strangely contrasted with his blunt and soldierly habits and manners.

The pavilion in which these personages were, had, as became the time, as well as the personal character of Richard, more of a warlike than a sumptuous or royal character. Weapons offensive and defensive, several of them of strange and newly-invented construction, were scattered about the tented apartment, or disposed upon the pillars which supported it. Skins of animals slain in the chase were stretched on the ground, or extended along the sides of the pavilion, and upon a heap of these silvan spoils lay three *alans*, as they were then called, (wolf-greyhounds, that is,) of the largest size, and as white as snow. Their faces, marked with many a scar from clutch and fang, showed their share in collecting the trophies upon which they reposed, and their eyes, fixed from time to time with an expressive stretch and yawn upon the bed of Richard, evinced how much they marvelled at, and regretted the unwonted inactivity which they were compelled to share. These were but the accompaniments of the soldier and huntsman; but on a small table close by the bed, was placed a shield of wrought steel, of triangular form, bearing the three lions passant, first assumed by the chivalrous monarch, and before it the golden circlet, resembling much a ducal coronet, only that it was higher in front than behind, which, with the purple velvet and embroidered tiara that lined it, formed then the emblem of England's sovereignty. Beside it, as if prompt for defending the regal symbol, lay a mighty curtal axe, which would have wearied the arm of any other than Cœur de Lion.

In an outer partition of the pavilion waited two or three officers of the royal household, depressed, anxious for their master's health, and not less so for their own safety, in case of his decease. Their gloomy apprehensions spread themselves to the warders without, who paced about in downcast and silent contemplation, or, resting on their halberds, stood motionless on their post, rather like armed trophies than living warriors.

"So thou hast no better news to bring me from without, Sir Thomas?" said the King, after a long and perturbed silence, spent in the feverish agitation which we have endeavoured to describe. "All our knights turned women, and our ladies become devotees, and neither a spark of valour nor of gallantry to enlighten a camp, which contains the choicest of Europe's chivalry—Ha!"

"The truce, my lord," said De Vaux, with the same patience with which he had twenty times repeated the explanation,— "the truce prevents us bearing ourselves as men of action; and for the ladies, I am no great reveller, as is well known to your Majesty, and seldom exchange steel and buff for velvet and gold—but thus far I know, that our choicest beauties are waiting upon the Queen's Majesty and the Princess, to a pilgrimage to the convent of Engaddi, to accomplish their vows for your Highness's deliverance from this trouble."

"And is it thus," said Richard, with the impatience of indisposition, "that royal matrons and maidens should risk themselves, where the dogs who defile the land have as little truth to man, as they have faith towards God?"

"Nay, my lord," said De Vaux, "they have Saladin's word for their safety."

"True, true!" replied Richard, "and I did the heathen Soldan injustice—I owe him reparation for it. Would God I were but fit to offer it him upon my body between the two hosts — Christendom and Heathenesse both looking on!"

As Richard spoke, he thrust his right arm out of bed, naked to the shoulder, and, painfully raising himself in his couch, shook his clenched hand, as if it grasped sword or battle-axe, and was then brandished over the jewelled turban of the Soldan. It was not without a gentle degree of violence, which the King would scarce have endured from another, that De Vaux, in his character of sick-nurse, compelled his royal master to replace himself in the couch, and covered his sinewy arm, neck, and shoulders, with the care which a mother bestows upon an impatient child.

"Thou art a rough nurse, though a willing one, De Vaux," said the King, laughing with a bitter expression, while he submitted to the strength which he was unable to resist; "methinks a coif would become thy lowering features as well as a child's biggin would beseem mine. We should be a babe and nurse to frighten girls with!"

"We have frightened men in our time, my liege," said De Vaux; "and, I trust, may live to frighten them again. What is a fever-fit, that we should not endure it patiently, in order to get rid of it easily?"

"Fever-fit!" exclaimed Richard, impetuously; "thou mayst think, and justly, that it is a fever-fit with me: but what is it with all the other Christian princes—with Philip of France—with that dull Austrian—with him of Montserrat—with the Hospitallers—with the Templars—what is it with all them?—I will tell thee: it is a cold palsy—a dead lethargy—a disease that deprives them of speech and action—a canker that has eaten into the heart of all that is noble, and chivalrous, and virtuous among them—that has made them false to the noblest vow ever knights were sworn to—has made them indifferent to their fame, and forgetful of their God!"

"For the love of Heaven, my liege," said De Vaux, "take it less violently! you will be heard without doors, where such speeches are but too current already among the common soldiery, and engender discord and contention in the Christian host. Bethink you that your illness mars the mainspring of their enterprise ; a mangonel will work without screw and lever better than the Christian host without King Richard."

"Thou flatterest me, De Vaux," said Richard ; and, not insensible to the power of praise, he reclined his head on the pillow, with a more deliberate attempt to repose than he had yet exhibited. But Thomas de Vaux was no courtier; the phrase which had offered had risen spontaneously to his lips; and he knew not how to pursue the pleasing theme, so as to soothe and prolong the vein which he had excited. He was silent, therefore, until, relapsing into his moody contemplations, the King demanded of him sharply, "Despardieux! This is smoothly said to soothe a sick man; but does a league of monarchs, an assemblage of nobles, a convocation of all the chivalry of Europe, droop with the sickness of one man, though he chances to be King of England? Why should Richard's illness, or Richard's death, check the march of thirty thousand men, as brave as himself? When the master stag is struck down, the herd do not disperse upon his fall—when the falcon strikes the leading crane, another takes the guidance of the phalanx.—Why do not the powers assemble and choose some one to whom they may intrust the guidance of the host?"

"Forsooth, and if it please your Majesty," said De Vaux, "I hear consultations have been held among the royal leaders for some such purpose."

"Ha!" exclaimed Richard, his jealousy awakened, giving his mental irritation another direction.—"Am I forgot by my allies ere I have taken the last sacrament?—Do they hold me dead already?—But no, no—they are right.—And whom do they select as leader of the Christian host?"

"Rank and dignity," said De Vaux, "point to the King of France."

"Oh, ay," answered the English monarch, "Philip of France and Navarre—Dennis Mountjoie, his Most Christian Majesty! —mouth-filling words these! There is but one risk—that he might mistake the words *En arrière* for *En avant*, and lead us back to Paris, instead of marching to Jerusalem. His politic head has learned by this time that there is more to be gotten by oppressing his feudatories, and pillaging his allies, than fighting with the Turks for the Holy Sepulchre."

"They might choose the Archduke of Austria," said De Vaux.

"What! because he is big and burly like thyself, Thomas— nearly as thick-headed, but without thy indifference to danger, and carelessness of offence? I tell thee that Austria has in all that mass of flesh no bolder animation than is afforded by the peevishness of a wasp, and the courage of a wren. Out upon him!—*He* a leader of chivalry to deeds of glory!—Give him a flagon of Rhenish to drink with his besmirched baaren-hauters and lance-knechts."

"There is the Grand Master of the Templars," continued the baron, not sorry to keep his master's attention engaged on other topics than his own illness, though at the expense of the characters of prince and potentate—"There is the Grand Master of the Templars," he continued, "undaunted, skilful, brave in battle, and sage in council, having no separate kingdoms of his own to divert his exertions from the recovery of the Holy Land—what thinks your Majesty of the Master as a general leader of the Christian host?"

"Ha, Beau-Seant!" answered the King. "Oh, no exception can be taken to Brother Giles Amaury; he understands the ordering of a battle, and the fighting in front when it begins. But, Sir Thomas, were it fair to take the Holy Land from the heathen Saladin, so full of all the virtues which may distinguish unchristened man, and give it to Giles Amaury, a worse pagan than himself—an idolater—a devil-worshipper—a necromancer —who practises crimes the most dark and unnatural, in the vaults and secret places of abomination and darkness?"

"The Grand Master of the Hospitallers of St. John of Jerusalem is not tainted by fame, either with heresy or magic," said Thomas de Vaux.

"But is he not a sordid miser?" said Richard, hastily; "has he not been suspected—ay, more than suspected—of selling to the infidels those advantages which they would never have won by fair force? Tush, man, better give the army to be made merchandise of by Venetian skippers and Lombardy pedlars, than trust it to the Grand Master of St. John."

"Well, then, I will venture but another guess," said the Baron de Vaux—"What say you to the gallant Marquis of Montserrat, so wise, so elegant, such a good man-at-arms?"

"Wise? cunning, you would say," replied Richard; "elegant in a lady's chamber, if you will. Oh, ay, Conrade of Montserrat—who knows not the popinjay? Politic and versatile, he will change you his purposes as often as the trimmings of his doublet, and you shall never be able to guess the hue of his inmost vestments from their outward colours. A man-at-arms?

ay, a fine figure on horseback, and can bear him well in the tilt-yard, and at the barriers, when swords are blunted at point and edge, and spears are tipped with trenchers of wood, instead of steel pikes. Wert thou not with me, when I said to that same gay Marquis, 'Here we be, three good Christians, and on yonder plain there pricks a band of some threescore Saracens; what say you to charge them briskly? There are but twenty unbelieving miscreants to each true knight.'"

"I recollect the Marquis replied," said De Vaux, "that his limbs were of flesh, not of iron, and that he would rather bear the heart of a man than of a beast, though that beast were the lion. But I see how it is—we shall end where we began, without hope of praying at the Sepulchre, until Heaven shall restore King Richard to health."

At this grave remark, Richard burst out into a hearty fit of laughter, the first which he had for some time indulged in. "Why, what a thing is conscience," he said, "that through its means even such a thick-witted northern lord as thou canst bring thy sovereign to confess his folly! It is true, that, did they not propose themselves as fit to hold my leading-staff, little should I care for plucking the silken trappings off the puppets thou hast shown me in succession—What concerns it me what fine tinsel robes they swagger in, unless when they are named as rivals in the glorious enterprise to which I have vowed myself? Yes, De Vaux, I confess my weakness, and the wilfulness of my ambition. The Christian camp contains, doubtless, many a better knight than Richard of England, and it would be wise and worthy to assign to the best of them the leading of the host—but," continued the warlike monarch, raising himself in his bed, and shaking the cover from his head, while his eyes sparkled as they were wont to do on the eve of battle, "were such a knight to plant the banner of the Cross on the Temple of Jerusalem, while I was unable to bear my share in the noble task, he should, so soon as I was fit to lay lance in rest, undergo my challenge to mortal combat, for having diminished my fame, and pressed in before to the object of my enterprise.—But hark, what trumpets are those at a distance?"

"Those of King Philip, as I guess, my liege," said the stout Englishman.

"Thou art dull of ear, Thomas," said the King, endeavouring to start up—"hearest thou not that clash and clang? By Heaven, the Turks are in the camp, I hear their lelies."

He again endeavoured to get out of bed, and De Vaux was obliged to exercise his own great strength, and also to summon the assistance of the chamberlains from the inner tent, to restrain him.

"Thou art a false traitor, De Vaux," said the incensed monarch, when, breathless and exhausted with struggling, he was compelled to submit to superior strength, and to repose in quiet on his couch. "I would I were—I would I were but strong enough to dash thy brains out with my battle-axe!"

"I would you had the strength, my liege," said De Vaux, "and would even take the risk of its being so employed. The odds would be great in favour of Christendom, were Thomas Multon dead, and Cœur de Lion himself again."

"Mine honest faithful servant," said Richard, extending his hand, which the baron reverentially saluted, "forgive thy master's impatience of mood. It is this burning fever which chides thee, and not thy kind master, Richard of England. But go, I prithee, and bring me word what strangers are in the camp, for these sounds are not of Christendom."

De Vaux left the pavilion on the errand assigned, and in his absence, which he had resolved should be brief, he charged the chamberlains, pages, and attendants to redouble their attention on their sovereign, with threats of holding them to responsibility, which rather added to than diminished their timid anxiety in the discharge of their duty; for next perhaps to the ire of the monarch himself, they dreaded that of the stern and inexorable Lord of Gilsland.[1]

CHAPTER VII

> There never was a time on the March parts yet
> When Scottish with English met,
> But it was marvel if the red blood ran not
> As the rain does in the street.
>
> *Battle of Otterbourn.*

A CONSIDERABLE band of Scottish warriors had joined the Crusaders, and had naturally placed themselves under the command of the English monarch, being, like his native troops, most of them of Saxon and Norman descent, speaking the same languages, possessed, some of them, of English as well as Scottish demesnes, and allied, in some cases, by blood and intermarriage. The period also preceded that when the

[1] Note I.—Sir Thomas Multon of Gilsland.

grasping ambition of Edward I. gave a deadly and envenomed character to the wars betwixt the two nations; the English fighting for the subjugation of Scotland, and the Scottish, with all the stern determination and obstinacy which has ever characterized their nation, for the defence of their independence, by the most violent means, under the most disadvantageous circumstances, and at the most extreme hazard. As yet, wars betwixt the two nations, though fierce and frequent, had been conducted on principles of fair hostility, and admitted of those softening shades by which courtesy, and the respect for open and generous foemen, qualify and mitigate the horrors of war. In time of peace, therefore, and especially when both, as at present, were engaged in war, waged in behalf of a common cause, and rendered dear to them by their ideas of religion, the adventurers of both countries frequently fought side by side, their national emulation serving only to stimulate them to excel each other in their efforts against the common enemy.

The frank and martial character of Richard, who made no distinction betwixt his own subjects and those of William of Scotland, excepting as they bore themselves in the field of battle, tended much to conciliate the troops of both nations. But upon his illness, and the disadvantageous circumstances in which the Crusaders were placed, the national disunion between the various bands united in the Crusade, began to display itself, just as old wounds break out afresh in the human body, when under the influence of disease or debility.

The Scottish and English, equally jealous and high-spirited, and apt to take offence,—the former the more so, because the poorer and the weaker nation,—began to fill up, by internal dissension, the period when the truce forbade them to wreak their united vengeance on the Saracens. Like the contending Roman chiefs of old, the Scottish would admit no superiority, and their southern neighbours would brook no equality. There were charges and recriminations, and both the common soldiery, and their leaders and commanders, who had been good comrades in time of victory, lowered on each other in the period of adversity, as if their union had not been then more essential than ever, not only to the success of their common cause, but to their joint safety. The same disunion had begun to show itself betwixt the French and English, the Italians and the Germans, and even between the Danes and Swedes; but it is only that which divided the two nations whom one island bred, and who seemed more animated against each other for the very reason, that our narrative is principally concerned with.

Of all the English nobles who had followed their King to Palestine, De Vaux was most prejudiced against the Scottish; they were his near neighbours, with whom he had been engaged during his whole life in private or public warfare, and on whom he had inflicted many calamities, while he had sustained at their hands not a few. His love and devotion to the King was like the vivid affection of the old English mastiff to his master, leaving him churlish and inaccessible to all others, even towards those to whom he was indifferent, and rough and dangerous to any against whom he entertained a prejudice. De Vaux had never observed, without jealousy and displeasure, his King exhibit any mark of courtesy or favour to the wicked, deceitful, and ferocious race, born on the other side of a river, or an imaginary line drawn through waste and wilderness, and he even doubted the success of a Crusade in which they were suffered to bear arms, holding them in his secret soul little better than the Saracens, whom he came to combat. It may be added, that, as being himself a blunt and downright Englishman, unaccustomed to conceal the slightest movement either of love or of dislike, he accounted the fair-spoken courtesy, which the Scots had learned, either from imitation of their frequent allies, the French, or which might have arisen from their own proud and reserved character, as a false and astucious mark of the most dangerous designs against their neighbours, over whom he believed, with genuine English confidence, they could, by fair manhood, never obtain any advantage.

Yet, though De Vaux entertained these sentiments concerning his northern neighbours, and extended them, with little mitigation, even to such as had assumed the Cross, his respect for the King, and a sense of the duty imposed by his vow as a Crusader, prevented him from displaying them otherwise than by regularly shunning all intercourse with his Scottish brethren-at-arms, as far as possible,—by observing a sullen taciturnity when compelled to meet them occasionally,—and by looking scornfully upon them when they encountered on the march and in camp. The Scottish barons and knights were not men to bear his scorn unobserved or unreplied to; and it came to that pass, that he was regarded as the determined and active enemy of a nation, whom, after all, he only disliked, and in some sort despised. Nay, it was remarked by close observers, that if he had not towards them the charity of Scripture, which suffereth long, and judges kindly, he was by no means deficient in the subordinate and limited virtue, which alleviates and relieves the wants of others. The wealth of Thomas of Gilsland procured supplies of provisions and medicines, and some of these usually flowed by secret channels into the quarters of the Scottish; his surly benevolence proceeding on the principle, that, next to a man's friend, his foe was of most importance to him, passing over all the intermediate relations, as too indifferent to merit even a thought. This explanation is necessary, in order that the reader may fully understand what we are now to detail.

Thomas de Vaux had not made many steps beyond the entrance of the royal pavilion, when he was aware of what the far more acute ear of the English monarch, no mean proficient in the art of minstrelsy, had instantly discovered, that the musical strains, namely, which had reached their ears, were produced by the pipes, shalms, and kettledrums of the Saracens; and, at the bottom of an avenue of tents, which formed a broad access to the pavilion of Richard, he could see a crowd of idle soldiers assembled around the spot from which the music was heard, almost in the centre of the camp; and he saw, with great surprise, mingled amid the helmets of various forms worn by the Crusaders of different nations, white turbans and long pikes, announcing the presence of armed Saracens, and the huge deformed heads of several camels or dromedaries, overlooking the multitude by aid of their long disproportioned necks.

Wondering and displeased at a sight so unexpected and singular,—for it was customary to leave all flags of truce and other communications from the enemy at an appointed place without the barriers,—the baron looked eagerly round for some one of whom he might enquire the cause of this alarming novelty.

The first person whom he met advancing to him, he set down at once, by his grave and haughty step, as a Spaniard or a Scot; and presently after muttered to himself, "And a Scot it is—he of the Leopard.—I have seen him fight indifferently well, for one of his country."

Loath to ask even a passing question, he was about to pass Sir Kenneth, with that sullen and lowering port which seems to say, "I know thee, but I will hold no communication with thee;" but his purpose was defeated by the northern knight, who moved forward directly to him, and accosting him with formal courtesy, said, "My Lord de Vaux of Gilsland, I have in charge to speak with you."

"Ha!" returned the English baron, "with me? But say your pleasure, so it be shortly spoken; I am on the King's errand."

"Mine touches King Richard yet more nearly," answered Sir Kenneth; "I bring him, I trust, health."

The Lord of Gilsland measured the Scot with incredulous eyes, and replied, "Thou art no leech, I think, Sir Scot—I had as soon thought of your bringing the King of England wealth."

Sir Kenneth, though displeased with the manner of the baron's reply, answered calmly, "Health to Richard is glory and wealth to Christendom.—But my time presses; I pray you, may I see the King?"

"Surely not, fair sir," said the baron, "until your errand be told more distinctly. The sick chambers of princes open not to all who enquire, like a northern hostelry."

"My lord," said Kenneth, "the cross which I wear in common with yourself, and the importance of what I have to tell, must, for the present, cause me to pass over a bearing which else I were unapt to endure. In plain language, then, I bring with me a Moorish physician, who undertakes to work a cure on King Richard."

"A Moorish physician!" said De Vaux; "and who will warrant that he brings not poisons instead of remedies?"

"His own life, my lord—his head, which he offers as a guarantee."

"I have known many a resolute ruffian," said De Vaux, "who valued his own life as little as it deserved, and would troop to the gallows as merrily as if the hangman were his partner in a dance."

"But thus it is, my lord," replied the Scot; "Saladin, to whom none will deny the credit of a generous and valiant enemy, hath sent this leech hither with an honourable retinue and guard, befitting the high estimation in which El Hakim is held by the Soldan, and with fruits and refreshments for the King's private chamber, and such message as may pass betwixt honourable enemies, praying him to be recovered of his fever, that he may be the fitter to receive a visit from the Soldan, with his naked scimitar in his hand, and an hundred thousand cavaliers at his back. Will it please you, who are of the King's secret council, to cause these camels to be discharged of their burdens, and some order taken as to the reception of the learned physician?"

"Wonderful!" said De Vaux, as speaking to himself.—"And who will vouch for the honour of Saladin, in a case when bad faith would rid him at once of his most powerful adversary?"

"I myself," replied Sir Kenneth, "will be his guarantee, with honour, life and fortune."

"Strange!" again ejaculated De Vaux; "the North vouches for the South—the Scot for the Turk!—May I crave of you, Sir Knight, how you became concerned in this affair?"

"I have been absent on a pilgrimage, in the course of which," replied Sir Kenneth, "I had a message to discharge towards the holy hermit of Engaddi."

"May I not be intrusted with it, Sir Kenneth, and with the answer of the holy man?"

"It may not be, my lord," answered the Scot.

"I am of the secret council of England," said the Englishman, haughtily.

"To which land I owe no allegiance," said Kenneth. "Though I have voluntarily followed in this war the personal fortunes of England's sovereign, I was dispatched by the General Council of the kings, princes, and supreme leaders of the army of the Blessed Cross, and to them only I render my errand."

"Ha! say'st thou?" said the proud Baron de Vaux. "But know, messenger of the kings and princes as thou mayst be, no leech shall approach the sick-bed of Richard of England, without the consent of him of Gilsland; and they will come on evil errand who dare to intrude themselves against it."

He was turning loftily away, when the Scot, placing himself closer, and more opposite to him, asked, in a calm voice, yet not without expressing his share of pride, whether the Lord of Gilsland esteemed him a gentleman and a good knight.

"All Scots are ennobled by their birthright," answered Thomas de Vaux, something ironically; but, sensible of his own injustice, and perceiving that Kenneth's colour rose, he added, "For a good knight it were sin to doubt you, in one at least who has seen you well and bravely discharge your devoir."

"Well, then," said the Scottish knight, satisfied with the frankness of the last admission, "and let me swear to you, Thomas of Gilsland, that as I am true Scottish man, which I hold a privilege equal to my ancient gentry, and as sure as I am a belted knight, and come hither to acquire *los* and fame in this mortal life, and forgiveness of my sins in that which is to come— so truly, and by the blessed Cross which I wear, do I protest unto you, that I desire but the safety of Richard Cœur de Lion in recommending the ministry of this Moslem physician."

The Englishman was struck with the solemnity of the obtestation, and answered with more cordiality than he had yet exhibited, "Tell me, Sir Knight of the Leopard, granting (which I do not doubt) that thou art thyself satisfied in this matter, shall I do well, in a land where the art of poisoning is as general as that of cooking, to bring this unknown physician to practise with his drugs on a health so valuable to Christendom?"

"My lord," replied the Scot, "thus only can I reply; that my squire, the only one of my retinue whom war and disease had left in attendance on me, has been of late suffering dangerously under this same fever, which, in valiant King Richard, has disabled the principal limb of our holy enterprise. This leech, this El Hakim, hath ministered remedies to him not two hours since, and already he hath fallen into a refreshing sleep. That he *can* cure the disorder, which has proved so fatal, I nothing doubt; that he hath the purpose to do it, is, I think, warranted by his mission from the royal Soldan, who is true-hearted and loyal, so far as a blinded infidel may be called so; and, for his eventual success, the certainty of reward in case of succeeding, and punishment in case of voluntary failure, may be a sufficient guarantee."

The Englishman listened with downcast looks, as one who doubted, yet was not unwilling to receive conviction. At length he looked up and said, "May I see your sick squire, fair sir?"

The Scottish knight hesitated and coloured, yet answered at last, "Willingly, my Lord of Gilsland; but you must remember, when you see my poor quarter, that the nobles and knights of Scotland feed not so high, sleep not so soft, and care not for the magnificence of lodgment, which is proper to their southern neighbours. I am *poorly* lodged, my Lord of Gilsland," he added, with a haughty emphasis on the word, while, with some unwillingness, he led the way to his temporary place of abode.

Whatever were the prejudices of De Vaux against the nation of his new acquaintance, and though we undertake not to deny that some of these were excited by its proverbial poverty, he had too much nobleness of disposition to enjoy the mortification of a brave individual, thus compelled to make known wants which his pride would gladly have concealed.

"Shame to the soldier of the Cross," he said, "who thinks of worldly splendour, or of luxurious accommodation, when pressing forward to the conquest of the Holy City. Fare as hard as we may, we shall yet be better than the host of martyrs and of saints, who having trod these scenes before us, now hold golden lamps, and evergreen palms."

This was the most metaphorical speech which Thomas of Gilsland was ever known to utter, the rather perhaps (as will sometimes happen), that it did not entirely express his own sentiments, being somewhat a lover of good cheer and splendid accommodation. By this time they reached the place of the camp, where the Knight of the Leopard had assumed his abode.

Appearances here did indeed promise no breach of the laws of mortification, to which the Crusaders, according to the opinion expressed by him of Gilsland, ought to subject themselves. A space of ground, large enough to accommodate perhaps thirty tents, according to the Crusaders' rules of castrametation, was partly vacant—because, in ostentation, the knight had demanded ground to the extent of his original retinue—partly occupied by a few miserable huts, hastily constructed of boughs and covered with palm leaves. These habitations seemed entirely deserted, and several of them were ruinous. The central hut, which represented the pavilion of the leader, was distinguished by his swallow-tailed pennon, placed on the point of a spear, from which its long folds dropt motionless to the ground, as if sickening under the scorching rays of the Asiatic sun. But no pages or squires, not even a solitary warder, was placed by the emblem of feudal power and knightly degrees. If its reputation defended it not from insult, it had no other guard.

Sir Kenneth cast a melancholy look around him, but, suppressing his feelings, entered the hut, making a sign to the Baron of Gilsland to follow. He also cast around a glance of examination, which implied pity not altogether unmingled with contempt, to which, perhaps, it is as nearly akin as it is said to be to love. He then stooped his lofty crest, and entered a lowly hut, which his bulky form seemed almost entirely to fill.

The interior of the hut was chiefly occupied by two beds. One was empty, but composed of collected leaves, and spread with an antelope's hide. It seemed, from the articles of armour laid beside it, and from a crucifix of silver, carefully and reverentially disposed at the head, to be the couch of the knight himself. The other contained the invalid of whom Sir

Kenneth had spoken, a strong-built and harsh-featured man, past, as his looks betokened, the middle age of life. His couch was trimmed more softly than his master's, and it was plain that the more courtly garments of the latter, the loose robe, in which the knights showed themselves on pacific occasions, and the other little spare articles of dress and adornment, had been applied by Sir Kenneth to the accommodation of his sick domestic. In an outward part of the hut, which yet was within the range of the English baron's eye, a boy, rudely attired with buskins of deer's hide, a blue cap or bonnet, and a doublet, whose original finery was much tarnished, sat on his knees by a chafing-dish filled with charcoal, cooking upon a plate of iron the cakes of barley-bread, which were then, and still are, a favourite food with the Scottish people. Part of an antelope was suspended against one of the main props of the hut, nor was it difficult to know how it had been procured; for a large stag greyhound, nobler in size and appearance than those even which guarded King Richard's sick-bed, lay eyeing the process of baking the cake. The sagacious animal, on their first entrance, uttered a stifled growl, which sounded from his deep chest like distant thunder. But he saw his master, and acknowledged his presence by wagging his tail and couching his head, abstaining from more tumultuous or noisy greeting, as if his noble instinct had taught him the propriety of silence in a sick man's chamber.

Beside the couch sat on a cushion, also composed of skins, the Moorish physician of whom Sir Kenneth had spoken, cross-legged, after the Eastern fashion. The imperfect light showed little of him, save that the lower part of his face was covered with a long black beard, which descended over hiss breast—that he wore a high *tolpach*, a Tartar cap of the lambs' wool manufactured at Astracan, bearing the same dusky colour, and that his ample caftan, or Turkish robe, was also of a dark hue. Two piercing eyes, which gleamed with unusual lustre, were the only lineaments of his visage that could be discerned amid the darkness in which he was enveloped. The English lord stood silent with a sort of reverential awe; for, notwithstanding the roughness of his general bearing, a scene of distress and poverty, firmly endured without complaint or murmur, would at any time have claimed more reverence from Thomas de Vaux, than would all the splendid formalities of a royal presence-chamber, unless that presence-chamber were King Richard's own. Nothing was, for a time, heard, but the heavy and regular breathings of the invalid, who seemed in profound repose.

"He hath not slept for six nights before," said Sir Kenneth, "as I am assured by the youth, his attendant."

"Noble Scot," said Thomas de Vaux, grasping the Scottish knight's hand, with a pressure which had more of cordiality than he permitted his words to utter, "this gear must be amended—Your esquire is but too evil fed and looked to."

In the latter part of this speech, he naturally raised his voice to its usual decided tone. The sick man was disturbed in his slumbers.

"My master," he said, murmuring as in a dream, "noble Sir Kenneth, taste not, to you as to me, the waters of the Clyde cold and refreshing, after the brackish springs of Palestine?"

"He dreams of his native land, and is happy in his slumbers," whispered Sir Kenneth to De Vaux; but had scarce uttered the words, when the physician, arising from the place which he had taken near the couch of the sick, and laying the hand of the patient, whose pulse he had been carefully watching, quietly upon the couch, came to the two knights, and taking them each by the arm, while he intimated to them to remain silent, led them to the front of the hut.

"In the name of Issa Ben Mariam," he said, "whom we honour as you, though not with the same blinded superstition, disturb not the effect of the blessed medicine of which he hath partaken. To awaken him now is death or deprivation of reason; but return at the hour when the Muezzin calls from the minaret to evening prayer in the mosque, and, if left undisturbed until then, I promise you, this same Frankish soldier shall be able, without prejudice to his health, to hold some brief converse with you, on any matters on which either, and especially his master, may have to question him."

The knights retreated before the authoritative commands of the leech, who seemed fully to comprehend the importance of the Eastern proverb, that the sick chamber of the patient is the kingdom of the physician.

They paused, and remained standing together at the door of the hut, Sir Kenneth, with the air of one who expected his visitor to say farewell, and De Vaux, as if he had something on his mind which prevented him from doing so. The hound, however, had pressed out of the tent after them, and now thrust his long rough countenance into the hand of his master, as if modestly soliciting some mark of his kindness. He had no sooner received the notice which he desired, in the shape of a kind word and slight caress, than, eager to acknowledge his gratitude, and joy for his master's return, he flew off at full speed, galloping in full career, and with outstretched tail, here and there, about and around, crossways and endlong, through the decayed huts and the esplanade we have described, but never transgressing those precincts which his sagacity knew were protected by his master's pennon. After a few gambols of this kind, the dog, coming close up to his master, laid at once aside his frolicsome mood, relapsed into his usual gravity and slowness of gesture and deportment, and looked as if he were ashamed that any thing should have moved him to depart so far out of his sober self-control.

Both knights looked on with pleasure; for Sir Kenneth was justly proud of his noble hound, and the northern English baron was of course an admirer of the chase, and a judge of the animal's merits.

"A right able dog," he said; "I think, fair sir, King Richard hath not an *alan* which may match him, if he be as stanch as he is swift. But let me pray you—speaking in all honour and kindness—have you not heard the proclamation, that no one, under the rank of earl, shall keep hunting dogs within King Richard's camp, without the royal license, which, I think, Sir Kenneth, hath not been issued to you?—I speak as Master of the Horse."

"And I answer as a free Scottish knight," said Kenneth, sternly. "For the present I follow the banner of England, but I cannot remember that I have ever subjected myself to the forest-laws of that kingdom, nor have I such respect for them as would incline me to do so. When the trumpet sounds to arms, my foot is in the stirrup as soon as any; when it clangs for the charge, my lance has not yet been the last laid in the rest. But for my hours of liberty or of idleness, King Richard has no title to bar my recreation."

"Nevertheless," said De Vaux, "it is a folly to disobey the King's ordinance—so, with your good leave, I, as having authority in that matter, will send you a protection for my friend here."

"I thank you," said the Scot, coldy; "but he knows my allotted quarters, and within these I can protect him myself.—

And yet," he said, suddenly changing his manner, "this is but a cold return for a well-meant kindness. I thank you, my lord, most heartily. The King's equerries, or prickers, might find Roswal at disadvantage, and do him some injury, which I should not, perhaps, be slow in returning, and so ill might come of it. You have seen so much of my house-keeping, my lord," he added with a smile, "that I need not shame to say that Roswal is our principal purveyor; and well I hope our Lion Richard will not be like the lion in the minstrel fable, that went a-hunting, and kept the whole booty to himself. I cannot think he would grudge a poor gentleman who follows him faithfully, his hour of sport, and his morsel of game, more especially when other food is hard enough to come by."

"By my faith, you do the King no more than justice—and yet," said the baron, "there is something in these words, vert and venison, that turns the very brains of our Norman princes."

"We have heard of late," said the Scot, "by minstrels and pilgrims, that your outlawed yeomen have formed great bands in the shires of York and Nottingham, having at their head a most stout archer, called Robin Hood, with his lieutenant, Little John. Methinks it were better that Richard relaxed his forest-code in England, than endeavoured to enforce it in the Holy Land."

"Wild work, Sir Kenneth," replied De Vaux, shrugging his shoulders, as one who would avoid a perilous or unpleasing topic—"a mad world, sir.—I must now bid you adieu, having presently to return to the King's pavilion. At vespers, I will again, with your leave, visit your quarters, and speak with this same infidel physician. I would, in the meantime, were it no offence, willingly send you what would somewhat mend your cheer."

"I thank you, sir," said Sir Kenneth, "but it needs not; Roswal hath already stocked my larder for two weeks, since the sun of Palestine, if it brings diseases, serves also to dry venison."

The two warriors parted much better friends than they had met; but ere they separated, Thomas de Vaux informed himself at more length of the circumstances attending the mission of the Eastern physician, and received from the Scottish knight the credentials which he had brought to King Richard on the part of Saladin.

CHAPTER VIII

A wise physician, skill'd our wounds to heal,
Is more than armies to the common weal.

POPE's *Iliad*.

"THIS is a strange tale, Sir Thomas," said the sick monarch, when he had heard the report of the trusty Baron of Gilsland; "art thou sure this Scottish man is a tall man and true?"

"I cannot say, my lord," replied the jealous borderer; "I live a little too near the Scots to gather much truth among them, having found them ever fair and false. But this man's bearing is that of a true man, were he a devil as well as a Scot—that I must needs say for him in conscience."

"And for his carriage as a knight, how say'st thou, De Vaux?" demanded the King.

"It is your Majesty's business more than mine to note men's bearings; and I warrant you have noted the manner in which this man of the Leopard hath borne himself. He hath been full well spoken of."

"And justly Thomas," said the King. "We have ourselves witnessed him. It is indeed our purpose in placing ourselves ever in the front of battle, to see how our liegemen and followers acquit themselves, and not from a desire to accumulate vainglory to ourselves, as some have supposed. We know the vanity of the praise of man, which is but a vapour, and buckle on our armour for other purposes than to win it."

De Vaux was alarmed when he heard the King make a declaration so inconsistent with his nature, and believed at first that nothing short of the approach of death could have brought him to speak in depreciating terms of military renown, which was the very breath of his nostrils. But recollecting he had met the royal confessor in the outer pavilion, he was shrewd enough to place this temporary self-abasement to the effect of the reverend man's lesson, and suffered the King to proceed without reply.

"Yes," continued Richard, "I have indeed marked the manner in which this knight does his devoir. My leading-staff were not worth a fool's bauble, had he escaped my notice—and he had ere now tasted of our bounty, but that I have also marked his overweening and audacious presumption."

"My liege," said the Baron of Gilsland, observing the

King's countenance change, "I fear I have transgressed your pleasure in lending some countenance to his transgression."

"How, De Multon, thou?" said the King, contracting his brows, and speaking in a tone of angry surprise,—"Thou countenance his insolence?—It cannot be."

"Nay, your Majesty will pardon me to remind you that I have by mine office right to grant liberty to men of gentle blood, to keep them a hound or two within the camp, just to cherish the noble art of venerie; and besides, it were a sin to have maimed or harmed a thing so noble as this gentleman's dog."

"Has he then a dog so handsome?" said the King.

"A most perfect creature of Heaven," said the baron, who was an enthusiast in field sports—"of the noblest northern breed, deep in the chest, strong in the stern, black colour, and brindled on the breast and legs—not spotted with white, but just shaded into grey—strength to pull down a bull, swiftness to cote an antelope."

The King laughed at his enthusiasm. "Well, thou hast given him leave to keep the hound, so there is an end of it. Be not, however, liberal of your licenses among those knights adventurers who have no prince or leader to depend upon— they are ungovernable, and leave no game in Palestine.—But to this piece of learned heathenesse—say'st thou the Scot met him in the desert?"

"No, my liege, the Scot's tale runs thus:—He was dispatched to the old hermit of Engaddi, of whom men talk so much——"

"'Sdeath and hell!" said Richard, starting up, "by whom dispatched, and for what? Who dared send any one thither, when our Queen was in the Convent of Engaddi, upon her pilgrimage for our recovery?"

"The Council of the Crusade sent him, my lord," answered the Baron de Vaux; "for what purpose, he declined to account to me. I think it is scarce known in the camp that your royal consort is on a pilgrimage—and even the princes may not have been aware, as the Queen has been sequestered from company since your love prohibited her attendance in case of infection."

"Well, it shall be looked into," said Richard. "So this Scottish man, this envoy, met with a wandering physician at the grotto of Engaddi—ha?"

"Not so, my liege," replied De Vaux; "but he met, I

think, near that place, with a Saracen Emir, with whom he had some *mêlée* in the way of proof of valour, and finding him worthy to bear brave men company, they went together, as errant knights are wont, to the grotto of Engaddi."

Here De Vaux stopped, for he was not one of those who can tell a long story in a sentence.

"And did they there meet the physician?" demanded the King impatiently.

"No, my liege," replied De Vaux; "but the Saracen, learning your Majesty's grievous illness, undertook that Saladin should send his own physician to you, and with many assurances of his eminent skill; and he came to the grotto accordingly, after the Scottish knight had tarried a day for him and more. He is attended as if he were a prince, with drums and atabals, and servants on horse and foot, and brings with him letters of credence from Saladin."

"Have they been examined by Giacomo Loredani?"

"I showed them to the interpreter ere bringing them hither, and behold their contents in English."

Richard took a scroll, in which were inscribed these words:
—"The blessing of Allah and his Prophet Mahommed!" ["Out upon the hound!" said Richard, spitting in contempt, by way of interjection;] "Saladin, king of kings, Soldan of Egypt and of Syria, the light and refuge of the earth, to the great Melech Ric, Richard of England, greeting. Whereas, we have been informed that the hand of sickness hath been heavy upon thee, our royal brother, and that thou hast with thee only such Nazarene and Jewish mediciners as work without the blessing of Allah and our holy Prophet," [Confusion on his head!" again muttered the English monarch,] "we have therefore sent to tend and wait upon thee at this time the physician to our own person, Adonbec el Hakim, before whose face the angel Azrael spreads his wings, and departs from the sick chamber; who knows the virtues of herbs and stones, the path of the sun, moon, and stars, and can save man from all that is not written on his forehead. And this we do, praying you heartily to honour and make use of his skill, not only that we may do service to thy worth and valour, which is the glory of all the nations of Frangistan, but that we may bring the controversy which is at present between us to an end, either by honourable agreement, or by open trial thereof with our weapons, in a fair field; seeing that it neither becomes thy place and courage to die the death of a slave

who hath been overwrought by his taskmaster, nor befits it our
fame that a brave adversary be snatched from our weapon by
such a disease. And, therefore, may the holy——"

"Hold, hold," said Richard, "I will have no more of his
dog of a Prophet! It makes me sick to think the valiant and
worthy Soldan should believe in a dead dog.—Yes, I will see
his physician. I will put myself into the charge of this Hakim
—I will repay the noble Soldan his generosity—I will meet
Saladin in the field, as he so worthily proposes, and he shall
have no cause to term Richard of England ungrateful. I will
strike him to the earth with my battle-axe—I will convert him
to Holy Church with such blows as he has rarely endured—
he shall recant his errors before my good cross-handled sword,
and I will have him baptized in the battlefield, from my own
helmet, though the cleansing waters were mixed with the blood
of us both.—Haste, De Vaux, why dost thou delay a conclusion so pleasing? Fetch the Hakim hither."

"My lord," said the baron, who perhaps saw some accession
of fever in this overflow of confidence, "bethink you, the
Soldan is a pagan, and that you are his most formidable
enemy——"

"For which reason he is the more bound to do me service
in this matter, lest a paltry fever end the quarrel betwixt two
such kings. I tell thee, he loves me as I love him—as noble
adversaries ever love each other—by my honour, it were sin
to doubt his good faith!"

"Nevertheless, my lord, it were well to wait the issue of
these medicines upon the Scottish squire," said the Lord
of Gilsland; "my own life depends upon it, for worthy were I
to die like a dog, did I proceed rashly in this matter, and
make shipwreck of the weal of Christendom."

"I never knew thee before hesitate for fear of life," said
Richard, upbraidingly.

"Nor would I now, my liege," replied the stout-hearted
baron, "save that yours lies at pledge as well as my
own."

"Well, thou suspicious mortal," answered Richard, "begone
then, and watch the progress of this remedy. I could almost
wish it might either cure or kill me, for I am weary of lying
here like an ox dying of the murrain, when tambours are
beating, horses stamping, and trumpets sounding without."

The baron hastily departed, resolved, however, to communicate his errand to some churchman, as he felt something

burdened in conscience at the idea of his master being attended by an unbeliever.

The Archbishop of Tyre was the first to whom he confided his doubts, knowing his interest with his master, Richard, who both loved and honoured that sagacious prelate. The bishop heard the doubts which De Vaux stated, with that acuteness of intelligence which distinguishes the Roman Catholic clergy. The religious scruples of De Vaux he treated with as much lightness as propriety permitted him to exhibit on such a subject to a layman.

"Mediciners," he said, "like the medicines which they employed, were often useful, though the one were by birth or manners the vilest of humanity, as the others are, in many cases, extracted from the basest materials. Men may use the assistance of pagans and infidels," he continued, "in their need, and there is reason to think, that one cause of their being permitted to remain on earth is that they might minister to the convenience of true Christians—Thus, we lawfully make slaves of heathen captives.—Again," proceeded the prelate, "there is no doubt that the primitive Christians used the services of the unconverted heathen—thus, in the ship of Alexandria, in which the blessed Apostle Paul sailed to Italy, the sailors were doubtless pagans, yet what said the holy saint when their ministry was needful, '*Nisi hi in navi manserint, vos salvi fieri non potestis*—Unless these men abide in the ship, ye cannot be saved.' Again, Jews are infidels to Christianity as well as Mahommedans. But there are few physicians in the camp excepting Jews, and such are employed without scandal or scruple. Therefore, Mahommedans may be used for their service in that capacity—*quod erat demonstrandum.*"

This reasoning entirely removed the scruples of Thomas de Vaux, who was particularly moved by the Latin quotation, as he did not understand a word of it.

But the bishop proceeded with far less fluency, when he considered the possibility of the Saracen's acting with bad faith ; and here he came not to a speedy decision. The baron showed him the letters of credence. He read and re-read them, and compared the original with the translation.

"It is a dish choicely cooked," he said, "to the palate of King Richard, and I cannot but have my suspicions of the wily Saracen. They are curious in the art of poisons, and can so temper them that they shall be weeks in acting upon the party, during which time the perpetrator has leisure to escape. They can impregnate cloth and leather, nay, even paper and parchment, with the most subtle venom—Our Lady forgive me!—And wherefore, knowing this, hold I these letters of credence so close to my face?—Take them, Sir Thomas, take them speedily."

Here he gave them at arm's-length, and with some appearance of haste, to the baron. "But come, my Lord De Vaux," he continued, "wend we to the tent of this sick squire, where we shall learn whether this Hakim hath really the art of curing which he professeth, ere we consider whether there be safety in permitting him to exercise his art upon King Richard.—Yet, hold! let me first take my pouncet-box, for these fevers spread like an infection. I would advise you to use dried rosemary steeped in vinegar, my lord. I, too, know something of the healing art."

"I thank your reverend lordship," replied Thomas of Gilsland; "but had I been accessible to the fever, I had caught it long since by the bed of my master."

The Bishop of Tyre blushed, for he had rather avoided the presence of the sick monarch; and he bid the baron lead on.

As they passed before the wretched hut in which Kenneth of the Leopard and his follower abode, the bishop said to De Vaux, "Now, of a surety, my lord, these Scottish knights have worse care of their followers than we of our dogs. Here is a knight, valiant they say in battle, and thought fitting to be graced with charges of weight in time of truce, whose esquire of the body is lodged worse than in the worst dog-kennel in England. What say you of your neighbours?"

"That a master doth well enough for his servant, when he lodgeth him in no worse dwelling than his own," said De Vaux, and entered the hut.

The bishop followed, not without evident reluctance; for though he lacked not courage in some respects, yet it was tempered with a strong and lively regard for his own safety. He recollected, however, the necessity there was for judging personally of the skill of the Arabian physician, and entered the hut with a stateliness of manner, calculated, as he thought, to impose respect on the stranger.

The prelate was, indeed, a striking and commanding figure. In his youth he had been eminently handsome, and even in age was unwilling to appear less so. His episcopal dress was of the richest fashion, trimmed with costly fur, and surrounded by a cope of curious needlework. The rings on his fingers

were worth a goodly barony, and the hood which he wore,
though now unclasped and thrown back for heat, had studs
of pure gold to fasten it around his throat and under his chin,
when he so inclined. His long beard, now silvered with age,
descended over his breast. One of two youthful acolytes who
attended him, created an artificial shade, peculiar then to the
East, by bearing over his head an umbrella of palmetto leaves,
while the other refreshed his reverend master by agitating a fan
of peacock feathers.

When the Bishop of Tyre entered the hut of the Scottish
knight, the master was absent; and the Moorish physician,
whom he had come to see, sat in the very posture in which De
Vaux had left him several hours before, cross-legged upon a
mat made of twisted leaves, by the side of the patient, who
appeared in deep slumber, and whose pulse he felt from time
to time. The bishop remained standing before him in silence
for two or three minutes, as if expecting some honourable
salutation, or at least that the Saracen would seem struck with
the dignity of his appearance. But Adonbec el Hakim took
no notice of him beyond a passing glance, and when the prelate at length saluted him in the lingua franca current in the
country, he only replied by the ordinary Oriental greeting,
" *Salam alicum*—peace be with you."

" Art thou a physician, infidel ? " said the bishop, somewhat
mortified at this cold reception. " I would speak to thee on
that art."

"If thou knewest aught of medicine," answered El Hakim,
"thou wouldst be aware that physicians hold no counsel or
debate in the sick chamber of their patient. Hear," he added,
as the low growling of the stag-hound was heard from the
inner hut, "even the dog might teach thee reason, Ulemat.
His instinct teaches him to suppress his barking in the sick
man's hearing. Come without the tent," said he, rising and
leading the way, "if thou hast aught to say with me."

Notwithstanding the plainness of the Saracen leech's dress,
and his inferiority of size, when contrasted with the tall prelate
and gigantic English baron, there was something striking in
his manner and countenance, which prevented the Bishop of
Tyre from expressing strongly the displeasure he felt at this
unceremonious rebuke. When without the hut, he gazed upon
Adonbec in silence for several minutes, before he could fix on
the best manner to renew the conversation. No locks were
seen under the high bonnet of the Arabian, which hid also

part of a brow that seemed lofty and expanded, smooth, and free from wrinkles, as were his cheeks, where they were seen under the shade of his long beard. We have elsewhere noticed the piercing quality of his dark eyes.

The prelate, struck with his apparent youth, at length broke a pause, which the other seemed in no haste to interrupt, by demanding of the Arabian how old he was?

"The years of ordinary men," said the Saracen, "are counted by their wrinkles; those of sages by their studies. I dare not call myself older than an hundred revolutions of the Hegira."[1]

The Baron of Gilsland, who took this for a literal assertion that he was a century old, looked doubtfully upon the prelate, who, though he better understood the meaning of El Hakim, answered his glance by mysteriously shaking his head. He resumed an air of importance, when he again authoritatively demanded, what evidence Adonbec could produce of his medical proficiency.

"Ye have the word of the mighty Saladin," said the sage, touching his cap in sign of reverence; "a word which was never broken towards friend or foe—what, Nazarene, wouldst thou demand more?"

"I would have ocular proof of thy skill," said the baron, "and without it thou approachest not to the couch of King Richard."

"The praise of the physician," said the Arabian, "is in the recovery of his patient. Behold this sergeant, whose blood has been dried up by the fever which has whitened your camp with skeletons, and against which the art of your Nazarene leeches hath been like a silken doublet against a lance of steel. Look at his fingers and arms, wasted like the claws and shanks of the crane. Death had this morning his clutch on him; but had Azrael been on one side of the couch, I being on the other, his soul should not have been reft from his body. Disturb me not with further questions, but await the critical minute, and behold in silent wonder the marvellous event."

The physician had then recourse to his astrolabe, the oracle of Eastern science, and, watching with grave precision until the precise time of the evening prayer had arrived, he sunk on his knees, with his face turned to Mecca, and recited the petitions which close the Moslemah's day of toil. The bishop and the

[1] Meaning that his attainments were those which might have been made in a hundred years.

English baron looked on each other, meanwhile, with symptoms of contempt and indignation, but neither judged it fit to interrupt El Hakim in his devotions, unholy as they considered them to be.

The Arab arose from the earth, on which he had prostrated himself, and, walking into the hut where the patient lay extended, he drew a sponge from a small silver box, dipt perhaps in some aromatic distillation; for when he put it to the sleeper's nose, he sneezed, awoke, and looked wildly around. He was a ghastly spectacle, as he sat up almost naked on his couch, the bones and cartilages as visible through the surface of his skin, as if they had never been clothed with flesh; his face was long, and furrowed with wrinkles, but his eye, though it wandered at first, became gradually more settled. He seemed to be aware of the presence of his dignified visitors, for he attempted feebly to pull the covering from his head, in token of reverence, as he enquired, in a subdued and submissive voice, for his master.

" Do you know us, vassal ? " said the Lord of Gilsland.

" Not perfectly, my lord," replied the squire, faintly. " My sleep has been long and full of dreams. Yet I know that you are a great English lord, as seemeth by the red cross, and this a holy prelate, whose blessing I crave on me a poor sinner."

" Thou hast it—*Benedictio Domini sit vobiscum*," said the prelate, making the sign of the cross, but without approaching nearer to the patient's bed.

" Your eyes witness," said the Arabian, " the fever hath been subdued—he speaks with calmness and recollection—his pulse beats composedly as yours—try its pulsations yourself."

The prelate declined the experiment; but Thomas of Gilsland, more determined on making the trial, did so, and satisfied himself that the fever was indeed gone.

" This is most wonderful," said the knight, looking to the bishop; " the man is assuredly cured. I must conduct this mediciner presently to King Richard's tent—What thinks your reverence ? "

" Stay, let me finish one cure ere I commence another," said the Arab; " I will pass with you when I have given my patient the second cup of this most holy elixir."

So saying, he pulled out a silver cup, and filling it with water from a gourd which stood by the bedside, he next drew forth a small silken bag made of network, twisted with silver, the contents of which the bystanders could not discover, and immersing it in the cup, continued to watch it in silence during the space of five minutes. It seemed to the spectators as if some effervescence took place during the operation, but if so, it instantly subsided.

"Drink," said the physician to the sick man, "sleep, and awaken free from malady."

"And with this simple-seeming draught, thou wilt undertake to cure a monarch?" said the Bishop of Tyre.

"I have cured a beggar, as you may behold," replied the sage. "Are the kings of Frangistan made of other clay than the meanest of their subjects?"

"Let us have him presently to the King," said the Baron of Gilsland. "He hath shown that he possesses the secret which may restore his health. If he fails to exercise it, I will put himself past the power of medicine."

As they were about to leave the hut, the sick man, raising his voice as much as his weakness permitted, exclaimed, "Reverend father, noble knight, and you, kind leech, if you would have me sleep and recover, tell me in charity what has become of my dear master?"

"He is upon a distant expedition, friend," replied the prelate; "on an honourable embassy, which may detain him for some days."

"Nay," said the Baron of Gilsland, "why deceive the poor fellow? Friend, thy master has returned to the camp, and you will presently see him."

The invalid held up, as if in thankfulness, his wasted hands to Heaven, and, resisting no longer the soporiferous operation of the elixir, sunk down in a gentle sleep.

"You are a better physician than I, Sir Thomas," said the prelate; "a soothing falsehood is fitter for a sick-room than an unpleasing truth."

"How mean you, my reverend lord?" said De Vaux, hastily. "Think you I would tell a falsehood to save the lives of a dozen such as he?"

"You said," replied the bishop, with manifest symptoms of alarm, "you said the esquire's master was returned—he, I mean, of the Couchant Leopard?"

"And he *is* returned," said De Vaux. "I spoke with him but a few hours since. This learned leech came in his company."

"Holy Virgin! why told you not of his return to me?" said the bishop, in evident perturbation.

"Did I not say that this same Knight of the Leopard had returned in company with the physician?—I thought I had," replied De Vaux, carelessly; "but what signified his return to the skill of the physician, or the cure of his Majesty?"

"Much, Sir Thomas, it signified much," said the bishop, clenching his hands, pressing his foot against the earth, and giving signs of impatience, as if in an involuntary manner. "But where can he be gone now, this same knight?—God be with us—here may be some fatal errors!"

"Yonder serf in the outer space," said De Vaux, not without wonder at the bishop's emotion, "can probably tell us whither his master has gone."

The lad was summoned, and, in a language nearly incomprehensible to them, gave them at length to understand, that an officer had summoned his master to the royal tent, some time before their arrival at that of his master. The anxiety of the bishop appeared to rise to the highest, and became evident to De Vaux, though neither an acute observer, nor of a suspicious temper. But with his anxiety seemed to increase his wish to keep it subdued and unobserved. He took a hasty leave of De Vaux, who looked after him with astonishment; and, after shrugging up his shoulders in silent wonder, proceeded to conduct the Arabian physician to the tent of King Richard.

CHAPTER IX

This is the Prince of Leeches; fever, plague,
Cold rheum, and hot podagra, do but look on him,
And quit their grasp upon the tortured sinews.
Anonymous.

THE Baron of Gilsland walked with slow step and an anxious countenance towards the royal pavilion. He had much diffidence of his own capacity, except in a field of battle, and, conscious of no very acute intellect, was usually contented to wonder at circumstances, which a man of livelier imagination would have endeavoured to investigate and understand, or at least would have made the subject of speculation. But it seemed very extraordinary, even to him, that the attention of the bishop should have been at once abstracted from all reflection on the marvellous cure which they had witnessed, and upon the probability it afforded of Richard being restored to health, by what seemed a very trivial piece of information, announcing the motions of a beggarly Scottish knight, than whom Thomas of Gilsland knew nothing within the circle of gentle blood more unimportant or contemptible ; and, despite his usual habit of passively beholding passing events, the baron's spirit toiled with unwonted attempts to form conjectures on the cause.

At length the idea occurred at once to him, that the whole might be a conspiracy against King Richard, formed within the camp of the allies, and to which the bishop, who was by some represented as a politic and unscrupulous person, was not unlikely to have been accessary.　It was true that, in his own opinion, there existed no character so perfect as that of his master ; for Richard being the flower of chivalry, and the chief of Christian leaders, and obeying in all points the commands of Holy Church, De Vaux's ideas of perfection went no farther.　Still he knew that, however unworthily, it had been always his master's fate to draw as much reproach and dislike, as honour and attachment from the display of his great qualities ; and that in the very camp, and amongst those princes bound by oath to the Crusade, were many who would have sacrificed all hope of victory over the Saracens, to the pleasure of ruining, or at least of humbling, Richard of England.

"Wherefore," said the baron to himself, "it is in no sense impossible that this El Hakim, with this his cure, or seeming cure, wrought on the body of the Scottish squire, may mean nothing but a trick, to which he of the Leopard may be accessary, and wherein the Bishop of Tyre, prelate as he is, may have some share."

This hypothesis, indeed, could not be so easily reconciled with the alarm manifested by the bishop, on learning that, contrary to his expectation, the Scottish knight had suddenly returned to the Crusaders' camp.　But De Vaux was influenced only by his general prejudices, which dictated to him the assured belief that a wily Italian priest, a false-hearted Scot, and an infidel physician, formed a set of ingredients from which all evil, and no good, was likely to be extracted.　He resolved, however, to lay his scruples bluntly before the King, of whose judgment he had nearly as high an opinion as of his valour.

Meantime, events had taken place very contrary to the suppositions which Thomas de Vaux had entertained.　Scarce had he left the royal pavilion, when, betwixt the impatience of the fever, and that which was natural to his disposition, Richard began to murmur at his delay, and express an earnest desire for his return. He had seen enough to try to reason himself out of this irritation, which greatly increased his bodily malady. He wearied his attendants by demanding from them amusements, and the breviary of the priest, the romance of the clerk, even the harp of his favourite minstrel, were had recourse to in vain. At length, some two hours before sundown, and long, therefore, ere he could expect a satisfactory account of the process of the cure which the Moor or Arabian had undertaken, he sent, as we have already heard, a messenger, commanding the attendance of the Knight of the Leopard, determined to soothe his impatience by obtaining from Sir Kenneth a more particular account of the cause of his absence from the camp, and the circumstances of his meeting with this celebrated physician.

The Scottish knight, thus summoned, entered the royal presence as one who was no stranger to such scenes. He was scarcely known to the King of England, even by sight, although, tenacious of his rank, as devout in the adoration of the lady of his secret heart, he had never been absent on those occasions when the munificence and hospitality of England opened the court of its monarch to all who held a certain rank in chivalry. The King gazed fixedly on Sir Kenneth approaching his bedside, while the knight bent his knee for a moment, then arose and stood before him, as became an officer in the presence of his sovereign, in a posture of deference, but not of subservience or humility.

" Thy name," said the King, " is Kenneth of the Leopard.— From whom hadst thou degree of knighthood ? "

" I took it from the sword of William the Lion, King of Scotland," replied the Scot.

" A weapon," said the King, " well worthy to confer honour, nor has it been laid on an undeserving shoulder. We have seen thee bear thyself knightly and valiantly in press of battle, when most need there was ; and thou hadst not been yet to learn that thy deserts were known to us, but that thy presumption in other points has been such, that thy services can challenge no better reward than that of pardon for thy transgression. What say'st thou—ha ? "

Kenneth attempted to speak, but was unable to express himself distinctly ; the consciousness of his too ambitious love, and the keen falcon glance with which Cœur de Lion seemed to penetrate his inmost soul, combining to disconcert him.

"And yet," said the King, "although soldiers should obey command, and vassals be respectful towards their superiors, we might forgive a brave knight greater offence than the keeping a simple hound, though it were contrary to our express public ordinance."

Richard kept his eye fixed on the Scot's face, beheld, and beholding smiled inwardly at the relief produced by the turn he had given to his general accusation.

"So please you, my lord," said the Scot, "your Majesty must be good to us poor gentlemen of Scotland in this matter. We are far from home, scant of revenues, and cannot support ourselves as your wealthy nobles, who have credit of the Lombards. The Saracens shall feel our blows the harder that we eat a piece of dried venison from time to time, with our herbs and barley-cakes."

"It skills not asking my leave," said Richard, "since Thomas de Vaux, who doth, like all around me, that which is fittest in his own eyes, hath already given thee permission for hunting and hawking."

"For hunting only, and please you," said the Scot; "but, if it please your Majesty to indulge me with the privilege of hawking also, and you list to trust me with a falcon on fist, I trust I could supply your royal mess with some choice water-fowl."

"I dread me, if thou hadst but the falcon," said the King, "thou would scarce wait for the permission. I wot well it is said abroad that we of the line of Anjou resent offence against our forest laws, as highly as we would do treason against our crown. To brave and worthy men, however, we could pardon either misdemeanour.—But enough of this.—I desire to know of you, Sir Knight, wherefore, and by whose authority, you took this recent journey to the wilderness of the Red Sea, and Engaddi?"

"By order," replied the knight, "of the Council of Princes of the Holy Crusade."

"And how dared any one to give such an order, when I —not the least, surely, in the league—was unacquainted with it?"

"It was not my part, please your Highness," said the Scot, "to enquire into such particulars. I am a soldier of the Cross —serving, doubtless, for the present, under your Highness's banner, and proud of the permission to do so, but still one who hath taken on him the holy symbol for the rights of Christianity, and the recovery of the Holy Sepulchre, and bound, therefore, to obey, without question, the orders of the princes and chiefs by whom the blessed enterprise is directed. That indisposition should seclude, I trust for but a short time, your Highness from their councils, in which you hold so potential a voice, I must lament with all Christendom ; but, as a soldier, I must obey those on whom the lawful right of command devolves, or set but an evil example in the Christian camp."

"Thou say'st well," said King Richard; "and the blame rests not with thee, but with those with whom, when it shall please Heaven to raise me from this accursed bed of pain and inactivity, I hope to reckon roundly. What was the purport of thy message?"

"Methinks, and please your Highness," replied Sir Kenneth, "that were best asked of those who sent me, and who can render the reasons of mine errand; whereas, I can only tell its outward form and purport."

"Palter not with me, Sir Scot—it were ill for thy safety," said the irritable monarch.

"My safety, my lord," replied the knight, firmly, "I cast behind me as a regardless thing when I vowed myself to this enterprise, looking rather to my immortal welfare than to that which concerns my earthly body."

"By the mass," said King Richard, "thou art a brave fellow! Hark thee, Sir Knight, I love the Scottish people ; they are hardy, though dogged and stubborn, and, I think, true men in the main, though the necessity of State has sometimes constrained them to be dissemblers. I deserve some love at their hand, for I have voluntarily done what they could not by arms have extorted from me, any more than from my predecessors— I have re-established the fortresses of Roxburgh and Berwick, which lay in pledge to England—I have restored your ancient boundaries—and, finally, I have renounced a claim to homage upon the crown of England, which I thought unjustly forced on you. I have endeavoured to make honourable and independent friends, where former kings of England attempted only to compel unwilling and rebellious vassals."

"All this you have done, my Lord King," said Sir Kenneth, bowing—"All this you have done by your royal treaty with our **sovereign at Canterbury**. Therefore have you me, and many

better Scottish men, making war against the infidels, under
your banners, who would else have been ravaging your frontiers
in England. If their numbers are now few, it is because their
lives have been freely waged and wasted."

"I grant it true," said the King; "and for the good offices
I have done your land, I require you to remember, that, as a
principal member of the Christian League, I have a right to
know the negotiations of my confederates. Do me, therefore,
the justice to tell me what I have a title to be acquainted with,
and which I am certain to know more truly from you than from
others."

"My lord," said the Scot, "thus conjured, I will speak the
truth; for I well believe that your purposes towards the
principal object of our expedition are single-hearted and
honest; and it is more than I dare warrant for others of
the Holy League. Be pleased, therefore, to know, my charge
was to propose, through the medium of the hermit of Engaddi
—a holy man, respected and protected by Saladin himself——"

"A continuation of the truce, I doubt not," said Richard,
hastily interrupting him.

"No, by Saint Andrew, my liege," said the Scottish knight;
"but the establishment of a lasting peace, and the withdrawing
our armies from Palestine."

"Saint George!" said Richard, in astonishment—"Ill as I
have justly thought of them, I could not have dreamed they
would have humbled themselves to such dishonour. Speak,
Sir Kenneth, with what will did you carry such a message?"

"With right good-will, my lord," said Kenneth; because,
when we had lost our noble leader, under whose guidance
alone I hoped for victory, I saw none who could succeed him
likely to lead us to conquest, and I accounted it well in such
circumstances to avoid defeat."

"And on what conditions was this hopeful peace to be contracted?" said King Richard, painfully suppressing the passion
with which his heart was almost bursting.

"These were not intrusted to me, my lord," answered the
Knight of the Couchant Leopard. "I delivered them sealed
to the hermit."

"And for what hold you this reverend hermit?—for fool,
madman, traitor, or saint?" said Richard.

"His folly, sire," replied the shrewd Scottish man, "I hold
to be assumed to win favour and reverence from the Paynimrie,
who regard madmen as the inspired of Heaven; at least it

seemed to me as exhibited only occasionally, and not as mixing, like natural folly, with the general tenor of his mind."

"Shrewdly replied," said the monarch, throwing himself back on his couch, from which he had half-raised himself.— "Now of his penitence?"

"His penitence," continued Kenneth, "appears to me sincere, and the fruits of remorse for some dreadful crime, for which he seems, in his own opinion, condemned to reprobation."

"And for his policy?" said King Richard.

"Methinks, my lord," said the Scottish knight, "he despairs of the security of Palestine, as of his own salvation, by any means short of a miracle—at least, since the arm of Richard of England hath ceased to strike for it."

"And therefore the coward policy of this hermit is like that of these miserable princes who, forgetful of their knighthood and their faith, are only resolved and determined when the question is retreat, and, rather than go forward against an armed Saracen, would trample in their flight over a dying ally!"

"Might I so far presume, my Lord King," said the Scottish knight, "this discourse but heats your disease, the enemy from which Christendom dreads more evil than from armed hosts of infidels."

The countenance of King Richard was, indeed, more flushed, and his action became more feverishly vehement, as, with clenched hand, expanded arm, and flashing eyes, he seemed at once to suffer under bodily pain, and at the same time under vexation of mind, while his high spirit led him to speak on, as if in contempt of both.

"You can flatter, Sir Knight," he said, "but you escape me not. I must know more from you than you have yet told me. Saw you my royal consort when at Engaddi?"

"To my knowledge—no, my lord," replied Sir Kenneth, with considerable perturbation; for he remembered the midnight procession in the chapel of the rocks.

"I ask you," said the King, in a sterner voice, "whether you were not in the chapel of the Carmelite Nuns at Engaddi, and there saw Berengaria, Queen of England, and the ladies of her Court, who went thither on pilgrimage?"

"My lord," said Sir Kenneth, "I will speak the truth as in the confessional. In a subterranean chapel, to which the anchorite conducted me, I beheld a choir of ladies do homage to a relic of the highest sanctity; but as I saw not their faces, nor heard their voices, unless in the hymns which they chanted, I cannot tell whether the Queen of England was of the bevy."

"And was there no one of these ladies known to you?"

Sir Kenneth stood silent.

"I ask you," said Richard, raising himself on his elbow, "as a knight and a gentleman—and I shall know by your answer how you value either character—did you, or did you not, know any lady amongst that band of worshippers?"

"My lord," said Kenneth, not without much hesitation, "I might guess."

"And I also may guess," said the King, frowning sternly; "but it is enough. Leopard as you are, Sir Knight, beware tempting the lion's paw. Hark ye—to become enamoured of the moon would be but an act of folly; but to leap from the battlements of a lofty tower, in the wild hope of coming within her sphere, were self-destructive madness."

At this moment some bustling was heard in the outer apartment, and the King, hastily changing to his more natural manner, said, "Enough—begone—speed to De Vaux, and send him hither with the Arabian physician. My life for the faith of the Soldan! Would he but abjure his false law, I would aid him with my sword to drive this scum of French and Austrians from his dominions, and think Palestine as well ruled by him as when her kings were anointed by the decree of Heaven itself."

The Knight of the Leopard retired, and presently afterwards the chamberlain announced a deputation from the Council, who had come to wait on the Majesty of England.

"It is well they allow that I am living yet," was his reply. "Who are the reverend ambassadors?"

"The Grand Master of the Templars, and the Marquis of Montserrat."

"Our brother of France loves not sick-beds," said Richard: "yet, had Philip been ill, I had stood by his couch long since. —Jocelyn, lay me the couch more fairly, it is tumbled like a stormy sea—reach me yonder steel mirror—pass a comb through my hair and beard. They look, indeed, liker a lion's mane than a Christian man's locks—bring water."

"My lord," said the trembling chamberlain, "the leeches say that cold water may be fatal."

"To the foul fiend with the leeches!" replied the monarch; "if they cannot cure me, think you I will allow them to torment me?—There, then," he said, after having made his ablutions, "admit the worshipful envoys; they will now, I think, scarcely see that disease has made Richard negligent of his person."

The celebrated Master of the Templars was a tall, thin, war-worn man, with a slow yet penetrating eye, and a brow on which a thousand dark intrigues had stamped a portion of their obscurity. At the head of that singular body, to whom their order was every thing and their individuality nothing— seeking the advancement of its power, even at the hazard of that very religion which the fraternity were originally associated to protect—accused of heresy and witchcraft, although by their character Christian priests—suspected of secret league with the Soldan, though by oath devoted to the protection of the Holy Temple, or its recovery—the whole order, and the whole personal character of its commander, or Grand Master, was a riddle, at the exposition of which most men shuddered. The Grand Master was dressed in his white robes of solemnity, and he bare the *abacus*, a mystic staff of office, the peculiar form of which has given rise to such singular conjectures and com-mentaries, leading to suspicions that this celebrated fraternity of Christian knights were embodied under the foulest symbols of Paganism.

Conrade of Montserrat had a much more pleasing exterior than the dark and mysterious priest-soldier by whom he was accompanied. He was a handsome man, of middle age, or something past that term, bold in the field, sagacious in council, gay and gallant in times of festivity; but, on the other hand he was generally accused of versatility, of a narrow and selfish ambition, of a desire to extend his own principality without regard to the weal of the Latin kingdom of Palestine, and of seeking his own interest, by private negotiations with Saladin, to the prejudice of the Christian leaguers.

When the usual salutations had been made by these dignitaries, and courteously returned by King Richard, the Marquis of Montserrat commenced an explanation of the motives of their visit, sent, as he said they were, by the anxious kings and princes who composed the Council of the Crusaders, to "enquire into the health of their magnanimous ally, the valiant King of England."

"We know the importance in which the princes of the Council hold our health," replied the English King; "and are well aware how much they must have suffered by suppressing all curiosity concerning it for fourteen days, for fear, doubtless, of aggravating our disorder by showing their anxiety regarding the event."

The flow of the Marquis's eloquence being checked, and he himself thrown into some confusion by this reply, his more austere companion took up the thread of the conversation, and, with as much dry and brief gravity as was consistent with the presence which he addressed, informed the King that they came from the Council, to pray, in the name of Christendom, "that he would not suffer his health to be tampered with by an infidel physician, said to be dispatched by Saladin, until the Council had taken measures to remove or confirm the suspicion, which they at present conceived did attach itself to the mission of such a person."

"Grand Master of the holy and valiant Order of Knights Templars, and you, Most Noble Marquis of Montserrat," replied Richard, "if it please you to retire into the adjoining pavilion, you shall presently see what account we make of the tender remonstrances of our royal and princely colleagues in this religious warfare."

The Marquis and Grand Master retired accordingly; nor had they been many minutes in the outward pavilion when the Eastern physician arrived, accompanied by the Baron of Gilsland, and Kenneth of Scotland. The baron, however, was a little later of entering the tent than the other two, stopping, perchance, to issue some orders to the warders without.

As the Arabian physician entered, he made his obeisance, after the Oriental fashion, to the Marquis and Grand Master, whose dignity was apparent, both from their appearance and their bearing. The Grand Master returned the salutation with an expression of disdainful coldness; the Marquis, with the popular courtesy which he habitually practised to men of every rank and nation. There was a pause; for the Scottish knight, waiting for the arrival of De Vaux, presumed not, of his own authority, to enter the tent of the King of England, and during this interval the Grand Master sternly demanded of the Moslem, "Infidel, hast thou the courage to practise thine art upon the person of an anointed sovereign of the Christian host?"

"The sun of Allah," answered the sage, "shines on the Nazarene as well as on the true believer, and his servant dare make no distinction betwixt them, when called on to exercise the art of healing."

"Misbelieving Hakim," said the Grand Master, "or whatsoever they call thee for an unbaptized slave of darkness, dost thou well know that thou shalt be torn asunder by wild horses should King Richard die under thy charge?"

"That were hard justice," answered the physician; "seeing that I can but use human means, and that the issue is written in the book of light."

"Nay, reverend and valiant Grand Master," said the Marquis of Montserrat, "consider that this learned man is not acquainted with our Christian order, adopted in the fear of God, and for the safety of his anointed.—Be it known unto thee, grave physician, whose skill we doubt not, that your wisest course is to repair to the presence of the illustrious Council of our Holy League, and there to give account and reckoning to such wise and learned leeches as they shall nominate, concerning your means of process and cure of this illustrious patient, so shall you escape all the danger which, rashly taking such a high matter upon your sole answer, you may else most likely incur."

"My lords," said El Hakim, "I understand you well. But knowledge hath its champions as well as your military art,— nay, hath sometimes had its martyrs as well as religion. I have the command of my sovereign, the Soldan Saladin, to heal this Nazarene King, and with the blessing of the Prophet, I will obey his commands. If I fail, ye wear swords thirsting for the blood of the faithful, and I proffer my body to your weapons. But I will not reason with one uncircumcised upon the virtue of the medicines of which I have obtained knowledge, through the grace of the Prophet, and I pray you interpose no delay between me and my office."

"Who talks of delay?" said the Baron de Vaux, hastily entering the tent; "we have had but too much already.—I salute you, my Lord of Montserrat, and you, valiant Grand Master. But I must presently pass with this learned physician to the bedside of my master."

"My lord," said the Marquis, in Norman-French, or the language of Ouie, as it was then called, "are you well advised that we came to expostulate, on the part of the Council of the monarchs and princes of the Crusade, against the risk of permitting an infidel and Eastern physician to tamper with a health so valuable as that of your master King Richard?"

"Noble Lord Marquis," replied the Englishman, bluntly, "I can neither use many words, nor do I delight in listening to them; moreover, I am much more ready to believe what my eyes have seen than what my ears have heard. I am satisfied that this heathen can cure the sickness of King Richard, and I believe and trust he will labour to do so. Time is precious. If Mahommed—may God's curse be on him!—stood at the door of the tent, with such fair purpose as this Adonbec el Hakim entertains, I would hold it sin to delay him for a minute—So, give ye God'en, my lords."

"Nay, but," said Conrade of Montserrat, "the King himself said we should be present when this same physician dealt upon him."

The baron whispered the chamberlain, probably to know whether the Marquis spoke truly, and then replied, "My lords, if you will hold your patience, you are welcome to enter with us; but if you interrupt, by action or threat, this accomplished physician in his duty, be it known, that, without respect to your high quality, I will enforce your absence from Richard's tent; for know, I am so well satisfied of the virtue of this man's medicines, that were Richard himself to refuse them, by Our Lady of Lanercost, I think I could find in my heart to force him to take the means of his cure whether he would or no.—Move onward, El Hakim."

The last word was spoken in the lingua franca, and instantly obeyed by the physician. The Grand Master looked grimly on the unceremonious old soldier, but, on exchanging a glance with the Marquis, smoothed his frowning brow as well as he could, and both followed De Vaux and the Arabian into the inner tent, where Richard lay expecting them, with that impatience with which the sick man watches the step of his physician. Sir Kenneth, whose attendance seemed neither asked nor prohibited, felt himself, by the circumstances in which he stood, entitled to follow these high dignitaries, but, conscious of his inferior power and rank, remained aloof during the scene which took place.

Richard, when they entered his apartment, immediately exclaimed, "So ho! a goodly fellowship come to see Richard take his leap in the dark.—My noble allies, I greet you as the representatives of our assembled League; Richard will again be amongst you in his former fashion, or ye shall bear to the grave what is left of him.—De Vaux, lives he or dies he, thou hast the thanks of thy prince.—There is yet another—but this fever hath wasted my eyesight—What, the bold Scot, who would climb Heaven without a ladder?—he is welcome too. Come, Sir Hakim, to the work, to the work."

The physician, who had already informed himself of the

various symptoms of the King's illness, now felt his pulse for a long time, and with deep attention, while all around stood silent and in breathless expectation. The sage next filled a cup with spring water, and dipt into it the small red purse, which, as formerly, he took from his bosom. When he seemed to think it sufficiently medicated, he was about to offer it to the sovereign, who prevented him, by saying, " Hold an instant. —Thou hast felt my pulse, let me lay my finger on thine.—I too, as becomes a good knight, know something of thine art."

The Arabian yielded his hand without hesitation, and his long slender dark fingers were, for an instant, enclosed, and almost buried, in the large enfoldment of King Richard's hand.

" His blood beats calm as an infant's," said the King ; "so throb not theirs who poison princes. De Vaux, whether we live or die, dismiss this Hakim with honour and safety— Commend us, friend, to the noble Saladin. Should I die, it is without doubt of his faith—should I live, it will be to thank him as a warrior would desire to be thanked."

He then raised himself in bed, took the cup in his hand, and turning to the Marquis and the Grand Master, " Mark what I say, and let my royal brethren pledge me in Cyprus wine—'To the immortal honour of the first Crusader who shall strike lance or sword on the gate of Jerusalem ; and to the shame and eternal infamy of whomsoever shall turn back from the plough on which he hath laid his hand !'"

He drained the cup to the bottom, resigned it to the Arabian, and sunk back, as if exhausted, upon the cushions which were arranged to receive him. The physician, then, with silent but expressive signs, directed that all should leave the tent, excepting himself and De Vaux, whom no remonstrance could induce to withdraw. The apartment was cleared accordingly.

CHAPTER X

And now I will unclasp a secret book,
And, to your quick-conceiving discontent,
I'll read you matter deep and dangerous.
                              Henry IV Part I.

THE Marquis of Montserrat and the Grand Master of the Knights Templars stood together in the front of the royal pavilion, within which this singular scene had passed, and beheld a strong guard of bills and bows drawn out to form a circle around it, and keep at distance all which might disturb the sleeping monarch. The soldiers wore the downcast, silent, and sullen looks, with which they trail their arms at a funeral, and stepped with such caution that you could not hear a buckler ring, or a sword clatter, though so many men in armour were moving around the tent. They lowered their weapons in deep reverence, as the dignitaries passed through their files, but with the same profound silence.

"There is a change of cheer among these island dogs," said the Grand Master to Conrade, when they had passed Richard's guards. "What hoarse tumult and revel used to be before this pavilion! nought but pitching the bar, hurling the ball, wrestling, roaring of songs, clattering of wine-pots, and quaffing of flagons, among these burly yeomen, as if they were holding some country wake, with a Maypole in the midst of them, instead of a royal standard."

"Mastiffs are a faithful race," said Conrade; "and the King their master has won their love by being ready to wrestle, brawl, or revel amongst the foremost of them, whenever the humour seized him."

"He is totally compounded of humours," said the Grand Master. "Marked you the pledge he gave us, instead of a prayer, over his grace-cup yonder?"

"He would have felt it a grace-cup, and a well-spiced one too," said the Marquis, "were Saladin like any other Turk that ever wore turban, or turned him to Mecca at call of the Muezzin. But he affects faith, and honour, and generosity,— as if it were for an unbaptized dog like him to practise the virtuous bearing of a Christian knight! It is said he hath applied to Richard to be admitted within the pale of chivalry."

"By Saint Bernard!" exclaimed the Grand Master, "it were time then to throw off our belts and spurs, Sir Conrade, deface our armorial bearings, and renounce our burgonets, if the highest honour of Christianity were conferred on an unchristened Turk of tenpence."

"You rate the Soldan cheap," replied the Marquis; "yet though he be a likely man, I have seen a better heathen sold for forty pence at the bagnio."

They were now near their horses, which stood at some distance from the royal tent, prancing among the gallant train of esquires and pages by whom they were attended, when Conrade, after a moment's pause, proposed that they should enjoy the coolness of the evening breeze which had arisen, and,

dismissing their steeds and attendants, walk homewards to
their own quarters, through the lines of the extended Christian
camp. The Grand Master assented, and they proceeded to
walk together accordingly, avoiding, as if by mutual consent,
the more inhabited parts of the canvas city, and tracing the
broad esplanade which lay between the tents and the external
defences, where they could converse in private, and unmarked,
save by the sentinels as they passed them.

They spoke for a time upon the military points and preparations for defence; but this sort of discourse, in which neither
seemed to take interest, at length died away, and there was a
long pause, which terminated by the Marquis of Montserrat
stopping short, like a man who has formed a sudden resolution, and, gazing for some moments on the dark, inflexible
countenance of the Grand Master, he at length addressed him
thus— "Might it consist with your valour and sanctity,
reverend Sir Giles Amaury, I would pray you for once to lay
aside the dark vizor which you wear, and to converse with a
friend barefaced."

The Templar half-smiled.

"There are light-coloured masks," he said, "as well as dark
vizors, and the one conceals the natural features as completely
as the other."

"Be it so," said the Marquis, putting his hand to his chin,
and withdrawing it with the action of one who unmasks
himself; "there lies my disguise. And now, what think you,
as touching the interests of your own Order, of the prospects
of this Crusade?"

"This is tearing the veil from *my* thoughts rather than
exposing your own," said the Grand Master; "yet I will reply
with a parable told to me by a santon of the desert.—'A
certain farmer prayed to Heaven for rain, and murmured when
it fell not at his need. To punish his impatience, Allah,' said
the santon, 'sent the Euphrates upon his farm, and he was
destroyed with all his possessions, even by the granting of his
own wishes.'"

"Most truly spoken," said the Marquis Conrade; "would
that the ocean had swallowed up nineteen parts of the
armaments of these Western princes! what remained would
better have served the purpose of the Christian nobles of
Palestine, the wretched remnant of the Latin kingdom of
Jerusalem. Left to ourselves, we might have bent to the
storm, or, moderately supported with money and troops, we

might have compelled Saladin to respect our valour, and grant us peace and protection on easy terms. But, from the extremity of danger with which this powerful Crusade threatens the Soldan, we cannot suppose, should it pass over, that the Saracen will suffer any one of us to hold possessions or principalities in Syria, far less permit the existence of the Christian military fraternities, from whom they have experienced so much mischief."

"Ay, but," said the Templar, "these adventurous Crusaders may succeed, and again plant the Cross on the bulwarks of Zion."

"And what will that advantage either the Order of the Templars, or Conrade of Montserrat?" said the Marquis.

"You it may advantage," replied the Grand Master. "Conrade of Montserrat might become Conrade King of Jerusalem."

"That sounds like something," said the Marquis, "and yet it rings but hollow.—Godfrey of Bouillon might well choose the crown of thorns for his emblem. Grand Master, I will confess to you I have caught some attachment to the Eastern form of government: a pure and simple monarchy should consist but of King and subjects. Such is the simple and primitive structure — a shepherd and his flock. All this internal chain of feudal dependence is artificial and sophisticated, and I would rather hold the baton of my poor marquisate with a firm gripe, and wield it after my pleasure, than the sceptre of a monarch, to be in effect restrained and curbed by the will of as many proud feudal barons as hold land under the Assize of Jerusalem.[1] A King should tread freely, Grand Master, and should not be controlled by here a ditch, and there a fence—here a feudal privilege, and there a mail-clad baron, with his sword in his hand to maintain it. To sum the whole, I am aware that Guy de Lusignan's claims to the throne would be preferred to mine, if Richard recovers, and has aught to say in the choice."

"Enough," said the Grand Master; "thou hast indeed convinced me of thy sincerity. Others may hold the same opinions,

[1] The Assises de Jerusalem were the digest of feudal law, composed by Godfrey of Boulogne, for the government of the Latin kingdom of Palestine, when reconquered from the Saracens. "It was composed with advice of the patriarch and barons, the clergy and laity, and is," says the historian Gibbon, "a precious monument of feudatory jurisprudence, founded upon those principles of freedom which were essential to the system."

but few, save Conrade of Montserrat, dared frankly avow that he desires not the restitution of the kingdom of Jerusalem, but rather prefers being master of a portion of its fragments, like the barbarous islanders, who labour not for the deliverance of a goodly vessel from the billows, expecting rather to enrich themselves at the expense of the wreck."

"Thou wilt not betray my counsel?" said Conrade, looking sharply and suspiciously. "Know for certain that my tongue shall never wrong my head, nor my hand forsake the defence of either. Impeach me if thou wilt—I am prepared to defend myself in the lists against the best Templar who ever laid lance in rest."

"Yet thou start'st somewhat suddenly for so bold a steed," said the Grand Master. "However, I swear to thee by the Holy Temple, which our Order is sworn to defend, that I will keep counsel with thee as a true comrade."

"By which Temple?" said the Marquis of Montserrat, whose love of sarcasm often outran his policy and discretion. "Swearest thou by that on the hill of Zion, which was built by King Solomon, or by that symbolical, emblematical edifice which is said to be spoken of in the councils held in the vaults of your Preceptories, as something which infers the aggrandizement of thy valiant and venerable Order?"

The Templar scowled upon him with an eye of death, but answered calmly, "By whatever Temple I swear, be assured, Lord Marquis, my oath is sacred. I would I knew how to bind *thee* by one of equal obligation."

"I will swear truth to thee," said the Marquis, laughing, "by the Earl's coronet, which I hope to convert, ere these wars are over, into something better. It feels cold on my brow, that same slight coronal; a duke's cap of maintenance were a better protection against such a night-breeze as now blows, and a king's crown more preferable still, being lined with comfortable ermine and velvet. In a word, our interests bind us together; for think not, Lord Grand Master, that, were these allied princes to regain Jerusalem, and place a king of their own choosing there, they would suffer your Order, any more than my poor marquisate, to retain the independence which we now hold. No, by Our Lady! In such case the proud Knights of Saint John must again spread plasters, and dress plague-sores, in the hospitals; and you, most puissant and venerable Knights of the Temple, must return to your condition of simple men-at-arms, sleep three on a pallet, and mount two upon one horse, as your present seal still expresses to have been your ancient most simple custom."

"The rank, privileges, and opulence of our Order prevent so much degradation as you threaten," said the Templar, haughtily.

"These are your bane," said Conrade of Montserrat; "and you, as well as I, reverend Grand Master, know, that were the allied princes to be successful in Palestine, it would be their first point of policy to abate the independence of your Order, which, but for the protection of our holy father the Pope, and the necessity of employing your valour in the conquest of Palestine, you would long since have experienced. Give them complete success, and you will be flung aside, as the splinters of a broken lance are tossed out of the tilt-yard."

"There may be truth in what you say," said the Templar, darkly smiling; "but what were our hopes should the allies withdraw their forces, and leave Palestine in the grasp of Saladin?"

"Great and assured," replied Conrade; "the Soldan would give large provinces to maintain at his behest a body of well-appointed Frankish lances. In Egypt, in Persia, an hundred such auxiliaries, joined to his own light cavalry, would turn the battle against the most fearful odds. This dependence would be but for a time—perhaps during the life of this enterprising Soldan—but, in the East, empires arise like mushrooms. Suppose him dead, and us strengthened with a constant succession of fiery and adventurous spirits from Europe, what might we not hope to achieve, uncontrolled by these monarchs, whose dignity throws us at present into the shade—and, were they to remain here, and succeed in this expedition, would willingly consign us for ever to degradation and dependence?"

"You say well, my Lord Marquis," said the Grand Master; "and your words find an echo in my bosom. Yet must we be cautious; Philip of France is wise as well as valiant."

"True, and will be therefore the more easily diverted from an expedition, to which, in a moment of enthusiasm, or urged by his nobles, he rashly bound himself. He is jealous of King Richard, his natural enemy, and longs to return to prosecute plans of ambition nearer to Paris than Palestine. Any fair pretence will serve him for withdrawing from a scene, in which he is aware he is wasting the force of his kingdom."

"And the Duke of Austria?" said the Templar.

"Oh, touching the Duke," returned Conrade, "his self-conceit and folly lead him to the same conclusions as do Philip's policy and wisdom. He conceives himself, God help the while! ungratefully treated, because men's mouths—even those of his own *minne-singers*—are filled with the praises of King Richard, whom he fears and hates, and in whose harm he would rejoice, like those unbred dastardly curs, who, if the foremost of the pack is hurt by the gripe of the wolf, are much more likely to assail the sufferer from behind, than to come to his assistance.—But wherefore tell I this to thee, save to show that I am in sincerity in desiring that this League be broken up, and the country freed of these great monarchs with their hosts? And thou well knowest, and hast thyself seen, how all the princes of influence and power, one alone excepted, are eager to enter into treaty with the Soldan."

"I acknowledge it," said the Templar; "he were blind that had not seen this in their last deliberations. But lift yet thy mask an inch higher, and tell me thy real reason for pressing upon the Council that northern Englishman, or Scot, or whatever you call yonder Knight of the Leopard, to carry their proposals for a treaty?"

"There was a policy in it," replied the Italian; "his character of native of Britain was sufficient to meet what Saladin required, who knew him to belong to the band of Richard, while his character of Scot, and certain other personal grudges which I wot of, rendered it most unlikely that our envoy should, on his return, hold any communication with the sick-bed of Richard, to whom his presence was ever unacceptable."

"Oh, too fine-spun policy," said the Grand Master; "trust me, that Italian spiders' webs will never bind this unshorn Samson of the Isle—well if you can do it with new cords, and those of the toughest. See you not that the envoy whom you have selected so carefully hath brought us, in this physician, the means of restoring the lion-hearted, bull-necked Englishman, to prosecute his crusading enterprise; and so soon as he is able once more to rush on, which of the princes dare hold back?—They must follow him for very shame, although they would march under the banner of Satan as soon."

"Be content," said Conrade of Montserrat; "ere this physician, if he work by any thing short of miraculous agency, can accomplish Richard's cure, it may be possible to put some open rupture betwixt the Frenchman, at least the Austrian, and his allies of England, so that the breach shall be irreconcilable; and Richard may arise from his bed, perhaps to command his own native troops, but never again, by his sole energy, to wield the force of the whole Crusade."

"Thou art a willing archer," said the Templar; "but, Conrade of Montserrat, thy bow is over slack to carry an arrow to the mark."

He then stopt short, cast a suspicious glance to see that no one overheard him, and taking Conrade by the hand, pressed it eagerly as he looked the Italian in the face, and repeated slowly, "Richard arise from his bed, say'st thou?—Conrade, he must never rise!"

The Marquis of Montserrat started—"What!—spoke you of Richard of England, of Cœur de Lion, the champion of Christendom?"

His cheek turned pale, and his knees trembled as he spoke. The Templar looked at him, with his iron visage contorted into a smile of contempt.

"Know'st thou what thou look'st like, Sir Conrade, at this moment? Not like the politic and valiant Marquis of Montserrat—not like him who would direct the Council of Princes, and determine the fate of empires—but like a novice, who, stumbling upon a conjuration in his master's book of gramarye, has raised the devil when he least thought of it, and now stands terrified at the spirit which appears before him."

"I grant you," said Conrade, recovering himself, "that, unless some other sure road could be discovered, thou hast hinted at that which leads most direct to our purpose. But, blessed Mary! we shall become the curse of all Europe, the malediction of every one, from the Pope on his throne to the very beggar at the church gate, who, ragged and leprous, in the last extremity of human wretchedness, shall bless himself that he is neither Giles Amaury nor Conrade of Montserrat."

"If thou takest it thus," said the Grand Master, with the same composure which characterized him all through this remarkable dialogue, "let us hold there has nothing passed between us—that we have spoken in our sleep—have awakened, and the vision is gone."

"It never can depart," answered Conrade.

"Visions of ducal crowns and kingly diadems are, indeed, somewhat tenacious of their place in the imagination," replied the Grand Master.

"Well," answered Conrade, "let me but first try to break peace between Austria and England."

They parted. Conrade remained standing still upon the spot, and watching the flowing white cloak of the Templar, as he stalked slowly away, and gradually disappeared amid the fast-sinking darkness of the Oriental night. Proud, ambitious, unscrupulous, and politic, the Marquis of Montserrat was yet not cruel by nature. He was a voluptuary and an epicurean, and, like many who profess this character, was averse, even upon selfish motives, from inflicting pain, or witnessing acts of cruelty; and he retained also a general sense of respect for his own reputation, which sometimes supplies the want of the better principle by which reputation is to be maintained.

"I have," he said, as his eyes still watched the point at which he had seen the last slight wave of the Templar's mantle, "I have, in truth, raised the devil with a vengeance! Who would have thought this stern ascetic Grand Master, whose whole fortune and misfortune are merged in that of his Order, would be willing to do more for its advancement, than I who labour for my own interest? To check this wild Crusade was my motive, indeed, but I durst not think on the ready mode which this determined priest has dared to suggest —yet it is the surest—perhaps even the safest."

Such were the Marquis's meditations, when his muttered soliloquy was broken by a voice from a little distance, which proclaimed with the emphatic tone of a herald, "Remember the Holy Sepulchre!"

The exhortation was echoed from post to post, for it was the duty of the sentinels to raise this cry from time to time upon their periodical watch, that the host of the Crusaders might always have in their remembrance the purpose of their being in arms. But though Conrade was familiar with the custom, and had heard the warning voice on all former occasions as a matter of habit, yet it came at the present moment so strongly in contact with his own train of thought, that it seemed a voice from Heaven warning him against the iniquity which his heart meditated. He looked around anxiously, as if, like the patriarch of old, though from very different circumstances, he was expecting some ram caught in a thicket—some substitution for the sacrifice, which his comrade proposed to offer, not to the Supreme Being, but to the Moloch of their own ambition. As he looked, the broad folds of the ensign of England, heavily distending itself to the failing night-breeze, caught his eye. It was displayed upon an artificial mound, nearly in the midst of the camp, which perhaps of old some Hebrew chief or champion had chosen as a memorial of his place of rest. If so, the name was now forgotten, and the Crusaders had christened it Saint George's Mount, because from that commanding height the banner of England was super-eminently displayed, as if an emblem of sovereignty over the many distinguished, noble, and even royal ensigns, which floated in lower situations.

A quick intellect like that of Conrade catches ideas from the glance of a moment. A single look on the standard seemed to dispel the uncertainty of mind which had affected him. He walked to his pavilion with the hasty and determined step of one who has adopted a plan which he is resolved to achieve, dismissed the almost princely train who waited to attend him, and, as he committed himself to his couch, muttered his amended resolution, that the milder means are to be tried before the more desperate are resorted to.

"To-morrow," he said, "I sit at the board of the Archduke of Austria—we will see what can be done to advance our purpose, before prosecuting the dark suggestions of this Templar."

CHAPTER XI

One thing is certain in our Northern land,
Allow that birth, or valour, wealth, or wit,
Give each precedence to their possessor,
Envy, that follows on such eminence,
As comes the lyme-hound on the roebuck's trace,
Shall pull them down each one.
                                                SIR DAVID LINDSAY.

LEOPOLD, Grand Duke of Austria, was the first possessor of that noble country to whom the princely rank belonged. He had been raised to the ducal sway in the German empire, on account of his near relationship to the emperor, Henry the Stern, and held under his government the finest provinces which are watered by the Danube. His character has been stained in history, on account of one action of violence and perfidy, which arose out of these very transactions in the Holy Land; and yet the shame of having made Richard a prisoner, when he returned through his dominions, unattended and in disguise, was not one which flowed from Leopold's natural disposition. He was rather a weak and a vain, than an ambitious or tyrannical prince. His mental powers resembled the qualities of his person. He was tall, strong, and handsome, with a complexion in which red and white was strongly contrasted, and had long flowing locks of fair hair. But there was an awkwardness in his gait, which seemed as if his size was not animated by energy sufficient to put in motion such a mass; and in the same manner, wearing the richest dresses, it always seemed as if they became him not. As a prince, he appeared too little familiar with his own dignity; and, being often at a loss how to assert his authority when the occasion demanded it, he frequently thought himself obliged to recover, by acts and expressions of ill-timed violence, the ground which might have been easily and gracefully maintained by a little more presence of mind in the beginning of the controversy.

Not only were these deficiencies visible to others, but the Archduke himself could not but sometimes entertain a painful consciousness that he was not altogether fit to maintain and assert the high rank which he had acquired; and to this was joined the strong, and sometimes the just suspicion, that others esteemed him lightly accordingly.

When he first joined the Crusade, with a most princely attendance, Leopold had desired much to enjoy the friendship and intimacy of Richard, and had made such advances towards cultivating his regard, as the King of England ought in policy to have received and answered. But the Archduke, though not deficient in bravery, was so infinitely inferior to Cœur de Lion in that ardour of mind which wooed danger as a bride, that the King very soon held him in a certain degree of contempt. Richard, also, as a Norman prince, a people with whom temperance was habitual, despised the inclination of the German for the pleasures of the table, and particularly his liberal indulgence in the use of wine. For these, and other personal reasons, the King of England very soon looked upon the Austrian prince with feelings of contempt, which he was at no pains to conceal or modify, and which, therefore, were speedily remarked, and returned with deep hatred, by the suspicious Leopold. The discord between them was fanned by the secret and politic arts of Philip of France, one of the most sagacious monarchs of the time, who, dreading the fiery and overbearing character of Richard, considering him as his natural rival, and feeling offended, moreover, at the dictatorial manner in which he, a vassal of France for his continental domains, conducted himself towards his liege lord, endeavoured to strengthen his own party, and weaken that of Richard by uniting the crusading princes of inferior degree, in resistance to what he termed the usurping authority of the King of England. Such was the state of politics and opinions entertained by the Archduke of Austria, when Conrade of Montserrat resolved upon employing his jealousy of England as a means of dissolving, or loosening at least, the league of the Crusaders.

The time which he chose for his visit was noon, and the pretence, to present the Archduke with some choice Cyprus wine which had lately fallen into his hands, and discuss its comparative merits with those of Hungary and of the Rhine. An intimation of his purpose was of course answered by a courteous invitation to partake of the archducal meal, and every effort was used to render it fitting the splendour of a sovereign prince. Yet the refined taste of the Italian saw more cumbrous profusion, than elegance or splendour, in the display of provisions under which the board groaned.

The Germans, though still possessing the martial and frank character of their ancestors, who subdued the Roman empire, had retained withal no slight tinge of their barbarism. The practices and principles of chivalry were not carried to such a nice pitch amongst them, as amongst the French and English knights, nor were they strict observers of the prescribed rules of society, which among those nations were supposed to express the height of civilisation. Sitting at the table of the Archduke, Conrade was at once stunned and amused with the clang of Teutonic sounds assaulting his ears on all sides, notwithstanding the solemnity of a princely banquet. Their dress seemed equally fantastic to him, many of the Austrian nobles retaining their long beards, and almost all of them wearing short jerkins of various colours, cut, and flourished, and fringed, in a manner not common in Western Europe.

Numbers of dependents, old and young, attended in the pavilion, mingled at times in the conversation, received from their masters the relics of the entertainment, and devoured them as they stood behind the backs of the company. Jesters, dwarfs, and minstrels were there in unusual numbers, and more noisy and intrusive than they were permitted to be in better regulated society. As they were allowed to share freely in the wine, which flowed round in large quantities, their licensed tumult was the more excessive.

All this while, and in the midst of a clamour and confusion, which would better have become a German tavern during a fair, than the tent of a sovereign prince, the Archduke was waited upon with a minuteness of form and observance, which showed how anxious he was to maintain rigidly the state and character to which his elevation had entitled him. He was served on the knee, and only by pages of noble blood, fed upon plate of silver, and drank his Tokay and Rhenish wines from a cup of gold. His ducal mantle was splendidly adorned with ermine, his coronet might have equalled in value a royal crown, and his feet, cased in velvet shoes, (the length of which, peaks included, might be two feet,) rested upon a footstool of solid silver. But it served partly to intimate the character of the man, that, although desirous to show attention to the Marquis of Montserrat, whom he had courteously placed at his right hand, he gave much more of his attention to his *spruch-sprecher*, that is, his man of conversation, or *sayer of sayings*, who stood behind the Duke's right shoulder.

This personage was well attired, in a cloak and doublet of black velvet, the last of which was decorated with various silver and gold coins, stitched upon it, in memory of the munificent princes who had conferred them, and bearing a short staff to which also bunches of silver coins were attached by rings, which he jingled by way of attracting attention, when he was about to say any thing which he judged worthy of it. This person's capacity in the household of the Archduke was somewhat betwixt that of a minstrel and a counsellor: he was by turns a flatterer, a poet, and an orator; and those who desired to be well with the Duke generally studied to gain the good-will of the *spruch-sprecher*.

Lest too much of this officer's wisdom should become tiresome, the Duke's other shoulder was occupied by his *hoff-narr*, or court jester, called Jonas Schwanker, who made almost as much noise with his fool's cap, bells, and bauble, as did the orator, or man of talk, with his jingling baton.

These two personages threw out grave and comic nonsense alternately, while their master, laughing or applauding them himself, yet carefully watched the countenance of his noble guest, to discern what impressions so accomplished a cavalier received from this display of Austrian eloquence and wit. It is hard to say whether the man of wisdom or the man of folly contributed most to the amusement of the party, or stood

highest in the estimation of their princely master; but the
sallies of both seemed excellently well received. Sometimes
they became rivals for the conversation, and clanged their
flappers in emulation of each other, with a most alarming
contention; but, in general, they seemed on such good terms,
and so accustomed to support each other's play, that the
spruch-sprecher often condescended to follow up the jester's
witticisms with an explanation, to render them more obvious
to the capacity of the audience; so that his wisdom became
a sort of commentary on the buffoon's folly. And sometimes,
in requital, the *hoff-narr*, with a pithy jest, wound up the
conclusion of the orator's tedious harangue.

Whatever his real sentiments might be, Conrade took
especial care that his countenance should express nothing but
satisfaction with what he heard, and smiled or applauded as
zealously, to all appearance, as the Archduke himself, at the
solemn folly of the *spruch-sprecher*, and the gibbering wit of the
fool. In fact, he watched carefully until the one or other
should introduce some topic, favourable to the purpose which
was uppermost in his mind.

It was not long ere the King of England was brought on
the carpet by the jester, who had been accustomed to consider
Dickon of the Broom (which irreverent epithet he substituted
for Richard Plantagenet) as a subject of mirth, acceptable and
inexhaustible. The orator, indeed, was silent, and it was only
when applied to by Conrade, that he observed, "The *genista*,
or broom-plant, was an emblem of humility; and it would
be well when those who wore it would remember the
warning."

The allusion to the illustrious badge of Plantagenet was
thus rendered sufficiently manifest, and Jonas Schwanker
observed, that they who humbled themselves had been exalted
with a vengeance.

"Honour unto whom honour is due," answered the Marquis
of Montserrat; "we have all had some part in these marches
and battles, and methinks other princes might share a little
in the renown which Richard of England engrosses amongst
minstrels and *minne-singers*. Has no one of the *joyeuse science*
here present a song in praise of the royal Archduke of Austria,
our princely entertainer?"

Three minstrels emulously stepped forward with voice and
harp. Two were silenced with difficulty by the *spruch-sprecher*,
who seemed to act as master of the revels, and a hearing was

at length procured for the poet preferred, who sung, in High German, stanzas which may be thus translated—

> What brave chief shall head the forces,
>   Where the red-cross legions gather?
> Best of horsemen, best of horses,
>   Highest head and fairest feather.

Here the orator, jingling his staff, interrupted the bard to intimate to the party, what they might not have inferred from the description, that their royal host was the party indicated, and a full-crowned goblet went round to the acclamation—*Hoch lebe der Herzog Leopold!* Another stanza followed—

> Ask not Austria why, 'midst princes,
>   Still her banner rises highest;
> Ask as well the strong-wing'd eagle,
>   Why to Heaven he soars the nighest.

"The eagle," said the expounder of dark sayings, "is the cognisance of our noble lord the Archduke—of his royal Grace, I would say — and the eagle flies the highest and nearest to the sun of all the feathered creation."

"The lion hath taken a spring above the eagle," said Conrade, carelessly.

The Archduke reddened, and fixed his eyes on the speaker, while the *spruch-sprecher* answered, after a minute's consideration, "The Lord Marquis will pardon me—a lion cannot fly above an eagle, because no lion hath got wings."

"Except the lion of Saint Mark," responded the jester.

"That is the Venetian's banner," said the Duke; "but assuredly that amphibious race, half nobles, half merchants, will not dare to place their rank in comparison with ours?"

"Nay, it was not of the Venetian lion that I spoke," said the Marquis of Montserrat, "but of the three lions passant of England—formerly, it is said, they were leopards, but now they are become lions at all points, and must take precedence of beast, fish, or fowl, or woe worth the gainstander."

"Mean you seriously, my lord?" said the Austrian, now considerably flushed with wine; "think you that Richard of England asserts any pre-eminence over the free sovereigns who have been his voluntary allies in this Crusade?"

"I know not but from circumstances," answered Conrade; "yonder hangs his banner alone in the midst of our camp, as if he were king and generalissimo of our whole Christian army."

"And do you endure this so patiently, and speak of it so coldly?" said the Archduke.

"Nay, my lord," answered Conrade, "it cannot concern the poor Marquis of Montserrat to contend against an injury, patiently submitted to by such potent princes as Philip of France and Leopold of Austria. What dishonour you are pleased to submit to, cannot be a disgrace to me."

Leopold closed his fist, and struck on the table with violence.

"I have told Philip of this," he said; "I have often told him it was our duty to protect the inferior princes against the usurpation of this Islander—but he answers me ever with cold respects of their relations together as suzerain and vassal, and that it were impolitic in him to make an open breach at this time and period."

"The world knows that Philip is wise," said Conrade, "and will judge his submission to be policy.—Yours, my lord, you can yourself alone account for; but I doubt not you have deep reasons for submitting to English domination."

"*I* submit!" said Leopold, indignantly—"*I*, the Archduke of Austria, so important and vital a limb of the Holy Roman empire—*I* submit myself to this king of half an island—this grandson of a Norman bastard!—No, by Heaven! The camp, and all Christendom, shall see that I know how to right myself, and whether I yield ground one inch to the English bandog.—Up, my lieges and merry-men, up and follow me! We will—and that without losing one instant—place the eagle of Austria where she shall float as high as ever floated the cognisance of king or kaisar."

With that he started from his seat, and, amidst the tumultuous cheering of his guests and followers, made for the door of the pavilion, and seized his own banner, which stood pitched before it.

"Nay, my lord," said Conrade, affecting to interfere, "it will blemish your wisdom to make an affray in the camp at this hour, and perhaps it is better to submit to the usurpation of England a little longer than to——"

"Not an hour—not a moment longer," vociferated the Duke; and, with the banner in his hand, and followed by his shouting guests and attendants, marched hastily to the central mount, from which the banner of England floated, and laid his hand on the standard-spear, as if to pluck it from the ground.

"My master, my dear master!" said Jonas Schwanker, throwing his arms about the Duke—"take heed, lions have teeth——"

"And eagles have claws!" said the Duke, not relinquishing his hold on the banner-staff, yet hesitating to pull it from the ground.

The speaker of sentences, notwithstanding such was his occupation, had nevertheless some intervals of sound sense. He clashed his staff loudly, and Leopold, as if by habit, turned his head towards his man of counsel.

"The eagle is king among the fowls of the air," said the *spruch-sprecher*, "as is the lion among the beasts of the field—each has his dominion, separated as wide as England and Germany—do thou, noble eagle, no dishonour to the princely lion, but let your banners remain floating in peace side by side."

Leopold withdrew his hand from the banner-spear, and looked round for Conrade of Montserrat, but he saw him not; for the Marquis, so soon as he saw the mischief afoot, had withdrawn himself from the crowd, taking care, in the first place, to express before several neutral persons his regret that the Archduke should have chosen the hours after dinner to avenge any wrong of which he might think he had a right to complain. Not seeing his guest, to whom he wished more particularly to have addressed himself, the Archduke said aloud, that, having no wish to breed dissension in the army of the Cross, he did but vindicate his own privileges and right to stand upon an equality with the King of England, without desiring, as he might have done, to advance his banner, which he derived from emperors, his progenitors, above that of a mere descendant of the Counts of Anjou; and, in the meantime, he commanded a cask of wine to be brought hither and pierced, for regaling the bystanders, who, with tuck of drum and sound of music, quaffed many a carouse round the Austrian standard.

This disorderly scene was not acted without a degree of noise, which alarmed the whole camp.

The critical hour had arrived, at which the physician, according to the rules of his art, had predicted that his royal patient might be awakened with safety, and the sponge had been applied for that purpose; and the leech had not made many observations ere he assured the Baron of Gilsland that the fever had entirely left his sovereign, and that such was the happy strength of his constitution, it would not be even necessary, as in most cases, to give a second dose of the powerful medicine. Richard himself seemed to be of the same opinion, for, sitting up and rubbing his eyes, he demanded of De Vaux what present sum of money was in the royal coffers.

The baron could not exactly inform him of the amount.

"It matters not," said Richard; "be it greater or smaller, bestow it all on this learned leech, who hath, I trust, given me back again to the service of the Crusade. If it be less than a thousand byzants, let him have jewels to make it up."

"I sell not the wisdom with which Allah has endowed me," answered the Arabian physician; "and be it known to you, great Prince, that the divine medicine of which you have partaken would lose its effects in my unworthy hands, did I exchange its virtues either for gold or diamonds."

"The physician refuseth a gratuity!" said De Vaux to himself. "This is more extraordinary than his being an hundred years old."

"Thomas de Vaux," said Richard, "thou knowest no courage but what belongs to the sword, no bounty and virtue but what are used in chivalry—I tell thee that this Moor, in his independence, might set an example to them who account themselves the flower of knighthood."

"It is reward enough for me," said the Moor, folding his arms on his bosom, and maintaining an attitude at once respectful and dignified, "that so great a king as the Melech Ric[1] should thus speak of his servant.—But now, let me pray you again to compose yourself on your couch; for though I think there needs no further repetition of the divine draught, yet injury might ensue from any too early exertion, ere your strength be entirely restored."

"I must obey thee, Hakim," said the King; "yet, believe me, my bosom feels so free from the wasting fire, which for so many days hath scorched it, that I care not how soon I expose it to a brave man's lance.—But hark! what mean these shouts, and that distant music in the camp? Go, Thomas de Vaux, and make enquiry."

"It is the Archduke Leopold," said De Vaux, returning after a minute's absence, "who makes with his pot-companions some procession through the camp."

"The drunken fool!" exclaimed King Richard, "can he not keep his brutal inebriety within the veil of his pavilion, that he

[1] Richard was thus called by the Eastern nations.

must needs show his shame to all Christendom?—What say you, Sir Marquis?" he added, addressing himself to Conrade of Montserrat, who at that moment entered the tent.

"Thus much, honoured Prince," answered the Marquis, "that I delight to see your Majesty so well, and so far recovered; and that is a long speech for any one to make who has partaken of the Duke of Austria's hospitality."

"What! you have been dining with the Teutonic wine-skin," said the monarch; "and what frolic has he found out to cause all this disturbance? Truly, Sir Conrade, I have still held you so good a reveller, that I wonder at your quitting the game."

De Vaux, who had got a little behind the King, now exerted himself, by look and sign, to make the Marquis understand that he should say nothing to Richard of what was passing without. But Conrade understood not, or heeded not, the prohibition.

"What the Archduke does," he said, "is of little consequence to any one, least of all to himself, since he probably knows not what he is acting; yet, to say truth, it is a gambol I should not like to share in, since he is pulling down the banner of England from Saint George's Mount in the centre of the camp yonder, and displaying his own in its stead."

"What say'st thou?" exclaimed the King, in a tone which might have waked the dead.

"Nay," said the Marquis, "let it not chafe your Highness that a fool should act according to his folly——"

"Speak not to me," said Richard, springing from his couch, and casting on his clothes with a dispatch which seemed marvellous—"speak not to me, Lord Marquis!—De Multon, I command thee speak not a word to me—he that breathes but a syllable is no friend to Richard Plantagenet.—Hakim, be silent, I charge thee!"

All this while the King was hastily clothing himself, and, with the last word, snatched his sword from the pillar of the tent, and without any other weapon, or calling any attendance, he rushed out of the pavilion. Conrade, holding up his hands as if in astonishment, seemed willing to enter into conversation with De Vaux, but Sir Thomas pushed rudely past him, and calling to one of the royal equerries, said hastily, "Fly to Lord Salisbury's quarters, and let him get his men together, and follow me instantly to Saint George's Mount. Tell him the King's fever has left his blood, and settled in his brain."

Imperfectly heard, and still more imperfectly comprehended, by the startled attendant whom De Vaux addressed thus hastily, the equerry and his fellow-servants of the royal chamber rushed hastily into the tents of the neighbouring nobility, and quickly spread an alarm, as general as the cause seemed vague, through the whole British forces. The English soldiers, waked in alarm from that noon-day rest which the heat of the climate had taught them to enjoy as a luxury, hastily asked each other the cause of the tumult, and, without waiting an answer, supplied by the force of their own fancy the want of information. Some said the Saracens were in the camp, some that the King's life was attempted, some that he had died of the fever the preceding night, many that he was assassinated by the Duke of Austria. The nobles and officers, at an equal loss with the common men to ascertain the real cause of the disorder, laboured only to get their followers under arms and under authority, lest their rashness should occasion some great misfortune to the crusading army. The English trumpets sounded loud, shrill, and continuously. The alarm-cry of "Bows and bills—bows and bills!" was heard from quarter to quarter, again and again shouted, and again and again answered by the presence of the ready warriors and their national invocation, "Saint George for Merry England!"

The alarm went through the nearest quarter of the camp, and men of all the various nations assembled, where, perhaps, every people in Christendom had their representatives, flew to arms, and drew together under circumstances of general confusion, of which they knew neither the cause nor the object. It was, however, lucky, amid a scene so threatening, that the Earl of Salisbury, while he hurried after De Vaux's summons, with a few only of the readiest English men at-arms, directed the rest of the English host to be drawn up and kept under arms, to advance to Richard's succour if necessity should require, but in fit array, and under due command, and not with the tumultuary haste which their own alarm, and zeal for the King's safety, might have dictated.

In the meanwhile, without regarding for one instant the shouts, the cries, the tumult, which began to thicken around him, Richard, with his dress in the last disorder, and his sheathed blade under his arm, pursued his way with the utmost speed, followed only by De Vaux, and one or two household servants, to Saint George's Mount.

He outsped even the alarm which his impetuosity only had

excited, and passed the quarter of his own gallant troops of Normandy, Poitou, Gascony, and Anjou, before the disturbance had reached them, although the noise accompanying the German revel had induced many of the soldiery to get on foot to listen. The handful of Scots were also quartered in the vicinity, nor had they been disturbed by the uproar. But the King's person, and his haste, were both remarked by the Knight of the Leopard, who, aware that danger must be afoot, and hastening to share in it, snatched his shield and sword, and united himself to De Vaux, who with some difficulty kept pace with his impatient and fiery master. De Vaux answered a look of curiosity, which the Scottish knight directed towards him, with a shrug of his broad shoulders, and they continued, side by side, to pursue Richard's steps.

The King was soon at the foot of Saint George's Mount, the sides as well as platform of which were now surrounded and crowded, partly by those belonging to the Duke of Austria's retinue, who were celebrating with shouts of jubilee the act which they considered as an assertion of national honour; partly by bystanders of different nations, whom dislike to the English, or mere curiosity, had assembled together to witness the end of these extraordinary proceedings. Through this disorderly troop Richard burst his way, like a goodly ship under full sail, which cleaves her forcible passage through the rolling billows, and heeds not that they unite after her passage, and roar upon her stern.

The summit of the eminence was a small level space, on which were pitched the rival banners, surrounded still by the Archduke's friends and retinue. In the midst of the circle was Leopold himself, still contemplating with self-satisfaction the deed he had done, and still listening to the shouts of applause which his partisans bestowed with no sparing breath. While he was in this state of self-gratulation, Richard burst into the circle, attended, indeed, only by two men, but in his own headlong energies an irresistible host.

"Who has dared," he said, laying his hands upon the Austrian standard, and speaking in a voice like the sound which precedes an earthquake, "who has dared to place this paltry rag beside the banner of England?"

The Archduke wanted not personal courage, and it was impossible he could hear this question without reply. Yet, so much was he troubled and surprised by the unexpected arrival of Richard, and affected by the general awe inspired by his ardent and unyielding character, that the demand was twice repeated, in a tone which seemed to challenge heaven and earth, ere the Archduke replied, with such firmness as he could command, "It was I, Leopold of Austria."

"Then shall Leopold of Austria," replied Richard, "presently see the rate at which his banner and his pretensions are held by Richard of England."

So saying, he pulled up the standard-spear, splintered it to pieces, threw the banner itself on the ground, and placed his foot upon it.

"Thus," said he, "I trample on the banner of Austria!—Is there a knight among your Teutonic chivalry dare impeach my deed?"

There was a momentary silence; but there are no braver men than the Germans.

"I!" and "I!" and "I!" was heard from several knights of the Duke's followers; and he himself added his voice to those which accepted the King of England's defiance.

"Why do we dally thus?" said the Earl Wallenrode, a gigantic warrior from the frontiers of Hungary: "Brethren, and noble gentlemen, this man's foot is on the honour of your country—Let us rescue it from violation, and down with the pride of England!"

So saying, he drew his sword, and struck at the King a blow which might have proved fatal, had not the Scot intercepted and caught it upon his shield.

"I have sworn," said King Richard—and his voice was heard above all the tumult, which now waxed wild and loud—"never to strike one whose shoulder bears the cross; therefore live, Wallenrode—but live to remember Richard of England."

As he spoke, he grasped the tall Hungarian round the waist, and, unmatched in wrestling, as in other military exercises, hurled him backwards with such violence that the mass flew, as if discharged from a military engine, not only through the ring of spectators who witnessed the extraordinary scene, but over the edge of the mount itself, down the steep side of which Wallenrode rolled headlong, until, pitching at length upon his shoulder, he dislocated the bone, and lay like one dead. This almost supernatural display of strength did not encourage either the Duke or any of his followers to renew a personal contest so inauspiciously commenced. Those who stood farthest back did, indeed, clash their swords, and cry out,

"Cut the island mastiff to pieces!" but those who were nearer, veiled, perhaps, their personal fears under an affected regard for order, and cried for the most part, "Peace! peace! the peace of the Cross! the peace of Holy Church, and our father the Pope!"

These various cries of the assailants, contradicting each other, showed their irresolution; while Richard, his foot still on the archducal banner, glared round him, with an eye that seemed to seek an enemy, and from which the angry nobles shrunk appalled, as from the threatened grasp of a lion. De Vaux and the Knight of the Leopard kept their places beside him; and though the swords which they held were still sheathed, it was plain that they were prompt to protect Richard's person to the very last, and their size and remarkable strength plainly showed the defence would be a desperate one.

Salisbury and his attendants were also now drawing near, with bills and partisans brandished, and bows already bended.

At this moment King Philip of France, attended by one or two of his nobles, came on the platform to enquire the cause of the disturbance, and made gestures of surprise at finding the King of England raised from his sick-bed, and confronting their common ally the Duke of Austria, in such a menacing and insulting posture. Richard himself blushed at being discovered by Philip, whose sagacity he respected as much as he disliked his person, in an attitude neither becoming his character as a monarch, nor as a Crusader; and it was observed that he withdrew his foot, as if accidentally, from the dishonoured banner, and exchanged his look of violent emotion for one of affected composure and indifference. Leopold also struggled to attain some degree of calmness, mortified as he was by having been seen by Philip in the act of passively submitting to the insults of the fiery King of England.

Possessed of many of those royal qualities for which he was termed by his subjects the august, Philip might be termed the Ulysses, as Richard was indisputably the Achilles, of the Crusade. The King of France was sagacious, wise, deliberate in council, steady and calm in action, seeing clearly, and steadily pursuing, the measures most for the interest of his kingdom—dignified and royal in his deportment, brave in person, but a politician rather than a warrior. The Crusade would have been no choice of his own, but the spirit was contagious, and the expedition was enforced upon him by the

Church, and by the unanimous wish of his nobility. In any other situation, or in a milder age, his character might have stood higher than that of the adventurous Cœur de Lion; but in the Crusade, itself an undertaking wholly irrational, sound reason was the quality of all others least estimated, and the chivalric valour which both the age and the enterprise demanded was considered as debased if mingled with the least touch of discretion. So that the merit of Philip, compared with that of his haughty rival, showed like the clear but minute flame of a lamp, placed near the glare of a huge blazing torch, which, not possessing half the utility, makes ten times more impression on the eye. Philip felt his inferiority in public opinion, with the pain natural to a high-spirited prince; and it cannot be wondered at if he took such opportunities as offered, for placing his own character in more advantageous contrast with that of his rival. The present seemed one of those occasions in which prudence and calmness might reasonably expect to triumph over obstinacy and impetuous violence.

"What means this unseemly broil betwixt the sworn brethren of the Cross—the royal Majesty of England and the princely Duke Leopold? How is it possible that those who are the chiefs and pillars of this holy expedition——"

"A truce with thy remonstrance, France," said Richard, enraged inwardly at finding himself placed on a sort of equality with Leopold, yet not knowing how to resent it; "this Duke, or prince, or pillar, if you will, hath been insolent, and I have chastised him—that is all. Here is a coil, forsooth, because of spurning a hound!"

"Majesty of France," said the Duke, "I appeal to you and every sovereign prince against the foul indignity which I have sustained. This King of England hath pulled down my banner—torn and trampled on it."

"Because he had the audacity to plant it beside mine," said Richard.

"My rank as thine equal entitled me," replied the Duke, emboldened by the presence of Philip.

"Assert such equality for thy person," said King Richard, "and, by Saint George, I will treat thy person as I did thy broidered kerchief there, fit but for the meanest use to which kerchief may be put."

"Nay, but patience, brother of England," said Philip, "and I will presently show Austria that he is wrong in this matter.— Do not think, noble Duke," he continued, "that, in permitting the standard of England to occupy the highest point in our camp, we, the independent sovereigns of the Crusade, acknowledge any inferiority to the royal Richard. It were inconsistent to think so; since even the Oriflamme itself—the great banner of France, to which the royal Richard himself, in respect of his French possessions, is but a vassal—holds for the present an inferior place to the Lions of England. But as sworn brethren of the Cross, military pilgrims, who, laying aside the pomp and pride of this world, are hewing with our swords the way to the Holy Sepulchre, I myself, and the other princes, have renounced to King Richard, from respect to his high renown and great feats of arms, that precedence, which elsewhere and upon other motives would not have been yielded. I am satisfied, that when your royal Grace of Austria shall have considered this, you will express sorrow for having placed your banner on this spot, and that the royal Majesty of England will then give satisfaction for the insult he has offered."

The *spruch-sprecher* and the jester had both retired to a safe distance when matters seemed coming to blows, but returned when words, their own commodity, seemed again about to become the order of the day.

The man of proverbs was so delighted with Philip's politic speech, that he clashed his baton at the conclusion, by way of emphasis, and forgot the presence in which he was, so far as to say aloud, that he himself had never said a wiser thing in his life.

"It may be so," whispered Jonas Schwanker, "but we shall be whipt if you speak so loud."

The Duke answered sullenly, that he would refer his quarrel to the General Council of the Crusade—a motion which Philip highly applauded, as qualified to take away a scandal most harmful to Christendom.

Richard, retaining the same careless attitude, listened to Philip until his oratory seemed exhausted, and then said aloud, "I am drowsy—this fever hangs about me still. Brother of France, thou art acquainted with my humour, and that I have at all times but few words to spare—know, therefore, at once, I will submit a matter touching the honour of England neither to prince, pope, nor council. Here stands my banner—whatsoever pennon shall be reared within three butts' length of it—ay, were it the Oriflamme, of which you were, I think, but now speaking—shall be treated as that dishonoured rag; nor will I yield other satisfaction than that which these poor limbs can render in the lists to any bold challenge—ay, were it against five champions instead of one."

"Now," said the jester, whispering his companion, "that is as complete a piece of folly, as if I myself had said it; but yet, I think, there may be in this matter a greater fool than Richard yet."

"And who may that be?" asked the man of wisdom.

"Philip," said the jester, "or our own royal Duke, should either accept the challenge—But oh, most sage *spruch-sprecher*, what excellent kings would thou and I have made, since those on whose heads these crowns have fallen, can play the proverb-monger and the fool as completely as ourselves!"

While these worthies plied their offices apart, Philip answered calmly to the almost injurious defiance of Richard—"I came not hither to awaken fresh quarrels, contrary to the oath we have sworn, and the holy cause in which we have engaged. I part from my brother of England as brothers should part, and the only strife between the Lions of England and the Lilies of France shall be, which shall be carried deepest into the ranks of the infidels."

"It is a bargain, my royal brother," said Richard, stretching out his hand with all the frankness which belonged to his rash but generous disposition; "and soon may we have the opportunity to try this gallant and fraternal wager."

"Let this noble Duke also partake in the friendship of this happy moment," said Philip; and the Duke approached, half-sullenly, half-willing to enter into some accommodation.

"I think not of fools, nor of their folly," said Richard, carelessly; and the Archduke, turning his back on him, withdrew from the ground.

Richard looked after him as he retired.

"There is a sort of glow-worm courage," he said, "that shows only by night. I must not leave this banner unguarded in darkness; by daylight the look of the Lions will alone defend it. Here, Thomas of Gilsland, I give thee the charge of the standard—watch over the honour of England."

"Her safety is yet more dear to me," said De Vaux, "and the life of Richard is the safety of England—I must have your Highness back to your tent, and that without further tarriance."

"Thou art a rough and peremptory nurse, De Vaux," said the King, smiling; and then added, addressing Sir Kenneth, "Valiant Scot, I owe thee a boon, and I will pay it richly.

There stands the banner of England! Watch it as a novice does his armour on the night before he is dubbed. Stir not from it three spears' length, and defend it with thy body against injury or insult—Sound thy bugle, if thou art assailed by more than three at once. Dost thou undertake the charge?"

"Willingly," said Kenneth; "and will discharge it upon penalty of my head. I will but arm me, and return hither instantly."

The Kings of France and England then took formal leave of each other, hiding, under an appearance of courtesy, the grounds of complaint which either had against the other—Richard against Philip for what he deemed an officious interference betwixt him and Austria, and Philip against Cœur de Lion for the disrespectful manner in which his mediation had been received. Those whom this disturbance had assembled, now drew off in different directions, leaving the contested mount in the same solitude which had subsisted till interrupted by the Austrian bravado. Men judged of the events of the day according to their partialities; and while the English charged the Austrian with having afforded the first ground of quarrel, those of other nations concurred in casting the greater blame upon the insular haughtiness and assuming character of Richard.

"Thou seest," said the Marquis of Montserrat to the Grand Master of the Templars, "that subtle courses are more effective than violence. I have unloosed the bonds which held together this bunch of sceptres and lances—thou wilt see them shortly fall asúnder."

"I would have called thy plan a good one," said the Templar, "had there been but one man of courage among yonder cold-blooded Austrians, to sever the bonds of which you speak, with his sword. A knot that is unloosed may again be fastened, but not so the cord which has been cut to pieces."

CHAPTER XII

'Tis woman that seduces all mankind—GAY.

IN the days of chivalry, a dangerous post, or a perilous adventure, was a reward frequently assigned to military bravery as a compensation for its former trials; just as, in ascending a precipice, the surmounting one crag only lifts the climber to points yet more dangerous.

It was midnight, and the moon rode clear and high in heaven, when Kenneth of Scotland stood upon his watch on Saint George's Mount, beside the banner of England, a solitary sentinel, to protect the emblem of that nation against the insults which might be meditated among the thousands whom Richard's pride had made his enemies. High thoughts rolled, one after each other, upon the mind of the warrior. It seemed to him as if he had gained some favour in the eyes of the chivalrous monarch, who till now had not seemed to distinguish him among the crowds of brave men whom his renown had assembled under his banner, and Sir Kenneth little recked that the display of royal regard consisted in placing him upon a post so perilous. The devotion of his ambitious and high-placed affection inflamed his military enthusiasm. Hopeless as that attachment was, in almost any conceivable circumstances, those which had lately occurred had, in some degree, diminished the distance between Edith and himself. He upon whom Richard had conferred the distinction of guarding his banner was no longer an adventurer of slight note, but placed within the regard of a princess, although he was as far as ever from her level. An unknown and obscure fate could not now be his. If he was surprised and slain on the post which had been assigned him, his death—and he resolved it should be glorious—must deserve the praises, as well as call down the vengeance, of Cœur de Lion, and be followed by the regrets, and even the tears, of the high-born beauties of the English court. He had now no longer reason to fear that he should die as a fool dieth.

Sir Kenneth had full leisure to enjoy these and similar high-souled thoughts, fostered by that wild spirit of chivalry, which, amid its most extravagant and fantastic flights, was still pure from all selfish alloy—generous, devoted, and perhaps only thus far censurable, that it proposed objects and courses of action inconsistent with the frailties and imperfections of man. All nature around him slept in calm moonshine or in deep shadow. The long rows of tents and pavilions, glimmering or darkening as they lay in the moonlight or in the shade, were still and silent as the streets of a deserted city. Beside the banner-staff lay the large stag-hound already mentioned, the sole companion of Kenneth's watch, on whose vigilance he trusted for early warning of the approach of any hostile footstep.

The noble animal seemed to understand the purpose of their watch, for he looked from time to time at the rich folds of the heavy pennon, and, when the cry of the sentinels came from the distant lines and defences of the camp, he answered them with one deep and reiterated bark, as if to affirm that he too was vigilant in his duty. From time to time, also, he lowered his lofty head, and wagged his tail, as his master passed and repassed him in the short turns which he took upon his post; or, when the knight stood silent and abstracted, leaning on his lance, and looking up towards heaven, his faithful attendant ventured sometimes, in the phrase of romance, "to disturb his thoughts," and awaken him from his reverie, by thrusting his large rough snout into the knight's gauntleted hand, to solicit a transitory caress.

Thus passed two hours of the knight's watch without any thing remarkable occurring. At length, and upon a sudden, the gallant stag-hound bayed furiously, and seemed about to dash forward where the shadow lay the darkest, yet waited, as if in the slips, till he should know the pleasure of his master.

"Who goes there?" said Sir Kenneth, aware that there was something creeping forward on the shadowy side of the mount.

"In the name of Merlin and Maugis," answered a hoarse, disagreeable voice, "tie up your four-footed demon there, or I come not at you."

"And who art thou, that would approach my post?" said Sir Kenneth, bending his eyes as keenly as he could on some object, which he could just observe at the bottom of the ascent, without being able to distinguish its form. "Beware—I am here for death and life."

"Take up thy long-fanged Sathanas," said the voice, "or I will conjure him with a bolt from my arblast."

At the same time was heard the sound of a spring or check, as when a crossbow is bent.

"Unbend thy arblast, and come into the moonlight," said the Scot, "or, by Saint Andrew, I will pin thee to the earth, be what or whom thou wilt!"

As he spoke, he poised his long lance by the middle, and, fixing his eye upon the object which seemed to move, he brandished the weapon, as if meditating to cast it from his hand—a use of the weapon sometimes, though rarely, resorted to when a missile was necessary. But Sir Kenneth was ashamed of his purpose, and grounded his weapon, when there stepped from the shadow into the moonlight, like an actor entering upon the stage, a stunted decrepit creature, whom, by his fantastic dress and deformity, he recognised, even at some distance, for the male of the two dwarfs whom he had seen at the chapel of Engaddi. Recollecting, at the same moment, the other, and far different, visions of that extraordinary night, he gave his dog a signal, which he instantly understood, and, returning to the standard, laid himself down beside it with a stifled growl.

The little distorted miniature of humanity, assured of his safety from an enemy so formidable, came panting up the ascent, which the shortness of his legs rendered laborious, and, when he arrived on the platform at the top, shifted to his left hand the little crossbow, which was just such a toy as children at that period were permitted to shoot small birds with, and, assuming an attitude of great dignity, gracefully extended his right hand to Sir Kenneth, in an attitude as if he expected he would salute it. But such a result not following, he demanded, in a sharp and angry tone of voice, "Soldier, wherefore renderest thou not to Nectabanus the homage due to his dignity?—Or, is it possible that thou canst have forgotten him?"

"Great Nectabanus," answered the knight, willing to soothe the creature's humour, "that were difficult for any one who has ever looked upon thee. Pardon me, however, that being a soldier upon my post, with my lance in my hand, I may not give to one of thy puissance the advantage of coming within my guard, or of mastering my weapon. Suffice it, that I reverence thy dignity, and submit myself to thee as humbly as a man-at-arms in my place may."

"It shall suffice," said Nectabanus, "so that you presently attend me to the presence of those who have sent me hither to summon you."

"Great sir," replied the knight, "neither in this can I gratify thee, for my orders are to abide by this banner till daybreak—so I pray you to hold me excused in that matter also."

So saying, he resumed his walk upon the platform; but the dwarf did not suffer him so easily to escape from his importunity.

"Look you," he said, placing himself before Sir Kenneth, so as to interrupt his way, "either obey me, Sir Knight, as in duty bound, or I will lay the command upon thee, in the name of one whose beauty could call down the genii from their sphere, and whose grandeur could command the immortal race when they had descended."

A wild and improbable conjecture arose in the knight's mind, but he repelled it. It was impossible, he thought, that the lady of his love should have sent him such a message by such a messenger—yet his voice trembled as he said, "Go to, Nectabanus. Tell me at once, and as a true man, whether this sublime lady, of whom thou speakest, be other than the houri with whose assistance I beheld thee sweeping the chapel at Engaddi?"

"How! presumptuous knight," replied the dwarf, "think'st thou the mistress of our own royal affections, the sharer of our greatness, and the partner of our comeliness, would demean herself by laying charge on such a vassal as thou? No, highly as thou art honoured, thou hast not yet deserved the notice of Queen Guenevra, the lovely bride of Arthur, from whose high seat even princes seem but pigmies. But look thou here, and as thou knowest or disownest this token, so obey or refuse her commands, who hath deigned to impose them on thee."

So saying, he placed in the knight's hands a ruby ring, which, even in the moonlight, he had no difficulty to recognise as that which usually graced the finger of the high-born lady to whose service he had devoted himself. Could he have doubted the truth of the token, he would have been convinced by the small knot of carnation-coloured ribbon which was fastened to the ring. This was his lady's favourite colour, and more than once had he himself, assuming it for that of his own liveries, caused the carnation to triumph over all other hues in the lists and in the battle.

Sir Kenneth was struck nearly mute by seeing such a token in such hands.

"In the name of all that is sacred, from whom didst thou receive this witness?" said the knight; "bring, if thou canst, thy wavering understanding to a right settlement for a minute or two, and tell me the person by whom thou art sent, and the real purpose of thy message—and take heed what thou say'st, for this is no subject for buffoonery."

"Fond and foolish knight," said the dwarf, "wouldst thou know more of this matter, than that thou art honoured with commands from a princess, delivered to thee by a king?— We list not to parley with thee further than to command thee, in the name, and by the power of that ring, to follow us to her who is the owner of the ring. Every minute that thou tarriest is a crime against thy allegiance."

"Good Nectabanus, bethink thyself," said the knight. "Can my lady know where and upon what duty I am this night engaged—Is she aware that my life—Pshaw, why should I speak of life—but that my honour depends on my guarding this banner till daybreak—and can it be her wish that I should leave it even to pay homage to her?—It is impossible—the princess is pleased to be merry with her servant, in sending him such a message; and I must think so the rather that she hath chosen such a messenger."

"Oh, keep your belief," said Nectabanus, turning round as if to leave the platform; "it is little to me whether you be traitor or true man to this royal lady—so fare thee well."

"Stay, stay—I entreat you stay," said Sir Kenneth; "answer me but one question—Is the lady who sent thee near to this place?"

"What signifies it?" said the dwarf. "Ought fidelity to reckon furlongs, or miles, or leagues,—like the poor courier, who is paid for his labour by the distance which he traverses? Nevertheless, thou soul of suspicion, I tell thee, the fair owner of the ring, now sent to so unworthy a vassal, in whom there is neither truth nor courage, is not more distant from this place, than this arblast can send a bolt."

The knight gazed again on the ring, as if to ascertain that there was no possible falsehood in the token.—"Tell me," he said to the dwarf, "is my presence required for any length of time?"

"Time!" answered Nectabanus, in his flighty manner; "what call you time? I see it not—I feel it not—it is but a shadowy name—a succession of breathings measured forth by night by the clank of a bell, by day by a shadow crossing along a dial-stone. Know'st thou not a true knight's time should only be reckoned by the deeds that he performs in behalf of God and his lady?"

"The words of truth, though in the mouth of folly," said the knight. "And doth my lady really summon me to some deed of action, in her name and for her sake?—and may it not be postponed for even the few hours till daybreak?"

"She requires thy presence instantly," said the dwarf, "and without the loss of so much time as would be told by ten grains of the sand-glass.—Hearken, thou cold-blooded and suspicious knight, these are her very words—'Tell him that the hand which dropped roses can bestow laurels.'"

This allusion to their meeting in the chapel of Engaddi, sent a thousand recollections through Sir Kenneth's brain, and convinced him that the message delivered by the dwarf was genuine. The rosebuds, withered as they were, were still treasured under his cuirass, and nearest to his heart. He paused, and could not resolve to forego an opportunity—the only one which might ever offer, to gain grace in her eyes whom he had installed as sovereign of his affections. The dwarf, in the meantime, augmented his confusion by insisting either that he must return the ring, or instantly attend him.

"Hold, hold, yet a moment hold," said the knight, and proceeded to mutter to himself, "Am I either the subject or slave of King Richard, more than as a free knight sworn to the service of the Crusade? And whom have I come hither to honour with lance and sword? Our holy cause, and my transcendent lady!"

"The ring, the ring!" exclaimed the dwarf, impatiently; "false and slothful knight, return the ring, which thou art unworthy to touch or to look upon."

"A moment, a moment, good Nectabanus," said Sir Kenneth; "disturb not my thoughts.—What if the Saracens were just now to attack our lines? Should I stay here like a sworn vassal of England, watching that her king's pride suffered no humiliation; or should I speed to the breach, and fight for the Cross?—To the breach, assuredly; and next to the cause of God, come the commands of my liege lady.—And yet, Cœur de Lion's behest—my own promise!—Nectabanus, I conjure thee once more to say, are you to conduct me far from hence?"

"But to yonder pavilion; and, since you must needs know," replied Nectabanus, "the moon is glimmering on the gilded ball which crowns its roof, and which is worth a king's ransom."

"I can return in an instant," said the knight, shutting his eyes desperately to all further consequences. "I can hear from thence the bay of my dog, if any one approaches the standard—I will throw myself at my lady's feet, and pray her leave to return to conclude my watch.—Here, Roswal," (calling his hound, and throwing down his mantle by the side of the standard-spear,) "watch thou here, and let no one approach."

The majestic dog looked in his master's face, as if to be sure that he understood his charge, then sat down beside the mantle, with ears erect and head raised, like a sentinel, understanding perfectly the purpose for which he was stationed there.

"Come now, good Nectabanus," said the knight, "let us hasten to obey the commands thou hast brought."

"Haste he that will," said the dwarf, sullenly; "thou hast not been in haste to obey my summons, nor can I walk fast enough to follow your long strides—you do not walk like a man, but bound like an ostrich in the desert."

There were but two ways of conquering the obstinacy of Nectabanus, who, as he spoke, diminished his walk into a snail pace. For bribes Sir Kenneth had no means—for soothing no time; so in his impatience he snatched the dwarf up from the ground, and bearing him along, notwithstanding his entreaties and his fear, reached nearly to the pavilion pointed out as that of the Queen. In approaching it, however, the Scot observed there was a small guard of soldiers sitting on the ground, who had been concealed from him by the intervening tents. Wondering that the clash of his own armour had not yet attracted their attention, and supposing that his motions might, on the present occasion, require to be conducted with secrecy, he placed the little panting guide upon the ground to recover his breath, and point out what was next to be done. Nectabanus was both frightened and angry; but he had felt himself as completely in the power of the robust knight, as an owl in the claws of an eagle, and therefore cared not to provoke him to any further display of his strength.

He made no complaints, therefore, of the usage he had received, but turning amongst the labyrinth of tents, he led the knight in silence to the opposite side of the pavilion, which thus screened them from the observation of the warders, who seemed either too negligent or too sleepy to discharge their duty with much accuracy. Arrived there, the dwarf raised the under part of the canvas from the ground, and made signs to Sir Kenneth that he should introduce himself to the inside of the tent, by creeping under it. The knight hesitated—there seemed an indecorum in thus privately introducing himself into a pavilion, pitched, doubtless, for the accommodation of noble ladies; but he recalled to remembrance the assured tokens which the dwarf had exhibited, and concluded that it was not for him to dispute his lady's pleasure.

He stoopt accordingly, crept beneath the canvas enclosure of the tent, and heard the dwarf whisper from without,— "Remain there until I call thee."

CHAPTER XIII

You talk of Gaiety and Innocence!
The moment when the fatal fruit was eaten,
They parted ne'er to meet again; and Malice
Has ever since been playmate to light Gaiety,
From the first moment when the smiling infant
Destroys the flower or butterfly he toys with,
To the last chuckle of the dying miser,
Who on his deathbed laughs his last to hear
His wealthy neighbour has become a bankrupt.
Old Play.

SIR KENNETH was left for some minutes alone, and in darkness. Here was another interruption, which must prolong his absence from his post, and he began almost to repent the facility with which he had been induced to quit it. But to return without seeing the Lady Edith, was now not to be thought of. He had committed a breach of military discipline, and was determined at least to prove the reality of the seductive expectations which had tempted him to do. so. Meanwhile, his situation was unpleasant. There was no light to show him into what sort of apartment he had been led—the Lady Edith was in immediate attendance on the Queen of England—and the discovery of his having introduced himself thus furtively into the royal pavilion, might, were it discovered, lead to much and dangerous suspicion. While he gave way to these unpleasant reflections, and began almost to wish that he could achieve his retreat unobserved, he heard a noise of female voices, laughing, whispering, and speaking, in an adjoining apartment, from which, as the sounds gave him reason to judge, he could only be separated by a canvas partition. Lamps were burning, as he might perceive by the shadowy light which extended itself even to his side of the veil which divided the tent, and he could see shades of several figures sitting and moving in the adjoining apartment. It cannot be termed discourtesy in Sir Kenneth, that, situated as he was, he overheard a conversation, in which he found himself deeply interested.

"Call her—call her, for Our Lady's sake," said the voice of one of these laughing invisibles. "Nectabanus, thou shalt be made ambassador to Prester John's court, to show them how wisely thou canst discharge thee of a mission."

The shrill tone of the dwarf was heard, yet so much subdued, that Sir Kenneth could not understand what he said, except that he spoke something of the means of merriment given to the guard.

" But how shall we rid us of the spirit which Nectabanus hath raised, my maidens?"

" Hear me, royal madam," said another voice; " if the sage and princely Nectabanus be not over-jealous of his most transcendent bride and empress, let us send her to get us rid of this insolent knight-errant, who can be so easily persuaded that high-born dames may need the use of his insolent and over-weening valour."

"It were but justice, methinks," replied another, "that the Princess Guenevra should dismiss, by her courtesy, him whom her husband's wisdom has been able to entice hither."

Struck to the heart with shame and resentment at what he had heard, Sir Kenneth was about to attempt his escape from the tent at all hazards, when what followed arrested his purpose.

"Nay, truly," said the first speaker, "our cousin Edith must first learn how this vaunted wight hath conducted himself, and we must reserve the power of giving her ocular proof that he hath failed in his duty. It may be a lesson will do good upon her; for, credit me, Calista, I have sometimes thought she has let this northern adventurer sit nearer her heart than prudence would sanction."

One of the other voices was then heard to mutter something of the Lady Edith's prudence and wisdom.

"Prudence, wench!" was the reply—"It is mere pride, and the desire to be thought more rigid than any of us. Nay, I will not quit my advantage. You know well, that when she has us at fault, no one can, in a civil way, lay your error before you more precisely than can my Lady Edith.—But here she comes."

A figure, as if entering the apartment, cast upon the partition a shade, which glided along slowly until it mixed with those which already clouded it. Despite of the bitter disappointment which he had experienced—despite the insult and injury with which it seemed he had been visited by the malice, or at best by the idle humour of Queen Berengaria, (for he already concluded that she who spoke loudest, and in a commanding tone, was the wife of Richard,) the knight felt something so soothing to his feelings in learning that Edith had been no partner to the fraud practised on him, and so interesting to his curiosity in the scene which was about to take place, that, instead of prosecuting his more prudent purpose of an instant retreat, he looked anxiously, on the contrary, for some rent or crevice, by means of which he might be made eye as well as ear-witness to what was to go forward.

"Surely," said he to himself, "the Queen, who hath been pleased for an idle frolic to endanger my reputation, and perhaps my life, cannot complain if I avail myself of the chance which fortune seems willing to afford me, to obtain knowledge of her further intentions."

It seemed, in the meanwhile, as if Edith were waiting for the commands of the Queen, and as if the other were reluctant to speak, for fear of being unable to command her laughter, and that of her companions; for Sir Kenneth could only distinguish a sound as of suppressed tittering and merriment.

"Your Majesty," said Edith, at last, "seems in a merry mood, though, methinks, the hour of night prompts a sleepy one. I was well disposed bedward, when I had your Majesty's commands to attend you."

"I will not long delay you, cousin, from your repose," said the Queen; "though I fear you will sleep less soundly when I tell you your wager is lost."

"Nay, royal madam," said Edith, "this, surely, is dwelling on a jest which has rather been worn out. I laid no wager, however it was your Majesty's pleasure to suppose, or to insist, that I did so."

"Nay, now, despite our pilgrimage, Satan is strong with you, my gentle cousin, and prompts thee to leasing. Can you deny that you gaged your ruby ring against my golden bracelet, that yonder Knight of the Libbard, or how call you him, could not be seduced from his post?"

"Your Majesty is too great for me to gainsay you," replied Edith; "but these ladies can, if they will, bear me witness, that it was your Highness who proposed such a wager, and took the ring from my finger, even while I was declaring that I did not think it maidenly to gage any thing on such a subject."

"Nay, but, my Lady Edith," said another voice, "you must needs grant, under your favour, that you expressed yourself very confident of the valour of that same Knight of the Leopard."

"And if I did, minion," said Edith, angrily, "is that a good reason why thou shouldst put in thy word to flatter her Majesty's humour? I spoke of that knight but as all men speak who have seen him in the field, and had no more interest in defending than thou in detracting from him. In a camp, what can women speak of save soldiers and deeds of arms?"

"The noble Lady Edith," said a third voice, "hath never forgiven Calista and me, since we told your Majesty that she dropped two rose-buds in the chapel."

"If your Majesty," said Edith, in a tone which Sir Kenneth could judge to be that of respectful remonstrance, "have no other commands for me than to hear the gibes of your waiting-women, I must crave your permission to withdraw."

"Silence, Florise," said the Queen, "and let not our indulgence lead you to forget the difference betwixt youself and the kinswoman of England.—But you, my dear cousin," she continued, resuming her tone of raillery, "how can you, who are so good-natured, begrudge us poor wretches a few minutes' laughing, when we have had so many days devoted to weeping and gnashing of teeth?"

"Great be your mirth, royal lady," said Edith; "yet would I be content not to smile for the rest of my life, rather than——"

She stopped, apparently out of respect; but Sir Kenneth could hear that she was in much agitation.

"Forgive me," said Berengaria, a thoughtless but good-humoured princess of the House of Navarre; "but what is the great offence after all? A young knight has been wiled hither, has stolen, or has *been* stolen, from his post, which no one will disturb in his absence, for the sake of a fair lady; for, to do your champion justice, sweet one, the wisdom of Nectabanus could conjure him hither in no name but yours."

"Gracious Heaven! your Majesty does not say so?" said Edith, in a voice of alarm quite different from the agitation she had previously evinced,—"you cannot say so, consistently with respect for your own honour, and for mine, your husband's kinswoman!—Say you were jesting with me, my royal mistress, and forgive me that I could, even for a moment, think it possible you could be in earnest!"

"The Lady Edith," said the Queen, in a displeased tone of voice, "regrets the ring we have won of her.—We will restore the pledge to you, gentle cousin, only you must not grudge us in turn a little triumph over the wisdom which has been so often spread over us, as a banner over a host."

"A triumph!" exclaimed Edith, indignantly; "a triumph! —The triumph will be with the infidel when he hears that the Queen of England can make the reputation of her husband's kinswoman the subject of a light frolic."

"You are angry, fair cousin, at losing your favourite ring," said the Queen. "Come, since you grudge to pay your wager, we will renounce our right; it was your name and that pledge brought him hither, and we care not for the bait after the fish is caught."

"Madam," replied Edith, impatiently, "you know well that your Grace could not wish for any thing of mine but it becomes instantly yours. But I would give a bushel of rubies ere ring or name of mine had been used to bring a brave man into a fault, and perhaps to disgrace and punishment."

"O, it is for the safety of our true knight that we fear!" said the Queen. "You rate our power too low, fair cousin, when you speak of a life being lost for a frolic of ours. O, Lady Edith, others have influence on the iron breasts of warriors as well as you—the heart even of a lion is made of flesh, not of stone; and, believe me, I have interest enough with Richard to save this knight, in whose fate Lady Edith is so deeply concerned, from the penalty of disobeying his royal commands."

"For the love of the blessed Cross, most royal lady," said Edith—and Sir Kenneth, with feelings which it were hard to unravel, heard her prostrate herself at the Queen's feet— "for the love of our blessed Lady, and of every holy saint in the calendar, beware what you do! You know not King Richard—you have been but shortly wedded to him—your breath might as well combat the west wind when it is wildest, as your words persuade my royal kinsman to pardon a military offence. Oh, for God's sake, dismiss this gentleman, if indeed you have lured him hither! I could almost be content to rest with the shame of having invited him, did I know that he was returned again where his duty calls him!"

"Arise, cousin, arise," said Queen Berengaria, "and be assured all will be better than you think. Rise, dear Edith; I am sorry I have played my foolery with a knight in whom you take such deep interest—Nay, wring not thy hands; I will believe thou carest not for him, believe any thing rather than see thee look so wretchedly miserable. I tell thee, I will take the blame on myself with King Richard in behalf of thy fair northern friend—thine acquaintance, I would say, since thou own'st him not as a friend.—Nay, look not so reproachfully—We will send Nectabanus to dismiss this Knight of the Standard to his post; and we ourselves will grace him on some future day, to make amends for his wild-goose chase. He is, I warrant, but lying perdue in some neighbouring tent."

"By my crown of lilies, and my sceptre of a specially good water-reed," said Nectabanus, "your Majesty is mistaken—he is nearer at hand than you wot—he lieth ensconced there behind that canvas partition."

"And within hearing of each word we have said!" exclaimed the Queen, in her turn violently surprised and agitated. "Out, monster of folly and malignity!"

As she uttered these words, Nectabanus fled from the pavilion with a yell of such a nature, as leaves it still doubtful whether Berengaria had confined her rebuke to words, or added some more emphatic expression of her displeasure.

"What can now be done?" said the Queen to Edith, in a whisper of undisguised uneasiness.

"That which must," said Edith, firmly. "We must see this gentleman, and place ourselves in his mercy."

So saying, she began hastily to undo a curtain, which at one place covered an entrance or communication.

"For Heaven's sake, forbear—consider," said the Queen, "my apartment—our dress—the hour—my honour!"

But ere she could detail her remonstrances, the curtain fell, and there was no division any longer betwixt the armed knight and the party of ladies. The warmth of an Eastern night occasioned the undress of Queen Berengaria and her household to be rather more simple and unstudied than their station, and the presence of a male spectator of rank, required. This the Queen remembered, and with a loud shriek fled from the apartment where Sir Kenneth was disclosed to view in a copartment of the ample pavilion, now no longer separated from that in which they stood. The grief and agitation of the Lady Edith, as well as the deep interest she felt in a hasty explanation with the Scottish knight, perhaps occasioned her forgetting that her locks were more dishevelled, and her person less heedfully covered, than was the wont of high-born damsels, in an age which was not, after all, the most prudish or scrupulous period of the ancient time. A thin loose garment of pink-coloured silk made the principal part of her vestments, with Oriental slippers, into which she had hastily thrust her bare feet, and a scarf hurriedly and loosely thrown about her shoulders. Her head had no other covering than the veil of rich and dishevelled locks falling round it on every side, that half hid a countenance, which a mingled sense of modesty, and of resentment, and other deep and agitating feelings, had covered with crimson.

But although Edith felt her situation with all that delicacy which is her sex's greatest charm, it did not seem that for a moment she placed her own bashfulness in comparison with the duty, which, as she thought, she owed to him who had been led into error and danger on her account. She drew, indeed, her scarf more closely over her neck and bosom, and she hastily laid from her hand a lamp, which shed too much lustre over her figure; but, while Sir Kenneth stood motionless on the same spot in which he was first discovered, she rather stepped towards than retired from him, as she exclaimed, "Hasten to your post, valiant knight! You are deceived in being trained hither; ask no questions."

"I need ask none," said the knight, sinking upon one knee, with the reverential devotion of a saint at the altar, and bending his eyes on the ground, lest his looks should increase the lady's embarrassment.

"Have you heard all?" said Edith, impatiently—"Gracious saints! then wherefore wait you here, when each minute that passes is loaded with dishonour?"

"I have heard that I am dishonoured, lady, and I have heard it from you," answered Kenneth. "What reck I how soon punishment follows? I have but one petition to you, and then I seek, among the sabres of the infidels, whether dishonour may not be washed out with blood."

"Do not so, neither," said the lady. "Be wise, dally not here; all may yet be well, if you will but use dispatch."

"I wait but for your forgiveness," said the knight, still kneeling, "for my presumption in believing that my poor services could have been required or valued by you."

"I do forgive you—O, I have nothing to forgive!—I have been the means of injuring you—But O, begone!—I will forgive —I will value you—that is, as I value every brave Crusader—if you will but begone!"

"Receive first this precious yet fatal pledge," said the knight, tendering the ring to Edith, who now showed gestures of impatience.

"Oh, no, no," she said, declining to receive it. "Keep it, keep it as a mark of my regard—my regret, I would say. O begone, if not for your own sake, for mine !"

Almost recompensed for the loss even of honour, which her voice had denounced to him, by the interest which she seemed to testify in his safety, Sir Kenneth rose from his knee, and, casting a momentary glance on Edith, bowed low and seemed about to withdraw. At the same instant, that maidenly bashfulness, which the energy of Edith's feelings had till then triumphed over, became conqueror in its turn, and she hastened from the apartment, extinguishing her lamp as she went, and leaving, in Sir Kenneth's thoughts, both mental and natural gloom behind her.

She must be obeyed, was the first distinct idea which waked him from his reverie, and he hastened to the place by which he had entered the pavilion. To pass under the canvas in the manner he had entered, required time and attention, and he made a readier aperture by slitting the canvas wall with his poniard. When in the free air, he felt rather stupified and overpowered by a conflict of sensations, than able to ascertain what was the real import of the whole. He was obliged to spur himself to action, by recollecting that the commands of the Lady Edith had required haste. Even then, engaged as he was amongst tent-ropes and tents, he was compelled to move with caution until he should regain the path or avenue, aside from which the dwarf had led him, in order to escape the observations of the guards before the Queen's pavilion ; and he was obliged also to move slowly, and with precaution, to avoid giving an alarm, either by falling or by the clashing of his armour. A thin cloud had obscured the moon, too, at the very instant of his leaving the tent, and Sir Kenneth had to struggle with this inconvenience at a moment when the dizziness of his head, and the fulness of his heart, scarce left him powers of intelligence sufficient to direct his motions.

But at once sounds came upon his ear, which instantly recalled him to the full energy of his faculties. These proceeded from the Mount of Saint George. He heard first a single fierce, angry, and savage bark, which was immediately followed by a yell of agony. No deer ever bounded with a wilder start at the voice of Roswal, than did Sir Kenneth at what he feared was the death-cry of that noble hound, from whom no ordinary injury could have extracted even the slightest acknowledgment of pain. He surmounted the space which divided him from the avenue, and, having attained it, began to run towards the mount, although loaded with his mail, faster than most men could have accompanied him even if unarmed, relaxed not his pace for the steep sides of the artificial mound, and in a few minutes stood on the platform upon its summit.

The moon broke forth at this moment, and showed him that the standard of England was vanished, that the spear on which it had floated lay broken on the ground, and beside it was his faithful hound, apparently in the agonies of death.

CHAPTER XIV

——All my long arrear of honour lost,
Heap'd up in youth, and hoarded up for age!
Hath Honour's fountain then suck'd up the stream?
He hath—and hooting boys may barefoot pass,
And gather pebbles from the naked ford!

Don Sebastian.

AFTER a torrent of afflicting sensations, by which he was at first almost stunned and confounded, Sir Kenneth's first thought was to look for the authors of this violation of the English banner; but in no direction could he see traces of them. His next—which to some persons, but scarce to any who have made intimate acquaintances among the canine race, may appear strange—was to examine the condition of his faithful Roswal, mortally wounded, as it seemed, in discharging the duty which his master had been seduced to abandon. He caressed the dying animal, who, faithful to the last, seemed to forget his own pain in the satisfaction he received from his master's presence, and continued wagging his tail and licking his hand, even while by low moanings he expressed that his agony was increased by the attempts which Sir Kenneth made to withdraw from the wound the fragment of the lance, or javelin, with which it had been inflicted; then redoubled his feeble endearments, as if fearing he had offended his master by showing a sense of the pain to which his interference had subjected him. There was something in the display of the dying creature's attachment which mixed as a bitter ingredient with the sense of disgrace and desolation by which Sir Kenneth was oppressed. His only friend seemed removed from him, just when he had incurred the contempt and hatred of all besides. The knight's strength of mind gave way to a burst of agonized distress, and he groaned and wept aloud.

While he thus indulged his grief, a clear and solemn voice, close beside him, pronounced these words in the sonorous tone of the readers of the mosque, and in the lingua franca, mutually understood by Christians and Saracens :—

"Adversity is like the period of the former and of the latter rain—cold, comfortless, unfriendly to man and to animal; yet from that season have their birth the flower and the fruit, the date, the rose, and the pomegranate."

Sir Kenneth of the Leopard turned towards the speaker, and beheld the Arabian physician, who, approaching unheard, had seated himself a little behind him cross-legged, and uttered with gravity, yet not without a tone of sympathy, the moral sentences of consolation with which the Koran and its commentators supplied him ; for, in the East, wisdom is held to consist less in a display of the sage's own inventive talents than in his ready memory, and happy application of, and reference to, "that which is written."

Ashamed at being surprised in a woman-like expression of sorrow, Sir Kenneth dashed his tears indignantly aside, and again busied himself with his dying favourite.

"The poet hath said," continued the Arab, without noticing the knight's averted looks and sullen deportment—"' the ox for the field, and the camel for the desert.' Were not the hand of the leech fitter than that of the soldier to cure wounds, though less able to inflict them ?"

"This patient, Hakim, is beyond thy help," said Sir Kenneth ; "and besides, he is, by thy law, an unclean animal."

"Where Allah hath deigned to bestow life, and a sense of pain and pleasure," said the physician, "it were sinful pride should the sage, whom he has enlightened, refuse to prolong existence, or assuage agony. To the sage, the cure of a miserable groom, of a poor dog, and of a conquering monarch, are events of little distinction. Let me examine this wounded animal."

Sir Kenneth acceded in silence, and the physician inspected and handled Roswal's wound with as much care and attention as if he had been a human being. He then took forth a case of instruments, and, by the judicious and skilful application of pincers, withdrew from the wounded shoulder the fragment of the weapon, and stopped with styptics and bandages the effusion of blood which followed; the creature all the while suffering him patiently to perform these kind offices, as if he had been aware of his kind intentions.

"The animal may be cured," said El Hakim, addressing himself to Sir Kenneth, "if you will permit me to carry him to my tent, and treat him with the care which the nobleness of his nature deserves. For know, that thy servant Adonbec is no less skilful in the race and pedigree, and distinctions of good dogs and of noble steeds, than in the diseases which affect the human race."

"Take him with you," said the knight. "I bestow him on you freely if he recovers. I owe thee a reward for attendance on my squire, and have nothing else to pay it with. For myself, —I will never again wind bugle, or halloo to hound!"

The Arabian made no reply, but gave a signal with a clapping of his hands, which was instantly answered by the appearance of two black slaves. He gave them his orders in Arabic, received the answer, that "to hear was to obey," when, taking the animal in their arms, they removed him, without much resistance on his part; for, though his eyes turned to his master, he was too weak to struggle.

"Fare thee well, Roswal, then," said Sir Kenneth; "fare thee well, my last and only friend; thou art too noble a possession to be retained by one such as I must in future call myself.—I would," he said, as the slaves retired, "that, dying as he is, I could exchange conditions with that noble animal!"

"It is written," answered the Arabian, although the exclamation had not been addressed to him, "that all creatures are fashioned for the service of man; and the master of the earth speaketh folly when he would exchange, in his impatience, his hopes here and to come, for the servile condition of an inferior being."

"A dog who dies in discharging his duty," said the knight, sternly, "is better than a man who survives the desertion of it. Leave me, Hakim; thou hast, on this side of miracle, the most wonderful science which man ever possessed, but the wounds of the spirit are beyond thy power."

"Not if the patient will explain his calamity, and be guided by the physician," said Adonbec el Hakim.

"Know, then," said Sir Kenneth, "since thou art so importunate, that last night the banner of England was displayed from this mound—I was its appointed guardian— morning is now breaking—there lies the broken banner-spear —the standard itself is lost—and here sit I a living man!"

"How!" said El Hakim, examining him; "thy armour is whole, there is no blood on thy weapons, and report speaks thee one unlikely to return thus from fight.—Thou hast been trained from thy post—ay, trained by the rosy cheek and black eye of one of those houris, to whom you Nazarenes vow rather such service as is due to Allah, than such love as may lawfully be rendered to forms of clay like our own. It has been thus assuredly; for so hath man ever fallen, even since the days of Sultan Adam."

"And if it were so, physician," said Sir Kenneth, sullenly, "what remedy?"

"Knowledge is the parent of power," said El Hakim, "as valour supplies strength.—Listen to me. Man is not as a tree, bound to one spot of earth, nor is he framed to cling to one bare rock, like the scarce animated shell-fish. Thine own Christian writings command thee, when persecuted in one city, to flee to another; and we Moslems also know that Mohammed, the Prophet of Allah, driven forth from the holy city of Mecca, found his refuge and his helpmates at Medina."

"And what does this concern me?" said the Scot.

"Much," answered the physician. "Even the sage flies the tempest which he cannot control. Use thy speed, therefore, and fly from the vengeance of Richard to the shadow of Saladin's victorious banner."

"I might indeed hide my dishonour," said Sir Kenneth, ironically, "in a camp of infidel heathens, where the very phrase is unknown. But had I not better partake more fully in their reproach? Does not thy advice stretch so far as to recommend me to take the turban?—Methinks I want but apostasy to consummate my infamy."

"Blaspheme not, Nazarene," said the physician, sternly. "Saladin makes no converts to the law of the Prophet, save those on whom its precepts shall work conviction. Open thine eyes to the light, and the great Soldan, whose liberality is as boundless as his power, may bestow on thee a kingdom; remain blinded if thou wilt, and, being one whose second life is doomed to misery, Saladin will yet, for this span of present time, make thee rich and happy. But fear not that thy brows shall be bound with the turban, save at thine own free choice."

"My choice were rather," said the knight, "that my writhen features should blacken, as they are like to do, in this evening's setting sun."

"Yet thou art not wise, Nazarene," said El Hakim, "to

reject this fair offer; for I have power with Saladin, and can raise thee high in his grace. Look you, my son, this Crusade, as you call your wild enterprise, is like a large dromond parting asunder in the waves. Thou thyself hast borne terms of truce from the kings and princes, whose force is here assembled, to the mighty Soldan, and knew'st not, perchance, the full tenor of thine own errand."

"I knew not, and I care not," said the knight, impatiently; "what avails it to me that I have been of late the envoy of princes, when, ere night, I shall be a gibbeted and dishonoured corse?"

"Nay, I speak that it may not be so with thee," said the physician. "Saladin is courted on all sides; the combined princes of this league formed against him have made such proposals of composition and peace as, in other circumstances, it might have become his honour to have granted to them. Others have made private offers, on their own separate account, to disjoin their forces from the camp of the kings of Frangistan, and even to lend their arms to the defence of the standard of the Prophet. But Saladin will not be served by such treacherous and interested defection. The King of kings will treat only with the Lion King. Saladin will hold treaty with none but the Melech Ric, and with him he will treat like a prince, or fight like a champion. To Richard he will yield such conditions of his free liberality, as the swords of all Europe could never compel from him by force or terror. He will permit a free pilgrimage to Jerusalem, and all the places where the Nazarenes list to worship; nay, he will so far share even his empire with his brother Richard, that he will allow Christian garrisons in the six strongest cities of Palestine, and one in Jerusalem itself, and suffer them to be under the immediate command of the officers of Richard, who, he consents, shall bear the name of King Guardian of Jerusalem. Yet further, strange and incredible as you may think it, know, Sir Knight—for to your honour I can commit even that almost incredible secret—know that Saladin will put a sacred seal on this happy union betwixt the bravest and noblest of Frangistan and Asia, by raising to the rank of his royal spouse a Christian damsel, allied in blood to King Richard, and known by the name of the Lady Edith of Plantagenet."[1]

[1] This may appear so extraordinary and improbable a proposition, that it is necessary to say such a one was actually made. The historians, however, substitute the widowed Queen of Naples, sister of Richard, for

"Ha!—say'st thou?" exclaimed Sir Kenneth, who, listening with indifference and apathy to the preceding part of El Hakim's speech, was touched by this last communication, as the thrill of a nerve, unexpectedly jarred, will awaken the sensation of agony even in the torpor of palsy. Then, moderating his tone, by dint of much effort, he restrained his indignation, and, veiling it under the appearance of contemptuous doubt, he prosecuted the conversation, in order to get as much knowledge as possible of the plot, as he deemed it, against the honour and happiness of her whom he loved not the less that his passion had ruined, apparently, his fortunes at once and his honour. "And what Christian," he said, with tolerable calmness, "would sanction a union so unnatural, as that of a Christian maiden with an unbelieving Saracen?"

"Thou art but an ignorant, bigoted Nazarene," said the Hakim. "Seest thou not how the Mohammedan princes daily intermarry with the noble Nazarene maidens in Spain, without scandal either to Moor or Christian? And the noble Soldan will, in his full confidence in the blood of Richard, permit the English maid the freedom which your Frankish manners have assigned to women. He will allow her the free exercise of her religion,—seeing that, in very truth, it signifies but little to which faith females are addicted,—and he will assign her such place and rank over all the women of his zenana, that she shall be in every respect his sole and absolute Queen."

"What!" said Sir Kenneth, "darest thou think, Moslem, that Richard would give his kinswoman—a high-born and virtuous princess—to be, at best, the foremost concubine in the harem of a misbeliever! Know, Hakim, the meanest free Christian noble would scorn, on his child's behalf, such splendid ignominy."

"Thou errest," said the Hakim; "Philip of France, and Henry of Champagne, and others of Richard's principal allies, have heard the proposal without starting, and have promised, as far as they may, to forward an alliance that may end these wasteful wars; and the wise arch-priest of Tyre hath undertaken to break the proposal to Richard, not doubting that he shall be able to bring the plan to good issue. The Soldan's wisdom hath as yet kept his proposition secret from others,

the bride, and Saladin's brother for the bridegroom. They appear to have been ignorant of the existence of Edith of Plantagenet.—See MILL'S *History of the Crusades*, vol. ii. p. 61.

such as he of Montserrat, and the Master of the Templars, because he knows they seek to thrive by Richard's death or disgrace, not by his life or honour.—Up, therefore, Sir Knight, and to horse. I will give thee a scroll which shall advance thee highly with the Soldan; and deem not that you are leaving your country, or her cause, or her religion, since the interest of the two monarchs will speedily be the same. To Saladin thy counsel will be most acceptable, since thou canst make him aware of much concerning the marriages of the Christians, the treatment of their wives, and other points of their laws and usages, which, in the course of such treaty, it much concerns him that he should know. The right hand of the Soldan grasps the treasures of the East, and it is the fountain of generosity. Or, if thou desirest it, Saladin, when allied with England, can have but little difficulty to obtain from Richard not only thy pardon and restoration to favour, but an honourable command in the troops which may be left of the King of England's host, to maintain their joint government in Palestine. Up, then, and mount—there lies a plain path before thee."

"Hakim," said the Scottish knight, "thou art a man of peace—also, thou hast saved the life of Richard of England—and, moreover, of my own poor esquire, Strauchan. I have, therefore, heard to an end a matter, which, being propounded by another Moslem than thyself, I would have cut short with a blow of my dagger! Hakim, in return for thy kindness, I advise thee to see that the Saracen, who shall propose to Richard a union betwixt the blood of Plantagenet and that of his accursed race, do put on a helmet, which is capable to endure such a blow of a battle-axe as that which struck down the gate of Acre. Certes, he will be otherwise placed beyond the reach even of thy skill."

"Thou art, then, wilfully determined not to fly to the Saracen host?" said the physician—"Yet, remember, thou stayest to certain destruction; and the writings of thy law, as well as ours, prohibit man from breaking into the tabernacle of his own life."

"God forbid!" replied the Scot, crossing himself; "but we are also forbidden to avoid the punishment which our crimes have deserved. And, since so poor are thy thoughts of fidelity, Hakim, it grudges me that I have bestowed my good hound on thee, for, should he live, he will have a master ignorant of his value."

"A gift that is begrudged, is already recalled," said El Hakim, "only we physicians are sworn not to send away a patient uncured. If the dog recover, he is once more yours."

"Go to, Hakim," answered Sir Kenneth; "men speak not of hawk and hound when there is but an hour of day-breaking betwixt them and death. Leave me to recollect my sins and reconcile myself to Heaven."

"I leave thee in thine obstinacy," said the physician. "The mist hides the precipice from those who are doomed to fall over it."

He withdrew slowly, turning from time to time his head, as if to observe whether the devoted knight might not recall him either by word or signal. At last his turbaned figure was lost among the labyrinth of tents which lay extended beneath, whitening in the pale light of the dawning, before which the moonbeam had now faded away.

But although the physician Adonbec's words had not made that impression upon Kenneth which the sage desired, they had inspired the Scot with a motive for desiring life, which, dishonoured as he conceived himself to be, he was before willing to part from, as from a sullied vestment no longer becoming his wear. Much that had passed betwixt himself and the hermit, besides what he had observed between the anchorite and Sheerkohf, (or Ilderim,) he now recalled to recollection, and it tended to confirm what the Hakim had told him of the secret article of the treaty.

"The reverend impostor!" he exclaimed to himself; "the hoary hypocrite! He spoke of the unbelieving husband converted by the believing wife; and what do I know but that the traitor exhibited to the Saracen, accursed of God, the beauties of Edith Plantagenet, that the hound might judge if the princely Christian lady were fit to be admitted into the harem of a misbeliever? If I had yonder infidel Ilderim, or whatsoever he is called, again in the gripe with which I once held him fast as ever hound held hare, never again should *he* at least come on errand disgraceful to the honour of Christian king, or noble and virtuous maiden. But I—my hours are fast dwindling into minutes—yet, while I have life and breath, something must be done and speedily."

He paused for a few minutes, threw from him his helmet, then strode down the hill, and took the road to King Richard's pavilion.

CHAPTER XV

The feather'd songster, chanticleer,
   Had wound his bugle-horn,
And told the early villager
   The coming of the morn.
King Edward saw the ruddy streaks
   Of light eclipse the grey,
And heard the raven's croaking throat
   Proclaim the fated day.
"Thou'rt right," he said, "for, by the God
   That sit s enthroned on high,
Charles Bawdwin, and his fellows t wain,
   This day shall surely die."

                              CHATTERTON.

ON the evening on which Sir Kenneth assumed his post, Richard, after the stormy event which disurbed its tranquillity, had retired to rest in the plenitude of confidence inspired by his unbounded courage, and the superiority which he had displayed in carrying the point he aimed at in presence of the whole Christian host, and leaders, many of whom, he was aware, regarded in their secret souls the disgrace of the Austrian Duke as a triumph over themselves; so that his pride felt gratified, that in prostrating one enemy he had mortified a hundred.

Another monarch would have doubled his guards on the evening after such a scene, and kept at least a part of his troops under arms. But Cœur de Lion dismissed, upon the occasion, even his ordinary watch, and assigned to his soldiers a donative of wine to celebrate his recovery, and to drink to the banner of Saint George; and his quarter of the camp would have assumed a character totally devoid of vigilance and military preparation, but that Sir Thomas de Vaux, the Earl of Salisbury, and other nobles, took precautions to preserve order and discipline among the revellers.

The physician attended the King from his retiring to bed till midnight was past, and twice administered medicine to him during that period, always previously observing the quarter of heaven occupied by the full moon, whose influences he declared to be most sovereign, or most baleful, to the effect of his drugs. It was three hours after midnight ere El Hakim withdrew from the royal tent, to one which had been pitched for himself and his retinue. In his way thither he visited the tent of Sir Kenneth of the Leopard, in order to see the condition of his first patient in the Christian camp, old Strauchan, as the knight's esquire was named. Enquiring there for Sir

Kenneth himself, El Hakim learned on what duty he was employed, and probably this information led him to Saint George's Mount, where he found him whom he sought in the disastrous circumstances alluded to in the last chapter.

It was about the hour of sunrise, when a slow armed tread was heard approaching the King's pavilion; and ere De Vaux, who slumbered beside his master's bed as lightly as ever sleep sat upon the eyes of a watch-dog, had time to do more than arise and say, "Who comes?" the Knight of the Leopard entered the tent, with a deep and devoted gloom seated upon his manly features.

"Whence this bold intrusion, Sir Knight?" said De Vaux, sternly, yet in a tone which respected his master's slumbers.

"Hold, De Vaux!" said Richard, awakening on the instant; "Sir Kenneth cometh like a good soldier to render an account of his guard,—to such the General's tent is ever accessible." Then, rising from his slumbering posture, and leaning on his elbow, he fixed his large bright eye upon the warrior. "Speak, Sir Scot; thou comest to tell me of a vigilant, safe, and honourable watch, dost thou not? The rustling of the folds of the banner of England were enough to guard it, even without the body of such a knight as men hold thee."

"As men will hold me no more," said Sir Kenneth; "my watch hath neither been vigilant, safe, nor honourable. The banner of England has been carried off."

"And thou alive to tell it?" said Richard, in a tone of derisive incredulity. "Away, it cannot be. There is not even a scratch on thy face. Why dost thou stand thus mute? Speak the truth—it is ill jesting with a king—yet I will forgive thee if thou hast lied."

"Lied, Sir King!" returned the unfortunate knight, with fierce emphasis, and one glance of fire from his eye, bright and transient as the flash from the cold and stony flint. "But this also must be endured—I have spoken the truth."

"By God, and by Saint George!" said the King, bursting into fury, which, however, he instantly checked—"De Vaux, go view the spot—This fever has disturbed his brain—This cannot be—The man's courage is proof—It *cannot* be! Go—speedily—or send, if thou wilt not go."

The King was interrupted by Sir Henry Neville, who came, breathless, to say that the banner was gone, and the knight who guarded it overpowered, and most probably murdered, as there was a pool of blood where the banner-spear lay shivered.

"But whom do I see here?" said Neville, his eyes suddenly resting upon Sir Kenneth.

"A traitor," said the King, starting to his feet and seizing the curtal-axe, which was ever near his bed—"a traitor! whom thou shalt see die a traitor's death." And he drew back the weapon as in act to strike.

Colourless, but firm as a marble statue, the Scot stood before him, with his bare head uncovered by any protection, his eyes cast down to the earth, his lips scarcely moving, yet muttering probably in prayer. Opposite to him, and within the due reach for a blow, stood King Richard, his large person wrapped in the folds of his camiscia, or ample gown of linen, except where the violence of his action had flung the covering from his right arm, shoulder, and a part of his breast, leaving to view a specimen of a frame which might have merited his Saxon predecessor's epithet of Ironside. He stood for an instant prompt to strike, then, sinking the head of the weapon towards the ground, he exclaimed, "But there was blood, Neville—there was blood upon the place. Hark thee, Sir Scot—brave thou wert once, for I have seen thee fight. Say thou hast slain two of the thieves in defence of the standard—say but one—say thou hast struck but a good blow in our behalf, and get thee out of the camp with thy life and thy infamy!"

"You have called me liar, my Lord King," replied Kenneth, firmly; "and therein, at least, you have done me wrong. Know that there was no blood shed in defence of the standard save that of a poor hound, which, more faithful than his master, defended the charge which he deserted."

"Now, by Saint George!" said Richard, again heaving up his arm—But De Vaux threw himself between the King and the object of his vengeance, and spoke with the blunt truth of his character, "My liege, this must not be—here, nor by your own hand. It is enough of folly for one night and day, to have intrusted your banner to a Scot—said I not they were ever fair and false?"[1]

---

[1] Such were the terms in which the English used to speak of their poor northern neighbours, forgetting that their own encroachments u on the independence of Scotland obliged the weaker nation to defend themselves by policy as well as force. The disgrace must be divided between Edward I. and III., who enforced their domination over a free country, and the Scots, who were compelled to take compulsory oaths, without any purpose of keeping them.

"Thou didst, De Vaux; thou wast right, and I confess it," said Richard. "I should have known him better—I should have remembered how the fox William deceived me touching this Crusade."

"My lord," said Sir Kenneth, "William of Scotland never deceived; but circumstances prevented his bringing his forces."

"Peace, shameless!" said the King; "thou sulliest the name of a prince, even by speaking it—And yet, De Vaux, it is strange," he added, "to see the bearing of the man. Coward or traitor he must be, yet he abode the blow of Richard Plantagenet, as our arm had been raised to lay knighthood on his shoulder. Had he shown the slightest sign of fear, had but a joint trembled, or an eyelid quivered, I had shattered his head like a crystal goblet. But I cannot strike where there is neither fear nor resistance."

There was a pause.

"My lord," said Kenneth——

"Ha!" replied Richard, interrupting him, "hast thou found thy speech? Ask grace from Heaven, but none from me, for England is dishonoured through thy fault; and wert thou mine own and only brother, there is no pardon for thy fault."

"I speak not to demand grace of mortal man," said the Scot; "it is in your Grace's pleasure to give or refuse me time for Christian shrift; if man denies it, may God grant me the absolution which I would otherwise ask of his Church! But whether I die on the instant, or half an hour hence, I equally beseech your Grace for one moment's opportunity to speak that to your royal person, which highly concerns your fame as a Christian King."

"Say on," said the King, making no doubt that he was about to hear some confession concerning the loss of the banner.

"What I have to speak," said Sir Kenneth, "touches the royalty of England, and must be said to no ears but thine own."

"Begone with yourselves, sirs," said the King to Neville and De Vaux.

The first obeyed, but the latter would not stir from the King's presence.

"If you said I was in the right," replied De Vaux to his sovereign, "I will be treated as one should be who hath been found to be right—that is, I will have my own will. I leave you not with this false Scot."

"How, De Vaux!" said Richard, angrily, and stamping slightly, "darest thou not venture our person with one traitor?"

"It is in vain you frown and stamp, my lord," said De Vaux; "I venture not a sick man with a sound one, a naked man with one armed in proof."

"It matters not," said the Scottish knight, "I seek no excuse to put off time—I will speak in presence of the Lord of Gilsland. He is good lord and true."

"But half an hour since," said De Vaux, with a groan, implying a mixture of sorrow and vexation, "and I had said as much for thee!"

"There is treason around you, King of England," continued Sir Kenneth.

"It may well be as thou say'st," replied Richard; "I have a pregnant example."

"Treason that will injure thee more deeply than the loss of an hundred banners in a pitched field. The—the—" Sir Kenneth hesitated, and at length continued, in a lower tone, "the Lady Edith——"

"Ha!" said the King, drawing himself suddenly into a state of haughty attention, and fixing his eye firmly on the supposed criminal; "What of her?—what of her?—what has she to do with this matter?"

"My lord," said the Scot, "there is a scheme on foot to disgrace your royal lineage, by bestowing the hand of the Lady Edith on the Saracen Soldan, and thereby to purchase a peace most dishonourable to Christendom, by an alliance most shameful to England."

This communication had precisely the contrary effect from that which Sir Kenneth expected. Richard Plantagenet was one of those, who, in Iago's words, would not serve God because it was the devil who bade him; advice or information often affected him less according to its real import, than through the tinge which it took from the supposed character and views of those by whom it was communicated. Unfortunately, the mention of his relative's name renewed his recollection of what he had considered as extreme presumption in the Knight of the Leopard, even when he stood high in the rolls of chivalry, but which, in his present condition, appeared an insult sufficient to drive the fiery monarch into a frenzy of passion.

"Silence," he said, "infamous and audacious! By Heaven,

I will have thy tongue torn out with hot pincers, for mentioning the very name of a noble Christian damsel! Know, degenerate traitor, that I was already aware to what height thou hadst dared to raise thine eyes, and endured it, though it were insolence, even when thou hadst cheated us—for thou art all a deceit—into holding thee as of some name and fame. But now, with lips blistered with the confession of thine own dishonour—that thou shouldst *now* dare to name our noble kinswoman as one in whose fate thou hast part or interest!— What is it to thee, if she marry Saracen or Christian?—what is it to thee, if in a camp where princes turn cowards by day, and robbers by night, where brave knights turn to paltry deserters and traitors—what is it, I say, to thee, or any one, if I should please to ally myself to truth, and to valour, in the person of Saladin?"

"Little to me, indeed, to whom all the world will soon be as nothing," answered Sir Kenneth, boldly; "but were I now stretched on the rack, I would tell thee, that what I have said is much to thine own conscience and thine own fame. I tell thee, Sir King, that if thou dost but in thought entertain the purpose of wedding thy kinswoman, the Lady Edith——"

"Name her not, and for an instant think not of her," said the King, again straining the curtal-axe in his gripe, until the muscles started above his brawny arm, like cordage formed by the ivy around the limb of an oak.

"Not name—not think of her!" answered Sir Kenneth, his spirits, stunned as they were by self-depression, beginning to recover their elasticity from this species of controversy. "Now, by the Cross, on which I place my hope, her name shall be the last word in my mouth, her image the last thought in my mind! Try thy boasted strength on this bare brow, and see if thou canst prevent my purpose."

"He will drive me mad!" said Richard, who, in his despite, was once more staggered in his purpose by the dauntless determination of the criminal.

Ere Thomas of Gilsland could reply, some bustle was heard without, and the arrival of the Queen was announced from the outer part of the pavilion.

"Detain her—detain her, Neville!" cried the King; "this is no sight for women—Fie, that I have suffered such a paltry traitor to chafe me thus!—Away with him, De Vaux," he whispered, "through the back-entrance of our tent; coop him up close, and answer for his safe custody with your life.—

And hark ye, he is presently to die; let him have a ghostly father, we would not kill soul and body.—And stay, hark thee, we will not have him dishonoured—he shall die knight-like, in his belt and spurs; for if his treachery be as black as hell, his boldness may match that of the devil himself."

De Vaux, right glad, if the truth may be guessed, that the scene ended without Richard's descending to the unkingly act of himself slaying an unresisting prisoner, made haste to remove Sir Kenneth by a private issue to a separate tent, where he was disarmed and put in fetters for security. De Vaux looked on with a steady and melancholy attention, while the provost's officers, to whom Sir Kenneth was now committed, took these severe precautions.

When they were ended, he said solemnly to the unhappy criminal, "It is King Richard's pleasure that you die undegraded—without mutilation of your body, or shame to your arms—and that your head be severed from the trunk by the sword of the executioner."

"It is kind," said the knight, in a low and rather submissive tone of voice, as one who received an unexpected favour; "my family will not then hear the worst of the tale—Oh, my father! my father!"

This muttered invocation did not escape the blunt but kindly-natured Englishman, and he brushed the back of his large hand over his rough features, ere he could proceed.

"It is Richard of England's further pleasure," he said, at length, "that you have speech with a holy man, and I have met on the passage hither with a Carmelite friar, who may fit you for your passage. He waits without, until you are in a frame of mind to receive him."

"Let it be instantly," said the knight. "In this also Richard is kind. I cannot be more fit to see the good father at any time than now; for life and I have taken farewell, as two travellers who have arrived at the crossway, where their roads separate."

"It is well," said De Vaux, slowly and solemnly; "for it irks me somewhat to say that which sums my message. It is King Richard's pleasure that you prepare for instant death."

"God's pleasure and the King's be done," replied the knight, patiently. "I neither contest the justice of the sentence, nor desire delay of the execution."

De Vaux began to leave the tent, but very slowly—paused

at the door, and looked back at the Scot, from whose aspect thoughts of the world seemed banished, as if he was composing himself into deep devotion. The feelings of the stout English baron were in general none of the most acute, and yet, on the present occasion, his sympathy overpowered him in an unusual manner. He came hastily back to the bundle of reeds on which the captive lay, took one of his fettered hands, and said, with as much softness as his rough voice was capable of expressing, "Sir Kenneth, thou art yet young; thou hast a father. My Ralph, whom I left training his little Galloway nag on the banks of the Irthing, may one day attain thy years—and, but for last night, would to God I saw his youth bear such promise as thine!—Can nothing be said or done in thy behalf?"

"Nothing," was the melancholy answer. "I have deserted my charge—the banner intrusted to me is lost—When the headsman and block are prepared, the head and trunk are ready to part company."

"Nay, then, God have mercy!" said De Vaux; "yet would I rather than my best horse I had taken that watch myself. There is mystery in it, young man, as a plain man may descry, though he cannot see through it. Cowardice? pshaw! No coward ever fought as I have seen thee do.—Treachery? I cannot think traitors die in their treason so calmly. Thou hast been trained from thy post by some deep guile—some well-devised stratagem—the cry of some distressed maiden has caught thine ear, or the laughful look of some merry one has taken thine eye. Never blush for it, we have all been led aside by such gear. Come, I pray thee, make a clean conscience of it to me, instead of the priest—Richard is merciful when his mood is abated. Hast thou nothing to intrust to me?"

The unfortunate knight turned his face from the kind warrior, and answered, "NOTHING."

And De Vaux, who had exhausted his topics of persuasion, arose and left the tent, with folded arms, and in melancholy deeper than he thought the occasion merited, even angry with himself, to find that so simple a matter as the death of a Scottish man could affect him so nearly.

"Yet," as he said to himself, "though the rough-footed knaves be our enemies in Cumberland, in Palestine one almost considers them as brethren."

CHAPTER XVI

'Tis not her sense—for sure, in that
    There's nothing more than common;
And all her wit is only chat,
    Like any other woman.
                  Song.

THE high-born Berengaria, daughter of Sanchez, King of
Navarre, and the Queen-Consort of the heroic Richard, was
accounted one of the most beautiful women of the period.
Her form was slight, though exquisitely moulded. She was
graced with a complexion not common in her country, a
profusion of fair hair, and features so extremely juvenile as
to make her look several years younger than she really was,
though in reality she was not above one-and-twenty. Perhaps
it was under the consciousness of this extremely juvenile
appearance, that she affected, or at least practised, a little
childish petulance and wilfulness of manner, not unbefitting,
she might suppose, a youthful bride, whose rank and age gave
her a right to have her fantasies indulged and attended to.
She was by nature perfectly good-humoured, and if her due
share of admiration and homage (in her opinion a very large
one) was duly resigned to her, no one could possess better
temper, or a more friendly disposition; but then, like all
despots, the more power that was voluntarily yielded to her,
the more she desired to extend her sway. Sometimes, even
when all her ambition was gratified, she chose to be a little
out of health, and a little out of spirits; and physicians had to
toil their wits to invent names for imaginary maladies, while
her ladies racked their imagination for new games, new head-
gear, and new court-scandal, to pass away those unpleasant
hours, during which their own situation was scarce to be
greatly envied. Their most frequent resource for diverting
this malady was some trick, or piece of mischief, practised
upon each other; and the good Queen, in the buoyancy of
her reviving spirits, was, to speak truth, rather too indifferent
whether the frolics thus practised were entirely befitting her
own dignity, or whether the pain which those suffered upon
whom they were inflicted, was not beyond the proportion of
pleasure which she herself derived from them. She was
confident in her husband's favour, in her high rank, and in
her supposed power to make good whatever such pranks might
cost others. In a word, she gamboled with the freedom of a

young lioness, who is unconscious of the weight of her own paws when laid on those whom she sports with.

The Queen Berengaria loved her husband passionately, but she feared the loftiness and roughness of his character, and as she felt herself not to be his match in intellect, was not much pleased to see that he would often talk with Edith Plantagenet in preference to herself, simply because he found more amusement in her conversation, a more comprehensive understanding, and a more noble cast of thoughts and sentiments, than his beautiful consort exhibited. Berengaria did not hate Edith on this account, far less meditate her any harm; for, allowing for some selfishness, her character was, on the whole, innocent and generous. But the ladies of her train, sharp-sighted in such matters, had for some time discovered, that a poignant jest at the expense of the Lady Edith was a specific for relieving her Grace of England's low spirits, and the discovery saved their imagination much toil.

There was something ungenerous in this, because the Lady Edith was understood to be an orphan; and though she was called Plantagenet, and the Fair Maid of Anjou, and admitted by Richard to certain privileges only granted to the royal family, and held her place in the circle accordingly, yet few knew, and none acquainted with the Court of England ventured to ask, in what exact degree of relationship she stood to Cœur de Lion. She had come with Eleanor, the celebrated Queen-Mother of England, and joined Richard at Messina, as one of the ladies destined to attend on Berengaria, whose nuptials then approached. Richard treated his kinswoman with much respectful observance, and the Queen made her her most constant attendant, and, even in despite of the petty jealousy which we have observed, treated her generally with suitable respect.

The ladies of the household had, for a long time, no further advantage over Edith, than might be afforded by an opportunity of censuring a less artfully disposed head attire, or an unbecoming robe; for the lady was judged to be inferior in these mysteries. The silent devotion of the Scottish knight did not, indeed, pass unnoticed; his liveries, his cognisances, his feats of arms, his mottoes and devices, were nearly watched, and occasionally made the subject of a passing jest. But then came the pilgrimage of the Queen and her ladies to Engaddi, a journey which the Queen had undertaken under a vow for the recovery of her husband's health, and which she had been encouraged to carry into effect by the Archbishop of Tyre for a political purpose. It was then, and in the chapel at that holy place, connected from above with a Carmelite nunnery, from beneath with the cell of the anchorite, that one of the Queen's attendants remarked that secret sign of intelligence which Edith had made to her lover, and failed not instantly to communicate it to her Majesty. The Queen returned from her pilgrimage enriched with this admirable recipe against dulness or ennui, and her train was at the same time augmented by a present of two wretched dwarfs from the dethroned Queen of Jerusalem, as deformed and as crazy (the excellence of that unhappy species) as any queen could have desired. One of Berengaria's idle amusements had been to try the effect of the sudden appearance of such ghastly and fantastic forms on the nerves of the knight when left alone in the chapel; but the jest had been lost by the composure of the Scot, and the interference of the anchorite. She had now tried another, of which the consequences promised to be more serious.

The ladies again met after Sir Kenneth had retired from the tent; and the Queen, at first little moved by Edith's angry expostulations, only replied to her by upbraiding her prudery, and by indulging her wit at the expense of the garb, nation, and, above all, the poverty, of the Knight of the Leopard, in which she displayed a good deal of playful malice, mingled with some humour, until Edith was compelled to carry her anxiety to her separate apartment. But when, in the morning, a female, whom Edith had intrusted to make enquiry, brought word that the standard was missing, and its champion vanished, she burst into the Queen's apartment, and implored her to rise and proceed to the King's tent without delay, and use her powerful mediation to prevent the evil consequences of her jest.

The Queen, frightened in her turn, cast, as is usual, the blame of her own folly on those around her, and endeavoured to comfort Edith's grief, and appease her displeasure, by a thousand inconsistent arguments. She was sure no harm had chanced; the knight was sleeping, she fancied, after his night-watch. What though, for fear of the King's displeasure, he had deserted with the standard—it was but a piece of silk, and he but a needy adventurer; or if he was put under warding for a time, she would soon get the King to pardon him—it was but waiting to let Richard's mood pass away.

Thus she continued talking thick and fast, and heaping together all sorts of inconsistencies, with the vain expectation of persuading both Edith and herself that no harm could come of a frolic, which in her heart she now bitterly repented. But while Edith in vain strove to intercept this torrent of idle talk, she caught the eye of one of the ladies who entered the Queen's apartment. There was death in her look of affright and horror, and Edith, at the first glance of her countenance, had sunk at once on the earth, had not strong necessity, and her own elevation of character, enabled her to maintain at least external composure.

"Madam," she said to the Queen, "lose not another word in speaking, but save life—if, indeed," she added, her voice choking as she said it, "life may yet be saved."

"It may be—it may," answered the Lady Calista. "I have just heard that he has been brought before the King—it is not yet over—but," she added, bursting into a vehement flood of weeping, in which personal apprehensions had some share, "it will soon, unless some course be taken."

"I will vow a golden candlestick to the Holy Sepulchre—a shrine of silver to Our Lady of Engaddi—a pall, worth one hundred bezants, to Saint Thomas of Orthez," said the Queen in extremity.

"Up, up, madam!" said Edith; "call on the saints if you list, but be your own best saint."

"Indeed, madam," said the terrified attendant, "the Lady Edith speaks truth. Up, madam, and let us to King Richard's tent, and beg the poor gentleman's life."

"I will go—I will go instantly," said the Queen, rising and trembling excessively; while her women, in as great confusion as herself, were unable to render her those duties which were indispensable to her levee. Calm, composed, only pale as death, Edith ministered to the Queen with her own hand, and alone supplied the deficiencies of her numerous attendants.

"How you wait, wenches!" said the Queen, not able even then to forget frivolous distinctions. "Suffer ye the Lady Edith to do the duties of your attendance?—Seest thou, Edith, they can do nothing—I shall never be attired in time. We will send for the Archbishop of Tyre, and employ him as a mediator."

"O no, no!" exclaimed Edith—"Go yourself, madam; you have done the evil, do you confer the remedy."

"I will go—I will go," said the Queen; "but if Richard be in his mood, I dare not speak to him—he will kill me!"

"Yet go, gracious madam," said the Lady Calista, who best knew her mistress's temper; "not a lion in his fury could look upon such a face and form, and retain so much as an angry thought, far less a love-true knight like the royal Richard, to whom your slightest word would be a command."

"Dost thou think so, Calista?" said the Queen. "Ah, thou little knowest—yet I will go. But see you here, what means this? You have bedizened me in green, a colour he detests. Lo you! let me have a blue robe, and search for the ruby carcanet, which was part of the King of Cyprus's ransom —it is either in the steel casket, or somewhere else."

"This, and a man's life at stake!" said Edith, indignantly; "it passes human patience. Remain at your ease, madam—I will go to King Richard. I am a party interested—I will know if the honour of a poor maiden of his blood is to be so far tampered with, that her name shall be abused to train a brave gentleman from his duty, bring him within the compass of death and infamy, and make, at the same time, the glory of England a laughing-stock to the whole Christian army."

At this unexpected burst of passion, Berengaria listened with an almost stupified look of fear and wonder. But as Edith was about to leave the tent, she exclaimed, though faintly, "Stop her, stop her!"

"You must indeed stop, noble Lady Edith," said Calista, taking her arm gently; "and you, royal madam, I am sure, will go, and without further dallying. If the Lady Edith goes alone to the King, he will be dreadfully incensed, nor will it be one life that will stay his fury."

"I will go—I will go," said the Queen, yielding to necessity; and Edith reluctantly halted to wait her movements.

They were now as speedy as she could have desired. The Queen hastily wrapped herself in a large loose mantle, which covered all inaccuracies of the toilet. In this guise, attended by Edith and her women, and preceded and followed by a few officers and men-at-arms, she hastened to the tent of her lion-like husband.

CHAPTER XVII

Were every hair upon his head a life,
And every life were to be supplicated
By numbers equal to those hairs quadrupled,
Life after life should out like waning stars
Before the daybreak—or as festive lamps,
Which have lent lustre to the midnight revel,
Each after each are quench'd when guests depart!
Old Play.

THE entrance of Queen Berengaria into the interior of Richard's pavilion was withstood, in the most respectful and reverential manner indeed, but still withstood, by the chamberlains who watched in the outer tent. She could hear the stern command of the King from within, prohibiting their entrance.

"You see," said the Queen, appealing to Edith, as if she had exhausted all means of intercession in her power—"I knew it—the King will not receive us."

At the same time they heard Richard speak to some one within,—"Go, speed thine office quickly, sirrah, for in that consists thy mercy; ten bezants if thou deal'st on him at one blow.—And, hark thee, villain, observe if his cheek loses colour, or his eye falters; mark me the smallest twitch of the features, or wink of the eyelid—I love to know how brave souls meet death."

"If he sees my blade waved aloft without shrinking, he is the first ever did so," answered a harsh deep voice, which a sense of unusual awe had softened into a sound much lower than its usual coarse tones.

Edith could remain silent no longer. "If your Grace," she said to the Queen, "make not your own way, I make it for you; or if not for your Majesty, for myself, at least.—Chamberlains, the Queen demands to see King Richard—the wife to speak with her husband."

"Noble lady," said the officer, lowering his wand of office, "it grieves me to gainsay you; but his Majesty is busied on matters of life and death."

"And we seek also to speak with him on matters of life and death," said Edith.—"I will make entrance for your Grace."—And putting aside the chamberlain with one hand, she laid hold on the curtain with the other.

"I dare not gainsay her Majesty's pleasure," said the chamberlain, yielding to the vehemence of the fair petitioner; and, as he gave way, the Queen found herself obliged to enter the apartment of Richard.

The monarch was lying on his couch, and at some distance, as awaiting his further commands, stood a man whose profession it was not difficult to conjecture. He was clothed in a jerkin of red cloth, which reached scantly below the shoulders, leaving the arms bare from about half-way above the elbow, and as an upper garment he wore, when about as at present to betake himself to his dreadful office, a coat or tabard without sleeves, something like that of a herald, made of dressed bull's hide, and stained in the front with many a broad spot and speckle of dull crimson. The jerkin, and the tabard over it, reached the knee, and the nether stocks, or covering of the legs, were of the same leather which composed the tabard. A cap of rough shag served to hide the upper part of a visage, which, like that of a screech-owl, seemed desirous to conceal itself from light—the lower part of the face being obscured by a huge red beard, mingling with shaggy locks of the same colour. What features were seen were stern and misanthropical. The man's figure was short, strongly made, with a neck like a bull, very broad shoulders, arms of great and disproportioned length, a huge square trunk, and thick bandy legs. This truculent official leant on a sword, the blade of which was nearly four feet and a half in length, while the handle of twenty inches, surrounded by a ring of lead plummets to counterpoise the weight of such a blade, rose considerably above the man's head, as he rested his arm upon its hilt, waiting for King Richard's further directions.

On the sudden entrance of the ladies, Richard, who was then lying on his couch with his face towards the entrance, and resting on his elbow as he spoke to his grisly attendant, flung himself hastily, as if displeased and surprised, to the other side, turning his back to the Queen and the females of her train, and drawing around him the covering of his couch, which, by his own choice, or more probably the flattering selection of his chamberlains, consisted of two large lions' skins, dressed in Venice with such admirable skill that they seemed softer than the hide of the deer.

Berengaria, such as we have described her, knew well—what woman knows not?—her own road to victory. After a hurried glance of undisguised and unaffected terror at the ghastly companion of her husband's secret councils, she rushed at once to the side of Richard's couch, dropped on her knees, flung her mantle from her shoulders, showing, as they hung down at their full length, her beautiful golden tresses, and while her countenance seemed like the sun bursting through a cloud, yet bearing on its pallid front traces that its splendours have been obscured, she seized upon the right hand of the King, which, as he assumed his wonted posture, had been employed in dragging the covering of his couch, and gradually pulling it to her with a force which was resisted, though but faintly, she possessed herself of that arm, the prop of Christendom, and the dread of Heathenesse, and, imprisoning its strength in both her little fairy hands, she bent upon it her brow, and united to it her lips.

"What needs this, Berengaria?" said Richard, his head still averted, but his hand remaining under her control.

"Send away that man — his look kills me!" muttered Berengaria.

"Begone, sirrah," said Richard, still without looking round. "What wait'st thou for? art thou fit to look on these ladies?"

"Your Highness's pleasure touching the head," said the man.

"Out with thee, dog!" answered Richard, "a Christian burial!"

The man disappeared, after casting a look upon the beautiful Queen, in her deranged dress and natural loveliness, with a smile of admiration more hideous in its expression than even his usual scowl of cynical hatred against humanity.

"And now, foolish wench, what wishest thou?" said Richard, turning slowly and half reluctantly round to his royal suppliant.

But it was not in nature for any one, far less an admirer of beauty like Richard, to whom it stood only in the second rank to glory, to look without emotion on the countenance and the tremor of a creature so beautiful as Berengaria, or to feel, without sympathy, that her lips, her brow, were on his hand, and that it was wetted by her tears. By degrees he turned on her his manly countenance, with the softest expression of which his large blue eye, which so often gleamed with insufferable light, was capable. Caressing her fair head, and mingling his large fingers in her beautiful and dishevelled locks, he raised and tenderly kissed the cherub countenance which seemed desirous to hide itself in his hand. The robust form, the broad, noble brow, and majestic looks, the naked arm and shoulder, the lions' skins among which he lay, and the fair fragile feminine creature that kneeled by his side, might have served for a model of Hercules reconciling himself, after a quarrel, to his wife Dejanira.

"And, once more, what seeks the lady of my heart in her knight's pavilion, at this early and unwonted hour?"

"Pardon, my most gracious liege, pardon!" said the Queen, whose fears began again to unfit her for the duty of intercessor.

"Pardon! for what?" asked the King.

"First, for entering your royal presence too boldly and unadvisedly——"

She stopped.

"*Thou* too boldly!—The sun might as well ask pardon because his rays entered the windows of some wretch's dungeon. But I was busied with work unfit for thee to witness, my gentle one, and I was unwilling, besides, that thou shouldst risk thy precious health where sickness has been so lately rife."

"But thou art now well?" said the Queen, still delaying the communication which she feared to make.

"Well enough to break a lance on the bold crest of that champion who shall refuse to acknowledge thee the fairest dame in Christendom."

"Thou wilt not then refuse me one boon—only one—only a poor life?"

"Ha!—proceed," said King Richard, bending his brows.

"This unhappy Scottish knight——" murmured the Queen.

"Speak not of him, madam," exclaimed Richard, sternly; "he dies—his doom is fixed."

"Nay, my royal liege and love, 'tis but a silken banner neglected. Berengaria will give thee another broidered with her own hand, and rich as ever dallied with the wind. Every pearl I have shall go to bedeck it, and with every pearl I will drop a tear of thankfulness to my generous knight!"

"Thou knowest not what thou say'st," said the King, interrupting her in anger—"Pearls! can all the pearls of the East atone for a speck upon England's honour—all the tears that ever woman's eye wept wash away a stain on Richard's fame? —Go to, madam, know your place, and your time, and your sphere. At present we have duties in which you cannot be our partner."

"Thou hear'st, Edith," whispered the Queen, "we shall but incense him."

"Be it so," said Edith, stepping forward.—"My lord—I, your poor kinswoman, crave you for justice rather than mercy; and to the cry of justice the ears of a monarch should be open at every time, place, and circumstance."

"Ha! our cousin Edith?" said Richard, rising and sitting

upright on the side of his couch, covered with his long camiscia
—"She speaks ever king-like, and king-like will I answer her,
so she bring no request unworthy of herself or me."

The beauty of Edith was of a more intellectual and less
voluptuous cast than that of the Queen; but impatience and
anxiety had given her countenance a glow which it sometimes
wanted, and her mien had a character of energetic dignity that
imposed silence for a moment even on Richard himself, who,
to judge by his looks, would willingly have interrupted her

"My lord," she said, "this good knight, whose blood you
are about to spill, hath done, in his time, service to Christendom.
He hath fallen from his duty, through a snare set for him in
mere folly and idleness of spirit. A message sent to him
in the name of one who—why should I not speak it?—it was in
my own—induced him for an instant to leave his post—And
what knight in the Christian camp might not have thus far
transgressed at command of a maiden, who, poor howsoever
in other qualities, hath yet the blood of Plantagenet in her
veins?"

"And you saw him, then, cousin?" replied the King, biting
his lips to keep down his passion.

"I did, my liege," said Edith. "It is no time to explain
wherefore; I am here neither to exculpate myself nor to blame
others."

"And where did you do him such a grace?"

"In the tent of her Majesty the Queen."

"Of our royal consort!" said Richard. "Now by Heaven,
by Saint George of England, and every other saint that treads
its crystal floor, this is too audacious! I have noticed and
overlooked this warrior's insolent admiration of one so far
above him, and I grudged him not that one of my blood
should shed from her high-born sphere such influence as the
sun bestows on the world beneath—But, heaven and earth!
that you should have admitted him to an audience by night, in
the very tent of our royal consort! and dare to offer this as an
excuse for his disobedience and desertion! By my father's
soul, Edith, thou shalt rue this thy life long in a monastery!"

"My liege," said Edith, "your greatness licenses tyranny.
My honour, Lord King, is as little touched as yours, and my
lady the Queen can prove it if she think fit.—But I have
already said, I am not here to excuse myself or inculpate
others.—I ask you but to extend to one, whose fault was
committed under strong temptation, that mercy which even

you yourself, Lord King, must one day supplicate at a higher tribunal, and for faults, perhaps, less venial."

"Can this be Edith Plantagenet?" said the King, bitterly, —"Edith Plantagenet, the wise and the noble?—Or is it some love-sick woman, who cares not for her own fame in comparison of the life of her paramour? Now, by King Henry's soul! little hinders but I order thy minion's skull to be brought from the gibbet, and fixed as a perpetual ornament by the crucifix in thy cell!"

"And if thou dost send it from the gibbet to be placed for ever in my sight," said Edith, "I will say it is a relic of a good knight, cruelly and unworthily done to death by"—(she checked herself)—"by one, of whom I shall only say he should have known better how to reward chivalry. Minion call'st thou him?" she continued, with increasing vehemence. "He was indeed my lover, and a most true one; but never sought he grace from me by look or word, contented with such humble observance as men pay to the saints.—And the good, the valiant, the faithful, must die for this!"

"Oh, peace, peace, for pity's sake," whispered the Queen; "you do but offend him more!"

"I care not," said Edith; "the spotless virgin fears not the raging lion! Let him work his will on this worthy knight. Edith, for whom he dies, will know how to weep his memory; to me no one shall speak more of politic alliances, to be sanctioned with this poor hand. I could not—I would not—have been his bride living—our degrees were too distant. But death unites the high and the low—I am henceforward the spouse of the grave."

The King was about to answer with much anger, when a Carmelite monk entered the apartment hastily, his head and person muffled in the long mantle and hood of striped cloth of the coarsest texture, which distinguished his order, and flinging himself on his knees before the King, conjured him, by every holy word and sign, to stop the execution.

"Now, by both sword and sceptre!" said Richard, "the world are leagued to drive me mad!—Fools, women, and monks, cross me at every step. How comes he to live still?"

"My gracious liege," said the monk, "I entreated of the Lord of Gilsland to stay the execution until I had thrown myself at your royal——"

"And he was wilful enough to grant thy request?" said the

King; "but it is of a piece with his wonted obstinacy—And what is it thou hast to say? Speak, in the fiend's name!"

"My lord, there is a weighty secret—but it rests under the seal of confession—I dare not tell or even whisper it—but I swear to thee by my holy order—by the habit which I wear, by the blessed Elias, our founder, even him who was translated without suffering the ordinary pangs of mortality—that this youth hath divulged to me a secret, which, if I might confide it to thee, would utterly turn thee from thy bloody purpose in regard to him."

"Good father," said Richard, "that I reverence the Church, let the arms which I now wear for her sake bear witness. Give me to know this secret, and I will do what shall seem fitting in the matter. But I am no blind Bayard, to take a leap in the dark under the stroke of a pair of priestly spurs."

"My lord," said the holy man, throwing back his cowl and upper vesture, and discovering under the latter a garment of goat-skin, and from beneath the former a visage so wildly wasted by climate, fast, and penance, as to resemble rather the apparition of an animated skeleton than a human face, "for twenty years have I macerated this miserable body in the caverns of Engaddi, doing penance for a great crime. Think you I, who am dead to the world, would contrive a falsehood to endanger my own soul, or that one, bound by the most sacred oaths to the contrary—one such as I, who have but one longing wish connected with earth, to wit, the rebuilding of our Christian Zion—would betray the secrets of the confessional? Both are alike abhorrent to my very soul."

"So," answered the King, "thou art that hermit of whom men speak so much? Thou art, I confess, like enough to those spirits which walk in dry places, but Richard fears no hobgoblins; and thou art he, too, as I bethink me, to whom the Christian princes sent this very criminal to open a communication with the Soldan, even while I, who ought to have been first consulted, lay on my sick-bed? Thou and they may content themselves—I will not put my neck into the loop of a Carmelite's girdle. And for your envoy, he shall die, the rather and the sooner that thou dost entreat for him."

"Now God be gracious to thee, Lord King!" said the hermit, with much emotion; "thou art setting that mischief on foot which thou wilt hereafter wish thou hadst stopped, though it had cost thee a limb. Rash, blinded man, yet forbear!"

"Away, away," cried the King, stamping; "the sun has risen on the dishonour of England, and it is not yet avenged.—Ladies and priest, withdraw, if ye would not hear orders which would displease you; for, by Saint George, I swear——"

"Swear NOT!" said the voice of one who had just then entered the pavilion.

"Ha! my learned Hakim," said the King; "come, I hope, to tax our generosity."

"I come to request instant speech with you—instant, and touching matters of deep interest."

"First look on my wife, Hakim, and let her know in you the preserver of her husband."

"It is not for me," said the physician, folding his arms with an air of Oriental modesty and reverence, and bending his eyes on the ground,—"It is not for me to look upon beauty unveiled, and armed in its splendours."

"Retire, then, Berengaria," said the monarch; "and, Edith, do you retire also. Nay, renew not your importunities! This I give to them, that the execution shall not be till high noon. —Go, and be pacified.—Dearest Berengaria, begone.—Edith," he added, with a glance which struck terror even into the courageous soul of his kinswoman, "go, if you are wise."

The females withdrew, or rather hurried from the tent, rank and ceremony forgotten, much like a flock of wild-fowl huddled together, against whom the falcon has made a recent stoop.

They returned from thence to the Queen's pavilion, to indulge in regrets and recriminations, equally unavailing. Edith was the only one who seemed to disdain these ordinary channels of sorrow. Without a sigh, without a tear, without a word of upbraiding, she attended upon the Queen, whose weak temperament showed her sorrow in violent hysterical ecstasies, and passionate hypochondriacal effusions, in the course of which Edith sedulously, and even affectionately, attended her.

"It is impossible she can have loved this knight," said Florise to Calista, her senior in attendance upon the Queen's person. "We have been mistaken; she is but sorry for his fate, as for a stranger who has come to trouble on her account."

"Hush, hush," answered her more experienced and more observant comrade; "she is of that proud house of Plantagenet, who never own that a hurt grieves them. While they have themselves been bleeding to death under a mortal wound, they have been known to bind up the scratches sustained by their more faint-hearted comrades. — Florise, we have done frightfully wrong; and for my own part, I would buy with every jewel I have, that our fatal jest had remained unacted."

CHAPTER XVIII

This work desires a planetary intelligence
Of Jupiter and Sol; and those great spirits
Are proud, fantastical. It asks great charges
To entice them from the guiding of their spheres,
To wait on mortals.

ALBUMAZAR.

THE hermit followed the ladies from the pavilion of Richard, as shadow follows a beam of sunshine when the clouds are driving over the face of the sun. But he turned on the threshold, and held up his hand towards the King in a warning, or almost a menacing posture, as he said, "Woe to him who rejects the counsel of the Church, and betaketh himself to the foul divan of the infidel! King Richard, I do not yet shake the dust from my feet and depart from thy encampment—the sword falls not—but it hangs but by a hair.—Haughty monarch, we shall meet again."

"Be it so, haughty priest," returned Richard, "prouder in thy goat-skins than princes in purple and fine linen."

The hermit vanished from the tent, and the King continued, addressing the Arabian, "Do the dervises of the East, wise Hakim, use such familiarity with their princes?"

"The dervise," replied Adonbec, "should be either a sage or a madman; there is no middle course for him who wears the khirkhah, who watches by night, and fasts by day. Hence, hath he either wisdom enough to bear himself discreetly in the presence of princes, or else, having no reason bestowed on him, he is not responsible for his own actions."

"Methinks our monks have adopted chiefly the latter character," said Richard—"But to the matter. In what can I pleasure you, my learned physician?"

"Great King," said El Hakim, making his profound Oriental obeisance, "let thy servant speak one word, and yet live. I would remind thee that thou owest—not to me, their humble instrument—but to the Intelligences, whose benefits I dispense to mortals, a life——"

"And I warrant me thou wouldst have another in requital, ha?" interrupted the King.

"Such is my humble prayer," said the Hakim, "to the great Melech Ric—even the life of this good knight who is doomed to die, and but for such fault as was committed by the Sultan Adam, surnamed Aboulbeschar, or the father of all men."

"And thy wisdom might remind thee, Hakim, that Adam died for it," said the King, somewhat sternly, and then began to pace the narrow space of his tent with some emotion, and to talk to himself. "Why, God-a-mercy! I knew what he desired as soon as ever he entered the pavilion! Here is one poor life justly condemned to extinction, and I, a king and a soldier, who have slain thousands by my command, and scores with my own hand, am to have no power over it, although the honour of my arms, of my house, of my very Queen, hath been attainied by the culprit—By Saint George, it makes me laugh!— By Saint Louis, it reminds me of Blondel's tale of an enchanted castle, where the destined knight was withstood successively in his purpose of entrance by forms and figures the most dissimilar, but all hostile to his undertaking! No sooner one sunk than another appeared—Wife—kinswoman—hermit— Hakim—each appears in the lists as soon as the other is defeated!—Why, this is a single knight fighting against the whole *mêlée* of the tournament—ha! ha! ha!"—And Richard laughed aloud; for he had, in fact, begun to change his mood, his resentment being usually too violent to be of long endurance.

The physician meanwhile looked on him with a countenance of surprise, not unmingled with contempt; for the Eastern people make no allowance for those mercurial changes in the temper, and consider open laughter, upon almost any account, as derogatory to the dignity of man, and becoming only to women and children. At length, the sage addressed the King, when he saw him more composed.

"A doom of death should not issue from laughing lips.— Let thy servant hope that thou hast granted him this man's life."

"Take the freedom of a thousand captives instead," said Richard; "restore so many of thy countrymen to their tents and families, and I will give the warrant instantly. This man's life can avail thee nothing, and it is forfeited."

"All our lives are forfeited," said the Hakim, putting his hand to his cap. "But the great Creditor is merciful, and exacts not the pledge rigorously nor untimely."

"Thou canst show me," said Richard, "no special interest

thou hast to become intercessor betwixt me and the execution of justice, to which I am sworn as a crowned king."

"Thou art sworn to the dealing forth mercy as well as justice," said El Hakim; "but what thou seekest, great King, is the execution of thine own will. And for the concern I have in this request, know that many a man's life depends upon thy granting this boon."

"Explain thy words," said Richard; "but think not to impose upon me by false pretexts."

"Be it far from thy servant!" said Adonbec. "Know, then, that the medicine to which thou, Sir King, and many one beside, owe their recovery, is a talisman, composed under certain aspects of the heavens, when the Divine Intelligences are most propitious. I am but the poor administrator of its virtues. I dip it in a cup of water, observe the fitting hour to adminster it to the patient, and the potency of the draught works the cure."

"A most rare medicine," said the King, "and a commodious! and, as it may be carried in the leech's purse, would save the whole caravan of camels which they require to convey drugs and physic-stuff—I marvel there is any other in use."

"It is written," answered the Hakim, with imperturbable gravity, "'Abuse not the steed which hath borne thee from the battle.' Know, that such talismans might indeed be framed, but rare has been the number of adepts who have dared to undertake the application of their virtue. Severe restrictions, painful observances, fasts, and penance, are necessary on the part of the sage who uses this mode of cure; and if, through neglect of these preparations, by his love of ease, or his indulgence of sensual appetite, he omits to cure at least twelve persons within the course of each moon, the virtue of the divine gift departs from the amulet, and both the last patient and the physician will be exposed to speedy misfortune, neither will they survive the year. I require yet one life to make up the appointed number."

"Go out into the camp, good Hakim, where thou wilt find a-many," said the King, "and do not seek to rob my headsman of *his* patients; it is unbecoming a mediciner of thine eminence to interfere with the practice of another.—Besides, I cannot see how delivering a criminal from the death he deserves, should go to make up thy tale of miraculous cures."

"When thou canst show why a draught of cold water should have cured thee, when the most precious drugs failed," said the Hakim, "thou mayst reason on the other mysteries attendant on this matter. For myself, I am inefficient to the great work, having this morning touched an unclean animal. Ask, therefore, no further questions; it is enough that, by sparing this man's life at my request, you will deliver yourself, great King, and thy servant, from a great danger."

"Hark thee, Adonbec," replied the King, "I have no objection that leeches should wrap their words in mist, and pretend to derive knowledge from the stars; but when you bid Richard Plantagenet fear that a danger will fall upon *him* from some idle omen, or omitted ceremonial, you speak to no ignorant Saxon, or doting old woman, who foregoes her purpose because a hare crosses the path, a raven croaks, or a cat sneezes."

"I cannot hinder your doubt of my words," said Adonbec; "but yet, let my lord the King grant that truth is on the tongue of his servant. Will he think it just to deprive the world, and every wretch who may suffer by the pains which so lately reduced him to that couch, of the benefit of this most virtuous talisman, rather than extend his forgiveness to one poor criminal? Bethink you, Lord King, that, though thou canst slay thousands, thou canst not restore one man to health. Kings have the power of Satan to torment, sages that of Allah to heal; beware how thou hinderest the good to humanity, which thou canst not thyself render. Thou canst cut off the head, but not cure the aching tooth."

"This is over insolent," said the King, hardening himself, as the Hakim assumed a more lofty and almost a commanding tone. "We took thee for our leech, not for our counsellor, or conscience-keeper."

"And is it thus the most renowned Prince of Frangistan repays benefit done to his royal person?" said El Hakim, exchanging the humble and stooping posture, in which he had hitherto solicited the King, for an attitude lofty and commanding. "Know, then," he said, "that through every court of Europe and Asia—to Moslem and Nazarene—to knight and lady—wherever harp is heard and sword worn—wherever honour is loved and infamy detested, to every quarter of the world will I denounce thee, Melech Ric, as thankless and ungenerous; and even the lands—if there be any such—that never heard of thy renown, shall yet be acquainted with thy shame!"

"Are these terms to me, vile infidel," said Richard, striding up to him in fury. "Art weary of thy life?"

"Strike!" said El Hakim; "thine own deed shall then paint thee more worthless than could my words, though each had an hornet's sting."

Richard turned fiercely from him, folded his arms, traversed the tent as before, and then exclaimed, "Thankless and ungenerous?—as well be termed coward and infidel!—Hakim, thou hast chosen thy boon; and though I had rather thou hadst asked my crown-jewels, yet I may not, king-like, refuse thee. Take this Scot, therefore, to thy keeping; the provost will deliver him to thee on this warrant."

He hastily traced one or two lines, and gave them to the physician. "Use him as thy bond-slave, to be disposed of as thou wilt—only, let him beware how he comes before the eyes of Richard. Hark thee, thou art wise; he hath been over bold among those in whose fair looks and weak judgments we trust our honour, as you of the East lodge your treasures in caskets of silver wire, as fine and as frail as the web of a gossamer."

"Thy servant understands the words of the King," said the sage, at once resuming the reverent style of address in which he had commenced. "When the rich carpet is soiled, the fool pointeth to the stain, the wise man covers it with his mantle. I have heard my lord's pleasure, and to hear is to obey."

"It is well," said the King; "let him consult his own safety, and never appear in my presence more.—Is there aught else in which I may do thee pleasure?"

"The bounty of the King hath filled my cup to the brim," said the sage; "yea, it hath been abundant as the fountain which sprung up amid the camp of the descendants of Israel, when the rock was stricken by the rod of Moussa Ben Amran."

"Ay, but," said the King, smiling, "it required, as in the desert, a hard blow on the rock ere it yielded its treasures. I would that I knew something to pleasure thee, which I might yield as freely as the natural fountain sends forth its waters."

"Let me touch that victorious hand," said the sage, "in token, that if Adonbec el Hakim should hereafter demand a boon of Richard of England, he may do so, yet plead his command."

"Thou hast hand and glove upon it, man," replied Richard; "only, if thou couldst consistently make up thy tale of patients without craving me to deliver from punishment those who have deserved it, I would more willingly discharge my debt in some other form."

"May thy days be multiplied!" answered the Hakim, and withdrew from the apartment after the usual deep obeisance.

King Richard gazed after him as he departed, like one but half-satisfied with what had passed.

"Strange pertinacity," he said, "in this Hakim, and a wonderful chance to interfere between that audacious Scot and the chastisement he has merited so richly. Yet, let him live! there is one brave man the more in the world.—And now for the Austrian.—Ho, is the Baron of Gilsland there without?"

Sir Thomas de Vaux thus summoned, his bulky form speedily darkened the opening of the pavilion, while behind him glided as a spectre, unannounced, yet unopposed, the savage form of the hermit of Engaddi, wrapped in his goat-skin mantle.

Richard, without noticing his presence, called in a loud tone to the baron, "Sir Thomas de Vaux of Lanercost and Gilsland, take trumpet and herald, and go instantly to the tent of him whom they call Archduke of Austria, and see that it be when the press of his knights and vassals is greatest around him,— as is likely at this hour, for the German boar breakfasts ere he hears mass,—enter his presence with as little reverence as thou mayst, and impeach him, on the part of Richard of England, that he hath this night, by his own hand, or that of others, stolen from its staff the banner of England. Wherefore, say to him our pleasure, that, within an hour from the time of my speaking, he restore the said banner with all reverence—he himself and his principal barons waiting the whilst with heads uncovered, and without their robes of honour; and that, more-over, he pitch beside it, on the one hand, his own banner of Austria reversed, as that which hath been dishonoured by theft and felony—and, on the other, a lance, bearing the bloody head of him who was his nearest counsellor, or assistant, in this base injury; and say that, such our behests being punctually dis-charged, we will, for the sake of our vow, and the weal of the Holy Land, forgive his other forfeits."

"And how if the Duke of Austria deny all accession to this act of wrong and of felony?" said Thomas de Vaux.

"Tell him," replied the King, "we will prove it upon his body—ay, were he backed with his two bravest champions. Knight-like will we prove it, on foot or on horse, in the desert or in the field, time, place, and arms, all at his own choice."

" Bethink you of the peace of God and the Church, my liege lord," said the Baron of Gilsland, " among those princes engaged in this holy Crusade."

" Bethink you how to execute my commands, my liege vassal," answered Richard, impatiently. " Methinks men expect to turn our purpose by their breath, as boys blow feathers to and fro—Peace of the Church!—who, I prithee, minds it? The peace of the Church, among Crusaders, implies war with the Saracens, with whom the princes have made truce, and the one ends with the other. And, besides, see you not how every prince of them is seeking his own several ends?— I will seek mine also, and that is honour. For honour I came hither, and if I may not win it upon the Saracens, at least I will not lose a jot from any respect to this paltry Duke, though he were bulwarked and buttressed by every prince in the Crusade."

De Vaux turned to obey the King's mandate, shrugging his shoulders at the same time, the bluntness of his nature being unable to conceal that its tenor went against his judgment. But the hermit of Engaddi stepped forward, and assumed the air of one charged with higher commands than those of a mere earthly potentate. Indeed, his dress of shaggy skins, his uncombed and untrimmed hair and beard, his lean, wild, and contorted features, and the almost insane fire which gleamed from under his bushy eyebrows, made him approach nearly to our idea of some seer of Scripture, who, charged with high mission to the sinful kings of Judah or Israel, descended from the rocks and caverns in which he dwelt in abstracted solitude, to abash earthly tyrants in the midst of their pride, by discharging on them the blighting denunciations of Divine Majesty, even as the cloud discharges the lightnings with which it is fraught, on the pinnacles and towers of castles and palaces. In the midst of his most wayward mood, Richard respected the Church and its ministers, and though offended at the intrusion of the hermit into his tent, he greeted him with respect; at the same time, however, making a sign to Sir Thomas de Vaux to hasten on his message.

But the hermit prohibited the baron, by gesture, look, and word, to stir a yard on such an errand; and holding up his bare arm, from which the goat-skin mantle fell back in the violence of his action, he waved it aloft, meagre with famine, and wealed with the blows of the discipline.

" In the name of God, and of the most holy Father, the vicegerent of the Christian Church upon earth, I prohibit this most profane, bloodthirsty, and brutal defiance, betwixt two Christian princes, whose shoulders are signed with the blessed mark under which they swore brotherhood. Woe to him by whom it is broken!—Richard of England, recall the most unhallowed message thou hast given to that baron—Danger and Death are nigh thee!—the dagger is glancing at thy very throat——!"

"Danger and Death are playmates to Richard," answered the monarch proudly; "and he hath braved too many swords to fear a dagger."

"Danger and Death are near," replied the seer; and sinking his voice to a hollow, unearthly tone, he added, "And after death the judgment!"

"Good and holy father," said Richard, "I reverence thy person and thy sanctity——"

"Reverence not me!" interrupted the hermit; "reverence sooner the vilest insect that crawls by the shores of the Dead Sea, and feeds upon its accursed slime. But reverence Him whose commands I speak—Reverence Him whose sepulchre you have vowed to rescue—Revere the oath of concord which you have sworn, and break not the silver cord of union and fidelity with which you have bound yourself to your princely confederates."

"Good father," said the King, "you of the Church seem to me to presume somewhat, if a layman may say so much, upon the dignity of your holy character. Without challenging your right to take charge of our conscience, methinks you might leave us the charge of our own honour."

"Presume!" repeated the hermit; "is it for me to presume, royal Richard, who am but the bell obeying the hand of the sexton—but the senseless and worthless trumpet, carrying the command of him who sounds it?—See, on my knees I throw myself before thee, imploring thee to have mercy on Christendom, on England, and on thyself!"

"Rise, rise," said Richard, compelling him to stand up; "it beseems not that knees, which are so frequently bended to the Deity, should press the ground in honour of man. What danger awaits us, reverend father? and when stood the power of England so low that the noisy bluster of this new-made Duke's displeasure should alarm her, or her monarch?"

"I have looked forth from my mountain turret upon the starry host of heaven, as each in his midnight circuit uttered wisdom to another, and knowledge to the few who can under-stand their voice. There sits an enemy in thy House of Life, Lord King, malign at once to thy fame, and thy prosperity—an emanation of Saturn, menacing thee with instant and bloody peril, and which, but thou yield thy proud will to the rule of thy duty, will presently crush thee, even in thy pride."

"Away, away! this is heathen science," said the King. "Christians practise it not—wise men believe it not.—Old man, thou dotest."

"I dote not, Richard," answered the hermit; "I am not so happy. I know my condition, and that some portion of reason is yet permitted me, not for my own use, but that of the Church, and the advancement of the Cross. I am the blind man who holds a torch to others, though it yields no light to himself. Ask me touching what concerns the weal of Christen-dom, and of this Crusade, and I will speak with thee as the wisest counsellor on whose tongue persuasion ever sat. Speak to me of my own wretched being, and my words shall be those of the maniac outcast which I am."

"I would not break the bands of unity asunder among the princes of the Crusade," said Richard, with a mitigated tone and manner; "but what atonement can they render me for the injustice and insult which I have sustained?"

"Even of that I am prepared and commissioned to speak by the Council, which, meeting hastily at the summons of Philip of France, have taken measures for that effect."

"Strange," replied Richard, "that others should treat of what is due to the wounded majesty of England!"

"They are willing to anticipate your demands, if it be possible," answered the hermit. "In a body, they consent that the banner of England be replaced on Saint George's Mount, and they lay under ban and condemnation the audacious criminal, or criminals, by whom it was outraged, and will announce a princely reward to any who shall denounce the delinquent's guilt, and give his flesh to the wolves and ravens."

"And Austria," said Richard, "upon whom rest such strong presumptions that he was the author of the deed?"

"To prevent discord in the host," replied the hermit, "Austria will clear himself of the suspicion, by submitting to whatsoever ordeal the Patriarch of Jerusalem shall impose."

"Will he clear himself by the trial by combat?" said King Richard.

"His oath prohibits it," said the hermit; "and, moreover, the Council of the Princes——"

"Will neither authorize battle against the Saracens," interrupted Richard, "nor against any one else. But it is enough, father; thou hast shown me the folly of proceeding as I designed in this matter. You shall sooner light your torch in a puddle of rain, than bring a spark out of a cold-blooded coward. There is no honour to be gained on Austria, and so let him pass.—I will have him perjure himself, however; I will insist on the ordeal.—How I shall laugh to hear his clumsy fingers hiss, as he grasps the red-hot globe of iron!—Ay, or his huge mouth riven, and his gullet swelling to suffocation, as he endeavours to swallow the consecrated bread!"

"Peace, Richard," said the hermit. "Oh, peace, for shame if not for charity! Who shall praise or honour princes who insult and calumniate each other? Alas! that a creature so noble as thou art—so accomplished in princely thoughts and princely daring — so fitted to honour Christendom by thy actions, and, in thy calmer mood, to rule her by thy wisdom, should yet have the brute and wild fury of the lion, mingled with the dignity and courage of that king of the forest!"

He remained an instant musing with his eyes fixed on the ground, and then proceeded,—"But Heaven, that knows our imperfect nature, accepts of our imperfect obedience, and hath delayed, though not averted, the bloody end of thy daring life. The destroying angel hath stood still, as of old, by the threshing-floor of Araunah the Jebusite, and the blade is drawn in his hand, by which, at no distant date, Richard the Lion-hearted shall be as low as the meanest peasant."

"Must it then be so soon?" said Richard. "Yet, even so be it. May my course be bright, if it be but brief."

"Alas! noble King," said the solitary, and it seemed as if a tear (unwonted guest) were gathering in his dry and glazened eye; "short and melancholy, marked with mortification, and calamity, and captivity, is the span that divides thee from the grave which yawns for thee—a grave in which thou shalt be laid, without lineage to succeed thee, without the tears of a people, exhausted by thy ceaseless wars, to lament thee, without having extended the knowledge of thy subjects, without having done aught to enlarge their happiness."

"But not without renown, monk, not without the tears of the lady of my love! These consolations, which thou canst neither know nor estimate, await upon Richard to his grave."

"*Do* I not know—*can* I not estimate, the value of minstrel's praise, and of lady's love!" retorted the hermit, in a tone which for a moment seemed to emulate the enthusiasm of Richard himself. "King of England," he continued, extending his emaciated arm, "the blood which boils in thy blue veins is not more noble than that which stagnates in mine. Few and cold as the drops are, they still are of the blood of the royal Lusignan—of the heroic and sainted Godfrey. I am —that is, I was when in the world—Alberick Mortemar——"

".Whose deeds," said Richard, "have so often filled Fame's trumpet! Is it so?—can it be so?—Could such a light as thine fall from the horizon of chivalry, and yet men be uncertain where its embers had alighted?"

"Seek a fallen star," said the hermit, "and thou shalt only light on some foul jelly, which, in shooting through the horizon, has assumed for a moment an appearance of splendour. Richard, if I thought that rending the bloody veil from my horrible fate could make thy proud heart stoop to the discipline of the Church, I could find in my heart to tell thee a tale, which I have hitherto kept gnawing at my vitals in conceal- ment, like the self-devoted youth of Heathenesse. Listen, then, Richard, and may the grief and despair, which cannot avail this wretched remnant of what was once a man, be powerful as an example to so noble, yet so wild a being as thou art! Yes, I will—I *will* tear open the long hidden wounds, although in thy very presence they should bleed to death!"

King Richard, upon whom the history of Alberick of Mortemar had made a deep impression in his early years, when minstrels were regaling his father's halls with legends of the Holy Land, listened with respect to the outlines of a tale, which, darkly and imperfectly sketched, indicated sufficiently the cause of the partial insanity of this singular and most unhappy being.

"I need not," he said, "tell thee that I was noble in birth, high in fortune, strong in arms, wise in counsel. All these I was ; but while the noblest ladies in Palestine strove which should wind garlands for my helmet, my love was fixed— unalterably and devotedly fixed—on a maiden of low degree. Her father, an ancient soldier of the Cross, saw our passion, and knowing the difference betwixt us, saw no other refuge for his daughter's honour than to place her within the shadow of the cloister. I returned from a distant expedition, loaded with spoils and honour, to find my happiness was destroyed for ever! I, too, sought the cloister, and Satan, who had marked me for his own, breathed into my heart a vapour of spiritual pride, which could only have had its source in his own infernal regions. I had risen as high in the Church as before in the State—I was, forsooth, the wise, the self-sufficient, the impeccable!—I was the counsellor of councils—I was the director of prelates—how should I stumble—wherefore should I fear temptation?—Alas! I became confessor to a sisterhood, and amongst that sisterhood I found the long-loved, the long-lost. Spare me further confession!—A fallen nun, whose guilt was avenged by self-murder, sleeps soundly in the vaults of Engaddi, while above her very grave, gibbers, moans, and roars a creature, to whom but so much reason is left as may suffice to render him completely sensible to his fate!"

"Unhappy man!" said Richard, "I wonder no longer at thy misery. How didst thou escape the doom, which the canons denounce against thy offence?"

"Ask one who is yet in the gall of worldly bitterness," said the hermit, "and he will speak of a life spared for personal respects, and from consideration to high birth. But, Richard, *I* tell thee, that Providence hath preserved me, to lift me on high as a light and beacon, whose ashes, when this earthly fuel is burnt out, must yet be flung into Tophet. Withered and shrunk as this poor form is, it is yet animated with two spirits—one active, shrewd, and piercing, to advocate the cause of the Church of Jerusalem; one mean, abject, and despairing, fluctuating between madness and misery, to mourn over my own wretchedness, and to guard holy relics, on which it would be most sinful for me even to cast my eye. Pity me not!—it is but sin to pity the loss of such an abject—pity me not, but profit by my example. Thou standest on the highest, and therefore on the most dangerous pinnacle, occupied by any Christian prince. Thou art proud of heart, loose of life, bloody of hand. Put from thee the sins which are to thee as daughters; though they be dear to the sinful Adam, expel these adopted furies from thy breast—thy pride, thy luxury, thy blood-thirstiness!"

"He raves," said Richard, turning from the solitary to De Vaux, as one who felt some pain from a sarcasm which yet he could not resent; then turned him calmly, and somewhat scornfully, to the anchoret, as he replied, "Thou hast found a fair bevy of daughters, reverend father, to one who hath been but few months married; but since I must put them from my roof, it were but like a father to provide them with suitable matches. Wherefore, I will part with my pride to the noble Canons of the Church—my luxury, as thou call'st it, to the Monks of the rule—and my blood-thirstiness to the Knights of the Temple."

"Oh, heart of steel, and hand of iron," said the anchoret, "upon whom example, as well as advice, is alike thrown away! —Yet thou shalt be spared for a season, in case it so be thou shouldst turn and do that which is acceptable in the sight of Heaven.—For me, I must return to my place.—Kyrie Eleison! —I am he through whom the rays of heavenly grace dart like those of the sun through a burning-glass, concentrating them on other objects, until they kindle and blaze, while the glass itself remains cold and uninfluenced.—Kyrie Eleison!—the poor must be called, for the rich have refused the banquet.—Kyrie Eleison!"

So saying, he burst from the tent, uttering loud cries.

"A mad priest!" said Richard, from whose mind the frantic exclamations of the hermit had partly obliterated the impression produced by the detail of his personal history and misfortunes. "After him, De Vaux, and see he comes to no harm; for, Crusaders as we are, a juggler hath more reverence amongst our varlets than a priest or a saint, and they may, perchance, put some scorn upon him."

The knight obeyed, and Richard presently gave way to the thoughts which the wild prophecy of the monk had inspired. —"To die early, without lineage, without lamentation?—a heavy sentence, and well that it is not passed by a more competent judge. Yet the Saracens, who are accomplished in mystical knowledge, will often maintain that He, in whose eyes the wisdom of the sage is but as folly, inspires wisdom and prophecy into the seeming folly of the madman. Yonder hermit is said to read the stars too, an art generally practised in these lands, where the heavenly host was of yore the object of idolatry. I would I had asked him touching the loss of my banner; for not the blessed Tishbite, the founder of his order, could seem more wildly rapt out of himself, or speak with a tongue more resembling that of a prophet.—How now, De Vaux what news of the mad priest?"

"Mad priest, call you him, my lord?" answered De Vaux. "Methinks he resembles more the blessed Baptist himself, just issued from the wilderness. He has placed himself on one of the military engines, and from thence he preaches to the soldiers, as never man preached since the time of Peter the Hermit. The camp, alarmed by his cries, crowd around him in thousands; and, breaking off every now and then from the main thread of his discourse, he addresses the several nations, each in their own language, and presses upon each the arguments best qualified to urge them to perseverance in the delivery of Palestine."

"By this light, a noble hermit!" said King Richard. "But what else could come from the blood of Godfrey? *He* despair of safety, because he hath in former days lived *par amours?* I will have the Pope send him an ample remission, and I would not less willingly be intercessor had his *belle amie* been an abbess."

As he spoke, the Archbishop of Tyre craved audience, for the purpose of requesting Richard's attendance, should his health permit, on a secret conclave of the chiefs of the Crusade, and to explain to him the military and political incidents which had occurred during his illness.

CHAPTER XIX

> Must we then sheathe our still victorious sword;
> Turn back our forward step, which ever trode
> O'er foemen's necks the onward path of glory;
> Unclasp the mail, which with a solemn vow
> In God's own house, we hung upon our shoulders;
> That vow, as unaccomplish'd as the promise
> Which village nurses make to still their children,
> And after think no more of?——
>
> *The Crusade, a Tragedy.*

THE Archbishop of Tyre was an emissary well chosen to communicate to Richard tidings, which from another voice the lion-hearted King would not have brooked to hear, without the most unbounded explosions of resentment. Even this sagacious and reverend prelate found difficulty in inducing him to listen to news, which destroyed all his hopes of gaining back the Holy Sepulchre by force of arms, and acquiring the renown, which the universal all-hail of Christendom was ready to confer upon him, as the Champion of the Cross.

But by the Archbishop's report it appeared that Saladin was assembling all the force of his hundred tribes, and that the monarchs of Europe, already disgusted from various motives with the expedition, which had proved so hazardous, and was daily growing more so, had resolved to abandon their purpose. In this they were countenanced by the example of Philip of France, who, with many protestations of regard, and assurances that he would first see his brother of England in safety, declared his intention to return to Europe. His great vassal, the Earl of Champagne, had adopted the same resolution; and it could not excite surprise that Leopold of Austria, affronted as he had been by Richard, was glad to embrace an opportunity of deserting a cause in which his haughty opponent was to be considered as chief. Others announced the same purpose; so that it was plain that the King of England was to be left, if he chose to remain, supported only by such volunteers as might, under such depressing circumstances, join themselves to the English army; and by the doubtful aid of Conrade of Montserrat, and the military orders of the Temple, and of Saint John, who, though they were sworn to wage battle against the Saracens, were at least equally jealous of any European monarch achieving the conquest of Palestine, where, with short-sighted and selfish policy, they proposed to establish independent dominions of their own.

It needed not many arguments to show Richard the truth of his situation; and indeed, after his first burst of passion, he sat him calmly down, and with gloomy looks, head depressed, and arms folded on his bosom, listened to the Archbishop's reasoning on the impossibility of his carrying on the Crusade when deserted by his companions. Nay, he forebore interruption, even when the prelate ventured in measured terms to hint that Richard's own impetuosity had been one main cause of disgusting the princes with the expedition.

"*Confiteor*," answered Richard, with a dejected look, and something of a melancholy smile; "I confess, reverend father, that I ought on some accounts to sing *culpa mea*. But is it not hard that my frailties of temper should be visited with such a penance, that, for a burst or two of natural passion, I should be doomed to see fade before me ungathered such a rich harvest of glory to God, and honour to chivalry?—But it shall *not* fade.—By the soul of the Conqueror, I will plant the Cross on the towers of Jerusalem, or it shall be planted over Richard's grave!"

"Thou mayst do it," said the prelate, "yet not another drop of Christian blood be shed in the quarrel."

"Ah, you speak of compromise, Lord Prelate—but the

blood of the infidel hounds must also cease to flow," said Richard.

"There will be glory enough," replied the Archbishop, "in having extorted from Saladin, by force of arms, and by the respect inspired by your fame, such conditions as at once restore the Holy Sepulchre, open the Holy Land to pilgrims, secure their safety by strong fortresses, and, stronger than all, assure the safety of the Holy City, by conferring on Richard the title of King Guardian of Jerusalem."

"How!" said Richard, his eyes sparkling with unusual light, "I—I—I the King Guardian of the Holy City! Victory itself, but that it *is* victory, could not gain more, scarce so much, when won with unwilling and disunited forces. But Saladin still proposes to retain his interest in the Holy Land?"

"As a joint sovereign, the sworn ally," replied the prelate, "of the mighty Richard—his relative, if it may be permitted, by marriage."

"By marriage!" said Richard, surprised, yet less so than the prelate had expected. "Ha!—Ay, Edith Plantagenet. Did I dream this? or did some one tell me? My head is still weak from this fever, and has been agitated.—Was it the Scot, or the Hakim, or yonder holy hermit, that hinted such a wild bargain?"

"The hermit of Engaddi, most likely," said the Archbishop; "for he hath toiled much in this matter; and since the discontent of the princes has become apparent, and a separation of their forces unavoidable, he hath had many consultations, both with Christian and Pagan, for arranging such a pacification as may give to Christendom, at least in part, the objects of this holy warfare."

"My kinswoman to an infidel—Ha!" exclaimed Richard, as his eyes began to sparkle.

The prelate hastened to avert his wrath.

"The Pope's consent must doubtless be first attained, and the holy hermit, who is well known at Rome, will treat with the holy Father."

"How?—without our consent first given?" said the King.

"Surely no," said the bishop, in a quieting and insinuating tone of voice; "only with and under your especial sanction."

"My sanction to marry my kinswoman to an infidel?" said Richard; yet he spoke rather in a tone of doubt than as distinctly reprobating the measure proposed. "Could I have dreamed of such a composition when I leaped upon the Syrian shore from the prow of my galley, even as a lion springs on his prey! And now—But proceed, I will hear with patience."

Equally delighted and surprised to find his task so much easier than he had apprehended, the Archbishop hastened to pour forth before Richard the instances of such alliances in Spain, not without countenance from the Holy See, the incalculable advantages which all Christendom would derive from the union of Richard and Saladin, by a bond so sacred; and, above all, he spoke with great vehemence and unction on the probability that Saladin would, in case of the proposed alliance, exchange his false faith for the true one.

"Hath the Soldan shown any disposition to become Christian?" said Richard; "if so, the king lives not on earth to whom I would grant the hand of a kinswoman, ay, or sister, sooner than to my noble Saladin—ay, though the one came to lay crown and sceptre at her feet, and the other had nothing to offer but his good sword and better heart!"

"Saladin hath heard our Christian teachers," said the bishop, somewhat evasively, "my unworthy self, and others; and as he listens with patience, and replies with calmness, it can hardly be but that he be snatched as a brand from the burning. *Magna est veritas, et prevalebit!* Moreover, the hermit of Engaddi, few of whose words have fallen fruitless to the ground, is possessed fully with the belief that there is a calling of the Saracens and the other heathen approaching, to which this marriage shall be matter of induction. He readeth the course of the stars; and dwelling, with maceration of the flesh, in those divine places which the saints have trodden of old, the spirit of Elijah the Tishbite, the founder of his blessed order, hath been with him as it was with the prophet Elisha, the son of Shaphat, when he spread his mantle over him."

King Richard listened to the prelate's reasoning, with a downcast brow and a troubled look.

"I cannot tell," he said, "how it is with me; but methinks these cold counsels of the princes of Christendom have infected me too with a lethargy of spirit. The time hath been, that, had a layman proposed such alliance to me, I had struck him to earth—if a churchman, I had spit at him as a renegade and priest of Baal; yet now this counsel sounds not so strange in mine ear. For why should I not seek for brotherhood and alliance with a Saracen, brave, just, generous,—who loves and honours a worthy foe as if he were a friend, whilst the princes

of Christendom shrink from the side of their allies, and forsake
the cause of Heaven and good knighthood? But I will possess
my patience, and will not think of them. Only one attempt
will I make to keep this gallant brotherhood together, if it be
possible; and if I fail, Lord Archbishop, we will speak together
of thy counsel, which, as now, I neither accept nor altogether
reject. Wend we to the Council, my lord—the hour calls us.
Thou say'st Richard is hasty and proud—thou shalt see him
humble himself like the lowly broom-plant, from which he
derives his surname."

With the assistance of those of his privy chamber, the King
then hastily robed himself in a doublet and mantle of a dark
and uniform colour; and without any mark of regal dignity,
excepting a ring of gold upon his head, he hastened with the
Archbishop of Tyre, to attend the Council, which waited but
his presence to commence its sitting.

The pavilion of the Council was an ample tent, having before
it the large banner of the Cross displayed, and another, on
which was portrayed a female kneeling, with dishevelled hair
and disordered dress, meant to represent the desolate and
distressed Church of Jerusalem, and bearing the motto,
Afflictæ sponsæ ne obliviscaris. Warders, carefully selected,
kept every one at a distance from the nieghbourhood of this
tent, lest the debates, which were sometimes of a loud and
stormy character, should reach other ears than those they were
designed for.

Here, therefore, the princes of the Crusade were assembled,
awaiting Richard's arrival; and even the brief delay which
was thus interposed, was turned to his disadvantage by his
enemies; various instances being circulated of his pride, and
undue assumption of superiority, of which even the necessity of
the present short pause was quoted as an instance. Men
strove to fortify each other in their evil opinion of the King of
England, and vindicated the offence which each had taken, by
putting the most severe construction upon circumstances the
most trifling; and all this, perhaps, because they were conscious
of an instinctive reverence for the heroic monarch, which it
would require more than ordinary efforts to overcome.

They had settled, accordingly, that they should receive him
on his entrance with slight notice, and no more respect than
was exactly necessary to keep within the bounds of cold
ceremonial. But when they beheld that noble form, that
princely countenance, somewhat pale from his late illness, the

eye which had been called by minstrels the bright star of battle and victory; when his feats, almost surpassing human strength and valour, rushed on their recollection, the Council of Princes simultaneously arose—even the jealous King of France, and the sullen offended Duke of Austria arose with one consent—and the assembled princes burst forth with one voice in the acclamation, "God save King Richard of England!—Long life to the valiant Lion's-heart!"

With a countenance frank and open as the summer sun when it rises, Richard distributed his thanks around, and congratulated himself on being once more among his royal brethren of the Crusades.

"Some brief words he desired to say," such was his address to the assembly, "though on a subject so unworthy as himself, even at the risk of delaying for a few minutes their consultations for the weal of Christendom and the advancement of their holy enterprise."

The assembled princes resumed their seats, and there was a profound silence.

"This day," continued the King of England, "is a high festival of the Church; and well becomes it Christian men, at such a tide, to reconcile themselves with their brethren, and confess their faults to each other. Noble princes, and fathers of this holy expedition, Richard is a soldier—his hand is ever readier than his tongue, and his tongue is but too much used to the rough language of his trade. But do not, for Plantagenet's hasty speeches and ill-considered actions, forsake the noble cause of the redemption of Palestine—do not throw away earthly renown and eternal salvation, to be won here if ever they can be won by man, because the act of a soldier may have been hasty, and his speech as hard as the iron which he has worn from childhood. Is Richard in default to any of you, Richard will make compensation both by word and action. —Noble brother of France, have I been so unlucky as to offend you?"

"The Majesty of France has no atonement to seek from that of England," answered Philip, with kingly dignity, accepting, at the same time, the offered hand of Richard; "and whatever opinion I may adopt concerning the prosecution of this enterprise, will depend on reasons arising out of the state of my own kingdom, certainly on no jealousy or disgust at my royal and most valorous brother."

"Austria," said Richard, walking up to the Archduke, with

a mixture of frankness and dignity, while Leopold arose from his seat, as if involuntarily, and with the action of an automaton, whose motions depended upon some external impulse— "Austria thinks he hath reason to be offended with England; England, that he hath cause to complain of Austria. Let them exchange forgiveness, that the peace of Europe and the concord of this host may remain unbroken. We are now joint supporters of a more glorious banner than ever blazed before an earthly prince, even the Banner of Salvation; let not, therefore, strife be betwixt us, for the symbol of our more worldly dignities; but let Leopold restore the pennon of England, if he has it in his power, and Richard will say, though from no motive save his love for Holy Church, that he repents him of the hasty mood in which he did insult the standard of Austria."

The Archduke stood still, sullen and discontented, with his eyes fixed on the floor, and his countenance lowering with smothered displeasure, which awe, mingled with awkwardness, prevented his giving vent to in words.

The Patriarch of Jerusalem hastened to break the embarrassing silence, and to bear witness for the Archduke of Austria, that he had exculpated himself, by solemn oath, from all knowledge, direct or indirect, of the aggression done to the banner of England.

"Then we have done the noble Archduke the greater wrong," said Richard; "and, craving his pardon for imputing to him an outrage so cowardly, we extend our hand to him in token of renewed peace and amity.—But how is this? Austria refuses our uncovered hand, as he formerly refused our mailed glove? What! we are neither to be his mate in peace nor his antagonist in war? Well, let it be so. We will take the slight esteem in which he holds us, as a penance for aught which we may have done against him in heat of blood, and will therefore hold the account between us cleared."

So saying, he turned from the Archduke with an air rather of dignity than scorn, leaving the Austrian apparently as much relieved by the removal of his eye, as is a sullen and truant schoolboy when the glance of his severe pedagogue is withdrawn.

"Noble Earl of Champagne—Princely Marquis of Montserrat—Valiant Grand Master of the Templars—I am here a penitent in the confessional. Do any of you bring a charge, or claim amends from me?"

"I know not on what we could ground any," said the smooth-tongued Conrade, "unless it were that the King of England carries off from his poor brothers of the war all the fame which they might have hoped to gain in the expedition."

"My charge, if I am called on to make one," said the Master of the Templars, "is graver and deeper than that of the Marquis of Montserrat. It may be thought ill to beseem a military monk such as I to raise his voice where so many noble princes remain silent; but it concerns our whole host, and not least this noble King of England, that he should hear from some one to his face those charges, which there are enow to bring against him in his absence. We laud and honour the courage and high achievements of the King of England, but we feel aggrieved that he should, on all occasions, seize and maintain precedence and superiority over us, which it becomes not independent princes to submit to. Much we might yield of our free will to his bravery, his zeal, his wealth, and his power; but he who snatches all, as matter of right, and leaves nothing to grant out of courtesy and favour, degrades us from allies into retainers and vassals, and sullies, in the eyes of our soldiers and subjects, the lustre of our authority, which is no longer independently exercised. Since the royal Richard has asked the truth from us, he must neither be surprised nor angry when he hears one, to whom worldly pomp is prohibited, and secular authority is nothing, saving so far as it advances the prosperity of God's Temple, and the prostration of the lion which goeth about seeking whom he may devour—when he hears, I say, such a one as I tell him the truth in reply to his question; which truth, even while I speak it, is, I know, confirmed by the heart of every one who hears me, however respect may stifle their voices."

Richard coloured very highly while the Grand Master was making this direct and unvarnished attack upon his conduct, and the murmur of assent which followed it showed plainly, that almost all who were present acquiesced in the justice of the accusation. Incensed, and at the same time mortified, he yet foresaw that to give way to his headlong resentment would be to give the cold and wary accuser the advantage over him, which it was the Templar's principal object to obtain. He, therefore, with a strong effort, remained silent till he had repeated a paternoster, being the course which his confessor had enjoined him to pursue, when anger was likely to obtain dominion over him. The King then spoke with composure, though not without an embittered tone, especially at the outset.

"And is it even so? And are our brethren at such pains to note the infirmities of our natural temper, and the rough precipitance of our zeal, which may sometimes have urged us to issue commands when there was little time to hold council? I could not have thought that offences, casual and unpremeditated like mine, could find such deep root in the hearts of my allies in this most holy cause; that for my sake they should withdraw their hand from the plough when the furrow was near the end; for my sake turn aside from the direct path to Jerusalem which their swords have opened. I vainly thought that my small services might have outweighed my rash errors—that, if it were remembered that I pressed to the van in an assault, it would not be forgotten that I was ever the last in the retreat—that, if I elevated my banner upon conquered fields of battle, it was all the advantage that I sought, while others were dividing the spoil. I may have called the conquered city by my name, but it was to others that I yielded the dominion. If I have been headstrong in urging bold counsels, I have not, methinks, spared my own blood or my people's, in carrying them into as bold execution—or if I have, in the hurry of march or battle, assumed a command over the soldiers of others, such have been ever treated as my own, when my wealth purchased the provisions and medicines which their own sovereigns could not procure.—But it shames me to remind you of what all but myself seem to have forgotten.—Let us rather look forward to our future measures; and believe me, brethren," he continued, his face kindling with eagerness, "you shall not find the pride, or the wrath, or the ambition of Richard, a stumbling-block of offence in the path to which religion and glory summon you, as with the trumpet of an archangel. Oh, no, no! never would I survive the thought, that my frailties and infirmities had been the means to sever this goodly fellowship of assembled princes. I would cut off my left hand with my right, could my doing so attest my sincerity. I will yield up, voluntarily, all right to command in the host even mine own liege subjects. They shall be led by such sovereigns as you may nominate, and their King, ever but too apt to exchange the leader's baton for the adventurer's lance, will serve under the banner of Beau-Seant among the Templars—ay, or under that of Austria, if Austria will name a brave man to lead his forces. Or, if ye are yourselves a-weary of this war, and feel your armour chafe your tender bodies, leave but with Richard some ten or fifteen thousand of your soldiers to work out the accomplishment of your vow; and when Zion is won," he exclaimed, waving his hand aloft, as if displaying the standard of the Cross over Jerusalem—"when Zion is won, we will write upon her gates, NOT the name of Richard Plantagenet, but of those generous princes who intrusted him with the means of conquest!"

The rough eloquence and determined expression of the military monarch at once roused the drooping spirits of the Crusaders, reanimated their devotion, and, fixing their attention on the principal object of the expedition, made most of them who were present blush for having been moved by such petty subjects of complaint as had before engrossed them. Eye caught fire from eye, voice lent courage to voice. They resumed, as with one accord, the war-cry with which the sermon of Peter the Hermit was echoed back, and shouted aloud, "Lead us on, gallant Lion's-heart—none so worthy to lead where brave men follow. Lead us on—to Jerusalem! to Jerusalem! It is the will of God! it is the will of God! Blessed is he who shall lend an arm to its fulfilment!"

The shout, so suddenly and generally raised, was heard beyond the ring of sentinels who guarded the pavilion of Council, and spread among the soldiers of the host, who, inactive and dispirited by disease and climate, had begun, like their leaders, to droop in resolution; but the reappearance of Richard in renewed vigour, and the well-known shout which echoed from the assembly of the princes, at once rekindled their enthusiasm, and thousands and tens of thousands answered with the same shout of "Zion, Zion!—War, war!—instant battle with the infidels! It is the will of God! it is the will of God!"

The acclamations from without increased in their turn the enthusiasm which prevailed within the pavilion. Those who did not actually catch the flame were afraid, at least for the time, to seem colder than others. There was no more speech except of a proud advance towards Jerusalem upon the expiry of the truce, and the measures to be taken in the meantime for supplying and recruiting the army. The Council broke up, all apparently filled with the same enthusiastic purpose,—which, however, soon faded in the bosom of most, and never had an existence in that of others.

Of the latter class were the Marquis Conrade and the Grand

Master of the Templars, who retired together to their quarters ill at ease, and malcontent with the events of the day.

"I ever told it to thee," said the latter, with the cold sardonic expression peculiar to him, "that Richard would burst through the flimsy wiles you spread for him, as would a lion through a spider's web. Thou seest he has but to speak, and his breath agitates these fickle fools as easily as the whirlwind catcheth scattered straws, and sweeps them together, or disperses them at its pleasure."

"When the blast has passed away," said Conrade, "the straws, which it made dance to its pipe, will settle to earth again."

"But know'st thou not besides," said the Templar, "that it seems, if this new purpose of conquest shall be abandoned and pass away, and each mighty prince shall again be left to such guidance as his own scanty brain can supply, Richard may yet probably become King of Jerusalem by compact, and establish those terms of treaty with the Soldan, which thou thyself thought'st him so likely to spurn at?"

"Now, by Mahound and Termagaunt, for Christian oaths are out of fashion," said Conrade, "say'st thou the proud King of England would unite his blood with a heathen Soldan?—My policy threw in that ingredient to make the whole treaty an abomination to him.—As bad for us that he become our master by an agreement, as by victory."

"Thy policy hath ill calculated Richard's digestion," answered the Templar; "I know his mind by a whisper from the Archbishop. — And then thy master-stroke respecting yonder banner—it has passed off with no more respect than two cubits of embroidered silk merited. Marquis Conrade, thy wit begins to halt—I will trust thy fine-spun measures no longer, but will try my own. Know'st thou not the people whom the Saracens call Charegites?"

"Surely," answered the Marquis; "they are desperate and besotted enthusiasts, who devote their lives to the advancement of religion—somewhat like Templars — only they are never known to pause in the race of their calling."

"Jest not," answered the scowling monk; "know, that one of these men has set down, in his bloody vow, the name of the Island Emperor yonder, to be hewn down as the chief enemy of the Moslem faith."

"A most judicious Paynim," said Conrade. "May Mahomet send him his paradise for a reward!"

"He was taken in the camp by one of our squires, and in private examination frankly avowed his fixed and determined purpose to me," said the Grand Master.

"Now the Heavens pardon them who prevented the purpose of this most judicious Charegite!" answered Conrade.

"He is my prisoner," added the Templar, "and secluded from speech with others, as thou mayst suppose; but prisons have been broken——"

"Chains left unlocked, and captives have escaped," answered the Marquis. "It is an ancient saying, No sure dungeon but the grave."

"When loose he resumes his quest," continued the military priest; "for it is the nature of this sort of bloodhound never to quit the slot of the prey he has once scented."

"Say no more of it," said the Marquis; "I see thy policy—it is dreadful, but the emergency is imminent."

"I only told thee of it," said the Templar, "that thou mayst keep thyself on thy guard, for the uproar will be dreadful, and there is no knowing on whom the English may vent their rage—Ay, and there is another risk—my page knows the counsels of this Charegite," he continued; "and, moreover, he is a peevish, self-willed fool, whom I would I were rid of, as he thwarts me by presuming to see with his own eyes, not mine. But our holy Order gives me power to put a remedy to such inconvenience. Or stay—the Saracen may find a good dagger in his cell, and I warrant you he uses it as he breaks forth, which will be of a surety so soon as the page enters with his food."

"It will give the affair a colour," said Conrade; "and yet——"

"*Yet* and *but*," said the Templar, "are words for fools; wise men neither hesitate nor retract—they resolve and they execute."

CHAPTER XX

When beauty leads the lion in her toils,
Such are her charms, he dare not raise his mane,
Far less expand the terror of his fangs.
So great Alcides made his club a distaff,
And spun to please fair Omphalé.

Anonymous.

RICHARD, the unsuspicious object of the dark treachery detailed in the closing part of the last chapter, having effected, for the present at least, the triumphant union of the crusading princes, in a resolution to prosecute the war with vigour, had it next at heart to establish tranquillity in his own family; and now that he could judge more temperately, to enquire distinctly into the circumstances leading to the loss of his banner, and the nature and the extent of the connexion betwixt his kinswoman Edith and the banished adventurer from Scotland.

Accordingly, the Queen and her household were startled with a visit from Sir Thomas de Vaux, requesting the present attendance of the Lady Calista of Montfaucon, the Queen's principal bower-woman, upon King Richard.

"What am I to say, madam?" said the trembling attendant to the Queen. "He will slay us all."

"Nay, fear not, madam," said De Vaux. "His Majesty hath spared the life of the Scottish knight, who was the chief offender, and bestowed him upon the Moorish physician—he will not be severe upon a lady, though faulty."

"Devise some cunning tale, wench," said Berengaria. "My husband hath too little time to make enquiry into the truth."

"Tell the tale as it really happened," said Edith, "lest I tell it for thee."

"With humble permission of her Majesty," said De Vaux, "I would say Lady Edith adviseth well; for although King Richard is pleased to believe what it pleases your Grace to tell him, yet I doubt his having the same deference for the Lady Calista, and in this especial matter."

"The Lord of Gilsland is right," said the Lady Calista, much agitated at the thoughts of the investigation which was to take place; "and, besides, if I had presence of mind enough to forge a plausible story, beshrew me if I think I should have the courage to tell it."

In this candid humour, the Lady Calista was conducted by De Vaux to the King, and made, as she had proposed, a full confession of the decoy by which the unfortunate Knight of the Leopard had been induced to desert his post; exculpating the Lady Edith, who, she was aware, would not fail to exculpate herself, and laying the full burden on the Queen, her mistress, whose most venial share of the frolic, she well knew, would appear the most venial in the eyes of Cœur de Lion. In truth, Richard was a fond—almost an uxorious husband. The first burst of his wrath had long since passed away, and he was not disposed severely to censure what could not now be amended. The wily Lady Calista, accustomed from her earliest childhood to fathom the intrigues of a court, and watch the indications of a sovereign's will, hastened back to the Queen with the speed of a lapwing, charged with the King's commands that she should expect a speedy visit from him; to which the bower-lady added a commentary founded on her own observation, tending to show that Richard meant just to preserve so much severity as might bring his royal consort to repent of her frolic, and then to extend to her and all concerned his gracious pardon.

"Sits the wind in that corner, wench?" said the Queen, much relieved by this intelligence; "believe me, that, great commander as he is, Richard will find it hard to circumvent us in this matter; and that, as the Pyrenean shepherds are wont to say in my native Navarre, Many a one comes for wool, and goes back shorn."

Having possessed herself of all the information which Calista could communicate, the royal Berengaria arrayed herself in her most becoming dress, and awaited with confidence the arrival of the heroic Richard.

He arrived, and found himself in the situation of a prince entering an offending province, in the confidence that his business will only be to inflict rebuke, and receive submission, when he unexpectedly finds it in a state of complete defiance and insurrection. Berengaria well knew the power of her charms, and the extent of Richard's affection, and felt assured that she could make her own terms good, now that the first tremendous explosion of his anger had expended itself without mischief. Far from listening to the King's intended rebuke, as what the levity of her conduct had justly deserved, she extenuated, nay defended, as a harmless frolic, that which she was accused of. She denied, indeed, with many a pretty form of negation, that she had directed Nectabanus absolutely to entice the knight farther than the brink of the mount on which he kept watch; and indeed this was so far true, that she had not designed Sir Kenneth to be introduced into her tent; and then, eloquent in urging her own defence, the Queen was far more so in pressing upon Richard the charge of unkindness, in refusing her so poor a boon as the life of an unfortunate knight, who, by her thoughtless prank, had been brought within the danger of martial law. She wept and sobbed while she enlarged on her husband's obduracy on this score, as a rigour which had threatened to make her unhappy for life, whenever she should reflect that she had given, unthinkingly, the remote cause for such a tragedy. The vision of the slaughtered victim would have haunted her dreams—nay, for aught she knew, since such things often happened, his actual spectre might have stood by her waking couch. To all this misery of the mind was she exposed by the severity of one, who, while he pretended to dote upon her slightest glance, would not forego one act of poor revenge, though the issue was to render her miserable.

All this flow of female eloquence was accompanied with the usual arguments of tears and sighs, and uttered with such tone and action, as seemed to show that the Queen's resentment arose neither from pride nor sullenness, but from feelings hurt at finding her consequence with her husband less than she had expected to possess.

The good King Richard was considerably embarrassed. He tried in vain to reason with one, whose very jealousy of his affection rendered her incapable of listening to argument, nor could he bring himself to use the restraint of lawful authority to a creature so beautiful in the midst of her unreasonable displeasure. He was, therefore, reduced to the defensive, endeavoured gently to chide her suspicions, and soothe her displeasure, and recalled to her mind that she need not look back upon the past with recollections either of remorse or supernatural fear, since Sir Kenneth was alive and well, and had been bestowed by him upon the great Arabian physician, who, doubtless, of all men, knew best how to keep him living. But this seemed the unkindest cut of all, and the Queen's sorrow was renewed at the idea of a Saracen—a mediciner—obtaining a boon for which, with bare head and on bended knee, she had petitioned her husband in vain. At this new charge, Richard's patience began rather to give way, and he said, in a serious tone of voice, "Berengaria, the physician saved my life. If it is of value in your eyes, you will not grudge him a higher recompense than the only one I could prevail on him to accept."

The Queen was satisfied she had urged her coquettish displeasure to the verge of safety.

"My Richard," she said, "why brought you not that sage to me, that England's Queen might show how she esteemed him, who could save from extinction the lamp of chivalry, the glory of England, and the light of poor Berengaria's life and hope?"

In a word, the matrimonial dispute was ended; but, that

some penalty might be paid to justice, both King and Queen accorded in laying the whole blame on the agent Nectabanus, who (the Queen being by this time well weary of the poor dwarf's humour) was, with his royal consort Guenevra, sentenced to be banished from the court; and the unlucky dwarf only escaped a supplementary whipping, from the Queen's assurances that he had already sustained personal chastisement. It was decreed further, that as an envoy was shortly to be dispatched to Saladin, acquainting him with the resolution of the Council to resume hostilities so soon as the truce was ended, and as Richard proposed to send a valuable present to the Soldan, in acknowledgment of the high benefit he had derived from the services of El Hakim, the two unhappy creatures should be added to it as curiosities, which, from their extremely grotesque appearance, and the shattered state of their intellect, were gifts that might well pass between sovereign and sovereign.

Richard had that day yet another female encounter to sustain; but he advanced to it with comparative indifference, for Edith, though beautiful and highly esteemed by her royal relative—nay, although she had from his unjust suspicions actually sustained the injury of which Berengaria only affected to complain, still was neither Richard's wife nor mistress, and he feared her reproaches less, although founded in reason, than those of the Queen, though unjust and fantastical. Having requested to speak with her apart, he was ushered into her apartment, adjoining that of the Queen, whose two female Coptish slaves remained on their knees in the most remote corner during the interview. A thin black veil extended its ample folds over the tall and graceful form of the high-born maiden, and she wore not upon her person any female ornament of what kind soever. She arose and made a low reverence when Richard entered, resumed her seat at his command, and when he sat down beside her, waited without uttering a syllable until he should communicate his pleasure.

Richard, whose custom it was to be familiar with Edith, as their relationship authorized, felt this reception chilling, and opened the conversation with some embarrassment.

"Our fair cousin," he at length said, "is angry with us; and we own that strong circumstances have induced us, without cause, to suspect her of conduct alien to what we have ever known in her course of life. But while we walk in this misty valley of humanity, men will mistake shadows for substances.

Can my fair cousin not forgive her somewhat vehement kinsman, Richard?"

"Who can refuse forgiveness to *Richard*," answered Edith, "provided Richard can obtain pardon of the *King?*"

"Come, my kinswoman," replied Cœur de Lion, "this is all too solemn. By Our Lady, such a melancholy countenance, and this ample sable veil, might make men think thou wert a new-made widow, or had lost a betrothed lover, at least. Cheer up—thou hast heard, doubtless, that there is no real cause for woe—why then keep up the form of mourning?"

"For the departed honour of Plantagenet—for the glory which hath left my father's house."

Richard frowned. "Departed honour! glory which hath left our house!" he repeated, angrily; "but my cousin Edith is privileged. I have judged her too hastily, she has therefore a right to deem of me too harshly. But tell me at least in what I have faulted."

"Plantagenet," said Edith, "should have either pardoned an offence or punished it. It misbecomes him to assign free men, Christians and brave knights, to the fetters of the infidels. It becomes him not to compromise and barter, or to grant life under the forfeiture of liberty. To have doomed the unfortunate to death might have been severity, but had a show of justice; to condemn him to slavery and exile, was barefaced tyranny."

"I see, my fair cousin," said Richard, "you are of those pretty ones who think an absent lover as bad as none, or as a dead one. Be patient; half a score of light horsemen may yet follow and redeem the error, if thy gallant have in keeping any secret which might render his death more convenient than his banishment."

"Peace with thy scurrile jests!" answered Edith, colouring deeply. "Think rather, that for the indulgence of thy mood thou hast lopped from this great enterprise one goodly limb, deprived the Cross of one of its most brave supporters, and placed a servant of the true God in the hands of the heathen; hast given, too, to minds as suspicious as thou hast shown thine own in this matter, some right to say that Richard Cœur de Lion banished the bravest soldier in his camp, lest his name in battle might match his own."

"I—I!" exclaimed Richard, now indeed greatly moved, "am I one to be jealous of renown?—I would he were here to profess such an equality! I would waive my rank and my crown, and meet him man-like in the lists, that it might appear whether Richard Plantagenet had room to fear or to envy the prowess of mortal man. Come, Edith, thou think'st not as thou say'st. Let not anger or grief for the absence of thy lover make thee unjust to thy kinsman, who, notwithstanding all thy tetchiness, values thy good report as high as that of any one living."

"The absence of my lover?" said the Lady Edith. "But yes—he may be well termed my lover, who hath paid so dear for the title. Unworthy as I might be of such homage, I was to him like a light, leading him forward in the noble path of chivalry; but that I forgot my rank, or that he presumed beyond his, is false, were a king to speak it."

"My fair cousin," said Richard, "do not put words in my mouth which I have not spoken. I said not you had graced this man beyond the favour which a good knight may earn, even from a princess, whatever be his native condition. But, by Our Lady, I know something of this love-gear—it begins with mute respect and distant reverence; but, when opportunities occur, familiarity increases, and so—But it skills not talking with one who thinks herself wiser than all the world."

"My kinsman's counsels I willingly listen to, when they are such," said Edith, "as convey no insult to my rank and character."

"Kings, my fair cousin, do not counsel, but rather command," said Richard.

"Soldans do indeed command," said Edith, "but it is because they have slaves to govern."

"Come, you might learn to lay aside this scorn of Soldanrie, when you hold so high of a Scot," said the King. "I hold Saladin to be truer to his word than this William of Scotland, who must needs be called a Lion, forsooth; he hath foully faulted towards me, in failing to send the auxiliary aid he promised. Let me tell thee, Edith, thou mayst live to prefer a true Turk to a false Scot."

"No, never!" answered Edith, "not should Richard himself embrace the false religion which he crossed the seas to expel from Palestine."

"Thou wilt have the last word," said Richard, "and thou shalt have it. Even think of me what thou wilt, pretty Edith. I shall not forget that we are near and dear cousins."

So saying, he took his leave in fair fashion, but very little satisfied with the result of his visit.

It was the fourth day after Sir Kenneth had been dismissed from the camp; and King Richard sat in his pavilion, enjoying an evening breeze from the west, which, with unusual coolness on her wings, seemed breathed from merry England for the refreshment of her adventurous monarch, as he was gradually recovering the full strength which was necessary to carry on his gigantic projects. There was no one with him, De Vaux having been sent to Ascalon to bring up reinforcements and supplies of military munition, and most of his other attendants being occupied in different departments, all preparing for the re-opening of hostilities, and for a grand preparatory review of the army of the Crusaders, which was to take place the next day. The King sat listening to the busy hum among the soldiery, the clatter from the forges, where horse-shoes were preparing, and from the tents of the armourers, who were repairing harness; the voice of the soldiers, too, as they passed and repassed, was loud and cheerful, carrying with its very tone an assurance of high and excited courage, and an omen of approaching victory. While Richard's ear drank in these sounds with delight, and while he yielded himself to the visions of conquest and of glory which they suggested, an equerry told him that a messenger from Saladin waited without.

"Admit him instantly," said the King, "and with due honour, Josceline."

The English knight accordingly introduced a person, apparently of no higher rank than a Nubian slave, whose appearance was nevertheless highly interesting. He was of superb stature and nobly formed, and his commanding features, although almost jet-black, showed nothing of negro descent. He wore over his coal-black locks a milk-white turban, and over his shoulders a short mantle of the same colour, open in front and at the sleeves, under which appeared a doublet of dressed leopard's skin, reaching within a handbreadth of the knee. The rest of his muscular limbs, both legs and arms, were bare, excepting that he had sandals on his feet, and wore a collar and bracelets of silver. A straight broadsword, with a handle of boxwood, and a sheath covered with snake-skin, was suspended from his waist. In his right hand he held a short javelin, with a broad, bright, steel head, of a span in length, and in his left he led, by a leash of twisted silk and gold, a large and noble stag-hound.

The messenger prostrated himself, at the same time partially uncovering his shoulders, in sign of humiliation, and having touched the earth with his forehead, arose so far as to rest on one knee, while he delivered to the King a silken napkin, enclosing another of cloth of gold, within which was a letter from Saladin in the original Arabic, with a translation into Norman-English, which may be modernized thus:—

"Saladin, King of kings, to Melech Ric, the Lion of England. Whereas, we are informed by thy last message, that thou hast chosen war rather than peace, and our enmity rather than our friendship, we account thee as one blinded in this matter, and trust shortly to convince thee of thine error, by the help of our invincible forces of the thousand tribes, when Mohammed, the Prophet of God, and Allah, the God of the Prophet, shall judge the controversy betwixt us. In what remains we make noble account of thee, and of the gifts which thou hast sent us, and of the two dwarfs, singular in their deformity as Ysop, and mirthful as the lute of Isaack. And in requital of these tokens from the treasure-house of thy bounty, behold we have sent thee a Nubian slave, named Zohauk, of whom judge not by his complexion, according to the foolish ones of the earth, in respect the dark-rinded fruit hath the most exquisite flavour. Know that he is strong to execute the will of his master, as Rustan of Zablestan; also he is wise to give counsel when thou shalt learn to hold communication with him, for the Lord of Speech hath been stricken with silence betwixt the ivory walls of his palace. We commend him to thy care, hoping the hour may not be distant when he may render thee good service. And herewith we bid thee farewell; trusting that our most holy Prophet may yet call thee to a sight of the truth, failing which illumination, our desire is for the speedy restoration of thy royal health, that Allah may judge between thee and us in a plain field of battle."

And the missive was sanctioned by the signature and seal of the Soldan.

Richard surveyed the Nubian in silence as he stood before him, his looks bent upon the ground, his arms folded on his bosom, with the appearance of a black marble statue of the most exquisite workmanship, waiting life from the touch of a Prometheus. The King of England, who, as it was emphatically said of his successor, Henry the Eighth, loved to look upon A MAN, was well pleased with the thews, sinews, and symmetry of him whom he now surveyed, and questioned him in the lingua franca, "Art thou a pagan?"

The slave shook his head, and raising his finger to his brow, crossed himself in token of his Christianity, then resumed his posture of motionless humility.

"A Nubian Christian, doubtless," said Richard, "and mutilated of the organ of speech by these heathen dogs?"

The mute again slowly shook his head in token of negative, pointed with his forefinger to Heaven, and then laid it upon his own lips.

"I understand thee," said Richard; "thou dost suffer under the infliction of God, not by the cruelty of man. Canst thou clean an armour and belt, and buckle it in time of need?"

The mute nodded, and, stepping towards the coat of mail, which hung, with the shield and helmet of the chivalrous monarch, upon the pillar of the tent, he handled it with such nicety of address as sufficiently to show that he fully understood the business of the armour-bearer.

"Thou art an apt, and wilt doubtless be a useful knave; thou shalt wait in my chamber and on my person," said the King, "to show how much I value the gift of the royal Soldan. If thou hast no tongue, it follows thou canst carry no tales, neither provoke me to be sudden by any unfit reply."

The Nubian again prostrated himself till his brow touched the earth, then stood erect at some paces distant, as waiting for his new master's commands.

"Nay, thou shalt commence thy office presently," said Richard, "for I see a speck of rust darkening on that shield; and when I shake it in the face of Saladin it should be bright and unsullied as the Soldan's honour and mine own."

A horn was winded without, and presently Sir Henry Neville entered with a packet of dispatches.—"From England, my lord," he said, as he delivered it.

"From England, our own England!" repeated Richard, in a tone of melancholy enthusiasm. "Alas! they little think how hard their sovereign has been beset by sickness and sorrow—faint friends and forward enemies." Then opening the dispatches, he said, hastily, "Ha! this comes from no peaceful land; they, too, have their feuds.—Neville, begone. —I must peruse these tidings alone, and at leisure."

Neville withdrew accordingly, and Richard was soon absorbed in the melancholy details which had been conveyed to him from England, concerning the factions that were tearing to pieces his native dominions,—the disunion of his brothers, John and Geoffrey, and the quarrels of both with the High Justiciary Longchamp, Bishop of Ely,— the oppressions practised by the nobles upon the peasantry, and rebellion of the latter against their masters, which had produced everywhere scenes of discord, and in some instances the effusion of blood. Details of incidents mortifying to his pride, and derogatory from his authority, were intermingled with the earnest advice of his wisest and most attached counsellors, that he should presently return to England, as his presence offered the only hope of saving the kingdom from all the horrors of civil discord, of which France and Scotland were likely to avail themselves. Filled with the most painful anxiety, Richard read, and again read, the ill-omened letters, compared the intelligence which some of them contained with the same facts as differently stated in others, and soon became totally insensible to whatever was passing around him, although seated, for the sake of coolness, close to the entrance of his tent, and having the curtains withdrawn, so that he could see and be seen by the guards and others who were stationed without.

Deeper in the shadow of the pavilion, and busied with the task his new master had imposed, sat the Nubian slave, with his back rather turned towards the King. He had finished adjusting and cleaning the hauberk and brigandine, and was now busily employed on a broad pavesse, or buckler, of unusual size, and covered with steel-plating, which Richard often used in reconnoitring, or actually storming, fortified places, as a more effectual protection against missile weapons, than the narrow triangular shield used on horseback. This pavesse bore neither the royal lions of England, nor any other device, to attract the observation of the defenders of the walls against which it was advanced; the care, therefore, of the armourer was addressed to causing its surface to shine as bright as crystal, in which he seemed to be peculiarly successful. Beyond the Nubian, and scarce visible from without, lay the large dog, which might be termed his brother slave, and which, as if he felt awed by being transferred to a royal owner, was couched close to the side of the mute, with head and ears on the ground, and his limbs and tail drawn close around and under him.

While the monarch and his new attendant were thus occupied, another actor crept upon the scene and mingled among the group of English yeomen, about a score of whom, respecting the unusually pensive posture and close occupation of their sovereign, were, contrary to their wont, keeping a silent guard in front of his tent. It was not, however, more vigilant than usual. Some were playing at games of hazard with small pebbles, others spoke together in whispers of the approaching day of battle, and several lay asleep, their bulky limbs folded in their green mantles.

Amid these careless warders glided the puny form of a little old Turk, poorly dressed like a marabout or santon of the desert, a sort of enthusiasts, who sometimes ventured into the camp of the Crusaders, though treated always with contumely, and often with violence. Indeed, the luxury and profligate indulgence of the Christian leaders had occasioned a motley concourse in their tents, of musicians, courtezans, Jewish merchants, Copts, Turks, and all the varied refuse of the Eastern nations; so that the caftan and turban, though to drive both from the Holy Land was the professed object of the expedition, were nevertheless neither an uncommon nor an alarming sight in the camp of the Crusaders. When, however, the little insignificant figure we have described approached so nigh as to receive some interruption from the warders, he dashed his dusky green turban from his head, showed that his beard and eyebrows were shaved like those of a professed buffoon, and that the expression of his fantastic and writhen features, as well as of his little black eyes, which glittered like jet, was that of a crazed imagination.

"Dance, marabout," cried the soldiers, acquainted with the manners of these wandering enthusiasts, "dance, or we will scourge thee with our bow-strings, till thou spin as never top did under schoolboy's lash." — Thus shouted the reckless warders, as much delighted at having a subject to tease, as a child when he catches a butterfly, or a schoolboy upon discovering a bird's nest.

The marabout, as if happy to do their behests, bounded from the earth, and spun his giddy round before them with singular agility, which, when contrasted with his slight and wasted figure, and diminutive appearance, made him resemble a withered leaf twirled round and around at the pleasure of the winter's breeze. His single lock of hair streamed upwards from his bald and shaven head, as if some genie upheld him by it; and indeed it seemed as if supernatural art were necessary to the execution of the wild whirling dance, in which scarce the tiptoe of the performer was seen to touch the ground. Amid the vagaries of his performance, he flew here and there, from one spot to another, still approaching, however, though almost imperceptibly, to the entrance of the royal tent; so that, when at length he sunk exhausted on the earth, after two or three bounds still higher than those which he had yet executed, he was not above thirty yards from the King's person.

"Give him water," said one yeoman; "they always crave a drink after their merry-go-round."

"Aha, water, say'st thou, Long Allen?"—exclaimed another archer, with a most scornful emphasis on the despised element; "how wouldst like such beverage thyself, after such a morrice dancing?"

"The devil a water-drop he gets here," said a third. "We will teach the light-footed old infidel to be a good Christian, and drink wine of Cyprus."

"Ay, ay," said a fourth; "and in case he be restive, fetch thou Dick Hunter's horn, that he drenches his mare withal."

A circle was instantly formed around the prostrate and exhausted dervise, and while one tall yeoman raised his feeble form from the ground, another presented to him a huge flagon of wine. Incapable of speech, the old man shook his head, and waved away from him with his hand the liquor forbidden by the Prophet; but his tormentors were not thus to be appeased.

"The horn, the horn!" exclaimed one. "Little difference between a Turk and a Turkish horse, and we will use him conforming."

"By Saint George, you will choke him!" said Long Allen; "and, besides, it is a sin to throw away upon a heathen dog as much wine as would serve a good Christian for a treble night-cap."

"Thou know'st not the nature of these Turks and pagans, Long Allen," replied Henry Woodstall; "I tell thee, man, that this flagon of Cyprus will set his brains a-spinning, just in the opposite direction that they went whirling in the dancing, and so bring him, as it were, to himself again.— Choke? he will no more choke on it than Ben's black bitch on the pound of butter."

"And for grudging it," said Tomalin Blacklees, "why shouldst thou grudge the poor paynim devil a drop of drink on earth, since thou know'st he is not to have a drop to cool the tip of his tongue through a long eternity?"

"That were hard laws, look ye," said Long Allen, "only for being a Turk, as his father was before him. Had he been

Christian turned heathen, I grant you the hottest corner had been good winter quarters for him."

"Hold thy peace, Long Allen," said Henry Woodstall; "I tell thee that tongue of thine is not the shortest limb about thee, and I prophesy that it will bring thee into disgrace with Father Francis, as once about the black-eyed Syrian wench.—But here comes the horn.—Be active a bit, man, wilt thou, and just force open his teeth with the haft of thy dudgeon-dagger."

"Hold, hold—he is conformable," said Tomalin. "See, see, he signs for the goblet; give him room, boys. *Oop sey es*, quoth the Dutchman; down it goes like lamb's-wool! Nay, they are true topers when once they begin; your Turk never coughs in his cup, or stints in his liquoring."

In fact, the dervise, or whatever he was, drank, or at least seemed to drink, the large flagon to the very bottom at a single pull; and when he took it from his lips, after the whole contents were exhausted, only uttered, with a deep sigh, the words Allah kerim, or God is merciful. There was a laugh among the yeomen who witnessed this pottle-deep potation, so obstreperous as to rouse and disturb the King, who, raising his finger, said angrily, "How, knaves, no respect, no observance?"

All were at once hushed into silence, well acquainted with the temper of Richard, which at some times admitted of much military familiarity, and at others exacted the most precise respect, although the latter humour was of much more rare occurrence. Hastening to a more reverent distance from the royal person, they attempted to drag along with them the marabout, who, exhausted apparently by previous fatigue, or overpowered by the potent draught he had just swallowed, resisted being moved from the spot, both with struggles and groans.

"Leave him still, ye fools," whispered Long Allen to his mates; "by Saint Christopher, you will make our Dickon go beside himself, and we shall have his dagger presently fly at our costards. Leave him alone, in less than a minute he will sleep like a dormouse."

At the same moment, the monarch darted another impatient glance to the spot, and all retreated in haste, leaving the dervise on the ground, unable, as it seemed, to stir a single limb or joint of his body. In a moment afterward, all was as still and quiet as it had been before the intrusion.

CHAPTER XXI

——and wither'd Murder,
Alarum'd by his sentinel, the wolf,
Whose howl's his watch, thus with his stealthy pace,
With Tarquin's ravishing strides, towards his design
Moves like a ghost.
                                    Macbeth.

For the space of a quarter of an hour, or longer, after the incident related, all remained perfectly quiet in the front of the royal habitation. The King read and mused in the entrance of his pavilion; behind, and with his back turned to the same entrance, the Nubian slave still burnished the ample pavesse; in front of all, at an hundred paces distant, the yeomen of the guard stood, sat, or lay extended on the grass, attentive to their own sports, but pursuing them in silence, while on the esplanade betwixt them and the front of the tent, lay, scarcely to be distinguished from a bundle of rags, the senseless form of the marabout.

But the Nubian had the advantage of a mirror, from the brilliant reflection which the surface of the highly polished shield now afforded, by means of which he beheld, to his alarm and surprise, that the marabout raised his head gently from the ground, so as to survey all around him, moving with a well-adjusted precaution, which seemed entirely inconsistent with a state of ebriety. He couched his head instantly, as if satisfied he was unobserved, and began, with the slightest possible appearance of voluntary effort, to drag himself, as if by chance, ever nearer and nearer to the King, but stopping and remaining fixed at intervals, like the spider, which, moving towards her object, collapses into apparent lifelessness when she thinks she is the object of observation. This species of movement appeared suspicious to the Ethiopian, who, on his part, prepared himself, as quickly as possible, to interfere, the instant that interference should seem to be necessary.

The marabout meanwhile glided on gradually and imperceptibly, serpent-like, or rather snail-like, till he was about ten yards' distance from Richard's person, when, starting on his feet, he sprung forward with the bound of a tiger, stood at the King's back in less than an instant, and brandished aloft the cangiar, or poniard, which he had hidden in his sleeve. Not the presence of his whole army could have saved their heroic monarch; but the motions of the Nubian had been as well calculated as those of the enthusiast, and ere the latter could strike the former caught his uplifted arm. Turning his fanatical wrath upon what thus unexpectedly interposed betwixt him and his object, the Charegite, for such was the seeming marabout, dealt the Nubian a blow with the dagger, which, however, only grazed his arm, while the far superior strength of the Ethiopian easily dashed him to the ground. Aware of what had passed, Richard had now arisen, and with little more of surprise, anger, or interest of any kind in his countenance, than an ordinary man would show in brushing off and crushing an intrusive wasp, caught up the stool on which he had been sitting, and exclaiming only "Ha, dog!" dashed almost to pieces the skull of the assassin, who uttered twice, once in a loud, and once in a broken tone, the words "Allah ackbar!"—God is victorious—and expired at the King's feet.

"Ye are careful warders," said Richard to his archers, in a tone of scornful reproach, as, aroused by the bustle of what had passed, in terror and tumult they now rushed into his tent;—"watchful sentinels ye are, to leave me to do such hangman's work with my own hand.—Be silent all of you, and cease your senseless clamour! saw ye never a dead Turk before?—Here—cast that carrion out of the camp, strike the head from the trunk, and stick it on a lance, taking care to turn the face to Mecca, that he may the easier tell the foul impostor, on whose inspiration he came hither, how he has sped on his errand.—For thee, my swart and silent friend," he added, turning to the Ethiopian——"But how's this?—thou art wounded—and with a poisoned weapon, I warrant me, for by force of stab so weak an animal as that could scarce hope to do more than raze the lion's hide.—Suck the poison from his wound, one of you—the venom is harmless on the lips, though fatal when it mingles with the blood."

The yeomen looked on each other confusedly and with hesitation, the apprehension of so strange a danger prevailing with those who feared no other.

"How now, sirrahs," continued the King, "are you dainty-lipped, or do you fear death, that you dally thus?"

"Not the death of a man," said Long Allen, to whom the King looked as he spoke; "but methinks I would not die like a poisoned rat for the sake of a black chattel there, that is bought and sold in a market like a Martlemas ox."

"His Grace speaks to men of sucking poison," muttered

another yeoman, "as if he said, Go to, swallow a goose-berry!"

"Nay," said Richard, "I never bade man do that which I would not do myself."

And without further ceremony, and in spite of the general expostulations of those around, and the respectful opposition of the Nubian himself, the King of England applied his lips to the wound of the black slave, treating with ridicule all remonstrances, and overpowering all resistance. He had no sooner intermitted his singular occupation than the Nubian started from him, and, casting a scarf over his arm, intimated by gestures, as firm in purpose as they were respectful in manner, his determination not to permit the monarch to renew so degrading an employment. Long Allen also interposed, saying, that if it were necessary to prevent the King engaging again in a treatment of this kind, his own lips, tongue, and teeth, were at the service of the negro, (as he called the Ethiopian,) and that he would eat him up bodily, rather than King Richard's mouth should again approach him.

Neville, who entered with other officers, added his remonstrances.

"Nay, nay, make not a needless halloo about a hart that the hounds have lost, or a danger when it is over," said the King. "The wound will be a trifle, for the blood is scarce drawn. An angry cat had dealt a deeper scratch—and for me, I have but to take a drachm of orvietan by way of precaution, though it is needless."

Thus spoke Richard, a little ashamed, perhaps, of his own condescension, though sanctioned both by humanity and gratitude. But when Neville continued to make remonstrances on the peril to his royal person, the King imposed silence on him.

"Peace, I prithee—make no more of it—I did it but to show these ignorant prejudiced knaves how they might help each other when these cowardly caitiffs come against us with sarbacanes and poisoned shafts.—But," he added, "take thee this Nubian to thy quarters, Neville. I have changed my mind touching him; let him be well cared for. But, hark in thine ear—see that he escapes thee not—there is more in him than seems. Let him have all liberty, so that he leave not the camp.—And you, ye beef-devouring, wine-swilling English mastiffs, get ye to your guard again, and be sure you keep it more warily. Think not you are now in your own land of fair play, where men speak before they strike, and shake hands ere they cut throats. Danger in our land walks openly, and with his blade drawn, and defies the foe whom he means to assault; but here he challenges you, with a silk glove instead of a steel gauntlet, cuts your throat with the feather of a turtle-dove, stabs you with the tongue of a priest's brooch, or throttles you with the lace of my lady's bodice. Go to—keep your eyes open and your mouths shut—drink less and look sharper about you, or I will place your huge stomachs on such short allowance as would pinch that of a patient Scottishman."

The yeomen, abashed and mortified, withdrew to their post, and Neville was beginning to remonstrate with his master upon the risk of passing over thus slightly their negligence upon their duty, and the propriety of an example in a case so peculiarly aggravated as the permitting one so suspicious as the marabout to approach within dagger's length of his person, when Richard interrupted him with "Speak not of it, Neville; wouldst thou have me avenge a petty risk to myself more severely than the loss of England's banner? It has been stolen—stolen by a thief, or delivered up by a traitor, and no blood has been shed for it.—My sable friend, thou art an expounder of mysteries, saith the illustrious Soldan; now would I give thee thine own weight in gold, if, by raising one still blacker than thyself, or by what other means thou wilt, thou couldst show me the thief who did mine honour that wrong. What say'st thou? ha!"

The mute seemed desirous to speak, but uttered only that imperfect sound proper to his melancholy condition, then folded his arms, looked on the King with an eye of intelligence, and nodded in answer to his question.

"How!" said Richard, with joyful impatience. "Wilt thou undertake to make discovery in this matter?"

The Nubian slave repeated the same motion.

"But how shall we understand each other?" said the King. "Canst thou write, good fellow?"

The slave again nodded in assent.

"Give him writing-tools," said the King. "They were readier in my father's tent than mine; but they be somewhere about, if this scorching climate hath not dried up the ink.— Why, this fellow is a jewel, a black diamond, Neville."

"So please you, my liege," said Neville, "if I might speak my poor mind, it were ill dealing in this ware. This man must be a wizard, and wizards deal with the Enemy, who hath

most interest to sow tares among the wheat, and bring dis
sension into our councils, and——"

"Peace, Neville," said Richard. "Hollo to your northern
hound when he is close on the haunch of the deer, and hope
to recall him, but seek not to stop Plantagenet when he hath
hope to retrieve his honour."

The slave, who during this discussion had been writing, in
which art he seemed skilful, now arose, and pressing what he
had written to his brow, prostrated himself as usual, ere he
delivered it into the King's hands. The scroll was in French,
although their intercourse had hitherto been conducted by
Richard in the lingua franca.

"To Richard, the conquering and invincible King of
England, this from the humblest of his slaves. Mysteries are
the sealed caskets of Heaven, but wisdom may devise means
to open the lock. Were your slave stationed where the
leaders of the Christian host were made to pass before him in
order, doubt nothing, that if he who did the injury whereof
my King complains shall be among the number, he may be
made manifest in his iniquity, though it be hidden under
seven veils."

"Now, by Saint George!" said King Richard, "thou hast
spoken most opportunely.—Neville, thou know'st, that when
we muster our troops to-morrow, the princes have agreed, that
to expiate the affront offered to England in the theft of her
banner, the leaders should pass our new standard as it floats
on Saint George's Mount and salute it with formal regard.
Believe me, the secret traitor will not dare to absent himself
from an expurgation so solemn, lest his very absence should
be matter of suspicion. There will we place our sable man
of counsel, and, if his art can detect the villain, leave me to
deal with him."

"My liege," said Neville, with the frankness of an English
baron, "beware what work you begin. Here is the concord
of our Holy League unexpectedly renewed; will you, upon
such suspicion as a negro slave can instil, tear open wounds so
lately closed, or will you use the solemn procession, adopted
for the reparation of your honour, and establishment of
unanimity amongst the discording princes, as the means of
again finding out new cause of offence or reviving ancient
quarrels? It were scarce too strong to say, this were a breach
of the declaration your Grace made to the assembled Council
of the Crusade."

"Neville," said the King, sternly interrupting him, "thy zeal makes thee presumptuous and unmannerly. Never did I promise to abstain from taking whatever means were most promising, to discover the infamous author of the attack on my honour. Ere I had done so, I would have renounced my kingdom — my life. All my declarations were under this necessary and absolute qualification; only, if Austria had stepped forth and owned the injury like a man, I proffered, for the sake of Christendom, to have forgiven *him*."

"But," continued the baron, anxiously, "what hope that this juggling slave of Saladin will not palter with your Grace?"

"Peace, Neville," said the King; "thou think'st thyself mighty wise, and art but a fool. Mind thou my charge touching this fellow—there is more in him than thy Westmoreland wit can fathom. And thou, swart and silent, prepare to perform the feat thou hast promised, and, by the word of a King, thou shalt choose thine own recompense. Lo, he writes again."

The mute accordingly wrote and delivered to the King, with the same form as before, another slip of paper, containing these words, "The will of the King is the law to his slave, nor doth it become him to ask guerdon for discharge of his devoir."

"*Guerdon* and *devoir!*" said the King, interrupting himself as he read, and speaking to Neville in the English tongue with some emphasis on the words.—"These Eastern people will profit by the Crusaders,—they are acquiring the language of chivalry!—And see, Neville, how discomposed that fellow looks—were it not for his colour, he would blush. I should not think it strange if he understood what I say—they are perilous linguists."

"The poor slave cannot endure your Grace's eye," said Neville; "it is nothing more."

"Well, but," continued the King, striking the paper with his finger, as he proceeded, "this bold scroll proceeds to say, that our trusty mute is charged with a message from Saladin to the Lady Edith Plantagenet, and craves means and opportunity to deliver it. What think'st thou of a request so modest—ha, Neville?"

"I cannot say," said Neville, "how such freedom may relish with your Grace; but the lease of the messenger's neck would be a short one, who should carry such a request to the Soldan on the part of your Majesty."

"Nay, I thank Heaven that I covet none of his sunburnt beauties," said Richard; "and for punishing this fellow for discharging his master's errand, and that when he has just saved my life—methinks it were something too summary. I'll tell thee, Neville, a secret—for, although our sable and mute minister be present, he cannot, thou know'st, tell it over again, even if he should chance to understand us. I tell thee, that for this fortnight past I have been under a strange spell, and I would I were disenchanted. There has no sooner any one done me good service, but lo you, he cancels his interest in me by some deep injury; and, on the other hand, he who hath deserved death at my hands for some treachery or some insult, is sure to be the very person, of all others, who confers upon me some obligation that overbalances his demerits, and renders respite of his sentence a debt due from my honour. Thus, thou seest, I am deprived of the best part of my royal function, since I can neither punish men nor reward them. Until the influence of this disqualifying planet be passed away, I will say nothing concerning the request of this our sable attendant, save that it is an unusually bold one, and that his best chance of finding grace in our eyes will be, to endeavour to make the discovery which he proposes to achieve in our behalf. Meanwhile, Neville, do thou look well to him, and let him be honourably cared for.—And hark thee once more," he said, in a low whisper, "seek out yonder hermit of Engaddi, and bring him to me forthwith, be he saint or savage, madman or sane. Let me see him privately."

Neville retired from the royal tent, signing to the Nubian to follow him, and much surprised at what he had seen and heard, and especially at the unusual demeanour of the King. In general, no task was so easy as to discover Richard's immediate course of sentiment and feeling, though it might in some cases be difficult to calculate its duration; for no weathercock obeyed the changing wind more readily than the King his gusts of passion. But, on the present occasion, his manner seemed unusually constrained and mysterious, nor was it easy to guess whether displeasure or kindness predominated in his conduct towards his new dependent, or in the looks with which, from time to time, he regarded him. The ready service which the King had rendered to counteract the bad effects of the Nubian's wound might seem to balance the obligation conferred on him by the slave, when he intercepted the blow of the assassin; but it seemed, as a much longer account

remained to be arranged between them, that the monarch was
doubtful whether the settlement might leave him, upon the
whole, debtor or creditor, and that, therefore, he assumed in
the meantime a neutral demeanour, which might suit with
either character. As for the Nubian, by whatever means he
had acquired the art of writing the European languages, the
King remained convinced that the English tongue at least was
unknown to him, since, having watched him closely during the
last part of the interview, he conceived it impossible for any
one understanding a conversation, of which he was himself the
subject, to have so completely avoided the appearance of
taking an interest in it.

CHAPTER XXII

Who's there?—Approach—'tis kindly done—
My learned physician and a friend.
SIR EUSTACE GREY.

OUR narrative retrogrades to a period shortly previous to
the incidents last mentioned, when, as the reader must
remember, the unfortunate Knight of the Leopard, bestowed
upon the Arabian physician by King Richard, rather as a
slave than in any other capacity, was exiled from the camp of
the Crusaders, in whose ranks he had so often and so brilliantly
distinguished himself. He followed his new master, for so
we must now term the Hakim, to the Moorish tents which
contained his retinue and his property, with the stupified
feelings of one, who, fallen from the summit of a precipice,
and escaping unexpectedly with life, is just able to drag
himself from the fatal spot, but without the power of estimating
the extent of the damage which he has sustained. Arrived at
the tent, he threw himself, without speech of any kind, upon a
couch of dressed buffalo's hide, which was pointed out to him
by his conductor, and hiding his face betwixt his hands groaned
heavily, as if his heart was on the point of bursting. The
physician heard him, as he was giving orders to his numerous
domestics to prepare for their departure the next morning
before daybreak, and, moved with compassion, interrupted his
occupation, to sit down, cross-legged, by the side of his couch,
and administer comfort according to the Oriental manner.

"My friend," he said, "be of good comfort, for what sayeth
the poet—'It is better that a man should be the servant of a

kind master, than the slave of his own wild passions.' Again, be of good courage; because, whereas Ysouf Ben Yagoube was sold to a King by his brethren, even to Pharaoh King of Egypt, thy King hath, on the other hand, bestowed thee on one who will be to thee as a brother."

Sir Kenneth made an effort to thank the Hakim, but his heart was too full, and the indistinct sounds which accompanied his abortive attempts to reply induced the kind physician to desist from his premature endeavours at consolation. He left his new domestic, or guest, in quiet, to indulge his sorrows, and having commanded all the necessary preparations for their departure on the morning, sat down upon the carpet of the tent, and indulged himself in a moderate repast. After he had thus refreshed himself, similar viands were offered to the Scottish knight; but, though the slaves let him understand that the next day would be far advanced ere they would halt for the purpose of refreshment, Sir Kenneth could not overcome the disgust which he felt against swallowing any nourishment, and could be prevailed upon to taste nothing, saving a draught of cold water.

He was awake long after his Arab host had performed his usual devotions, and betaken himself to his repose, nor had sleep visited him at the hour of midnight, when a movement took place among the domestics, which, though attended with no speech, and very little noise, made him aware they were loading the camels and preparing for departure. In the course of these preparations the last person who was disturbed, excepting the physician himself, was the knight of Scotland, whom, about three in the morning, a sort of major-domo, or master of the household, acquainted that he must arise. He did so, without further answer, and followed him into the moonlight, where stood the camels, most of which were already loaded, and one only remained kneeling until its burden should be completed.

A little apart from the camels stood a number of horses ready bridled and saddled, and the Hakim himself coming forth, mounted on one of them with as much agility as the grave decorum of his character permitted, and directed another, which he pointed out, to be led towards Sir Kenneth. An English officer was in attendance, to escort them through the camp of the Crusaders, and to ensure their leaving it in safety, and all was ready for their departure. The pavilion which they had left, was, in the meanwhile, struck with singular dispatch, and the tent-poles and coverings composed the burden of the last camel, when the physician, pronouncing solemnly the verse of the Koran, "God be our guide, and Mahommed our protector, in the desert as in the watered field," the whole cavalcade was instantly in motion.

In traversing the camp they were challenged by the various sentinels who maintained guard there, and suffered to proceed in silence, or with a muttered curse upon their Prophet, as they passed the post of some more zealous Crusader. At length the last barriers were left behind them, and the party formed themselves for the march with military precaution. Two or three horsemen advanced in front as a vanguard; one or two remained a bowshot in the rear; and, wherever the ground admitted, others were detached to keep an outlook on the flanks. In this manner they proceeded onward, while Sir Kenneth, looking back on the moonlight camp, might now indeed seem banished, deprived at once of honour and of liberty, from the glimmering banners, under which he had hoped to gain additional renown, and the tented dwellings of chivalry, of Christianity, and—of Edith Plantagenet.

The Hakim, who rode by his side, observed, in his usual tone of sententious consolation, "It is unwise to look back when the journey lieth forward;" and as he spoke, the horse of the knight made such a perilous stumble, as threatened to add a practical moral to the tale.

The knight was compelled by this hint to give more attention to the management of his steed, which more than once required the assistance and support of the check-bridle, although in other respects nothing could be more easy at once, and active, than the ambling pace at which the animal (which was a mare) proceeded.

"The conditions of that horse," observed the sententious physician, "are like those of human fortune; seeing that amidst his most swift and easy pace, the rider must guard himself against a fall, and that it is when prosperity is at the highest, that our prudence should be awake and vigilant to prevent misfortune."

The overloaded appetite loathes even the honeycomb, and it is scarce a wonder that the knight, mortified and harassed with misfortunes and abasement, became something impatient of hearing his misery made, at every turn, the ground of proverbs and apophthegms, however just and apposite.

"Methinks," he said, rather peevishly, "I wanted no additional illustration of the instability of fortune, though I would thank thee, Sir Hakim, for thy choice of a steed for me, would the jade but stumble so effectually as at once to break my neck and her own."

"My brother," answered the Arab sage, with imperturbable gravity, "thou speakest as one of the foolish. Thou say'st in thy heart, that the sage should have given thee, as his guest, the younger and better horse, and reserved the old one for himself; but know, that the defects of the older steed may be compensated by the energies of the young rider, whereas the violence of the young horse requires to be moderated by the cold temper of the older."

So spoke the sage; but neither to this observation did Sir Kenneth return any answer which could lead to a continuance of their conversation, and the physician, wearied perhaps of administering comfort to one who would not be comforted, signed to one of his retinue.

"Hassan," he said, "hast thou nothing wherewith to beguile the way?"

Hassan, story-teller and poet by profession, spurred up, upon this summons, to exercise his calling. "Lord of the palace of life," he said, addressing the physician, "thou, before whom the angel Azrael spreadeth his wings for flight—thou, wiser than Solimaun Ben Daoud, upon whose signet was inscribed the REAL NAME which controls the spirits of the elements—forbid it, Heaven, that while thou travellest upon the track of benevolence, bearing healing and hope wherever thou comest, thine own course should be saddened for lack of the tale and of the song. Behold, while thy servant is at thy side, he will pour forth the treasures of his memory, as the fountain sendeth her stream beside the pathway, for the refreshment of him that walketh thereon."

After this exordium Hassan uplifted his voice, and began a tale of love and magic, intermixed with feats of warlike achievement, and ornamented with abundant quotations from the Persian poets, with whose compositions the orator seemed familiar. The retinue of the physician, such excepted as were necessarily detained in attendance on the camels, thronged up to the narrator, and pressed as close as deference for their master permitted, to enjoy the delight which the inhabitants of the East have ever derived from this species of exhibition.

At another time, notwithstanding his imperfect knowledge of the language, Sir Kenneth might have been interested in the recitation, which, though dictated by a more extravagant imagination, and expressed in more inflated and metaphorical language, bore yet a strong resemblance to the romances of chivalry, then so fashionable in Europe. But as matters stood with him, he was scarcely even sensible that a man in the centre of the cavalcade recited and sung, in a low tone, for nearly two hours, modulating his voice to the various moods of passion introduced into the tale, and receiving in return now low murmurs of applause, now muttered expressions of wonder, now sighs and tears, and sometimes—what it was far more difficult to extract from such an audience—a tribute of smiles, and even laughter.

During the recitation the attention of the exile, however abstracted by his own deep sorrow, was occasionally awakened by the low wail of a dog, secured in a wicker enclosure suspended on one of the camels, which, as an experienced woodsman, he had no hesitation in recognising to be that of his own faithful hound; and from the plaintive tone of the animal, he had no doubt that he was sensible of his master's vicinity, and in his way invoking his assistance for liberty and rescue.

"Alas! poor Roswal," he said, "thou callest for aid and sympathy upon one in stricter bondage than thou thyself art. I will not seem to heed thee, or return thy affection, since it would serve but to load our parting with yet more bitterness."

Thus passed the hours of night, and the space of dim hazy dawn, which forms the twilight of a Syrian morning. But when the very first line of the sun's disc began to rise above the level horizon, and when the very first level ray shot glimmering in dew along the surface of the desert, which the travellers had now attained, the sonorous voice of El Hakim himself overpowered and cut short the narrative of the tale-teller, while he caused to resound along the sands the solemn summons, which the muezzins thunder at morning from the minaret of every mosque.

"To prayer! to prayer! God is the one God —To prayer! to prayer! Mahommed is the prophet of God.—To prayer! to prayer! Time is flying from you. — To prayer! to prayer! Judgment is drawing nigh to you."

In an instant each Moslem cast himself from his horse, turned his face towards Mecca, and performed with sand an imitation of those ablutions which were elsewhere required to be made with water, while each individual, in brief but fervent ejaculations, recommended himself to the care, and his sins to the forgiveness, of God and the Prophet.

Even Sir Kenneth, whose reason at once and prejudices were offended by seeing his companions in that which he considered as an act of idolatry, could not help respecting the sincerity of their misguided zeal, and being stimulated by their fervour to apply supplications to Heaven in a purer form, wondering, meanwhile, what new-born feelings could teach him to accompany in prayer, though with varied invocation, those very Saracens, whose heathenish worship he had conceived a crime dishonourable to the land in which high miracles had been wrought, and where the day-star of redemption had arisen.

The act of devotion, however, though rendered in such strange society, burst purely from his natural feelings of religious duty, and had its usual effect in composing the spirits, which had been long harassed by so rapid a succession of calamities. The sincere and earnest approach of the Christian to the throne of the Almighty teaches the best lesson of patience under affliction; since wherefore should we mock the Deity with supplications, when we insult him by murmuring under his decrees? or how, while our prayers have in every word admitted the vanity and nothingness of the things of time in comparison to those of eternity, should we hope to deceive the Searcher of Hearts, by permitting the world and worldly passions to reassume the reins even immediately after a solemn address to Heaven? But Sir Kenneth was not of these. He felt himself comforted and strengthened, and better prepared to execute or submit to whatever his destiny might call upon him to do or to suffer.

Meanwhile, the party of Saracens regained their saddles, and continued their route, and the tale-teller, Hassan, resumed the thread of his narrative; but it was no longer to the same attentive audience. A horseman, who had ascended some high ground on the right hand of the little column, had returned on a speedy gallop to El Hakim, and communicated with him. Four or five more cavaliers had then been dispatched, and the little band, which might consist of about twenty or thirty persons, began to follow them with their eyes, as men from whose gestures, and advance or retreat, they were to augur good or evil. Hassan, finding his audience inattentive, or being himself attracted by the dubious appearances on the flank, stinted in his song; and the march became silent, save when a camel-driver called out to his patient charge, or some anxious follower of the Hakim communicated with his next neighbour in a hurried and low whisper.

This suspense continued until they had rounded a ridge composed of hillocks of sand, which concealed from their main body the object that had created this alarm among their scouts. Sir Kenneth could now see, at the distance of a mile or more, a dark object moving rapidly on the bosom of the desert, which his experienced eye recognised for a party of cavalry, much superior to their own in numbers, and, from the thick and frequent flashes which flung back the level beams of the rising sun, it was plain that these were Europeans in their complete panoply.

The anxious looks which the horsemen of El Hakim now cast upon their leader seemed to indicate deep apprehension; while he, with gravity as undisturbed as when he called his followers to prayer, detached two of his best-mounted cavaliers, with instructions to approach as closely as prudence permitted to these travellers of the desert, and observe more minutely their numbers, their character, and, if possible, their purpose. The approach of danger, or what was feared as such, was like a stimulating draught to one in apathy, and recalled Sir Kenneth to himself and his situation.

"What fear you from these Christian horseman, for such they seem?" he said to the Hakim.

"Fear!" said El Hakim, repeating the word disdainfully— "The sage fears nothing but Heaven, but ever expects from wicked men the worst which they can do,"

"They are Christians," said Sir Kenneth, "and it is the time of truce—why should you fear a breach of faith?"

"They are the priestly soldiers of the Temple," answered El Hakim, "whose vow limits them to know neither truce nor faith with the worshippers of Islam. May the Prophet blight them, both root, branch, and twig!—Their peace is war, and their faith is falsehood, Other invaders of Palestine have their times and moods of courtesy. The lion Richard will spare when he has conquered—the eagle Philip will close his wing when he has stricken a prey—even the Austrian bear will sleep when he is gorged; but this horde of ever-hungry wolves know neither pause nor satiety in their rapine —Seest thou not that they are detaching a party from their main body, and that they take an eastern direction? Yon are their pages and squires, whom they train up in their accursed mysteries, and whom, as lighter mounted, they send to cut us off from our watering-place. But they will be disappointed; *I* know the war of the desert yet better than they."

He spoke a few words to his principal officer, and his whole demeanour and countenance was at once changed from the solemn repose of an Eastern sage, accustomed more to contemplation than to action, into the prompt and proud expression of a gallant soldier, whose energies are roused by the near approach of a danger, which he at once foresees and despises.

To Sir Kenneth's eyes the approaching crisis had a different aspect, and when Adonbec said to him, "Thou must tarry close by my side," he answered solemnly in the negative.

"Yonder," he said, "are my comrades in arms—the men in whose society I have vowed to fight or fall—on their banner gleams the sign of our most blessed redemption—I cannot fly from the Cross in company with the Crescent."

"Fool!" said the Hakim; "their first action would be to do thee to death, were it only to conceal their breach of the truce."

"Of that I must take my chance," replied Sir Kenneth; "but I wear not the bonds of the infidels an instant longer than I can cast them from me."

"Then will I compel thee to follow me," said El Hakim.

"Compel!" answered Sir Kenneth, angrily. "Wert thou not my benefactor, or one who has showed will to be such, and were it not that it is to thy confidence I owe the freedom of these hands, which thou mightest have loaded with fetters, I would show thee that, unarmed as I am, compulsion would be no easy task."

"Enough, enough," replied the Arabian physician; "we lose time even when it is becoming precious."

So saying, he threw his arm aloft, and uttered a loud and shrill cry, as a signal to those of his retinue, who instantly dispersed themselves on the face of the desert, in as many different directions as a chaplet of beads when the string is broken. Sir Kenneth had no time to note what ensued; for at the same instant the Hakim seized the rein of his steed, and putting his own to its mettle, both sprung forth at once with the suddenness of light, and at a pitch of velocity which almost deprived the Scottish knight of the power of respiration, and left him absolutely incapable, had he been desirous, to have checked the career of his guide. Practised as Sir Kenneth was in horsemanship from his earliest youth, the speediest horse he had ever mounted was a tortoise in comparison to those of the

Arabian sage. They spurned the sand from behind them—they seemed to devour the desert before them—miles flew away with minutes, and yet their strength seemed unabated, and their respiration as free as when they first started upon the wonderful race. The motion, too, as easy as it was swift, seemed more like flying through the air than riding on the earth, and was attended with no unpleasant sensation, save the awe naturally felt by one who is moving at such astonishing speed, and the difficulty of breathing occasioned by their passing through the air so rapidly.

It was not until after an hour of this portentous motion, and when all human pursuit was far, far behind, that the Hakim at length relaxed his speed, and, slackening the pace of the horses into a hand gallop, began, in a voice as composed and even as if he had been walking for the last hour, a descant upon the excellence of his coursers to the Scot, who, breathless, half-blind, half-deaf, and altogether giddy from the rapidity of this singular ride, hardly comprehended the words which flowed so freely from his companion.

"These horses," he said, "are of the breed called the Winged, equal in speed to aught excepting the Borak of the Prophet. They are fed on the golden barley of Yemen, mixed with spices, and with a small portion of dried sheep's flesh. Kings have given provinces to possess them, and their age is active as their youth. Thou, Nazarene, art the first, save a true believer, that ever had beneath his loins one of this noble race, a gift of the Prophet himself to the blessed Ali, his kinsman and lieutenant, well called the Lion of God. Time lays his touch so lightly on these generous steeds, that the mare on which thou now sittest has seen five times five years pass over her, yet retains her pristine speed and vigour, only that in the career the support of a bridle, managed by a hand more experienced than thine, hath now become necessary. May the Prophet be blessed, who hath bestowed on the true believers the means of advance and retreat, which causeth their iron-clothed enemies to be worn out with their own ponderous weight! How the horses of yonder dog Templars must have snorted and blown, when they had toiled fetlock-deep in the desert for one-twentieth part of the space which these brave steeds have left behind them, without one thick pant, or a drop of moisture upon their sleek and velvet coats!"

The Scottish knight, who had now begun to recover his breath and powers of attention, could not help acknowledging in his heart the advantage possessed by these Eastern warriors in a race of animals, alike proper for advance or retreat, and so admirably adapted to the level and sandy deserts of Arabia and Syria. But he did not choose to augment the pride of the Moslem by acquiescing in his proud claim of superiority, and therefore suffered the conversation to drop, and looking around him could now, at the more moderate pace at which they moved, distinguish that he was in a country not unknown to him.

The blighted borders and sullen waters of the Dead Sea, the ragged and precipitous chain of mountains arising on the left, the two or three palms clustered together, forming the single green speck on the bosom of the waste wilderness,—objects which, once seen, were scarcely to be forgotten,—showed to Sir Kenneth that they were approaching the fountain called the Diamond of the Desert, which had been the scene of his interview, on a former occasion, with the Saracen Emir, Sheerkohf, or Ilderim. In a few minutes they checked their horses beside the spring, and the Hakim invited Sir Kenneth to descend from horseback, and repose himself as in a place of safety. They unbridled their steeds, El Hakim observing that further care of them was unnecessary, since they would be speedily joined by some of the best mounted among his slaves, who would do what further was needful.

"Meantime," he said, spreading some food on the grass, "eat and drink, and be not discouraged. Fortune may raise up or abuse the ordinary mortal, but the sage and the soldier should have minds beyond her control."

The Scottish knight endeavoured to testify his thanks by showing himself docile; but, though he strove to eat out of complaisance, the singular contrast between his present situation, and that which he had occupied on the same spot, when the envoy of princes, and the victor in combat, came like a cloud over his mind, and fasting, lassitude, and fatigue, oppressed his bodily powers. El Hakim examined his hurried pulse, his red and inflamed eye, his heated hand, and his shortened respiration.

"The mind," he said, "grows wise by watching, but her sister, the body, of coarser materials, needs the support of repose. Thou must sleep; and that thou mayst do so to refreshment thou must take a draught mingled with this elixir."

He drew from his bosom a small crystal vial, cased in silver fili gree-work, and dropped into a little golden drinking-cup a small portion of a dark-coloured fluid.

"This," he said, "is one of those productions which Allah hath sent on earth for a blessing, though man's weakness and wickedness have sometimes converted it into a curse. It is powerful as the wine-cup of the Nazarene to drop the curtain on the sleepless eye, and to relieve the burden of the overloaded bosom; but when applied to the purposes of indulgence and debauchery, it rends the nerves, destroys the strength, weakens the intellect, and undermines life. But fear not thou to use its virtues in the time of need, for the wise man warms him by the same firebrand with which the madman burneth the tent."[1]

"I have seen too much of thy skill, sage Hakim," said Sir Kenneth, "to debate thine hest;" and swallowed the narcotic, mingled as it was with some water from the spring, then wrapped him in the haick, or Arab cloak, which had been fastened to his saddle-pommel, and, according to the directions of the physician, stretched himself at ease in the shade to await the promised repose. Sleep came not at first, but in her stead a train of pleasing, yet not rousing or awakening sensations. A state ensued in which, still conscious of his own identity and his own condition, the knight felt enabled to consider them, not only without alarm and sorrow, but as composedly as he might have viewed the story of his misfortunes acted upon a stage, or rather as a disembodied spirit might regard the trans-actions of its past existence. From this state of repose, amounting almost to apathy respecting the past, his thoughts were carried forward to the future, which, in spite of all that existed to overcloud the prospect, glittered with such hues as under much happier auspices his unstimulated imagination had not been able to produce, even in its most exalted state. Liberty, fame, successful love, appeared to be the certain and not very distant prospect of the enslaved exile, the dishonoured knight, even of the despairing lover, who had placed his hopes of happiness so far beyond the prospect of chance, in her wildest possibilities, serving to countenance his wishes. Gradually, as the intellectual sight became overclouded, these gay visions became obscure, like the dying hues of sunset, until they were at last lost in total oblivion; and Sir Kenneth lay extended at the feet of El Hakim, to all appearance, but for his deep respiration, as inanimate a corpse as if life had actually departed.

[1] Some preparation of opium seems to be intimated.

CHAPTER XXIII

'Mid these wild scenes Enchantment waves her hand,
To change the face of the mysterious land ;
Till the bewildering scenes around us seem
The vain productions of a feverish dream.

                              Astolpho, a Romance.

WHEN the Knight of the Leopard awoke from his long and profound repose, he found himself in circumstances so different from those in which he had lain down to sleep, that he doubted whether he was not still dreaming, or whether the scene had not been changed by magic. Instead of the damp grass, he lay on a couch of more than Oriental luxury, and some kind hands had, during his repose, stripped him of the cassock of chamois which he wore under his armour, and substituted a night-dress of the finest linen, and a loose gown of silk. He had been canopied only by the palm-trees of the desert, but now he lay beneath a silken pavilion, which blazed with the richest colours of the Chinese loom, while a slight curtain of gauze, displayed around his couch, was calculated to protect his repose from the insects, to which he had, ever since his arrival in these climates, been a constant and passive prey. He looked around, as if to convince himself that he was actually awake, and all that fell beneath his eye partook of the splendour of his dormitory. A portable bath of cedar, lined with silver, was ready for use, and steamed with the odours which had been used in preparing it. On a small stand of ebony beside the couch, stood a silver vase, containing sherbet of the most exquisite quality, cold as snow, and which the thirst that followed the use of the strong narcotic rendered peculiarly delicious. Still further to dispel the dregs of intoxication which it had left behind, the knight resolved to use the bath, and experienced in doing so a delightful refreshment. Having dried himself with napkins of the Indian wool, he would willingly have resumed his own coarse garments, that he might go forth to see whether the world was as much changed without, as within the place of his repose. These, however, were nowhere to be seen, but in their place he found a Saracen dress of rich materials, with sabre and poniard, and all befitting an emir of distinction. He was able to suggest no motive to himself for this exuberance of care, excepting a suspicion that these attentions were intended to shake him in his religious profession ; as, indeed, it was well known that the high esteem of the

European knowledge and courage, made the Soldan unbounded in his gifts to those, who, having become his prisoners, had been induced to take the turban. Sir Kenneth, therefore, crossing himself devoutly, resolved to set all such snares at defiance; and, that he might do so the more firmly, conscientiously determined to avail himself as moderately as possible of the attentions and luxuries thus liberally heaped upon him. Still, however, he felt his head oppressed and sleepy, and aware, too, that his undress was not fit for appearing abroad, he reclined upon the couch, and was again locked in the arms of slumber.

But this time his rest was not unbroken; for he was awakened by the voice of the physician at the door of the tent, enquiring after his health, and whether he had rested sufficiently.— "May I enter your tent?" he concluded, "for the curtain is drawn before the entrance."

"The master," replied Sir Kenneth, determined to show that he was not surprised into forgetfulness of his own condition, "need demand no permission to enter the tent of the slave."

"But if I come not as a master?" said El Hakim, still without entering.

"The physician," answered the knight, "hath free access to the bedside of his patient."

"Neither come I now as a physician," replied El Hakim; "and therefore I still request permission, ere I come under the covering of thy tent."

"Whoever comes as a friend," said Sir Kenneth, "and such thou hast hitherto shown thyself to me, the habitation of the friend is ever open to him."

"Yet once again," said the Eastern sage, after the periphrastical manner of his countrymen, "supposing that I come not as a friend?"

"Come as thou wilt," said the Scottish knight, somewhat impatient of this circumlocution, "be what thou wilt—thou knowest well it is neither in my power nor my inclination to refuse thee entrance."

"I come, then," said El Hakim, "as your ancient foe; but a fair and a generous one."

He entered as he spoke; and when he stood before the bedside of Sir Kenneth, the voice continued to be that of Adonbec the Arabian physician, but the form, dress, and features, were those of Ilderim of Kurdistan, called Sheerkohf. Sir Kenneth gazed upon him, as if he expected the vision to depart, like something created by his imagination.

"Doth it so surprise thee," said Ilderim, "and thou an approved warrior, to see that a soldier knows somewhat of the art of healing?—I say to thee, Nazarene, that an accomplished cavalier should know how to dress his steed as well as how to ride him; how to forge his sword upon the stithy, as well as how to use it in battle; how to burnish his arms, as well as how to wear them; and, above all, how to cure wounds as well as how to inflict them."

As he spoke, the Christian knight repeatedly shut his eyes, and while they remained closed, the idea of the Hakim, with his long flowing dark robes, high Tartar cap, and grave gestures was present to his imagination; but so soon as he opened them, the graceful and richly-gemmed turban, the light hauberk of steel rings entwisted with silver, which glanced brilliantly as it obeyed every inflection of the body, the features freed from their formal expression, less swarthy, and no longer shadowed by the mass of hair (now limited to a well-trimmed beard,) announced the soldier and not the sage.

"Art thou still so much surprised," said the Emir, "and hast thou walked in the world with such little observance, as to wonder that men are not always what they seem?—Thou thyself—art thou what thou seemest?"

"No, by Saint Andrew!" exclaimed the knight; "for to the whole Christian camp I seem a traitor, and I know myself to be a true, though an erring man."

"Even so I judged thee," said Ilderim; "and as we had eaten salt together, I deemed myself bound to rescue thee from death and contumely.—But wherefore lie you still on your couch, since the sun is high in the heavens? or are the vestments which my sumpter-camels have afforded unworthy of your wearing?"

"Not unworthy, surely, but unfitting for it," replied the Scot. "Give me the dress of a slave, noble Ilderim, and I will don it with pleasure; but I cannot brook to wear the habit of the free Eastern warrior, with the turban of the Moslem."

"Nazarene," answered the Emir, "thy nation so easily entertains suspicion, that it may well render themselves suspected. Have I not told thee that Saladin desires no converts saving those whom the holy Prophet shall dispose to submit themselves to his law? violence and bribery are alike alien to his plan for extending the true faith. Hearken to me, my brother. When the blind man was miraculously restored to sight, the scales dropped from his eyes at the Divine pleasure—think'st thou that any earthly leech could have removed them? No. Such mediciner might have tormented the patient with his instruments, or perhaps soothed him with his balsams and cordials, but dark as he was must the darkened man have remained; and it is even so with the blindness of the understanding. If there be those among the Franks, who, for the sake of worldly lucre, have assumed the turban of the Prophet, and followed the laws of Islam, with their own consciences be the blame. Themselves sought out the bait —it was not flung to them by the Soldan. And when they shall hereafter be sentenced, as hypocrites, to the lowest gulf of hell, below Christian and Jew, magician and idolater, and condemned to eat the fruit of the tree Yacoun, which is the heads of demons, to themselves, not to the Soldan, shall their guilt and their punishment be attributed. Wherefore wear, without doubt or scruple, the vesture prepared for you, since, if you proceed to the camp of Saladin, your own native dress will expose you to troublesome observation, and perhaps to insult."

"*If* I go to the camp of Saladin?" said Sir Kenneth, repeating the words of the Emir. "Alas! am I a free agent, and rather must I *not* go wherever your pleasure carries me?"

"Thine own will may guide thine own motions," said the Emir, "as freely as the wind which moveth the dust of the desert in what direction it chooseth. The noble enemy who met, and well-nigh mastered my sword, cannot become my slave like him who has crouched beneath it. If wealth and power would tempt thee to join our people, I could ensure thy possessing them; but the man who refused the favours of the Soldan, when the axe was at his head, will not, I fear, now accept them, when I tell him he has his free choice."

"Complete your generosity, noble Emir," said Sir Kenneth, "by forbearing to show me a mode of requital, which conscience forbids me to comply with. Permit me rather to express, as bound in courtesy, my gratitude for this most chivalrous bounty, this undeserved generosity."

"Say not undeserved," replied the Emir Ilderim; "was it not through thy conversation, and thy account of the beauties which grace the court of the Melech Ric, that I ventured me thither in disguise, and thereby procured a sight the most blessed that I have ever enjoyed—that I ever shall enjoy, until the glories of Paradise beam on my eyes?"

"I understand you not," said Sir Kenneth, colouring

alternately, and turning pale, as one who felt that the conversation was taking a tone of the most painful delicacy.

"Not understand me!" exclaimed the Emir. "If the sight I saw in the tent of King Richard escaped thine observation, I will account it duller than the edge of a buffoon's wooden falchion. True, thou wert under sentence of death at the time; but, in my case, had my head been dropping from the trunk, the last strained glances of my eyeballs had distinguished with delight such a vision of loveliness, and the head would have rolled itself towards the incomparable houris, to kiss with its quivering lips the hem of their vestments.— Yonder royalty of England, who for her superior loveliness deserves to be Queen of the universe—what tenderness in her blue eye! what lustre in her tresses of dishevelled gold!— By the tomb of the Prophet, I scarce think that the houri who shall present to me the diamond cup of immortality, will deserve so warm a caress!"

"Saracen," said Sir Kenneth, sternly, "thou speakest of the wife of Richard of England, of whom men think not and speak not as a woman to be won, but as a Queen to be revered."

"I cry you mercy," said the Saracen. "I had forgotten your superstitious veneration for the sex, which you consider rather fit to be wondered at and worshipped, than wooed and possessed. I warrant, since thou exactest such profound respect to yonder tender piece of frailty, whose every motion, step, and look, bespeaks her very woman, less than absolute adoration must not be yielded to her of the dark tresses, and nobly speaking eye. *She*, indeed, I will allow, hath in her noble port and majestic mien something at once pure and firm—yet even she, when pressed by opportunity and a forward lover, would, I warrant thee, thank him in her heart rather for treating her as a mortal than as a goddess."

"Respect the kinswoman of Cœur de Lion!" said Sir Kenneth, in a tone of unrepressed anger.

"Respect her!" answered the Emir, in scorn; "by the Caaba, and if I do, it shall be rather as the bride of Saladin."

"The infidel Soldan is unworthy to salute even a spot that has been pressed by the foot of Edith Plantagenet!" exclaimed the Christian, springing from his couch.

"Ha! what said the Giaour?" exclaimed the Emir, laying his hand on his poniard hilt, while his forehead glowed like glancing copper, and the muscles of his lips and cheeks wrought till each curl of his beard seemed to twist and screw itself, as if alive with Instinctive wrath. But the Scottish knight, who had stood the lion-anger of Richard, was unappalled at the tiger-like mood of the chafed Saracen.

"What I have said," continued Sir Kenneth, with folded arms and dauntless look, "I would, were my hands loose, maintain on foot or horseback against all mortals, and would hold it not the most memorable deed of my life to support it with my good broadsword against a score of these sickles and bodkins," pointing at the curved sabre and small poniard of the Emir.

The Saracen recovered his composure as the Christian spoke, so far as to withdraw his hand from his weapon, as if the motion had been without meaning; but still continued in deep ire.

"By the sword of the Prophet," he said, "which is the key both of heaven and hell, he little values his own life, brother, who uses the language thou dost! Believe me, that were thine hands loose, as thou term'st it, one single true believer would find them so much to do, that thou wouldst soon wish them fettered again in manacles of iron."

"Sooner would I wish them hewn off by the shoulder-blades!" replied Sir Kenneth.

"Well. Thy hands are bound at present," said the Saracen, in a more amicable tone, "bound by thine own gentle sense of courtesy, nor have I any present purpose of setting them at liberty. We have proved each other's strength and courage ere now, and we may again meet in a fair field;—and shame befall him who shall be the first to part from his foeman! But now we are friends, and I look for aid from thee, rather than hard terms or defiances."

"We *are* friends," repeated the knight; and there was a pause, during which the fiery Saracen paced the tent, like the lion, who, after violent irritation, is said to take that method of cooling the distemperature of his blood, ere he stretches himself to repose in his den. The colder European remained unaltered in posture and aspect; yet he, doubtless, was also engaged in subduing the angry feelings which had been so unexpectedly awakened.

"Let us reason of this calmly," said the Saracen; "I am a physician, as thou knowest, and it is written, that he who would have his wound cured, must not shrink when the leech probes and tents it. Seest thou, I am about to lay my finger on the sore. Thou lovest this kinswoman of the

Melech Ric—Unfold the veil that shrouds thy thoughts—or unfold it not if thou wilt, for mine eyes see through its coverings."

"I *loved* her," answered Sir Kenneth, after a pause, "as a man loves Heaven's grace, and sued for her favour like a sinner for Heaven's pardon."

"And you love her no longer?" said the Saracen.

"Alas!" answered Sir Kenneth, "I am no longer worthy to love her.—I pray thee cease this discourse; thy words are poniards to me."

"Pardon me but a moment," continued Ilderim. "When thou, a poor and obscure soldier, didst so boldly and so highly fix thine affection, tell me, hadst thou good hope of its issue?"

"Love exists not without hope," replied the knight; "but mine was as nearly allied to despair, as that of the sailor swimming for his life, who, as he surmounts billow after billow, catches by intervals some gleam of the distant beacon, which shows him there is land in sight, though his sinking heart and wearied limbs assure him that he shall never reach it."

"And now," said Ilderim, "these hopes are sunk—that solitary light is quenched for ever?"

"For ever," answered Sir Kenneth, in the tone of an echo from the bosom of a ruined sepulchre.

"Methinks," said the Saracen, "if all thou lackest were some such distant meteoric glimpse of happiness as thou hadst formerly, thy beacon-light might be rekindled, thy hope fished up from the ocean in which it has sunk, and thou thyself, good knight, restored to the exercise and amusement of nourishing thy fantastic passion upon a diet as unsubstantial as moonlight; for, if thou stood'st to-morrow fair in reputation as ever thou wert, she whom thou lovest will not be less the daughter of princes, and the elected bride of Saladin."

"I would it so stood," said the Scot, "and if I did not——"

He stopt short, like a man who is afraid of boasting under circumstances which did not permit his being put to the test. The Saracen smiled as he concluded the sentence.

"Thou wouldst challenge the Soldan to single combat?" said he.

"And if I did," said Sir Kenneth, haughtily, "Saladin's would neither be the first nor the best turban that I have couched lance at."

"Ay, but methinks the Soldan might regard it as too unequal

a mode of perilling the chance of a royal bride, and the event
of a great war," said the Emir,

"He may be met with in the front of battle," said the knight,
his eyes gleaming with the ideas which such a thought inspired.

"He has been ever found there," said Ilderim; "nor is it
his wont to turn his horse's head from any brave encounter.—
But it was not of the Soldan that I meant to speak. In a
word, if it will content thee to be placed in such reputation as
may be attained by detection of the thief who stole the banner
of England, I can put thee in a fair way of achieving this task
—that is, if thou wilt be governed; for what says Lokman, 'If
the child would walk, the nurse must lead him—if the ignorant
would understand, the wise must instruct.'"

"And thou art wise, Ilderim," said the Scot, "wise though
a Saracen, and generous though an infidel. I have witnessed
that thou art both. Take, then, the guidance of this matter;
and so thou ask nothing of me contrary to my loyalty and my
Christian faith, I will obey thee punctually. Do what thou
hast said, and take my life when it is accomplished."

"Listen thou to me, then," said the Saracen. "Thy noble
hound is now recovered, by the blessing of that divine medicine
which healeth man and beast, and by his sagacity shall those
who assailed him be discovered."

"Ha!" said the knight, "methinks I comprehend thee; I
was dull not to think of this!"

"But tell me," added the Emir, "hast thou any followers or
retainers in the camp by whom the animal may be known?"

"I dismissed," said Sir Kenneth, "my old attendant, thy
patient, with a varlet that waited on him, at the time when I
expected to suffer death, giving him letters for my friends in
Scotland; there are none other to whom the dog is familiar.
But then my own person is well known; my very speech will
betray me, in camp where I have played no mean part for
many months."

"Both he and thou shalt be disguised, so as to escape even
close examination.—I tell thee," said the Saracen, "that not
thy brother in arms, not thy brother in blood, shall discover
thee, if thou be guided by my counsels. Thou hast seen me
do matters more difficult; he that can call the dying from the
darkness of the shadow of death, can easily cast a mist before
the eyes of the living. But mark me, there is still the condition
annexed to this service, that thou deliver a letter of Saladin to
the niece of the Melech Ric, whose name is as difficult to our

Eastern tongue and lips, as her beauty is delightful to our eyes."

Sir Kenneth paused before he answered, and the Saracen, observing his hesitation, demanded of him, " if he feared to undertake this message ? "

" Not if there were death in the execution," said Sir Kenneth; " I do but pause to consider whether it consists with my honour to bear the letter of the Soldan, or with that of the Lady Edith to receive it from a heathen prince."

" By the head of Mahommed, and by the honour of a soldier—by the tomb at Mecca, and by the soul of my father," said the Emir, " I swear to thee that the letter is written in all honour and respect. The song of the nightingale will sooner blight the rose-bower she loves, than will the words of the Soldan offend the ears of the lovely kinswoman of England."

" Then," said the knight, " I will bear the Soldan's letter faithfully, as if I were his born vassal—understanding, that beyond this simple act of service, which I will render with fidelity, from me of all men he can least expect mediation or advice in this his strange love-suit."

" Saladin is noble," answered the Emir, " and will not spur a generous horse to a leap which he cannot achieve.—Come with me to my tent," he added, " and thou shalt be presently equipped with a disguise as unsearchable as midnight ; so thou mayst walk the camp of the Nazarenes as if thou hadst on thy finger the signet of the Giaougi." [1]

CHAPTER XXIV

———A grain of dust
Soiling our cup, will make our sense reject
Fastidiously the draught which we did thirst for ;
A rusted nail, placed near the faithful compass,
Will sway it from the truth, and wreck the argosy.
Even this small cause of anger and disgust
Will break the bonds of amity 'mongst princes,
And wreck their noblest purposes.
                              The Crusade.

THE reader can now have little doubt who the Ethiopian slave really was, with what purpose he had sought Richard's camp, and wherefore and with what hope he now stood close to the person of that monarch, as, surrounded by his valiant peers of England and Normandy, Cœur de Lion stood on the summit

[1] Perhaps the same with Gyges.

or Saint George's Mount, with the banner of England by his side, borne by the most goodly person in the army, being his own natural brother, William with the Long Sword, Earl of Salisbury, the offspring of Henry the Second's amour with the celebrated Rosamond of Woodstock.

From several expressions in the King's conversation with Neville on the preceding day, the Nubian was left in anxious doubt whether his disguise had not been penetrated, especially as that the King seemed to be aware in what manner the agency of the dog was expected to discover the thief who stole the banner, although the circumstance of such an animal's having been wounded on the occasion, had been scarce mentioned in Richard's presence. Nevertheless, as the King continued to treat him in no other manner than his exterior required, the Nubian remained uncertain whether he was or was not discovered, and determined not to throw the disguise aside voluntarily.

Meanwhile, the powers of the various crusading princes, arrayed under their royal and princely leaders, swept in long order around the base of the little mound; and as those of each different country passed by, their commanders advanced a step or two up the hill, and made a signal of courtesy to Richard and to the standard of England, "in sign of regard and amity," as the protocol of the ceremony heedfully expressed it, "not of subjection or vassalage." The spiritual dignitaries, who in those days veiled not their bonnets to created being, bestowed on the King and his symbol of command their blessing instead of rendering obeisance.

Thus the long files marched on, and, diminished as they were by so many causes, appeared still an iron host, to whom the conquest of Palestine might seem an easy task. The soldiers, inspired by the consciousness of united strength, sat erect in their steel saddles, while it seemed that the trumpets sounded more cheerfully shrill, and the steeds, refreshed by rest and provender, chafed on the bit, and trode the ground more proudly. On they passed, troop after troop, banners waving, spears glancing, plumes dancing, in long perspective —a host composed of different nations, complexions, languages, arms, and appearances, but all fired, for the time, with the holy yet romantic purpose of rescuing the distressed daughter of Zion from her thraldom, and redeeming the sacred earth, which more than mortal had trodden, from the yoke of the unbelieving Pagan. And it must be owned, that if, in other circumstances, the species of courtesy rendered to the King of England by so many warriors, from whom he claimed no natural allegiance, had in it something that might have been thought humiliating, yet the nature and cause of the war was so fitted to his pre-eminently chivalrous character, and renowned feats in arms, that claims, which might elsewhere have been urged, were there forgotten ; and the brave did willing homage to the bravest, in an expedition where the most undaunted and energetic courage was necessary to success.

The good King was seated on horseback about half-way up the mount, a morion on his head, surmounted by a crown, which left his manly features exposed to public view, as with cool and considerate eye, he perused each rank as it passed him, and returned the salutation of the leaders. His tunic was of sky-coloured velvet, covered with plates of silver, and his hose of crimson silk, slashed with cloth of gold. By his side stood the seeming Ethiopian slave, holding the noble dog in a leash, such as was used in woodcraft. It was a circumstance which attracted no notice, for many of the princes of the Crusade had introduced black slaves into their household, in imitation of the barbarous splendour of the Saracens. Over the King's head streamed the large folds of the banner, and, as he looked to it from time to time, he seemed to regard a ceremony, indifferent to himself personally, as important, when considered as atoning an indignity offered to the kingdom which he ruled. In the background, and on the very summit of the mount, a wooden turret, erected for the occasion, held the Queen Berengaria and the principal ladies of the court. To this the King looked from time to time, and then ever and anon his eyes were turned on the Nubian and the dog, but only when such leaders approached, as, from circumstances of previous ill-will, he suspected of being accessary to the theft of the standard, or whom he judged capable of a crime so mean.

Thus, he did not look in that direction when Philip Augustus of France approached at the head of his splendid troops of Gallic chivalry—nay, he anticipated the motions of the French King, by descending the mount as the latter came up the ascent, so that they met in the middle space, and blended their greeting so gracefully that it appeared they met in fraternal equality. The sight of the two greatest princes in Europe, in rank at once and power, thus publicly avowing their concord, called forth bursts of thundering acclaim from the crusading host at many miles' distance, and made the roving Arab scouts of the desert alarm the camp of Saladin with intelligence, that the army of the Christians was in motion. Yet who but the King of kings can read the hearts of monarchs? Under this smooth show of courtesy, Richard nourished displeasure and suspicion against Philip, and Philip meditated withdrawing himself and his host from the army of the Cross, and leaving Richard to accomplish or fail in the enterprise with his own unassisted forces.

Richard's demeanour was different when the dark-armed knights and squires of the Temple chivalry approached—men with countenances bronzed to Asiatic blackness by the suns of Palestine, and the admirable state of whose horses and appointments far surpassed even that of the choicest troops of France and England. The King cast a hasty glance aside, but the Nubian stood quiet, and his trusty dog sat at his feet, watching, with a sagacious yet pleased look, the ranks which now passed before them. The King's look turned again on the chivalrous Templars, as the Grand Master, availing himself of his mingled character, bestowed his benediction on Richard as a priest, instead of doing him reverence as a military leader.

"The misproud and amphibious caitiff puts the monk upon me," said Richard to the Earl of Salisbury. "But, Longsword, we will let it pass. A punctilio must not lose Christendom the services of these experienced lances, because their victories have rendered them overweening.—Lo you, here comes our valiant adversary, the Duke of Austria; mark his manner and bearing, Longsword; and thou, Nubian, let the hound have full view of him. By Heaven, he brings his buffoons along with him!"

In fact, whether from habit, or, which is more likely, to intimate contempt of the ceremonial he was about to comply with, Leopold was attended by his *spruch-sprecher* and his jester, and as he advanced towards Richard he whistled in what he wished to be considered as an indifferent manner, though his heavy features evinced the sullenness, mixed with the fear, with which a truant schoolboy may be seen to approach his master.

As the reluctant dignitary made, with discomposed and sulky look, the obeisance required, the *spruch-sprecher* shook his baton, and proclaimed, like a herald, that, in what he was now doing, the Archduke of Austria was not to be held derogating from the rank and privileges of a sovereign prince;

to which the jester answered with a sonorous *amen*, which provoked much laughter among the bystanders.

King Richard looked more than once at the Nubian and his dog; but the former moved not, nor did the latter strain at the leash, so that Richard said to the slave with some scorn, "Thy success in this enterprise, my sable friend, even though thou hast brought thy hound's sagacity to back thine own, will not, I fear, place thee high in the rank of wizards, or much augment thy merits towards our person."

The Nubian answered, as usual, only by a lowly obeisance.

Meantime the troops of the Marquis of Montserrat next passed in order before the King of England. That powerful and wily baron, to make the greater display of his forces, had divided them into two bodies. At the head of the first, consisting of his vassals and followers, and levied from his Syrian possessions, came his brother Enguerrand, and he himself followed, leading on a gallant band of twelve hundred Stradiots, a kind of light cavalry raised by the Venetians in their Dalmatian possessions, and of which they had intrusted the command to the Marquis, with whom the republic had many bonds of connexion. These Stradiots were clothed in a fashion partly European, but partaking chiefly of the Eastern fashion. They wore, indeed, short hauberks, but had over them parti-coloured tunics of rich stuffs, with large wide pantaloons and half-boots. On their heads were straight upright caps, similar to those of the Greeks, and they carried small round targets, bows and arrows, scimitars, and poniards. They were mounted on horses, carefully selected, and well maintained at the expense of the State of Venice; their saddles and appointments resembled those of the Turks, and they rode in the same manner, with short stirrups and upon a high seat. These troops were of great use in skirmishing with the Arabs, though unable to engage in close combat, like the iron-sheathed men-at-arms of Western and Northern Europe.

Before this goodly band came Conrade, in the same garb with the Stradiots, but of such rich stuff that he seemed to blaze with gold and silver, and the milk-white plume fastened in his cap by a clasp of diamonds, seemed tall enough to sweep the clouds. The noble steed which he reined bounded and caracoled, and displayed his spirit and agility in a manner which might have troubled a less admirable horseman than the Marquis, who gracefully ruled him with the one hand, while the other displayed the baton, whose predominancy over the ranks which he led seemed equally absolute. Yet his authority over the Stradiots was more in show than in substance; for there paced beside him, on an ambling palfrey of soberest mood, a little old man, dressed entirely in black, without beard or moustaches, and having an appearance altogether mean and insignificant, when compared with the blaze of splendour around him. But this mean-looking old man was one of those deputies whom the Venetian government sent into camps to overlook the conduct of the generals to whom the leading was consigned, and to maintain that jealous system of espial and control which had long distinguished the policy of the republic.

Conrade, who, by cultivating Richard's humour, had attained a certain degree of favour with him, no sooner was come within his ken than the King of England descended a step or two to meet him, exclaiming, at the same time, "Ha, Lord Marquis, thou at the head of the fleet Stradiots, and thy black shadow attending thee as usual, whether the sun shines or not!—May not one ask thee whether the rule of the troops remains with the shadow or the substance?"

Conrade was commencing his reply with a smile, when Roswal, the noble hound, uttering a furious and savage yell, sprung forward. The Nubian at the same time slipped the leash, and the hound, rushing on, leapt upon Conrade's noble charger, and seizing the Marquis by the throat, pulled him down from the saddle. The plumed rider lay rolling on the sand, and the frightened horse fled in wild career through the camp.

"Thy hound hath pulled down the right quarry, I warrant him," said the King to the Nubian, "and I vow to Saint George he is a stag of ten tynes!—Pluck the dog off, lest he throttle him."

The Ethiopian, accordingly, though not without difficulty, disengaged the dog from Conrade, and fastened him up, still highly excited, and struggling in the leash. Meanwhile many crowded to the spot, especially followers of Conrade, and officers of the Stradiots, who, as they saw their leader lie gazing wildly on the sky, raised him up amid a tumultuary cry of—"Cut the slave and his hound to pieces!"

But the voice of Richard, loud and sonorous, was heard clear above all other exclamations, "He dies the death who injures the hound! He hath but done his duty, after the sagacity with which God and nature have endowed the brave animal.—Stand forward for a false traitor, thou Conrade, Marquis of Montserrat! I impeach thee of treason."

Several of the Syrian leaders had now come up, and Conrade, vexation, and shame, and confusion struggling with passion in his manner and voice, exclaimed, "What means this?—With what am I charged?—Why this base usage, and these reproachful terms?—Is this the league of concord which England renewed but so lately?"

"Are the princes of the Crusade turned hares or deers in the eyes of King Richard, that he should slip hounds on them?" said the sepulchral voice of the Grand Master of the Templars.

"It must be some singular accident, some fatal mistake," said Philip of France, who rode up at the same moment.

"Some deceit of the Enemy," said the Archbishop of Tyre.

"A stratagem of the Saracens," cried Henry of Champagne. "It were well to hang up the dog, and put the slave to the torture."

"Let no man lay hand upon them," said Richard, "as he loves his own life!—Conrade, stand forth, if thou darest, and deny the accusation which this mute animal hath in his noble instinct brought against thee, of injury done to him, and foul scorn to England?"

"I never touched the banner," said Conrade, hastily.

"Thy words betray thee, Conrade!" said Richard; "for how didst thou know, save from conscious guilt, that the question is concerning the banner?"

"Hast thou then not kept the camp in turmoil on that and no other score?" answered Conrade; "and dost thou impute to a prince and an ally a crime, which, after all, was probably committed by some paltry felon for the sake of the gold thread? Or wouldst thou now impeach a confederate on the credit of a dog?"

By this time the alarm was becoming general, so that Philip of France interposed.

"Princes and nobles," he said, "you speak in presence of those whose swords will soon be at the throats of each other, if they hear their leaders at such terms together. In the name of Heaven, let us draw off, each his own troops, into their separate quarters, and ourselves meet an hour hence in the Pavilion of Council, to take some order in this new state of confusion."

"Content," said King Richard, "though I should have liked to have interrogated that caitiff while his gay doublet was yet besmirched with sand. But the pleasure of France shall be ours in this matter."

The leaders separated as was proposed, each prince placing himself at the head of his own forces; and then was heard on all sides the crying of war-cries, and the sounding of gathering-notes upon bugles and trumpets, by which the different stragglers were summoned to their prince's banner; and the troops were shortly seen in motion, each taking different routes through the camp to their own quarters. But although any immediate act of violence was thus prevented, yet the accident which had taken place dwelt on every mind; and those foreigners, who had that morning hailed Richard as the worthiest to lead their army, now resumed their prejudices against his pride and intolerance, while the English, conceiving the honour of their country connected with the quarrel, of which various reports had gone about, considered the natives of other countries jealous of the fame of England and her King, and disposed to undermine it by the meanest arts of intrigue. Many and various were the rumours spread upon the occasion, and there was one which averred that the Queen and her ladies had been much alarmed by the tumult, and that one of them had swooned.

The Council assembled at the appointed hour. Conrade had in the meanwhile laid aside his dishonoured dress, and with it the shame and confusion which, in spite of his talents and promptitude, had at first overwhelmed him, owing to the strangeness of the accident, and suddenness of the accusation. He was now robed like a prince, and entered the council-chamber attended by the Archduke of Austria, the Grand Masters both of the Temple and of the Order of Saint John, and several other potentates, who made a show of supporting him and defending his cause, chiefly perhaps from political motives, or because they themselves nourished a personal enmity against Richard.

This appearance of union in favour of Conrade was far from influencing the King of England. He entered the Council with his usual indifference of manner, and in the same dress in which he had just alighted from horseback. He cast a careless and somewhat scornful glance on the leaders, who had with studied affectation arranged themselves around Conrade, as if owning his cause, and in the most direct terms charged

Conrade of Montserrat with having stolen the banner of England, and wounded the faithful animal who stood in its defence.

Conrade arose boldly to answer, and in despite, as he expressed himself, of man and brute, king or dog, avouched his innocence of the crime charged.

"Brother of England," said Philip, who willingly assumed the character of moderator of the assembly, "this is an unusual impeachment. We do not hear you avouch your own knowledge of this matter, further than your belief resting upon the demeanour of this hound towards the Marquis of Montserrat. Surely the word of a knight and a prince should bear him out against the barking of a cur?"

"Royal brother," returned Richard, "recollect that the Almighty, who gave the dog to be companion of our pleasures and our toils, hath invested him with a nature noble and incapable of deceit. He forgets neither friend nor foe—remembers, and with accuracy, both benefit and injury. He hath a share of man's intelligence, but no share of man's falsehood. You may bribe a soldier to slay a man with his sword, or a witness to take life by false accusation; but you cannot make a hound tear his benefactor—he is the friend of man, save when man justly incurs his enmity. Dress yonder Marquis in what peacock-robes you will—disguise his appearance—alter his complexion with drugs and washes—hide him amidst an hundred men—I will yet pawn my sceptre that the hound detects him, and expresses his resentment, as you have this day beheld. This is no new incident, although a strange one. Murderers and robbers have been, ere now, convicted, and suffered death under such evidence, and men have said that the finger of God was in it. In thine own land, royal brother, and upon such an occasion, the matter was tried by a solemn duel betwixt the man and the dog, as appellant and defendant in a challenge of murder. The dog was victorious, the man was punished, and the crime was confessed. Credit me, royal brother, that hidden crimes have often been brought to light by the testimony even of inanimate substances, not to mention animals far inferior in instinctive sagacity to the dog, who is the friend and companion of our race."

"Such a duel there hath indeed been, royal brother," answered Philip, "and that in the reign of one of our predecessors, to whom God be gracious. But it was in the olden time, nor can we hold it a precedent fitting for this occasion.

The defendant in that case was a private gentleman, of small rank or respect; his offensive weapons were only a club, his defensive, a leathern jerkin. But we cannot degrade a prince to the disgrace of using such rude arms, or to the ignominy of such a combat."

"I never meant that you should," said King Richard; "it were foul play to hazard the good hound's life against that of such a double-faced traitor as this Conrade hath proved himself. But there lies our own glove; we appeal him to the combat in respect of the evidence we brought forth against him. A king, at least, is more than the mate of a marquis."

Conrade made no hasty effort to seize on the pledge which Richard cast into the middle of the assembly, and King Philip had time to reply, ere the Marquis made a motion to lift the glove.

"A king," said he of France, "is as much more than a match for the Marquis Conrade as a dog would be less. Royal Richard, this cannot be permitted. You are the leader of our expedition—the sword and buckler of Christendom."

"I protest against such a combat," said the Venetian proveditore, "until the King of England shall have repaid the fifty thousand bezants which he is indebted to the republic. It is enough to be threatened with the loss of our debt, should our debtor fall by the hands of the pagans, without the additional risk of his being slain in brawls amongst Christians, concerning dogs and banners."

"And I," said William with the Long Sword, Earl of Salisbury, "protest in my turn against my royal brother periling his life, which is the property of the people of England, in such a cause.—Here, noble brother, receive back your glove, and think only as if the wind had blown it from your hand. Mine shall lie in its stead. A king's son, though with the bar sinister on his shield, is at least a match for this marmoset of a marquis."

"Princes and nobles," said Conrade, "I will not accept of King Richard's defiance. He hath been chosen our leader against the Saracens, and if *his* conscience can answer the accusation of provoking an ally to the field on a quarrel so frivolous, *mine*, at least, cannot endure the reproach of accepting it. But touching his bastard brother, William of Woodstock, or against any other who shall adopt, or shall dare to stand godfather to this most false charge, I will defend my honour in the lists, and prove whosoever impeaches it a false liar."

"The Marquis of Montserrat," said the Archbishop of Tyre, "hath spoken like a wise and moderate gentleman; and methinks this controversy might, without dishonour to any party, end at this point."

"Methinks it might so terminate," said the King of France, "provided King Richard will recall his accusation, as made upon over slight grounds."

"Philip of France," answered Cœur de Lion, "my words shall never do my thoughts so much injury. I have charged yonder Conrade as a thief, who, under cloud of night, stole from its place the emblem of England's dignity. I still believe and charge him to be such; and when a day is appointed for the combat, doubt not that, since Conrade declines to meet us in person, I will find a champion to appear in support of my challenge; for thou, William, must not thrust thy long sword into this quarrel without our special license."

"Since my rank makes me arbiter in this most unhappy matter," said Philip of France, "I appoint the fifth day from hence for the decision thereof, by way of combat, according to knightly usage; Richard, King of England, to appear by his champion as appellant, and Conrade, Marquis of Montserrat, in his own person, as defendant. Yet I own, I know not where to find neutral ground where such a quarrel may be fought out; for it must not be in the neighbourhood of this camp, where the soldiers would make faction on the different sides."

"It were well," said Richard, "to 'apply to the generosity of the royal Saladin, since, heathen as he is, I have never known knight more fulfilled of nobleness, or to whose good faith we may so peremptorily intrust ourselves. I speak thus for those who may be doubtful of mishap—for myself, wherever I see my foe, I make that spot my battle-ground."

"Be it so," said Philip; "we will make this matter known to Saladin, although it be showing to an enemy the unhappy spirit of discord which we would willingly hide from even ourselves, were it possible. Meanwhile, I dismiss this assembly, and charge you all, as Christian men and noble knights, that ye let this unhappy feud breed no further brawling in the camp, but regard it as a thing solemnly referred to the judgment of God, to whom each of you should pray that he will dispose of victory in the combat according to the truth of the quarrel; and therewith may his will be done!"

"Amen, Amen!" was answered on all sides; while the Templar whispered the Marquis, "Conrade, wilt thou not add a petition to be delivered from the power of the dog, as the Psalmist hath it?"

"Peace, thou——!" replied the Marquis; "there is a revealing demon abroad, which may report, amongst other tidings, how far thou dost carry thy motto of the order—*Feriatur Leo.*"

"Thou wilt stand the brunt of challenge?" said the Templar.

"Doubt me not," said Conrade. "I would not, indeed, have willingly met the iron arm of Richard himself, and I shame not to confess that I rejoice to be free of his encounter. But from his bastard brother downward the man breathes not in his ranks whom I fear to meet."

"It is well you are so confident," continued the Templar; "and in that case, the fangs of yonder hound have done more to dissolve this league of princes, than either thy devices, or the dagger of the Charegite. Seest thou how, under a brow studiously overclouded, Philip cannot conceal the satisfaction which he feels at the prospect of release from the alliance which sat so heavy on him? Mark how Henry of Champagne smiles to himself, like a sparkling goblet of his own wine; and see the chuckling delight of Austria, who thinks his quarrel is about to be avenged, without risk or trouble of his own. Hush, he approaches. — A most grievous chance, most royal Austria, that these breaches in the walls of our Zion——"

"If thou meanest this Crusade," replied the Duke, "I would it were crumbled to pieces, and each were safe at home!—I speak this in confidence."

"But," said the Marquis of Montserrat, "to think this disunion should be made by the hands of King Richard, for whose pleasure we have been contented to endure so much and to whom we have been as submissive as slaves to a master, in hopes that he would use his valour against our enemies instead of exercising it upon our friends!"

"I see not that he is so much more valorous than others," said the Archduke. "I believe, had the noble Marquis met him in the lists, he would have had the better; for, though the islander deals heavy blows with the pole-axe, he is not so very dexterous with the lance. I should have cared little to have met him myself on our old quarrel, had the weal of Christendom permitted to sovereign princes to breathe themselves in the lists—And if thou desirest it, noble Marquis, I will myself be your godfather in this combat."

" And I also," said the Grand Master.

"Come, then, and take your nooning in our tent, noble sirs," said the Duke, "and we'll speak of this business over some right *nierenstein*."

They entered together accordingly.

" What said our patron and these great folks together?" said Jonas Schwanker to his companion, the *spruch-sprecher*, who had used the freedom to press nigh to his master when the Council was dismissed, while the jester waited at a more respectful distance.

"Servant of Folly," said the *spruch-sprecher*, "moderate thy curiosity; it beseems not that I should tell to thee the counsels of our master."

" Man of Wisdom, you mistake," answered Jonas; "we are both the constant attendants on our patron, and it concerns us alike to know whether thou or I—Wisdom or Folly—have the deeper interest in him."

"He told to the Marquis," answered the *spruch-sprecher*, "and to the Grand Master, that he was a-weary of these wars, and would be glad he was safe at home."

" That is a drawn cast, and counts for nothing in the game," said the jester; " it was most wise to think thus, but great folly to tell it to others—proceed."

" Ha, hem!" said the *spruch-sprecher*; "he next said to them, that Richard was not more valorous than others, or over dexterous in the tilt-yard."

" Woodcock of my side," said Schwanker; "this was egregious folly. What next?"

"Nay, I am something oblivious," replied the man of wisdom; "he invited them to a goblet of *nierenstein*."

" That hath a show of wisdom in it," said Jonas, "thou mayst mark it to thy credit in the meantime; but an he drink too much, as is most likely, I will have it pass to mine. Any thing more?"

"Nothing worth memory," answered the orator, "only he wished he had taken the occasion to meet Richard in the lists."

"Out upon it—out upon it!" said Jonas; "this is such dotage of folly, that I am well-nigh ashamed of winning the game by it. Ne'ertheless, fool as he is, we will follow him, most sage *spruch-sprecher*, and have our share of the wine of *nierenstein*."

CHAPTER XXV

Yet this inconstancy is such,
    As thou, too, shalt adore ;
I could not love thee, love, so much,
    Loved I not honour more.
                    MONTROSE'S *Lines.*

WHEN King Richard returned to his tent, he commanded the Nubian to be brought before him. He entered with his usual ceremonial reverence, and, having prostrated himself, remained standing before the King, in the attitude of a slave awaiting the orders of his master. It was perhaps well for him, that the preservation of his character required his eyes to be fixed on the ground, since the keen glance with which Richard for some time surveyed him in silence, would, if fully encountered, have been difficult to sustain.

"Thou canst well of woodcraft," said the King, after a pause, "and hast started thy game and brought him to bay, as ably as if Tristrem himself had taught thee.[1] But this is not all—he must be brought down at force. I myself would have liked to have levelled my hunting-spear at him. There are, it seems, respects which prevent this. Thou art about to return to the camp of the Soldan, bearing a letter, requiring of his courtesy to appoint neutral ground for the deed of chivalry, and, should it consist with his pleasure, to concur with us in witnessing it. Now, speaking conjecturally, we think thou mightst find in that camp some cavalier, who, for the love of truth, and his own augmentation of honour, will do battle with this same traitor of Montserrat?"

The Nubian raised his eyes and fixed them on the King with a look of eager ardour ; then raised them to Heaven with such solemn gratitude that the water soon glistened in them, then bent his head, as affirming what Richard desired, and resumed his usual posture of submissive attention.

"It is well," said the King ; "and I see thy desire to oblige me in this matter. And herein, I must needs say, lies the excellence of such a servant as thou, who hast not speech either to debate our purpose, or to require explanation of what we have determined. An English serving-man, in thy place,

---

[1] A universal tradition, ascribed to Sir Tristrem, famous for his love of the fair Queen Yseult—the laws concerning the practice of woodcraft, or *venerie,* as it was called, being those that related to the rules of the chase, were deemed of much consequence during the middle ages.

had given me his dogged advice to trust the combat with some good lance of my household, who, from my brother Longsword downwards, are all on fire to do battle in my cause; and a chattering Frenchman had made a thousand attempts to discover wherefore I look for a champion from the camp of the infidels. But thou, my silent agent, canst do mine errand without questioning or comprehending it; with thee, to hear is to obey."

A bend of the body and a genuflection, were the appropriate answer of the Ethiopian to these observations.

"And now to another point," said the King, and speaking suddenly and rapidly.—"Have you yet seen Edith Plantagenet?"

The mute looked up as in the act of being about to speak—nay, his lips had begun to utter a distinct negative—when the abortive attempt died away in the imperfect murmurs of the dumb.

"Why, lo you there!" said the King. "The very sound of the name of a royal maiden, of beauty so surpassing as that of our lovely cousin, seems to have power enough well-nigh to make the dumb speak. What miracles then might her eye work upon such a subject! I will make the experiment, friend slave. Thou shalt see this choice beauty of our court, and do the errand of the princely Soldan."

Again a joyful glance, again a genuflection; but, as he arose, the King laid his hand heavily on his shoulder, and proceeded with stern gravity thus—"Let me in one thing warn you, my sable envoy. Even if thou shouldst feel that the kindly influence of her whom thou art soon to behold, should loosen the bonds of thy tongue, presently imprisoned, as the good Soldan expresses it, within the ivory walls of its castle, beware how thou changest thy taciturn character, or speakest a word in her presence, even if thy powers of utterance were to be miraculously restored. Believe me, that I should have thy tongue extracted by the roots, and its ivory palace, that is, I presume, its range of teeth, drawn out one by one. Wherefore, be wise and silent still."

The Nubian, so soon as the King had removed his heavy grasp from his shoulder, bent his head, and laid his hand on his lips, in token of silent obedience.

But Richard again laid his hand on him more gently, and added, "This behest we lay on thee as on a slave. Wert thou knight and gentleman, we would require thine honour in pledge of thy silence, which is one especial condition of our present trust."

The Ethiopian raised his body proudly, looked full at the King, and laid his right hand on his heart.

Richard then summoned his chamberlain.

"Go, Neville," he said, "with this slave, to the tent of our royal consort, and say it is our pleasure that he have an audience—a private audience—of our cousin Edith. He is charged with a commission to her. Thou canst show him the way also, in case he requires thy guidance, though thou mayst have observed it is wonderful how familiar he already seems to be with the purlieus of our camp.—And thou, too, friend Ethiop," the King continued, "what thou dost, do quickly, and return hither within the half-hour."

"I stand discovered," thought the seeming Nubian, as with downcast looks and folded arms he followed the hasty stride of Neville towards the tent of Queen Berengaria.—"I stand undoubtedly discovered and unfolded to King Richard; yet I cannot perceive that his resentment is hot against me. If I understand his words, and surely it is impossible to misinterpret them, he gives me a noble chance of redeeming my honour upon the crest of this false Marquis, whose guilt I read in his craven eye and quivering lip, when the charge was made against him.—Roswal, faithfully hast thou served thy master, and most dearly shall thy wrong be avenged!—But what is the meaning of my present permission to look upon her whom I had despaired ever to see again?—And why, or how, can the royal Plantagenet consent that I should see his divine kinswoman, either as the messenger of the heathen Saladin, or as the guilty exile whom he so lately expelled from his camp —his audacious avowal of the affection which is his pride, being the greatest enhancement of his guilt? That Richard should consent to her receiving a letter from an infidel lover, by the hands of one of such disproportioned rank, are either of them circumstances equally incredible, and at the same time inconsistent with each other. But Richard, when unmoved by his heady passions, is liberal, generous, and truly noble, and as such I will deal with him, and act according to his instructions, direct or implied, seeking to know no more than may gradually unfold itself without my officious enquiry. To him who has given me so brave an opportunity to vindicate my tarnished honour, I owe acquiescence and obedience, and, painful as it may be, the debt shall be paid. And yet,"—thus the proud swelling of his heart further suggested,—"Cœur de Lion, as he is called, might have measured the feelings of others by his own. *I* urge an address to his kinswoman! *I*, who never spoke word to her when I took a royal prize from her hand—when I was accounted not the lowest in feats of chivalry among the defenders of the Cross! *I* approach her when in a base disguise, and in a servile habit—and, alas! when my actual condition is that of a slave, with a spot of dishonour on that which was once my shield! *I* do this! He little knows me. Yet I thank him for the opportunity which may make us all better acquainted with each other."

As he arrived at this conclusion, they paused before the entrance of the Queen's pavilion.

They were of course admitted by the guards, and Neville, leaving the Nubian in a small apartment, or antechamber, which was but too well remembered by him, passed into that which was used as the Queen's presence-chamber. He communicated his royal master's pleasure in a low and respectful tone of voice, very different from the bluntness of Thomas de Vaux, to whom Richard was every thing, and the rest of the court, including Berengaria herself, was nothing. A burst of laughter followed the communication of his errand.

"And what like is the Nubian slave, who comes ambassador on such an errand from the Soldan?—a negro, De Neville, is he not?" said a female voice easily recognised for that of Berengaria. "A negro, is he not, De Neville, with black skin, a head curled like a ram's, a flat nose, and blubber lips—ha, worthy Sir Henry?"

"Let not your Grace forget the shin-bones," said another voice, "bent outwards like the edge of a Saracen scimitar."

"Rather like the bow of a Cupid, since he comes upon a lover's errand," said the Queen. "Gentle Neville, thou art ever prompt to pleasure us poor women, who have so little to pass away our idle moments. We must see this messenger of love. Turks and Moors have I seen many, but negro never."

"I am created to obey your Grace's commands, so you will bear me out with my sovereign for doing so," answered the debonair knight. "Yet, let me assure your Grace, you will see somewhat different from what you expect."

"So much the better—uglier yet than our imaginations can fancy, yet the chosen love-messenger of this gallant Soldan!"

"Gracious madam," said the Lady Calista, "may I implore you would permit the good knight to carry this messenger straight to the Lady Edith, to whom his credentials are addressed? We have already escaped hardly for such a frolic."

"Escaped?" repeated the Queen, scornfully. "Yet thou mayst be right, Calista, in thy caution; let this Nubian, as thou callest him, first do his errand to our cousin—Besides, he is mute too, is he not?"

"He is, gracious madam," answered the knight.

"Royal sport have these Eastern ladies," said Berengaria, "attended by those before whom they may say any thing, yet who can report ..othing. Whereas in our camp, as the prelate of Saint Jude's is wont to say, a bird of the air will carry the matter."

"Because," said De Neville, "your Grace forgets that you speak within canvas walls."

The voices sunk on this observation, and after a little whispering the English knight again returned to the Ethiopian, and made him a sign to follow. He did so, and Neville conducted him to a pavilion, pitched somewhat apart from that of the Queen, for the accommodation, it seemed, of the Lady Edith and her attendants. One of her Coptic maidens received the message communicated by Sir Henry Neville, and in the space of a very few minutes the Nubian was ushered into Edith's presence, while Neville was left on the outside of the tent. The slave who introduced him withdrew on a signal from her mistress, and it was with humiliation, not of the posture only, but of the very inmost soul, that the unfortunate knight, thus strangely disguised, threw himself on one knee, with looks bent on the ground and arms folded on his bosom, like a criminal who expects his doom. Edith was clad in the same manner as when she received King Richard, her long transparent dark veil hanging around her like the shade of a summer night on a beautiful landscape, disguising and rendering obscure the beauties which it could not hide. She held in her hand a silver lamp, fed with some aromatic spirit, which burned with unusual brightness.

When Edith came within a step of the kneeling and motionless slave, she held the light towards his face, as if to peruse his features more attentively, then turned from him and placed her lamp so as to throw the shadow of his face in profile upon the curtain which hung beside. She at length spoke in a voice composed, yet deeply sorrowful.

"Is it you?—Is it indeed you, brave Knight of the Leopard —gallant Sir Kenneth of Scotland—Is it indeed you?—thus servilely disguised, thus surrounded by an hundred dangers?"

At hearing the tones of his lady's voice thus unexpectedly addressed to him, and in a tone of compassion approaching to tenderness, a corresponding reply rushed to the knight's lips, and scarce could Richard's commands, and his own promised silence, prevent his answering, that the sight he saw, the sounds he just heard, were sufficient to recompense the slavery of a life, and dangers which threatened that life every hour. He *did* recollect himself, however, and a deep and impassioned sigh was his only reply to the high-born Edith's question.

"I see—I know I have guessed right," continued Edith; "I marked you from your first appearance near the platform on which I stood with the Queen. I knew, too, your valiant hound. She is no true lady, and is unworthy of the service of such a knight as thou art, from whom disguises of dress or hue could conceal a faithful servant. Speak, then, without fear, to Edith Plantagenet. She knows how to grace in adversity the good knight who served, honoured, and did deeds of arms in her name, when fortune befriended him.—Still silent! Is it fear or shame that keeps thee so? Fear should be unknown to thee; and for shame, let it remain with those who have wronged thee."

The knight, in despair at being obliged to play the mute in an interview so interesting, could only express his mortification by sighing deeply, and laying his finger upon his lips. Edith stepped back, as if somewhat displeased.

"What!" she said, "the Asiatic mute in very deed, as well as in attire? This I looked not for. Or thou mayst scorn me, perhaps, for thus boldly acknowledging that I have heedfully observed the homage thou hast paid me? Hold no unworthy thoughts of Edith on that account. She knows well the bounds which reserve and modesty prescribe to high-born maidens, and she knows when and how far they should give place to gratitude —to a sincere desire that it were in her power to repay services and repair injuries, arising from the devotion which a good knight bore towards her.—Why fold thy hands together, and wring them with so much passion?—Can it be," she added, shrinking back at the idea, "that their cruelty has actually deprived thee of speech? Thou shakest thy head. Be it a spell, be it obstinacy, I question thee no further, but leave thee to do thine errand after thine own fashion. I also can be mute.'

The disguised knight made an action as if at once lamenting his own condition, and deprecating her displeasure, while at the same time he presented to her, wrapped as usual in fine silk and cloth of gold, the letter of the Soldan. She took it, surveyed it carelessly, then laid it aside, and, bending her eyes once more on the knight, she said in a low tone, "Not even a word to do thine errand to me?"

He pressed both his hands to his brow, as if to intimate the pain which he felt at being unable to obey her; but she turned from him in anger.

"Begone!" she said. "I have spoken enough—too much—to one who will not waste on me a word in reply. Begone! —and say, if I have wronged thee, I have done penance; for if I have been the unhappy means of dragging thee down from a station of honour, I have, in this interview, forgotten my own worth, and lowered myself in thy eyes and in my own."

She covered her eyes with her hand, and seemed deeply agitated. Sir Kenneth would have approached, but she waved him back.

"Stand off! thou whose soul Heaven hath suited to its new station! Aught less dull and fearful than a slavish mute had spoken a word of gratitude, were it but to reconcile me to my own degradation. Why pause you?—begone!"

The disguised knight almost involuntarily looked towards the letter as an apology for protracting his stay. She snatched it up, saying, in a tone of irony and contempt, "I had forgotten—the dutiful slave waits an answer to his message.—How's this —from the Soldan!"

She hastily ran over the contents, which were expressed both in Arabic and French, and when she had done, she laughed in bitter anger.

"Now this passes imagination!" she said; "no jongleur can show so deft a transmutation! His legerdemain can transform zechins and bezants into doits and maravedies; but can his art convert a Christian knight, ever esteemed among the bravest of the Holy Crusade, into the dust-kissing slave of a heathen Soldan—the bearer of a Paynim's insolent proposals to a Christian maiden—nay, forgetting the laws of honourable chivalry, as well as of religion! But it avails not talking to the willing slave of a heathen hound. Tell your master, when his scourge shall have found thee a tongue, that which thou hast seen me do."—So saying, she threw the Soldan's letter on the ground, and placed her foot upon it.—"And say to him that Edith Plantagenet scorns the homage of an unchristened Pagan."

With these words she was about to shoot from the knight, when, kneeling at her feet in bitter agony, he ventured to lay his hand upon her robe and oppose her departure.

"Heardst thou not what I said, dull slave?" she said, turning short round on him, and speaking with emphasis; "tell the heathen Soldan, thy master, that I scorn his suit as much as I despise the prostration of a worthless renegade to religion and chivalry—to God and to his lady!"

So saying, she burst from him, tore her garment from his grasp, and left the tent.

The voice of Neville, at the same time, summoned him from without. Exhausted and stupified by the distress he had undergone during this interview, from which he could only have extricated himself by breach of the engagement which he had formed with King Richard, the unfortunate knight staggered rather than walked after the English baron, till they reached the royal pavilion, before which a party of horsemen had just dismounted. There was light and motion within the tent, and when Neville entered with his disguised attendant, they found the King, with several of his nobility, engaged in welcoming those who were newly arrived.

CHAPTER XXVI

"The tears I shed must ever fall!
I weep not for an absent swain,
For time may happier hours recall,
And parted lovers meet again.

"I weep not for the silent dead,
Their pains are past, their sorrows o'er,
And those that loved their steps must tread,
When death shall join to part no more."

But worse than absence, worse than death,
She wept her lover's sullied fame,
And, fired with all the pride of birth,
She wept a soldier's injured name.
                                    Ballad.

The frank and bold voice of Richard was heard in joyous gratulation.

"Thomas de Vaux! stout Tom of the Gills! by the head of King Henry, thou art welcome to me as ever was flask of wine to a jolly toper! I should scarce have known how to order my battle array, unless I had thy bulky form in mine eye as a landmark to form my ranks upon. We shall have blows anon, Thomas, if the saints be gracious to us; and had we fought in thine absence, I would have looked to hear of thy being found hanging upon an elder-tree."

"I should have borne my disappointment with more Christian patience, I trust," said Thomas de Vaux, "than to have died the death of an apostate. But I thank your Grace for my welcome, which is the more generous, as it respects a banquet of blows, of which, saving your pleasure, you are ever too apt to engross the larger share; but here have I brought one, to whom your Grace will, I know, give a yet warmer welcome."

The person who now stepped forward to make obeisance to Richard, was a young man of low stature and slight form. His dress was as modest as his figure was unimpressive, but he bore on his bonnet a gold buckle, with a gem, the lustre of which could only be rivalled by the brilliancy of the eye which the bonnet shaded. It was the only striking feature in his countenance; but, when once noticed, it uniformly made a strong impression on the spectator. About his neck there hung in a scarf of sky-blue silk a *wrest*, as it was called,—that is, the key with which a harp is tuned, and which was of solid gold.

This personage would have kneeled reverently to Richard, but the monarch raised him in joyful haste, pressed him to his bosom warmly, and kissed him on either side of the face.

"Blondel de Nesle!" he exclaimed joyfully—"welcome from Cyprus, my king of minstrels!—welcome to the King of England, who rates not his own dignity more highly than he does thine. I have been sick, man, and, by my soul, I believe it was for lack of thee; for, were I half-way to the gate of Heaven, methinks thy strains could call me back.—And what news, my gentle master, from the land of the lyre? Any thing fresh from the *trouveurs* of Provence?—any thing from the minstrels of merry Normandy?—above all, hast thou thyself been busy?— But I need not ask thee—thou canst not be idle, if thou wouldst —thy noble qualities are like a fire burning within, and compel thee to pour thyself out in music and song."

"Something I have learned, and something I have done, noble King," answered the celebrated Blondel, with a retiring modesty, which all Richard's enthusiastic admiration of his skill had been unable to banish.

"We will hear thee, man—we will hear thee instantly," said

the King; then, touching Blondel's shoulder kindly, he added,
"that is, if thou art not fatigued with thy journey; for I would
sooner ride my best horse to death, than injure a note of thy
voice."

"My voice is, as ever, at the service of my royal patron," said
Blondel; "but your Majesty," he added, looking at some papers
on the table, "seems more importantly engaged, and the hour
waxes late."

"Not a whit, man, not a whit, my dearest Blondel. I did
but sketch an array of battle against the Saracens, a thing of a
moment, almost as soon done as the routing of them."

"Methinks, however," said Thomas de Vaux, "it were not
unfit to enquire what soldiers your Grace hath to array. I
bring reports on that subject from Ascalon."

"Thou art a mule, Thomas," said the King, "a very mule
for dulness and obstinacy!—Come, nobles—a hall—a hall!—
range ye around him—Give Blondel the tabouret—Where is
his harp-bearer?—or, soft—lend him my harp, his own may be
damaged by the journey."

"I would your Grace would take my report," said Thomas
de Vaux. "I have ridden far, and have more list to my bed
than to have my ears tickled."

"*Thy* ears tickled!" said the King; "that must be with a
woodcock's feather, and not with sweet sounds. Hark thee,
Thomas, do thine ears know the singing of Blondel from the
braying of an ass?"

"In faith, my liege," replied Thomas, "I cannot well say;
but setting Blondel out of the question, who is a born
gentleman, and doubtless of high acquirements, I shall never,
for the sake of your Grace's question, look on a minstrel but I
shall think upon an ass."

"And might not your manners," said Richard, "have
excepted me, who am a gentleman born as well as Blondel, and,
like him, a guild-brother of the *joyeuse science*?"

"Your Grace should remember," said De Vaux, smiling, "that
'tis useless asking for manners from a mule."

"Most truly spoken," said the King; "and an ill-conditioned
animal thou art. But come hither, master mule, and be
unloaded, that thou mayst get thee to thy litter, without any
music being wasted on thee.—Meantime, do thou, good
brother of Salisbury, go to our consort's tent, and tell her that
Blondel has arrived, with his budget fraught with the newest
minstrelsy. Bid her come hither instantly, and do thou escort

her, and see that our cousin, Edith Plantagenet, remain not behind."

His eye then rested for a moment on the Nubian, with that expression of doubtful meaning which his countenance usually displayed when he looked at him.

"Ha, our silent and secret messenger returned? Stand up, slave, behind the back of De Neville, and thou shalt hear presently sounds which will make thee bless God that he afflicted thee rather with dumbness than deafness."

So saying, he turned from the rest of the company towards De Vaux, and plunged instantly into the military details which that baron laid before him.

About the time that the Lord of Gilsland had finished his audience, a messenger announced that the Queen and her attendants were approaching the royal tent.—"A flask of wine, ho!" said the King; "of old King Isaac's long-saved Cyprus, which we won when we stormed Famagosta. Fill to the stout Lord of Gilsland, gentles; a more careful and faithful servant never had any prince."

"I am glad," said Thomas de Vaux, "that your Grace finds the mule a useful slave, though his voice be less musical than horse-hair or wire."

"What, thou canst not yet digest that quip of the mule?" said Richard. "Wash it down with a brimming flagon, man, or thou wilt choke upon it. Why, so—well pulled!—and now I will tell thee, thou art a soldier as well as I, and we must brook each other's jests in the hall, as each other's blows in the tourney, and love each other the harder we hit. By my faith, if thou didst not hit me as hard as I did thee in our late encounter, thou gavest all thy wit to the thrust. But here lies the difference betwixt thee and Blondel. Thou art but my comrade, I might say my pupil, in the art of war; Blondel is my master in the science of minstrelsy and music. To thee I permit the freedom of intimacy—to him I must do reverence, as to my superior in his art. Come, man, be not peevish, but remain and hear our glee."

"To see your Majesty in such cheerful mood," said the Lord of Gilsland, "by my faith, I could remain till Blondel had achieved the great Romance of King Arthur, which lasts for three days."

"We will not tax your patience so deeply," said the King. "But see, yonder glare of torches without shows that our consort approaches.—Away to receive her, man, and win thyself grace in the brightest eyes of Christendom.—Nay, never stop to adjust thy cloak. See, thou hast let Neville come between the wind and the sails of thy galley!"

"He was never before me in the field of battle," said De Vaux, not greatly pleased to see himself anticipated by the more active service of the chamberlain.

"No, neither he nor any one went before thee there, my good Tom of the Gills," said the King, "unless it was ourself, now and then."

"Ay, my liege," said De Vaux, "and let us do justice to the unfortunate;—the unhappy Knight of the Leopard hath been before me, too, at a season; for, look you, he weighs less on horseback, and so——"

"Hush!" said the King, interrupting him in a peremptory tone—"not a word of him!"—and instantly stepped forward to greet his royal consort; and when he had done so, he presented to her Blondel, as king of minstrelsy, and his master in the gay science. Berengaria, who well knew that her royal husband's passion for poetry and music almost equalled his appetite for warlike fame, and that Blondel was his especial favourite, took anxious care to receive him with all the flattering distinctions due to one whom the King delighted to honour. Yet it was evident, that, though Blondel made suitable returns to the compliments showered on him something too abundantly by the royal beauty, he owned with deeper reverence and more humble gratitude the simple and graceful welcome of Edith, whose kindly greeting appeared to him, perhaps, sincere in proportion to its brevity and simplicity.

Both the Queen and her royal husband were aware of this distinction, and Richard, seeing his consort somewhat piqued at the preference assigned to his cousin, by which perhaps he himself did not feel much gratified, said in the hearing of both, "We minstrels, Berengaria, as thou mayst see by the bearing of our master Blondel, pay more reverence to a severe judge like our kinswoman, than to a kindly partial friend like thyself, who is willing to take our worth upon trust."

Edith was moved by this sarcasm of her royal kinsman, and hesitated not to reply, that, "To be a harsh and severe judge was not an attribute proper to her alone of all the Plantagenets."

She had perhaps said more, having some touch of the temper of that house, which, deriving their name and cognisance from the lowly broom, (*Planta genista*,) assumed as an emblem of humility, were perhaps one of the proudest families that ever ruled in England; but her eye, when kindling in her reply, suddenly caught those of the Nubian, although he endeavoured to conceal himself behind the nobles who were present, and she sunk upon a seat, turning so pale that the Queen Berengaria deemed herself obliged to call for water and essences, and to go through the other ceremonies appropriate to a lady's swoon. Richard, who better estimated Edith's strength of mind, called to Blondel to assume his seat and commence his lay, declaring that minstrelsy was worth every other recipe to recall a Plantagenet to life.—"Sing us," he said, "that song of the Bloody Vest, of which thou didst formerly give me the argument, ere I left Cyprus; thou must be perfect in it by this time, or, as our yeomen say, thy bow is broken."

The anxious eye of the minstrel, however, dwelt on Edith, and it was not till he observed her returning colour that he obeyed the repeated commands of the King. Then, accompanying his voice with the harp, so as to grace, but yet not drown, the sense of what he sung, he chanted in a sort of recitative, one of those ancient adventures of love and knighthood, which were wont of yore to win the public attention. So soon as he began to prelude, the insignificance of his personal appearance seemed to disappear, and his countenance glowed with energy and inspiration. His full, manly, mellow voice, so absolutely under command of the purest taste, thrilled on every ear, and to every heart. Richard, rejoiced as after victory, called out the appropriate summons for silence,

Listen, lords, in bower and hall;

while with the zeal of a patron at once and a pupil, he arranged the circle around, and hushed them into silence; and he himself sat down with an air of expectation and interest, not altogether unmixed with the gravity of the professed critic. The courtiers turned their eyes on the King, that they might be ready to trace and imitate the emotions his features should express, and Thomas de Vaux yawned tremendously, as one who submitted unwillingly, to a wearisome penance. The song of Blondel was of course in the Norman language; but the verses which follow, express its meaning and its manner.

THE BLOODY VEST

'Twas near the fair city of Benevent,
When the sun was setting on bough and bent,
And knights were preparing in bower and tent,
On the eve of the Baptist's tournament;

When in Lincoln green a stripling gent,
Well seeming a page by a princess sent,
Wander'd the camp, and, still as he went,
Enquired for the Englishman, Thomas à Kent.

Far hath he fared, and farther must fare,
Till he finds his pavilion nor stately nor rare—
Little save iron and steel was there;
And, as lacking the coin to pay armourer's care,
With his sinewy arms to the shoulders bare,
The good knight with hammer and file did repair
The mail that to-morrow must see him wear,
For the honour of Saint John and his lady fair.

"Thus speaks my lady," the page said he,
And the knight bent lowly both head and knee,
"She is Benevent's Princess so high in degree,
And thou art as lowly as knight may well be;
He that would climb so lofty a tree,
Or spring such a gulf as divides her from thee,
Must dare some high deed, by which all men may see
His ambition is back'd by his hie chivalrie.

"Therefore thus speaks my lady," the fair page he said,
And the knight lowly louted with hand and with head,
"Fling aside the good armour in which thou art clad,
And don thou this weed of her night-gear instead,
For a hauberk of steel, a kirtle of thread;
And charge, thus attired, in the tournament dread,
And fight as thy wont is where most blood is shed,
And bring honour away, or remain with the dead."

Untroubled in his look, and untroubled in his breast,
The knight the weed hath taken, and reverently hath kissed:—
"Now blessed be the moment, the messenger be blest!
Much honour'd do I hold me in my lady's high behest;
And say unto my lady, in this dear night-weed dress'd,
To the best armed champion I will not veil my crest;
But if I live and bear me well 'tis her turn to take the test."
Here, gentles, ends the foremost fytte of the Lay of the Bloody Vest.

"Thou hast changed the measure upon us unawares in that last couplet, my Blondel!" said the King.

"Most true, my lord," said Blondel. "I rendered the verses from the Italian of an old harper, whom I met in Cyprus, and not having had time either to translate it accurately, or commit it to memory, I am fain to supply gaps in the music and the verse as I can upon the spur of the moment, as you see boors mend a quickset fence with a fagot."

"Nay, on my faith," said the King, "I like these rattling rolling Alexandrines; methinks they come more twangingly off to the music than that briefer measure."

"Both are licensed, as is well known to your Grace," answered Blondel.

"They are so, Blondel," said Richard; "yet methinks the scene, where there is like to be fighting, will go best on in these same thundering Alexandrines, which sound like the charge of cavalry; while the other measure is but like the sidelong amble of a lady's palfrey."

"It shall be as your Grace pleases," replied Blondel, and began again to prelude.

"Nay, first cherish thy fancy with a cup of fiery Chios wine," said the King; "and hark thee, I would have thee fling away that new-fangled restriction of thine, of terminating in accurate and similar rhymes. They are a constraint on thy flow of fancy, and make thee resemble a man dancing in fetters."

"The fetters are easily flung off, at least," said Blondel, again sweeping his fingers over the strings, as one who would rather have played than listened to criticism.

"But why put them on, man?" continued the King. "Wherefore thrust thy genius into iron bracelets? I marvel how you got forward at all; I am sure I should not have been able to compose a stanza in yonder hampered measure."

Blondel looked down and busied himself with the strings of his harp, to hide an involuntary smile which crept over his features; but it escaped not Richard's observation.

"By my faith, thou laugh'st at me, Blondel," he said; "and in good truth, every man deserves it, who presumes to play the master when he should be the pupil; but we kings get bad habits of self-opinion.—Come, on with thy lay, dearest Blondel, on after thine own fashion, better than aught that we can suggest, though we must needs be talking."

Blondel resumed the lay; but, as extemporaneous composition was familiar to him, he failed not to comply with the King's hints, and was perhaps not displeased to show with how much ease he could new-model a poem even while in the act of recitation.

THE BLOODY VEST

FYTTE SECOND

The Baptist's fair morrow beheld gallant feats—
There was winning of honour, and losing of seats—
There was hewing with falchions, and splintering of staves,
The victors won glory, the vanquished won graves.

O, many a knight there fought bravely and well,
Yet one was accounted his peers to excel,
And 'twas he whose sole armour on body and breast,
Seem'd the weed of a damsel when bound for her rest.

There were some dealt him wounds that were bloody and sore,
But others respected his plight and forbore.
" It is some oath of honour," they said, " and I trow,
'Twere unknightly to slay him achieving his vow."
Then the Prince, for his sake, bade the tournament cease,
He flung down his warder, the trumpets sung peace ;
And the judges declare, and competitors yield,
That the Knight of the Night-gear was first in the field.

The feast it was nigh, and the mass it was nigher,
When before the fair Princess low louted a squire,
And deliver'd a garment unseemly to view,
With sword-cut and spear-thrust, all hack'd and pierced through ;
All rent and all tatter'd, all clotted with blood,
With foam of the horses, with dust, and with mud.
Not the point of that lady's small finger, I ween,
Could have rested on spot was unsullied and clean.

" This token, my master, Sir Thomas à Kent,
Restores to the Princess of fair Benevent.
He that climbs the tall tree has won right to the fruit,
He that leaps the wide gulf should prevail in his suit ;
Through life's utmost peril the prize I have won,
And now must the faith of my mistress be shown ;
For she who prompts knights on such danger to run
Must avouch his true service in front of the sun.

" ' I restore,' says my master, ' the garment I've worn,
And I claim of the Princess to don it in turn ;
For its stains and its rents she should prize it the more,
Since by shame 'tis unsullied, though crimson'd with gore.' "
Then deep blush'd the Princess, yet kiss'd she and press'd
The blood-spotted robes to her lips and her breast.
Go, tell my true knight, church and chamber shall show,
If I value the blood on this garment or no."

And when it was time for the nobles to pass,
In solemn procession to minster and mass,
The first walk'd the Princess in purple and pall,
But the blood-besmear'd night-robe she wore over all ;
And eke in the hall, where they all sat at dine,
When she knelt to her father and proffered the wine,
Over all her rich robes and state jewels, she wore
That wimple unseemly bedabbled with gore.

Then lords whisper'd ladies, as well you may think,
And ladies replied, with nod, titter, and wink ;
And the Prince, who in anger and shame had look'd down,
Turn'd at length to his daughter, and spoke with a frown :

"Now since thou hast publish'd thy folly and guilt,
E'en atone with thy hand for the blood thou hast spilt;
Yet sore for your boldness you both will repent,
When you wander as exiles from fair Benevent."

Then out spoke stout Thomas, in hall where he stood,
Exhausted and feeble, but dauntless of mood:
"The blood that I lost for this daughter of thine,
I pour'd forth as freely as flask gives its wine;
And if for my sake she brooks penance and blame,
Do not doubt I will save her from suffering and shame;
And light will she reck of thy princedom and rent,
While I hail her, in England, the Countess of Kent!"

A murmur of applause ran through the assembly, following the example of Richard himself, who loaded with praises his favourite minstrel, and ended by presenting him with a ring of considerable value. The Queen hastened to distinguish the favourite by a rich bracelet, and many of the nobles who were present followed the royal example.

"Is our cousin Edith," said the King, "become insensible to the sound of the harp she once loved?"

"She thanks Blondel for his lay," replied Edith, "but doubly the kindness of the kinsman who suggested it."

"Thou art angry, cousin," said the King; "angry because thou hast heard of a woman more wayward than thyself. But you escape me not—I will walk a space homeward with you towards the Queen's pavilion—we must have conference together ere the night has waned into morning."

The Queen and her attendants were now on foot, and the other guests withdrew from the royal tent. A train with blazing torches, and an escort of archers, awaited Berengaria without the pavilion, and she was soon on her way homeward. Richard, as he had proposed, walked beside his kinswoman, and compelled her to accept of his arm as her support, so that they could speak to each other without being overheard.

"What answer, then, am I to return to the noble Soldan?" said Richard. "The kings and princes are falling from me, Edith; this new quarrel hath alienated them once more. I would do something for the Holy Sepulchre by composition, if not by victory; and the chance of my doing this depends, alas! on the caprice of a woman. I would lay my single spear in the rest against ten of the best lances in Christendom, rather than argue with a wilful wench, who knows not what is for her own good. What answer, coz, am I to return to the Soldan? It must be decisive."

"Tell him," said Edith, "that the poorest of the Plantagenets will rather wed with misery than with misbelief."

"Shall I say with *slavery*, Edith?" said the King. "Methinks that is nearer thy thoughts."

"There is no room," said Edith, "for the suspicion you so grossly insinuate. Slavery of the body might have been pitied, but that of the soul is only to be despised. Shame to thee, King of merry England! Thou hast enthralled both the limbs and the spirit of a knight, once scarce less famed than thyself."

"Should I not prevent my kinswoman from drinking poison, by sullying the vessel which contained it, if I saw no other means of disgusting her with the fatal liquor?" replied the King.

"It is thyself," answered Edith, "that would press me to drink poison, because it is proffered in a golden chalice."

"Edith," said Richard, "I cannot force thy resolution; but beware you shut not the door which Heaven opens. The hermit of Engaddi, he whom Popes and Councils have regarded as a prophet, hath read in the stars that thy marriage shall reconcile me with a powerful enemy, and that thy husband shall be Christian, leaving thus the fairest ground to hope that the conversion of the Soldan, and the bringing in of the sons of Ishmael to the pale of the Church, will be the consequence of thy wedding with Saladin. Come, thou must make some sacrifice rather than mar such happy prospects."

"Men may sacrifice rams and goats," said Edith, "but not honour and conscience. I have heard that it was the dishonour of a Christian maiden which brought the Saracens into Spain; the shame of another is no likely mode of expelling them from Palestine."

"Dost thou call it shame to become an empress?" said the King.

"I call it shame and dishonour to profane a Christian sacrament, by entering into it with an infidel whom it cannot bind; and I call it foul dishonour, that I, the descendant of a Christian princess, should become of free-will the head of a harem of heathen concubines."

"Well, kinswoman," said the King, after a pause, "I must not quarrel with thee, though I think thy dependent condition might have dictated more compliance."

"My liege," replied Edith, "your Grace hath worthily succeeded to all the wealth, dignity, and dominion of the House of Plantagenet; do not, therefore, begrudge your poor kinswoman some small share of their pride."

"By my faith, wench," said the King, "thou hast unhorsed me with that very word! so we will kiss and be friends. I will presently dispatch thy answer to Saladin. But, after all, coz, were it not better to suspend your answer till you have seen him? Men say he is pre-eminently handsome."

"There is no chance of our meeting, my lord," said Edith.

"By Saint George, but there is next to a certainty of it," said the King; "for Saladin will doubtless afford us a free field for the doing of this new battle of the Standard, and will witness it himself. Berengaria is wild to behold it also, and I dare be sworn not a feather of you, her companions and attendants, will remain behind—least of all thou thyself, fair coz. But come, we have reached the pavilion, and must part, not in unkindness though—nay, thou must seal it with thy lip as well as thy hand, sweet Edith—it is my right as a sovereign to kiss my pretty vassals."

He embraced her respectfully and affectionately, and returned through the moonlight camp, humming to himself such snatches of Blondel's lay as he could recollect.

On his arrival, he lost no time in making up his dispatches for Saladin, and delivered them to the Nubian, with a charge to set out by peep of day on his return to the Soldan.

CHAPTER XXVII

We heard the Tecbir,—so these Arabs call
Their shout of onset, when, with loud acclaim,
They challenge Heaven to give them victory.
Siege of Damascus.

ON the subsequent morning, Richard was invited to a conference by Philip of France, in which the latter, with many expressions of his high esteem for his brother of England, communicated to him, in terms extremely courteous, but too explicit to be misunderstood, his positive intention to return to Europe, and to the cares of his kingdom, as entirely despairing of future success in their undertaking, with their diminished forces and civil discords. Richard remonstrated, but in vain; and when the conference ended, he received without surprise a manifesto from the Duke of Austria and several other princes, announcing a resolution similar to that of Philip, and in no modified terms, assigning, for their defection from the cause of the Cross, the inordinate ambition and arbitrary domination of Richard of England. All hopes of continuing the war with any prospect of ultimate success were now abandoned, and Richard, while he shed bitter tears over his disappointed hopes of glory, was little consoled by the recollection, that the failure was in some degree to be imputed to the advantages which he had given his enemies by his own hasty and imprudent temper.

"They had not dared to have deserted my father thus," he said to De Vaux, in the bitterness of his resentment. "No slanders they could have uttered against so wise a king would have been believed in Christendom ; whereas—fool that I am ! —I have not only afforded them a pretext for deserting me, but even a colour for casting all the blame of the rupture upon my unhappy foibles."

These thoughts were so deeply galling to the King, that De Vaux was rejoiced when the arrival of an ambassador from Saladin turned his reflections into a different channel.

This new envoy was an Emir much respected by the Soldan, whose name was Abdallah el Hadgi. He derived his descent from the family of the Prophet, and the race or tribe of Hashem, in witness of which genealogy he wore a green turban of large dimensions. He had also three times performed the journey to Mecca, from which he derived his epithet of El Hadgi, or the Pilgrim. Notwithstanding these various pretensions to sanctity, Abdallah was (for an Arab) a boon companion, who enjoyed a merry tale, and laid aside his gravity so far as to quaff a blithe flagon, when secrecy ensured him against scandal. He was likewise a statesman, whose abilities had been used by Saladin in various negotiations with the Christian princes, and particularly with Richard, to whom El Hadgi was personally known and acceptable. Animated by the cheerful acquiescence with which the envoy of Saladin afforded a fair field for the combat, a safe-conduct for all who might choose to witness it, and offered his own person as a guarantee of his fidelity, Richard soon forgot his disappointed hopes, and the approaching dissolution of the Christian league, in the interesting discussions preceding a combat in the lists.

The station, called the Diamond of the Desert, was assigned for the place of conflict, as being nearly at an equal distance betwixt the Christian and Saracen camps. It was agreed that Conrade of Montserrat, the defendant, with his godfathers, the Archduke of Austria and the Grand Master of the Templars, should appear there on the day fixed for the combat, with an hundred armed followers, and no more; that Richard of England, and his brother Salisbury, who supported the accusation, should attend with the same number, to protect his champion; and that the Soldan should bring with him a guard of five hundred chosen followers, a band considered as not more than equal to the two hundred Christian lances. Such persons of consideration as either party chose to invite to witness the contest, were to wear no other weapons than their swords, and to come without defensive armour. The Soldan undertook the preparation of the lists, and to provide accommodations and refreshments of every kind for all who were to assist at the solemnity; and his letters expressed, with much courtesy, the pleasure which he anticipated in the prospect of a personal and peaceful meeting with the Melech Ric, and his anxious desire to render his reception as agreeable as possible.

All preliminaries being arranged, and communicated to the defendant and his godfathers, Abdallah the Hadgi was admitted to a more private interview, where he heard with delight the strains of Blondel. Having first carefully put his green turban out of sight, and assumed a Greek cap in its stead, he requited the Norman minstrel's music with a drinking song from the Persian, and quaffed a hearty flagon of Cyprus wine, to show that his practice matched his principles. On the next day, grave and sober as the water-drinker Mirglip, he bent his brow to the ground before Saladin's footstool, and rendered to the Soldan an account of his embassy.

On the day before that appointed for the combat, Conrade and his friends set off by daybreak to repair to the place assigned, and Richard left the camp at the same hour, and for the same purpose; but, as had been agreed upon, he took his journey by a different route, a precaution which had been judged necessary to prevent the possibility of a quarrel betwixt their armed attendants.

The good King himself was in no humour for quarrelling with any one. Nothing could have added to his pleasurable anticipations of a desperate and bloody combat in the lists, except his being in his own royal person one of the combatants; and he was half in charity again even with Conrade of Montserrat. Lightly armed, richly dressed, and gay as a bridegroom on the eve of his nuptials, Richard caracoled along by the side of Queen Berengaria's litter, pointing out to her the various scenes through which they passed, and cheering with tale and song the bosom of the inhospitable wilderness. The former route of the Queen's pilgrimage to Engaddi had been on the other side of the chain of mountains, so that the ladies were strangers to the scenery of the desert; and though Berengaria knew her husband's disposition too well not to endeavour to seem interested in what he was pleased either to say or to sing, she could not help indulging some female fears when she found herself in the howling wilderness with so small an escort, which seemed almost like a moving speck on the bosom of the plain, and knew, at the same time, they were not so distant from the camp of Saladin but what they might be in a moment surprised and swept off by an overpowering host of his fiery-footed cavalry, should the pagan be faithless enough to embrace an opportunity thus tempting. But when she hinted these suspicions to Richard, he repelled them with displeasure and disdain. "It were worse than ingratitude," he said, "to doubt the good faith of the generous Soldan."

Yet the same doubts and fears recurred more than once, not to the timid mind of the Queen alone, but to the firmer and more candid soul of Edith Plantagenet, who had no such confidence in the faith of the Moslem as to render her perfectly at ease when so much in their power; and her surprise had been far less than her terror, if the desert around had suddenly resounded with the shout of Alla hu! and a band of Arab cavalry had pounced on them like vultures on their prey. Nor were these suspicions lessened, when, as evening approached, they were aware of a single Arab horseman, distinguished by his turban and long lance, hovering on the edge of a small eminence like a hawk poised in the air, and who instantly, on the appearance of the royal retinue, darted off with the speed of the same bird, when it shoots down the wind and disappears from the horizon.

"We must be near the station," said King Richard; "and yonder cavalier is one of Saladin's outposts—methinks I hear the noise of the Moorish horns and cymbals. Get you into order, my hearts, and form yourselves around the ladies soldier-like and firmly."

As he spoke, each knight, squire, and archer, hastily closed in upon his appointed ground, and they proceeded in the most compact order, which made their numbers appear still smaller; and to say the truth, though there might be no fear, there was anxiety as well as curiosity in the attention with which they listened to the wild bursts of Moorish music, which came ever and anon more distinctly from the quarter in which the Arab horseman had been seen to disappear.

De Vaux spoke in a whisper to the King—"Were it not well, my liege, to send a page to the top of that sand-bank? Or would it stand with your pleasure that I prick forward? Methinks, by all yonder clash and clang, if there be no more than five hundred men beyond the sand-hills, half of the Soldan's retinue must be drummers and cymbal-tossers.— Shall I spur on?"

The baron had checked his horse with the bit, and was just about to strike him with the spurs, when the King exclaimed, "Not for the world. Such a caution would express suspicion, and could do little to prevent surprise, which, however, I apprehend not."

They advanced accordingly in close and firm order till they surmounted the line of low sand-hills, and came in sight of the appointed station, when a splendid, but at the same time a startling, spectacle awaited them.

The Diamond of the Desert, so lately a solitary fountain, distinguished only amid the waste by solitary groups of palm-trees, was now the centre of an encampment, the embroidered flags and gilded ornaments of which glittered far and wide, and reflected a thousand rich tints against the setting sun. The coverings of the large pavilions were of the gayest colours, scarlet, bright yellow, pale blue, and other gaudy and gleaming hues, and the tops of their pillars, or tent-poles, were decorated with golden pomegranates and small silken flags. But, besides these distinguished pavilions, there were, what Thomas de Vaux considered as a portentous number of the ordinary black tents of the Arabs, being sufficient, as he conceived, to accommodate, according to the Eastern fashion, a host of five thousand men. A number of Arabs and Curds, fully corresponding to the extent of the encampment, were hastily assembling, each leading his horse in his hand, and their muster was accompanied by an astonishing clamour of their noisy instruments of martial music, by which, in all ages, the warfare of the Arabs has been animated.

They soon formed a deep and confused mass of dismounted cavalry in front of their encampment, when at the signal of a shrill cry, which arose high over the clangour of the music, each cavalier sprung to his saddle. A cloud of dust, arising at the moment of this manœuvre, hid from Richard and his attendants the camp, the palm-trees, and the distant ridge of mountains, as well as the troops whose sudden movement had raised the cloud, and ascending high over their heads, formed itself into the fantastic forms of writhed pillars, domes, and minarets. Another shrill yell was heard from the bosom of this cloudy tabernacle. It was the signal for the cavalry to advance, which they did at full gallop, disposing themselves as they came forward, so as to come in at once on the front, flanks, and rear, of Richard's little body-guard, who were thus surrounded, and almost choked, by the dense clouds of dust enveloping them on each side, through which were seen alternately, and lost, the grim forms and wild faces of the Saracens, brandishing and tossing their lances in every possible direction, with the wildest cries and halloos, and frequently only reining up their horses when within a spear's length of the Christians, while those in the rear discharged over the heads of both parties thick volleys of arrows. One of these struck the litter in which the Queen was seated, who loudly screamed, and the red spot was on Richard's brow in an instant.

"Ha! Saint George," he exclaimed, "we must take some order with this infidel scum!"

But Edith, whose litter was near, thrust her head out, and with her hand holding one of the shafts, exclaimed, "Royal Richard, beware what you do! see, these arrows are headless!"

"Noble, sensible wench!" exclaimed Richard; "by Heaven, thou shamest us all by thy readiness of thought and eye.—Be not moved, my English hearts," he exclaimed, to his followers, "their arrows have no heads, and their spears, too, lack the steel points. It is but a wild welcome, after their savage fashion, though doubtless they would rejoice to see us daunted or disturbed. Move onward, slow and steady."

The little phalanx moved forward accordingly, accompanied on all sides by the Arabs, with the shrillest and most piercing cries, the bowmen, meanwhile, displaying their agility by shooting as near the crests of the Christians as was possible, without actually hitting them, while the lancers charged each other with such rude blows of their blunt weapons, that more than one of them lost his saddle, and well-nigh his life, in this rough sport. All this, though designed to express welcome, had rather a doubtful appearance in the eyes of the Europeans.

As they had advanced nearly half-way towards the camp, King Richard and his suite forming, as it were, the nucleus round which this tumultuary body of horsemen howled, whooped, skirmished, and galloped, creating a scene of indescribable confusion, another shrill cry was heard, on which all these irregulars, who were on the front and upon the flanks of the little body of Europeans, wheeled off, and forming themselves into a long and deep column, followed with comparative order and silence in the rear of Richard's troop. The dust began now to dissipate in their front, when there advanced to meet them, through that cloudy veil, a body of cavalry of a different and more regular description, completely armed with offensive and defensive weapons, and who might well have served as a body-guard to the proudest of Eastern monarchs. This splendid troop consisted of five hundred men, and each horse which it contained was worth an earl's ransom. The riders were Georgian and Circassian slaves in the very prime of life; their helmets and hauberks were formed of steel rings, so bright that they shone like silver; their vestures were of the gayest colours, and some of cloth of gold or silver; the sashes were twisted with silk and gold, their rich turbans were plumed and jewelled, and their sabres and poniards, of Damascene steel, were adorned with gold and gems on hilt and scabbard.

This splendid array advanced to the sound of military music, and when they met the Christian body, they opened their files to the right and left, and let them enter between their ranks. Richard now assumed the foremost place in his troop, aware that Saladin himself was approaching. Nor was it long when, in the centre of his body-guard, surrounded by his domestic officers, and those hideous negroes who guard the Eastern harem, and whose misshapen forms were rendered yet more frightful by the richness of their attire, came the Soldan, with the look and manners of one on whose brow Nature had written, This is a king! In his snow-white turban, vest, and wide Eastern trowsers, wearing a sash of scarlet silk, without any other ornament, Saladin might have seemed the plainest dressed man in his own guard. But closer inspection discerned in his turban that inestimable gem, which was called by the poets, the Sea of Light; the diamond on which his signet was engraved, and which he wore in a ring, was probably worth all the jewels of the English crown, and a sapphire, which terminated the hilt of his canjiar, was not of much inferior value. It should be added, that to protect him from the dust, which in the vicinity of the Dead Sea, resembles the finest ashes, or perhaps out of Oriental pride, the Soldan wore a sort of veil attached to his turban, which partly obscured the view of his noble features. He rode a milk-white Arabian, which bore him as if conscious and proud of his noble burden.

There was no need of further introduction. The two heroic monarchs, for such they both were, threw themselves at once from horseback, and, the troops halting and the music suddenly ceasing, they advanced to meet each other in profound silence, and, after a courteous inclination on either side, they embraced as brethren and equals. The pomp and display upon both sides attracted no further notice—no one saw aught save Richard and Saladin, and they two beheld nothing but each other. The looks with which Richard surveyed Saladin, were, however, more intently curious than those which the Soldan fixed upon him; and the Soldan also was the first to break silence.

"The Melech Ric is welcome to Saladin as water to this desert! I trust he hath no distrust of this numerous array? Excepting the armed slaves of my household, those who surround you with eyes of wonder and of welcome, are, even the humblest of them, the privileged nobles of my thousand tribes; for who that could claim a title to be present, would remain at home when such a prince was to be seen as Richard, with the terrors of whose name, even on the sands of Yemen, the nurse stills her child, and the free Arab subdues his restive steed!"

"And these are all nobles of Araby?" said Richard, looking around on wild forms with their persons covered with haicks, their countenances swart with the sunbeams, their teeth as white as ivory, their black eyes glancing with fierce and preternatural lustre from under the shade of their turbans, and their dress being in general simple, even to meanness.

"They claim such rank," said Saladin; "but though numerous, they are within the conditions of the treaty, and bear no arms but the sabre—even the iron of their lances is left behind."

"I fear," muttered De Vaux in English, "they have left them where they can be soon found.—A most flourishing House of Peers, I confess, and would find Westminster Hall something too narrow for them."

"Hush, De Vaux," said Richard, "I command thee.— Noble Saladin," he said, "suspicion and thou cannot exist on the same ground.—Seest thou," pointing to the litters, "I too have brought some champions with me, though armed, perhaps, in breach of agreement, for bright eyes and fair features are weapons which cannot be left behind."

The Soldan, turning to the litters, made an obeisance as lowly as if looking towards Mecca, and kissed the sand in token of respect.

"Nay," said Richard, "they will not fear a closer encounter, brother; wilt thou not ride towards their litters, and the curtains will be presently withdrawn?"

"That may Allah prohibit!" said Saladin, "since not an Arab looks on who would not think it shame to the noble ladies to be seen with their faces uncovered."

"Thou shalt see them, then, in private, my royal brother," answered Richard.

"To what purpose?" answered Saladin, mournfully. "Thy last letter was, to the hopes which I had entertained, like water to fire; and wherefore should I again light a flame, which may indeed consume, but cannot cheer me?—But will not my brother pass to the tent which his servant hath prepared for him? My principal black slave hath taken order for the reception of the princesses—the officers of my household will attend your followers, and ourself will be the chamberlain of the royal Richard."

He led the way accordingly to a splendid pavilion, where was every thing that royal luxury could devise. De Vaux, who was in attendance, then removed the chappe, (*capa*,) or long riding-cloak which Richard wore, and he stood before Saladin in the close dress which showed to advantage the strength and symmetry of his person, while it bore a strong contrast to the flowing robes which disguised the thin frame of the Eastern monarch. It was Richard's two-handed sword that chiefly attracted the attention of the Saracen, a broad straight blade, the seemingly unwieldy length of which extended well-nigh from the shoulder to the heel of the wearer.

"Had I not," said Saladin, "seen this brand flaming in the front of battle, like that of Azrael, I had scarce believed that human arm could wield it. Might I request to see the Melech Ric strike one blow with it in peace, and in pure trial of strength?"

"Willingly, noble Saladin," answered Richard; and looking around for something whereon to exercise his strength, he saw a steel mace, held by one of the attendants, the handle being of the same metal, and about an inch and a half in diameter; this he placed on a block of wood.

The anxiety of De Vaux for his master's honour led him to whisper in English, "For the blessed Virgin's sake, beware what you attempt, my liege! Your full strength is not as yet returned; give no triumph to the infidel."

"Peace, fool!" said Richard, standing firm on his ground, and casting a fierce glance around; "thinkest thou that I can fail in *his* presence?"

The glittering broadsword, wielded by both his hands, rose aloft to the King's left shoulder, circled round his head, descended with the sway of some terrific engine, and the bar of iron rolled on the ground in two pieces, as a woodsman would sever a sapling with a hedging-bill.

"By the head of the Prophet, a most wonderful blow!" said the Soldan, critically and accurately examining the iron bar which had been cut asunder; and the blade of the sword was so well tempered as to exhibit not the least token of having suffered by the feat it had performed. He then took the King's hand, and, looking on the size and muscular strength which it exhibited, laughed as he placed it beside his own, so lank and thin, so inferior in brawn and sinew.

"Ay, look well," said De Vaux in English; "it will be long ere your long jackanape's fingers do such a feat with your fine gilded reaping-hook there."

"Silence, De Vaux," said Richard; "by Our Lady, he understands or guesses thy meaning—be not so broad, I pray thee."

The Soldan, indeed, presently said, "Something I would fain attempt—though, wherefore should the weak show their inferiority in presence of the strong? Yet, each land hath its own exercises, and this may be new to the Melech Ric."— So saying, he took from the floor a cushion of silk and down, and placed it upright on one end. "Can thy weapon, my brother, sever that cushion?" he said to King Richard.

"No, surely," replied the King; "no sword on earth, were it the Excalibar of King Arthur, can cut that which opposes no steady resistance to the blow."

"Mark, then," said Saladin; and, tucking up the sleeve of his gown, showed his arm, thin indeed and spare, but which constant exercise had hardened into a mass consisting of nought but bone, brawn, and sinew. He unsheathed his scimitar, a curved and narrow blade, which glittered not like the swords of the Franks, but was, on the contrary, of a dull blue colour, marked with ten millions of meandering lines, which showed how anxiously the metal had been welded by the armourer. Wielding this weapon, apparently so inefficient when compared to that of Richard, the Soldan stood resting his weight upon his left foot, which was slightly advanced; he balanced himself a little as if to steady his aim, then stepping at once forward, drew the scimitar across the cushion, applying the edge so dexterously, and with so little apparent effort, that the cushion seemed rather to fall asunder than to be divided by violence.

"It is a juggler's trick," said De Vaux, darting forward and snatching up the portion of the cushion which had been cut off, as if to assure himself of the reality of the feat; "there is gramarye in this."

The Soldan seemed to comprehend him, for he undid the sort of veil which he had hitherto worn, laid it double along the edge of his sabre, extended the weapon edgeways in the air, and drawing it suddenly through the veil, although it hung on the blade entirely loose, severed that also into two parts, which floated to different sides of the tent, equally displaying the extreme temper and sharpness of the weapon, and the exquisite dexterity of him who used it.

"Now, in good faith, my brother," said Richard, "thou art even matchless at the trick of the sword, and right perilous were it to meet thee! Still, however, I put some faith in a downright English blow, and what we cannot do by sleight, we eke out by strength. Nevertheless, in truth thou art as expert in inflicting wounds as my sage Hakim in curing them. I trust I shall see the learned leech—I have much to thank him for, and had brought some small present."

As he spoke, Saladin exchanged his turban for a Tartar cap. He had no sooner done so, than De Vaux opened at once his extended mouth and his large round eyes, and Richard gazed with scarce less astonishment, while the Soldan spoke in a grave and altered voice—"The sick man, sayeth the poet, while he is yet infirm, knoweth the physician by his step; but when he is recovered, he knoweth not even his face when he looks upon him."

"A miracle!—a miracle!" exclaimed Richard.

"Of Mahound's working, doubtless," said Thomas de Vaux.

"That I should lose my learned Hakim," said Richard,

"merely by absence of his cap and robe, and that I should find him again in my royal brother Saladin!"

"Such is oft the fashion of the world," answered the Soldan; "the tattered robe makes not always the dervish."

"And it was through thy intercession," said Richard, "that yonder Knight of the Leopard was saved from death, and by thy artifice that he revisited my camp in disguise?"

"Even so," replied Saladin; "I was physician enough to know, that unless the wounds of his bleeding honour were stanched, the days of his life must be few. His disguise was more easily penetrated than I had expected from the success of my own."

"An accident," said King Richard, (probably alluding to the circumstance of his applying his lips to the wound of the supposed Nubian,) "let me first know that his skin was artificially discoloured; and that hint once taken, detection became easy, for his form and person are not to be forgotten. I confidently expect that he will do battle on the morrow."

"He is full in preparation, and high in hope," said the Soldan. "I have furnished him with weapons and horse, thinking nobly of him from what I have seen under various disguises."

"Knows he now," said Richard, "to whom he lies under obligation?"

"He doth," replied the Saracen.—"I was obliged to confess my person when I unfolded my purpose."

"And confessed he aught to you?" said the King of England.

"Nothing explicit," replied the Soldan; "but from much that passed between us, I conceive his love is too highly placed to be happy in its issue."

"And thou knowest that his daring and insolent passion crossed thine own wishes?" said Richard.

"I might guess so much," said Saladin; "but his passion had existed ere my wishes had been formed—and, I must now add, is likely to survive them. I cannot, in honour, revenge me for my disappointment on him who had no hand in it. Or, if this high-born dame loved him better than myself, who can say that she did not justice to a knight of her own religion, who is full of nobleness?"

"Yet of too mean lineage to mix with the blood of Plantagenet," said Richard, haughtily.

"Such may be your maxims in Frangistan," replied the

Soldan. "Our poets of the Eastern countries say, that a valiant camel-driver is worthy to kiss the lip of a fair Queen, when a cowardly prince is not worthy to salute the hem of her garment.—But with your permission, noble brother, I must take leave of thee for the present, to receive the Duke of Austria and yonder Nazarene knight, much less worthy of hospitality, but who must yet be suitably entreated, not for their sakes, but for mine own honour—for what saith the sage Lokman? 'Say not that the food is lost unto thee which is given to the stranger—for if his body be strengthened and fattened therewithal, not less is thine own worship and good name cherished and augmented.'"

The Saracen monarch departed from King Richard's tent, and having indicated to him, rather with signs than with speech, where the pavilion of the Queen and her attendants was pitched, he went to receive the Marquis of Montserrat and his attendants, for whom, with less good-will, but with equal splendour, the magnificent Soldan had provided accommodations. The most ample refreshments, both in the Oriental, and after the European fashion, were spread before the royal and princely guests of Saladin, each in their own separate pavilion; and so attentive was the Soldan to the habits and taste of his visitors, that Grecian slaves were stationed to present them with the goblet, which is the abomination of the sect of Mahommed. Ere Richard had finished his meal, the ancient Omrah, who had brought the Soldan's letter to the Christian camp, entered with a plan of the ceremonial to be observed on the succeeding day of combat. Richard, who knew the taste of his old acquaintance, invited him to pledge him in a flagon of wine of Schiraz; but Abdallah gave him to understand, with a rueful aspect, that self-denial, in the present circumstances, was a matter in which his life was concerned; for that Saladin, tolerant in many respects, both observed and enforced by high penalties the laws of the Prophet.

"Nay, then," said Richard, "if he loves not wine, that lightener of the human heart, his conversion is not to be hoped for, and the prediction of the mad priest of Engaddi goes like chaff down the wind."

The King then addressed himself to settle the articles of combat, which cost a considerable time, as it was necessary on some points to consult with the opposite parties, as well as with the Soldan.

They were at length finally agreed upon, and adjusted by a

protocol in French and in Arabian, which was subscribed by Saladin as umpire of the field, and by Richard and Leopold as guarantees for the two combatants. As the Omrah took his final leave of King Richard for the evening, De Vaux entered.

"The good knight," he said, "who is to do battle to-morrow, requests to know, whether he may not to-night pay duty to his royal godfather?"

"Hast thou seen him, De Vaux?" said the King, smiling; "and didst thou know an ancient acquaintance?"

"By our Lady of Lanercost," answered De Vaux, "there are so many surprises and changes in this land, that my poor brain turns. I scarce knew Sir Kenneth of Scotland, till his good hound, that had been for a short while under my care, came and fawned on me; and even then I only knew the tyke by the depth of his chest, the roundness of his foot, and his manner of baying; for the poor gaze-hound was painted like any Venetian courtezan."

"Thou art better skilled in brutes than men, De Vaux," said the King.

"I will not deny," said De Vaux, "I have found them ofttimes the honester animals. Also, your Grace is pleased to term me sometimes a brute myself; besides that I serve the Lion, whom all men acknowledge the king of brutes."

"By Saint George, there thou brokest thy lance fairly on my brow," said the King. "I have ever said thou hast a sort of wit, De Vaux—marry, one must strike thee with a sledge-hammer ere it can be made to sparkle. But to the present gear—is the good knight well armed and equipped?"

"Fully, my liege, and nobly," answered De Vaux; "I know the armour well—it is that which the Venetian commissary offered your Highness, just ere you became ill, for five hundred bezants."

"And he hath sold it to the infidel Soldan, I warrant me, for a few ducats more, and present payment. These Venetians would sell the sepulchre itself!"

"The armour will never be borne in a nobler cause," said De Vaux.

"Thanks to the nobleness of the Saracen," said the King, "not to the avarice of the Venetians."

"I would to God your Grace would be more cautious," said the anxious De Vaux. "Here are we deserted by all our allies, for points of offence given to one or another; we cannot hope to prosper upon the land, and we have only to quarrel with the amphibious republic, to lose the means of retreat by sea!"

"I will take care," said Richard, impatiently; "but school me no more. Tell me rather, for it is of interest, hath the knight a confessor?"

"He hath," answered De Vaux; "the hermit of Engaddi, who erst did him that office when preparing for death, attends him on the present occasion; the fame of the duel having brought him hither."

"'Tis well," said Richard; "and now for the knight's request. Say to him, Richard will receive him when the discharge of his devoir beside the Diamond of the Desert shall have atoned for his fault beside the Mount of Saint George; and as thou passest through the camp, let the Queen know I will visit her pavilion; and tell Blondel to meet me there."

De Vaux departed, and in about an hour afterwards, Richard, wrapping his mantle around him, and taking his ghittern in his hand, walked in the direction of the Queen's pavilion. Several Arabs passed him, but always with averted heads, and looks fixed upon the earth, though he could observe that all gazed earnestly after him when he was past. This led him justly to conjecture that his person was known to them; but that either the Soldan's commands, or their own Oriental politeness, forbade them to seem to notice a sovereign who desired to remain incognito.

When the King reached the pavilion of his Queen, he found it guarded by those unhappy officials whom Eastern jealousy places around the zenana. Blondel was walking before the door, and touched his rote from time to time, in a manner which made the Africans show their ivory teeth, and bear burden with their strange gestures and shrill unnatural voices.

"What art thou after with this herd of black cattle, Blondel?" said the King; "wherefore goest thou not into the tent?"

"Because my trade can neither spare the head nor the fingers," said Blondel; "and these honest blackamoors threatened to cut me joint from joint if I pressed forward."

"Well, enter with me," said the King, "and I will be thy safeguard."

The blacks accordingly lowered pikes and swords to King Richard, and bent their eyes on the ground, as if unworthy to look upon him. In the interior of the pavilion, they found Thomas de Vaux in attendance on the Queen. While Berengaria welcomed Blondel, King Richard spoke for some time secretly and apart with his fair kinswoman.

At length, "Are we still foes, my fair Edith?" he said in a whisper.

"No, my liege," said Edith, in a voice just so low as not to interrupt the music; "none can bear enmity against King Richard, when he deigns to show himself, as he really is, generous and noble, as well as valiant and honourable."

So saying, she extended her hand to him. The King kissed it in token of reconciliation, and then proceeded.

"You think, my sweet cousin, that my anger in this matter was feigned; but you are deceived. The punishment I inflicted upon this knight was just; for he had betrayed—no matter for how tempting a bribe, fair cousin—the trust committed to him. But I rejoice, perchance as much as you, that to-morrow gives him a chance to win the field, and throw back the stain which for a time clung to him upon the actual thief and traitor. No!—future times may blame Richard for impetuous folly; but they shall say, that in rendering judgment, he was just when he should, and merciful when he could."

"Laud not thyself, cousin King," said Edith. "They may call thy justice cruelty, thy mercy caprice."

"And do not thou pride thyself," said the King, "as if thy knight, who hath not yet buckled on his armour, were unbelting it in triumph.—Conrade of Montserrat is held a good lance. What if the Scot should lose the day?"

"It is impossible!" said Edith, firmly. "My own eyes saw yonder Conrade tremble and change colour, like a base thief. He is guilty—and the trial by combat is an appeal to the justice of God.—I myself, in such a cause, would encounter him without fear."

"By the mass, I think thou wouldst, wench," said the King, "and beat him to boot; for there never breathed a truer Plantagenet than thou."

He paused, and added in a very serious tone, "See that thou continue to remember what is due to thy birth."

"What means that advice, so seriously given at this moment?" said Edith. "Am I of such light nature as to forget my name—my condition?"

"I will speak plainly, Edith," answered the King, "and as

to a friend—What will this knight be to you, should he come off victor from yonder lists?"

"To *me?*" said Edith, blushing deep with shame and displeasure,—"What *can* he be to me more than an honoured knight, worthy of such grace as Queen Berengaria might confer on him, had he selected her for his lady, instead of a more unworthy choice? The meanest knight may devote himself to the service of an empress, but the glory of his choice," she said proudly, "must be his reward."

"Yet he hath served and suffered much for you," said the King.

"I have paid his services with honour and applause, and his sufferings with tears," answered Edith. "Had he desired other reward, he would have done wisely to have bestowed his affections within his own degree."

"You would not then wear the bloody night-gear for his sake?" said King Richard.

"No more," answered Edith, "than I would have required him to expose his life by an action, in which there was more madness than honour."

"Maidens talk ever thus," said the King; "but when the favoured lover presses his suit, she says, with a sigh, her stars had decreed otherwise."

"Your Grace has now, for the second time, threatened me with the influence of my horoscope," Edith replied, with dignity. "Trust me, my liege, whatever be the power of the stars, your poor kinswoman will never wed either infidel, or obscure adventurer.—Permit me, that I listen to the music of Blondel, for the tone of your royal admonitions is scarce so grateful to the ear."

The conclusion of the evening offered nothing worthy of notice.

CHAPTER XXVIII

Heard ye the din of battle bray,
Lance to lance, and horse to horse?
GRAY.

IT had been agreed, on account of the heat of the climate, that the judicial combat, which was the cause of the present assemblage of various nations at the Diamond of the Desert, should take place at one hour after sunrise. The wide lists, which had been constructed under the inspection of the

Knight of the Leopard, enclosed a space of hard sand, which was one hundred and twenty yards long by forty in width. They extended in length from north to south, so as to give both parties the equal advantage of the rising sun. Saladin's royal seat was erected on the western side of the enclosure, just in the centre, where the combatants were expected to meet in mid encounter. Opposed to this was a gallery with closed casements, so contrived that the ladies, for whose accommodation it was erected, might see the fight without being themselves exposed to view. At either extremity of the lists was a barrier which could be opened or shut at pleasure. Thrones had been also erected, but the Archduke, perceiving that his was lower than King Richard's, refused to occupy it; and Cœur de Lion, who would have submitted to much ere any formality should have interfered with the combat, readily agreed that the sponsors, as they were called, should remain on horseback during the fight. At one extremity of the lists were placed the followers of Richard, and opposed to them were those who accompanied the defender, Conrade. Around the throne destined for the Soldan, were ranged his splendid Georgian Guards, and the rest of the enclosure was occupied by Christian and Mahommedan spectators.

Long before daybreak, the lists were surrounded by even a larger number of Saracens than Richard had seen on the preceding evening. When the first ray of the sun's glorious orb arose above the desert, the sonorous call, "To prayer, to prayer!" was poured forth by the Soldan himself, and answered by others, whose rank and zeal entitled them to act as muezzins. It was a striking spectacle to see them all sink to earth, for the purpose of repeating their devotions, with their faces turned to Mecca. But when they arose from the ground, the sun's rays, now strengthening fast, seemed to confirm the Lord of Gilsland's conjecture of the night before. They were flashed back from many a spear-head, for the pointless lances of the preceding day were certainly no longer such. De Vaux pointed it out to his master, who answered with impatience, that he had perfect confidence in the good faith of the Soldan; but if De Vaux was afraid of his bulky body, he might retire.

Soon after this the noise of timbrels was heard, at the sound of which the whole Saracen cavaliers threw themselves from their horses, and prostrated themselves, as if for a second morning prayer. This was to give an opportunity to the

Queen, with Edith and her attendants, to pass from the pavilion to the gallery intended for them. Fifty guards of Saladin's seraglio escorted them, with naked sabres, whose orders were, to cut to pieces whomsoever, were he prince or peasant, should venture to gaze on the ladies as they passed, or even presume to raise his head until the cessation of the music should make all men aware that they were lodged in their gallery, not to be gazed on by the curious eye.

This superstitious observance of Oriental reverence to the fair sex, called forth from Queen Berengaria some criticisms very unfavourable to Saladin and his country. But their den, as the royal fair called it, being securely closed and guarded by their sable attendants, she was under the necessity of contenting herself with seeing, and laying aside for the present the still more exquisite pleasure of being seen.

Meantime the sponsors of both champions went, as was their duty, to see that they were duly armed, and prepared for combat. The Archduke of Austria was in no hurry to perform this part of the ceremony, having had rather an unusually severe debauch upon wine of Schiraz the preceding evening. But the Grand Master of the Temple, more deeply concerned in the event of the combat, was early before the tent of Conrade of Montserrat. To his great surprise, the attendants refused him admittance.

"Do you not know me, ye knaves?" said the Grand Master, in great anger.

"We do, most valiant and reverend," answered Conrade's squire; "but even *you* may not at present enter—the Marquis is about to confess himself."

"Confess himself!" exclaimed the Templar, in a tone where alarm mingled with surprise and scorn; "and to whom, I pray thee?"

"My master bid me be secret," said the squire; on which the Grand Master pushed past him, and entered the tent almost by force.

The Marquis of Montserrat was kneeling at the feet of the hermit of Engaddi, and in the act of beginning his confession.

"What means this, Marquis?" said the Grand Master; "up, for shame; or, if you must needs confess, am not I here?"

"I have confessed to you too often already," replied Conrade, with a pale cheek and a faltering voice. "For God's sake, Grand Master, begone, and let me unfold my conscience to this holy man."

"In what is he holier than I am?" said the Grand Master. "Hermit, prophet, madman—say, if thou darest, in what thou excellest me?"

"Bold and bad man," replied the hermit, "know that I am like the latticed window, and the divine light passes through to avail others, though, alas! it helpeth not me. Thou art like the iron stanchions, which neither receive light themselves, nor communicate it to any one."

"Prate not to me, but depart from this tent," said the Grand Master; "the Marquis shall not confess this morning, unless it be to me, for I part not from his side."

"Is this *your* pleasure?" said the hermit to Conrade; "for think not I will obey that proud man, if you continue to desire my assistance."

"Alas!" said Conrade, irresolutely, "what would you have me say?—Farewell for a while—we will speak anon."

"Oh, procrastination!" exclaimed the hermit, "thou art a soul-murderer!—Unhappy man, farewell—not for a while, but until we shall both meet—no matter where.—And for thee," he added, turning to the Grand Master, "TREMBLE!"

"Tremble," replied the Templar, contemptuously; "I cannot if I would."

The hermit heard not his answer, having left the tent.

"Come! to this gear hastily," said the Grand Master, "since thou wilt needs go through the foolery.—Hark thee; I think I know most of thy frailties by heart, so we may omit the detail, which may be somewhat a long one, and begin with the absolution. What signifies counting the spots of dirt that we are about to wash from our hands?"

"Knowing what thou art thyself," said Conrade, "it is blasphemous to speak of pardoning another."

"That is not according to the canon, Lord Marquis," said the Templar; "thou art more scrupulous than orthodox. The absolution of the wicked priest is as effectual as if he were himself a saint—otherwise, God help the poor penitent! Wnat wounded man enquires whether the surgeon that tents his gashes have clean hands or no?—Come, shall we to this toy?"

"No," said Conrade, "I will rather die unconfessed than mock the sacrament."

"Come, noble Marquis," said the Templar, "rouse up your courage, and speak not thus. In an hour's time thou shalt stand victorious in the lists, or confess thee in thy helmet like a valiant knight."

"Alas, Grand Master!" answered Conrade, "all augurs ill for this affair. The strange discovery by the instinct of a dog —the revival of this Scottish knight, who comes into the lists like a spectre—all betokens evil."

"Pshaw!" said the Templar, "I have seen thee bend thy lance boldly against him in sport, and with equal chance of success—think thou art but in a tournament, and who bears him better in the tilt-yard than thou?—Come, squires and armourers, your master must be accoutred for the field."

The attendants entered accordingly, and began to arm the Marquis.

"What morning is without?" said Conrade.

"The sun rises dimly," answered a squire.

"Thou seest, Grand Master," said Conrade, "nought smiles on us."

"Thou wilt fight the more coolly, my son," answered the Templar; "thank Heaven, that hath tempered the sun of Palestine to suit thine occasion."

Thus jested the Grand Master; but his jests had lost their influence on the harassed mind of the Marquis, and, notwithstanding his attempts to seem gay, his gloom communicated itself to the Templar.

"This craven," he thought, "will lose the day in pure faintness and cowardice of heart, which he calls tender conscience. I, whom visions and auguries shake not—who am firm in my purpose as the living rock—I should have fought the combat myself. Would to God the Scot may strike him dead on the spot; it were next best to his winning the victory. But, come what will, he must have no other confessor than myself; our sins are too much in common, and he might confess my share with his own."

While these thoughts passed through his mind, he continued to assist the Marquis in arming, but it was in silence.

The hour at length arrived, the trumpets sounded, the knights rode into the lists armed at all points, and mounted like men who were to do battle for a kingdom's honour. They wore their vizors up, and riding around the lists three times, showed themselves to the spectators. Both were goodly persons, and both had noble countenances. But there was an air of manly confidence on the brow of the Scot—radiancy of hope, which amounted even to cheerfulness, while, although pride and effort had recalled much of Conrade's natural courage, there lowered still on his brow a cloud of ominous despondence.

Even his steed seemed to tread less lightly and blithely to the trumpet-sound than the noble Arab which was bestrode by Sir Kenneth; and the *spruch-sprecher* shook his head while he observed, that while the challenger rode around the lists in the course of the sun—that is, from right to left—the defender made the same circuit *widdersins*—that is, from left to right— which is in most countries held ominous.

A temporary altar was erected just beneath the gallery occupied by the Queen, and beside it stood the hermit in the dress of his order, as a Carmelite friar. Other churchmen were also present. To this altar the challenger and defender were successively brought forward, conducted by their respective sponsors. Dismounting before it, each knight avouched the justice of his cause by a solemn oath on the Evangelists, and prayed that his success might be according to the truth or falsehood of what he then swore. They also made oath, that they came to do battle in knightly guise, and with the usual weapons, disclaiming the use of spells, charms, or magical devices, to incline victory to their side. The challenger pronounced his vow with a firm and manly voice, and a bold and cheerful countenance. When the ceremony was finished, the Scottish knight looked at the gallery, and bent his head to the earth, as if in honour of those invisible beauties which were enclosed within; then, loaded with armour as he was, sprung to the saddle without the use of the stirrup, and made his courser carry him in a succession of caracoles to his station at the eastern extremity of the lists. Conrade also presented himself before the altar with boldness enough; but his voice, as he took the oath, sounded hollow, as if drowned in his helmet. The lips with which he appealed to Heaven to adjudge victory to the just quarrel, grew white as they uttered the impious mockery. As he turned to remount his horse, the Grand Master approached him closer, as if to rectify something about the sitting of his gorget, and whispered, "Coward and fool! recall thy senses, and do me this battle bravely, else, by Heaven, shouldst thou escape him, thou escapest not *me!*"

The savage tone in which this was whispered, perhaps completed the confusion of the Marquis's nerves, for he stumbled as he made to horse; and though he recovered his feet, sprung to the saddle with his usual agility, and displayed his address in horsemanship as he assumed his position opposite to the challenger's, yet the accident did not escape those who were on the watch for omens, which might predict the fate of the day.

The priests, after a solemn prayer, that God would show the rightful quarrel, departed from the lists. The trumpets of the challenger then rung a flourish, and a herald-at-arms proclaimed at the eastern end of the lists—"Here stands a good knight, Sir Kenneth of Scotland, champion for the royal King Richard of England, who accuseth Conrade, Marquis of Montserrat, of foul treason and dishonour done to the said King."

When the words Kenneth of Scotland announced the name and character of the champion, hitherto scarce generally known, a loud and cheerful acclaim burst from the followers of King Richard, and hardly, notwithstanding repeated commands of silence, suffered the reply of the defendant to be heard. He, of course, avouched his innocence, and offered his body for battle. The esquires of the combatants now approached, and delivered to each his shield and lance, assisting to hang the former around his neck, that his two hands might remain free, one for the management of the bridle, the other to direct the lance.

The shield of the Scot displayed his old bearing, the leopard, but with the addition of a collar and broken chain, in allusion to his late captivity. The shield of the Marquis bore, in reference to his title, a serrated and rocky mountain. Each shook his lance aloft, as if to ascertain the weight and toughness of the unwieldy weapon, and then laid it in the rest. The sponsors, heralds, and squires now retired to the barriers, and the combatants sat opposite to each other, face to face, with couched lance and closed vizor, the human form so completely enclosed, that they looked more like statues of molten iron, than beings of flesh and blood. The silence of suspense was now general—men breathed thicker, and their very souls seemed seated in their eyes, while not a sound was to be heard save the snorting and pawing of the good steeds, who, sensible of what was about to happen, were impatient to dash into career. They stood thus for perhaps three minutes, when, at a signal given by the Soldan, an hundred instruments rent the air with their brazen clamours, and each champion striking his horse with the spurs, and slacking the rein, the horses started into full gallop, and the knights met in mid space with a shock like a thunderbolt. The victory was not in doubt—no, not one moment. Conrade, indeed, showed himself a practised warrior; for he struck his antagonist knightly in the midst of his shield, bearing his lance so straight and true, that it shivered into splinters from the steel spear-head up to the very gauntlet. The horse of Sir Kenneth recoiled two or three yards and fell on his haunches, but the rider easily raised him with hand and rein. But for Conrade, there was no recovery. Sir Kenneth's lance had pierced through the shield, through a plated corslet of Milan steel, through a *secret*, or coat of linked mail, worn beneath the corslet, had wounded him deep in the bosom, and borne him from his saddle, leaving the truncheon of the lance fixed in the wound. The sponsors, heralds, and Saladin himself, descending from his throne, crowded around the wounded man; while Sir Kenneth, who had drawn his sword ere yet he discovered his antagonist was totally helpless, now commanded him to avow his guilt. The helmet was hastily unclosed, and the wounded man, gazing wildly on the skies, replied, "What would you more?—God hath decided justly—I am guilty; but there are worse traitors in the camp than I.—In pity to my soul, let me have a confessor!"

He revived as he uttered these words.

"The talisman—the powerful remedy, royal brother!" said King Richard to Saladin.

"The traitor," answered the Soldan, "is more fit to be dragged from the lists to the gallows by the heels, than to profit by its virtues; and some such fate is in his look," he added, after gazing fixedly upon the wounded man, "for though his wound may be cured, yet Azrael's seal is on the wretch's brow."

"Nevertheless," said Richard, "I pray you do for him what you may, that he may at least have time for confession. Slay not soul and body! To him one half-hour of time may be worth more, by ten thousand-fold, than the life of the oldest patriarch."

"My royal brother's wish shall be obeyed," said Saladin.— "Slaves, bear this wounded man to our tent."

"Do not so," said the Templar, who had hitherto stood gloomily looking on in silence. "The royal Duke of Austria and myself will not permit this unhappy Christian prince to be delivered over to the Saracens, that they may try their spells upon him. We are his sponsors, and demand that he be assigned to our care."

"That is, you refuse the certain means offered to recover him?" said Richard.

"Not so," said the Grand Master, recollecting himself. "If the Soldan useth lawful medicines, he may attend the patient in my tent."

"Do so, I pray thee, good brother," said Richard to Saladin, "though the permission be ungraciously yielded.—But now to a more glorious work.—Sound, trumpets—shout, England—in honour of England's champion!"

Drum, clarion, trumpet, and cymbal, rung forth at once, and the deep and regular shout which for ages has been the English acclamation, sounded amidst the shrill and irregular yells of the Arabs, like the diapason of the organ amid the howling of a storm. There was silence at length.

"Brave Knight of the Leopard," resumed Cœur de Lion, "thou hast shown that the Ethiopian *may* change his skin, and the leopard his spots, though clerks quote Scripture for the impossibility. Yet I have more to say to you when I have conducted you to the presence of the ladies, the best judges, and best rewarders, of deeds of chivalry."

The Knight of the Leopard bowed assent.

"And thou, princely Saladin, wilt also attend them. I promise thee our Queen will not think herself welcome, if she lacks the opportunity to thank her royal host for her most princely reception."

Saladin bent his head gracefully, but declined the invitation.

"I must attend the wounded man," he said. "The leech leaves not his patient more than the champion the lists, even if he be summoned to a bower like those of Paradise. And further, royal Richard, know that the blood of the East flows not so temperately in the presence of beauty, as that of your land. What saith the Book itself? 'Her eye is as the edge of the sword of the Prophet, who shall look upon it?' He that would not be burnt avoideth to tread on hot embers; wise men spread not the flax before a bickering torch. He, saith the sage, who hath forfeited a treasure, doth not wisely to turn back his head to gaze at it."

Richard, it may be believed, respected the motives of delicacy which flowed from manners so different from his own, and urged his request no further.

"At noon," said the Soldan, as he departed, "I trust ye will all accept a collation under the black camel-skin tent of a chief of Curdistan."

The same invitation was circulated among the Christians,

comprehending all those of sufficient importance to be admitted to sit at a feast made for princes.

"Hark!" said Richard, "the timbrels announce that our Queen and her attendants are leaving their gallery; and see, the turbans sink on the ground, as if struck down by a destroying angel. All lie prostrate, as if the glance of an Arab's eye could sully the lustre of a lady's cheek! Come, we will to the pavilion, and lead our conqueror thither in triumph.—How I pity that noble Soldan, who knows but of love as it is known to those of inferior nature!"

Blondel tuned his harp to its boldest measure, to welcome the introduction of the victor into the pavilion of Queen Berengaria. He entered, supported on either side by his sponsors, Richard and Thomas Longsword, and knelt gracefully down before the Queen, though more than half the homage was silently rendered to Edith, who sat on her right hand.

"Unarm him, my mistresses," said the King, whose delight was in the execution of such chivalrous usages—"Let Beauty honour Chivalry! Undo his spurs, Berengaria; Queen though thou be, thou owest him what marks of favour thou canst give. Unlace his helmet, Edith—by this hand thou shalt, wert thou the proudest Plantagenet of the line, and he the poorest knight on earth!"

Both ladies obeyed the royal commands,—Berengaria with bustling assiduity, as anxious to gratify her husband's humour, and Edith blushing and growing pale alternately, as slowly and awkwardly she undid, with Longsword's assistance, the fastenings which secured the helmet to the gorget.

"And what expect you from beneath this iron shell?" said Richard, as the removal of the casque gave to view the noble countenance of Sir Kenneth, his face glowing with recent exertion, and not less so with present emotion. "What think ye of him, gallants and beauties?" said Richard. "Doth he resemble an Ethiopian slave, or doth he present the face of an obscure and nameless adventurer? No, by my good sword!— Here terminate his various disguises. He hath knelt down before you unknown save by his worth; he arises, equally distinguished by birth and by fortune. The adventurous knight, Kenneth, arises David, Earl of Huntingdon, Prince Royal of Scotland!"

There was a general exclamation of surprise, and Edith dropped from her hand the helmet which she had just received.

"Yes, my masters," said the King, "it is even so. Ye knew

how Scotland deceived us when she proposed to send this valiant Earl, with a bold company of her best and noblest, to aid our arms in this conquest of Palestine, but failed to comply with her engagements. This noble youth, under whom the Scottish Crusaders were to have been arrayed, thought foul scorn that his arm should be withheld from the holy warfare, and joined us at Sicily with a small train of devoted and faithful attendants, which was augmented by many of his countrymen to whom the rank of their leader was unknown. The confidants of the royal prince had all, saving one old follower, fallen by death, when his secret, but too well kept, had nearly occasioned my cutting off, in a Scottish adventurer, one of the noblest hopes of Europe.—Why did you not mention your rank, noble Huntingdon, when endangered by my hasty and passionate sentence?—Was it that you thought Richard capable of abusing the advantage I possessed over the heir of a King whom I have so often found hostile?"

"I did you not that injustice, royal Richard," answered the Earl of Huntingdon; "but my pride brooked not that I should avow myself Prince of Scotland in order to save my life, endangered for default of loyalty. And, moreover, I had made my vow to preserve my rank unknown till the Crusade should be accomplished; nor did I mention it save *in articulo mortis*, and under the seal of confession, to yonder reverend hermit."

"It was the knowledge of that secret, then, which made the good man so urgent with me to recall my severe sentence?" said Richard. "Well did he say, that, had this good knight fallen by my mandate, I should have wished the deed undone though it had cost me a limb.—A limb!—I should have wished it undone had it cost me my life—since the world would have said that Richard had abused the condition in which the heir of Scotland had placed himself, by his confidence in his generosity."

"Yet, may we know of your Grace by what strange and happy chance this riddle was at length read?" said the Queen Berengaria.

"Letters were brought to us from England," said the King, "in which we learnt, among other unpleasant news, that the King of Scotland had seized upon three of our nobles, when on a pilgrimage to Saint Ninian, and alleged as a cause, that his heir, being supposed to be fighting in the ranks of the Teutonic Knights, against the heathen of Borussia, was, in fact, in our camp, and in our power; and, therefore, William proposed to hold these nobles as hostages for his safety. This gave me the first light on the real rank of the Knight of the Leopard, and my suspicions were confirmed by De Vaux, who, on his return from Ascalon, brought back with him the Earl of Huntingdon's sole attendant, a thick-sculled slave, who had gone thirty miles to unfold to De Vaux a secret he should have told to me."

"Old Strauchan must be excused," said the Lord of Gilsland. "He knew from experience that my heart is somewhat softer than if I wrote myself Plantagenet."

"Thy heart soft? thou commodity of old iron—and Cumberland flint, that thou art!" exclaimed the King. "It is we Plantagenets who boast soft and feeling hearts, Edith," turning to his cousin, with an expression which called the blood into her cheek—"Give me thy hand, my fair cousin, and, Prince of Scotland, thine."

"Forbear, my lord," said Edith, hanging back, and endeavouring to hide her confusion, under an attempt to rally her royal kinsman's credulity. "Remember you not that my hand was to be the signal of converting to the Christian faith the Saracen and Arab, Saladin and all his turbaned host?"

"Ay, but the wind of prophecy hath chopped about, and sits now in another corner," replied Richard.

"Mock not, lest your bonds be made strong," said the hermit, stepping forward. "The heavenly host write nothing but truth in their brilliant records; it is man's eyes which are too weak to read their characters aright. Know, that when Saladin and Kenneth of Scotland slept in my grotto, I read in the stars that there rested under my roof a prince, the natural foe of Richard, with whom the fate of Edith Plantagenet was to be united. Could I doubt that this must be the Soldan, whose rank was well known to me, as he often visited my cell to converse on the revolutions of the heavenly bodies?—Again, the lights of the firmament proclaimed that this Prince, the husband of Edith Plantagenet, should be a Christian; and I—weak and wild interpreter!—argued thence the conversion of the noble Saladin, whose good qualities seemed often to incline him towards the better faith. The sense of my weakness hath humbled me to the dust, but in the dust I have found comfort! I have not read aright the fate of others—who can assure me but that I may have miscalculated mine own? God will not have us break into his council-house, or spy out his hidden mysteries. We must wait his time with watching and prayer, with fear and with hope. I came hither the stern seer—the proud prophet—skilled, as I thought, to instruct princes, and gifted even with supernatural powers, but burdened with a weight which I deemed no shoulders but mine could have borne. But my bands have been broken! I go hence humble in mine ignorance, penitent, and not hopeless."

With these words he withdrew from the assembly; and it is recorded, that from that period his frenzy fits seldom occurred, and his penances were of a milder character, and accompanied with better hopes of the future. So much is there of self-opinion, even in insanity, that the conviction of his having entertained and expressed an unfounded prediction with so much vehemence seemed to operate like loss of blood on the human frame, to modify and lower the fever of the brain.

It is needless to follow into further particulars the conferences at the royal tent, or to enquire whether David, Earl of Huntingdon, was as mute in the presence of Edith Plantagenet, as when he was bound to act under the character of an obscure and nameless adventurer. It may be well believed that he there expressed, with suitable earnestness, the passion to which he had so often before found it difficult to give words.

The hour of noon now approached, and Saladin waited to receive the princes of Christendom in a tent which, but for its large size, differed little from that of the ordinary shelter of the common Curdman, or Arab; yet, beneath its ample and sable covering, was prepared a banquet after the most gorgeous fashion of the East, extended upon carpets of the richest stuffs, with cushions laid for the guests. But we cannot stop to describe the cloth of gold and silver—the superb embroidery in Arabesque—the shawls of Cashmere—and the muslins of India, which were here unfolded in all their splendour; far less to tell the different sweetmeats, ragouts edged with rice coloured in various manners, with all the other niceties of Eastern cookery. Lambs roasted whole, and game and poultry dressed in pilaus, were piled in vessels of gold, and silver, and porcelain, and intermixed with large mazers of sherbet, cooled in snow and ice from the caverns of Mount Lebanon. A magnificent pile of cushions at the head of the banquet, seemed prepared for the master of the feast, and such dignitaries as he might call to share that place of distinction, while from the roof of the tent in all quarters, but over this seat of eminence in particular, waved many a banner and pennon, the trophies of battles won, and kingdoms overthrown. But amongst and above them all, a long lance displayed a shroud, the banner of Death, with this impressive inscription— "SALADIN, KING OF KINGS—SALADIN, VICTOR OF VICTORS —SALADIN MUST DIE." Amid these preparations, the slaves who had arranged the refreshments stood with drooped heads and folded arms, mute and motionless as monumental statuary, or as automata, which waited the touch of the artist to put them in motion.

Expecting the approach of his princely guests, the Soldan, imbued, as most were, with the superstitions of his time, paused over a horoscope and corresponding scroll, which had been sent to him by the hermit of Engaddi when he departed from the camp.

"Strange and mysterious science," he muttered to himself, "which, pretending to draw the curtain of futurity, misleads those whom it seems to guide, and darkens the scene which it pretends to illuminate! Who would not have said that I was that enemy most dangerous to Richard, whose enmity was to be ended by marriage with his kinswoman? Yet it now appears that a union betwixt this gallant Earl and the lady will bring about friendship betwixt Richard and Scotland, an enemy more dangerous than I, as a wild-cat in a chamber is more to be dreaded than a lion in a distant desert.—But then," he continued to mutter to himself, "the combination intimates, that this husband was to be Christian.—"Christian?" he repeated, after a pause,—"That gave the insane fanatic star-gazer hopes that I might renounce my faith! but me, the faithful follower of our Prophet, me it should have undeceived. Lie there, mysterious scroll," he added, thrusting it under the pile of cushions; "strange are thy bodements, and fatal, since even when true in themselves, they work upon those who attempt to decipher their meaning, all the effects of falsehood. —How now! what means this intrusion?"

He spoke to the dwarf Nectabanus, who rushed into the tent fearfully agitated, with each strange and disproportioned feature wrenched by horror into still more extravagant ugliness, —his mouth open, his eyes staring, his hands, with their shrivelled and deformed fingers, wildly expanded.

"What now?" said the Soldan, sternly.

"*Accipe hoc!*" groaned out the dwarf.

"Ha! sayest thou?" answered Saladin.

"*Accipe hoc!*" replied the panic-struck creature, unconscious, perhaps, that he repeated the same words as before.

"Hence, I am in no vein for foolery," said the Emperor.

"Nor am I further fool," said the dwarf, "than to make my folly help out my wits to earn my bread, poor helpless wretch! —Hear, hear me, great Soldan!"

"Nay, if thou hast actual wrong to complain of," said Saladin, "fool or wise, thou art entitled to the ear of a King. Retire hither with me;" and he led him into the inner tent.

Whatever their conference related to, it was soon broken off by the fanfare of the trumpets, announcing the arrival of the various Christian princes, whom Saladin welcomed to his tent with a royal courtesy well becoming their rank and his own; but chiefly, he saluted the young Earl of Huntingdon, and generously congratulated him upon prospects, which seemed to have interfered with and overclouded those which he had himself entertained.

"But think not," said the Soldan, "thou noble youth, that the Prince of Scotland is more welcome to Saladin, than was Kenneth to the solitary Ilderim when they met in the desert, or the distressed Ethiop to the Hakim Adonbec. A brave and generous disposition like thine hath a value independent of condition and birth, as the cool draught, which I here proffer thee, is as delicious from an earthen vessel as from a goblet of gold."

The Earl of Huntingdon made a suitable reply, gratefully acknowledging the various important services he had received from the generous Soldan; but when he had pledged Saladin in the bowl of sherbet, which the Soldan had proffered to him, he could not help remarking with a smile, "The brave cavalier, Ilderim, knew not of the formation of ice, but the munificent Soldan cools his sherbet with snow."

"Wouldst thou have an Arab or a Curdman as wise as a Hakim?" said the Soldan. "He who does on a disguise must make the sentiments of his heart and the learning of his head accord with the dress which he assumes. I desired to see how a brave and single-hearted cavalier of Frangistan would conduct himself in debate with such a chief as I then seemed; and I questioned the truth of a well-known fact, to know by what arguments thou wouldst support thy assertion."

While they were speaking, the Archduke of Austria, who stood a little apart, was struck with the mention of iced sherbet, and took with pleasure and some bluntness the deep goblet, as the Earl of Huntingdon was about to replace it.

"Most delicious!" he exclaimed, after a deep draught, which the heat of the weather, and the feverishness following the debauch of the preceding day, had rendered doubly acceptable. He sighed as he handed the cup to the Grand Master of the Templars. Saladin made a sign to the dwarf, who advanced and pronounced, with a harsh voice, the words *Accipe hoc!* The Templar started, like a steed who sees a lion under a bush beside the pathway; yet instantly recovered, and to hide, perhaps, his confusion, raised the goblet to his lips—but those lips never touched that goblet's rim. The sabre of Saladin left its sheath as lightning leaves the cloud. It was waved in the air,—and the head of the Grand Master rolled to the extremity of the tent, while the trunk remained for a second standing, with the goblet still clenched in its grasp, then fell, the liquor mingling with the blood that spurted from the veins.[1]

There was a general exclamation of treason, and Austria, nearest to whom Saladin stood with the bloody sabre in his hand, started back as if apprehensive that his turn was to come next. Richard and others laid hand on their swords.

"Fear nothing, noble Austria," said Saladin, as composedly as if nothing had happened, "nor you, royal England, be wroth at what you have seen. Not for his manifold treasons;—not for the attempt which, as may be vouched by his own squire, he instigated against King Richard's life;—not that he pursued the Prince of Scotland and myself in the desert, reducing us to save our lives by the speed of our horses;—not that he had stirred up the Maronites to attack us upon this very occasion, had I not brought up unexpectedly so many Arabs as rendered the scheme abortive;—not for any or all of these crimes does he now lie there, although each were deserving such a doom; —but because, scarce half-an-hour ere he polluted our presence, as the simoom empoisons the atmosphere, he poniarded his comrade and accomplice, Conrade of Montserrat, lest he should confess the infamous plots in which they had both been engaged."

"How! Conrade murdered?—And by the Grand Master, his sponsor and most intimate friend!" exclaimed Richard. "Noble Soldan, I would not doubt thee; yet this must be proved, otherwise——"

"There stands the evidence," said Saladin, pointing to the

[1] Note II.—Death of Grand Master of the Templars.

terrified dwarf. "Allah, who sends the fire-fly to illuminate the night season, can discover secret crimes by the most contemptible means."

The Soldan proceeded to tell the dwarf's story, which amounted to this.—In his foolish curiosity, or, as he partly confessed, with some thoughts of pilfering, Nectabanus had strayed into the tent of Conrade, which had been deserted by his attendants, some of whom had left the encampment to carry the news of his defeat to his brother, and others were availing themselves of the means which Saladin had supplied for revelling. The wounded man slept under the influence of Saladin's wonderful talisman, so that the dwarf had opportunity to pry about at pleasure, until he was frightened into concealment by the sound of a heavy step. He skulked behind a curtain, yet could see the motions, and hear the words, of the Grand Master, who entered, and carefully secured the covering of the pavilion behind him. His victim started from sleep, and it would appear that he instantly suspected the purpose of his old associate, for it was in a tone of alarm that he demanded wherefore he disturbed him?

"I come to confess and to absolve thee," answered the Grand Master.

Of their further speech the terrified dwarf remembered little, save that Conrade implored the Grand Master not to break a wounded reed, and that the Templar struck him to the heart with a Turkish dagger, with the words *Accipe hoc*—words which long afterwards haunted the terrified imagination of the concealed witness.

"I verified the tale," said Saladin, "by causing the body to be examined; and I made this unhappy being, whom Allah hath made the discoverer of the crime, repeat in your own presence the words which the murderer spoke; and you yourselves saw the effect which they produced upon his con·cience."

The Soldan paused, and the King of England broke silence :—

"If this be true, as I doubt not, we have witnessed a great act of justice, though it bore a different aspect. But wherefore in this presence? wherefore with thine own hand?"

"I had designed otherwise," said Saladin ; "but had I not hastened his doom, it had been altogether averted, since, if I had permitted him to taste of my cup, as he was about to do, how could I, without incurring the brand of inhospitality, have done him to death as he deserved? Had he murdered my father, and afterwards partaken of my food and my bowl, not a hair of his head could have been injured by me. But enough of him—let his carcass and his memory be removed from amongst us."

The body was carried away, and the marks of the slaughter obliterated or concealed with such ready dexterity, as showed that the case was not altogether so uncommon as to paralyse the assistants and officers of Saladin's household.

But the Christian princes felt that the scene which they had beheld weighed heavily on their spirits, and although, at the courteous invitation of the Soldan, they assumed their seats at the banquet, yet it was with the silence of doubt and amazement. The spirits of Richard alone surmounted all cause for suspicion or embarrassment. Yet he, too, seemed to ruminate on some proposition, as if he were desirous of making it in the most insinuating and acceptable manner which was possible. At length he drank off a large bowl of wine, and, addressing the Soldan, desired to know whether it was not true that he had honoured the Earl of Huntingdon with a personal encounter.

Saladin answered with a smile, that he had proved his horse and his weapons with the heir of Scotland, as cavaliers are wont to do with each other when they meet in the desert, and modestly added, that though the combat was not entirely decisive, he had not, on his part, much reason to pride himself on the event. The Scot, on the other hand, disclaimed the attributed superiority, and wished to assign it to the Soldan.

"Enough of honour thou hast had in the encounter," said Richard, "and I envy thee more for that, than for the smiles of Edith Plantagenet, though one of them might reward a bloody day's work.—But what say you, noble princes; is it fitting that such a royal ring of chivalry should break up without something being done for future times to speak of? What is the overthrow and death of a traitor, to such a fair garland of honour as is here assembled, and which ought not to part without witnessing something more worthy of their regard? How say you, princely Soldan—What if we two should now, and before this fair company, decide the long-contended question for this land of Palestine, and end at once these tedious wars? Yonder are the lists ready, nor can Paynimrie ever hope a better champion than thou. I, unless worthier offers, will lay down my gauntlet in behalf of Christendom, and, in all love and honour, we will do mortal battle for the possession of Jerusalem."

There was a deep pause for the Soldan's answer. His cheek and brow coloured highly, and it was the opinion of many present, that he hesitated whether he should accept the challenge. At length he said, "Fighting for the Holy City against those whom we regard as idolaters, and worshippers of stocks and stones, and graven images, I might confide that Allah would strengthen my arm; or if I fell beneath the sword of the Melech Ric, I could not pass to Paradise by a more glorious death. But Allah has already given Jerusalem to the true believers, and it were a tempting the God of the Prophet to peril, upon my own personal strength and skill, that which I hold securely by the superiority of my forces."

"If not for Jerusalem, then," said Richard, in the tone of one who would entreat a favour of an intimate friend, "yet for the love of honour, let us run at least three courses with grinded lances."

"Even this," said Saladin, half smiling at Cœur de Lion's affectionate earnestness for the combat, "even this I may not lawfully do. The master places the shepherd over the flock, not for the shepherd's own sake, but for the sake of the sheep. Had I a son to hold the sceptre when I fell, I might have had the liberty, as I have the will, to brave this bold encounter; but your own Scripture sayeth, that when the herdsman is smitten, the sheep are scattered."

"Thou hast had all the fortune," said Richard, turning to the Earl of Huntingdon with a sigh. "I would have given the best year in my life for that one half-hour beside the Diamond of the Desert!"

The chivalrous extravagance of Richard awakened the spirits of the assembly, and when at length they arose to depart, Saladin advanced and took Cœur de Lion by the hand.

"Noble King of England," he said, "we now part, never to meet again. That your league is dissolved, no more to be reunited, and that your native forces are far too few to enable you to prosecute your enterprise, is as well known to me as to yourself. I may not yield you up that Jerusalem which you so much desire to hold. It is to us, as to you, a Holy City. But whatever other terms Richard demands of Saladin, shall be as willingly yielded as yonder fountain yields its waters. Ay, and the same should be as frankly afforded by Saladin, if Richard stood in the desert with but two archers in his train!"

The next day saw Richard's return to his own camp, and in a short space afterwards, the young Earl of Huntingdon was espoused by Edith Plantagenet. The Soldan sent, as a nuptial present on this occasion, the celebrated TALISMAN; but though many cures were wrought by means of it in Europe, none equalled in success and celebrity those which the Soldan achieved. It is still in existence, having been bequeathed by the Earl of Huntingdon to a brave knight of Scotland, Sir Simon of the Lee, in whose ancient and highly honoured family it is still preserved;[1] and although charmed stones have been dismissed from the modern Pharmacopœia, its virtues are still applied to for stopping blood, and in cases of canine madness.

Our story closes here, as the terms on which Richard relinquished his conquests are to be found in every history of the period.

Note III.—The Lee Penny.

NOTES

Note I. p. 79.—SIR THOMAS MULTON OF GILSLAND

He was a historical hero, faithfully attached, as is here expressed, to King Richard, and is noticed with distinction in the romance mentioned in the Introduction. At the beginning of the romance, mention is made of a tournament, in which the king returns three times with a fresh suit of armour, which acted as a disguise; and at each appearance some knight of great prowess had a sharp encounter with him. When Richard returned the second time, the following is Mr. Ellis's account of his proceedings:—" He now mounted a bay horse, assumed a suit of armour painted red, and a helmet, the crest of which was a red hound, with a long tail which reached to the earth; an emblem intended to convey his indignation against the heathen hounds who defiled the Holy Land, and his determination to attempt their destruction. Having sufficiently signalized himself in his new disguise, he rode into the ranks for the purpose of selecting a more formidable adversary; and delivering his spear to his squire, took his mace, and assaulted Sir Thomas de Multon, a knight whose prowess was deservedly held in the highest estimation. Sir Thomas, apparently not at all disordered by a blow which would have felled a common adversary, calmly advised him to go and amuse himself elsewhere; but Richard, having aimed at him a second and more violent stroke, by which his helmet was nearly crushed, he returned it with such vigour that the king lost his stirrups, and, recovering himself with some difficulty, rode off with all speed into the forest."—ELLIS's *Specimens*, pp. 193, 194.

Note II. p. 310.—DEATH OF GRAND MASTER OF THE TEMPLARS

The manner of the death of the supposed Grand Master of the Templars was taken from the real tragedy enacted by Saladin upon the person of Arnold or Reginald de Chatillon. This person, a soldier of fortune, had seized a castle on the verge of the desert, from whence he made plundering excursions, and insulted and abused the pilgrims who were on their journey to Mecca. It was chiefly on his account that Saladin declared war against Guy de Lusignan, the last Latin king of the Holy Land. The Christian monarch was defeated by Saladin with the loss of thirty thousand men, and having been made prisoner, with Chatillon and others, was conducted before the Soldan. The victor presented to his exhausted captive a cup of sherbet, cooled in snow. Lusignan, having drank, was about to hand the cup to Chatillon, when the Soldan interfered. "Your person," he said, "my royal prisoner, is sacred, but the cup of Saladin must not be profaned by a blasphemous robber and ruffian." So saying, he slew the captive knight by a blow of his scimitar.—See GIBBON's *History*.

Note III. p. 314.—THE LEE PENNY

Since the last sheet of this volume of the present edition was printed off, a kind friend has transmitted the following curious document, by which it would appear that the alleged virtues of the Lee Penny had at one time given uneasiness to our Presbyterian brethren of Clydesdale.

(Copy)

Extract from the Assemblie Books at Glasgow, anent the Lee Penny stone.

Apud Glasgow, 21 *of October*.[1]

SYNOD. SESS. 2.

QUHILK day, amongest the referries of the Brethren of the Ministry of Lanark, it was proposed to the Synod that Gavin Hamilton of Raploch had pursueit an Complaint before them against Sir James Lockhart of Lee, anent the superstitious using of an Stone, set in silver, for the curing of deseased Cattle, q^{lk} the said Gavin affirmed could not be lawfully usit, and that they had deferrit to give ony decisionne thairin till the advice of the Assemblie might be had concerning the same. The Assemblie having inquirit of the manner of using thereof, and particularly understood, be examination of the said Laird of Lee and otherwise, that the custom is only to cast the stone in some water, and give the deseasit Cattle thereof to drink, and that the same is done without using any words, such as Charmers and Sorcereirs use in thair unlawfull practices; and considering that in nature thair are many things seen to work strange effects, whereof no human wit can give a reason, it having pleast God to give to stones and herbs a speciall vertue for healing of many infirmities in man and beast, advises the Brethren to surcease thair process, as therein they perceive no ground of Offence, and admonishes the said Laird of Lee, in the using of the said stone, to take heid that it be usit hereafter with the least scandle that possibly maybe. Extract out of the Books of the Assemblie holden at Glasgow, and subscribed at thair command

M. ROBERT YOUNG, Clerk to the
Assemblie at Glasgow.

---

[1] The year is unfortunately not given; but the Sir James Lockhart named in the extract was born in 1596, and died in 1674.

GLOSSARY

A', all.

Abacus, mystic wand of office.

Abouten, about.

Accipe hoc (Lat.), 'take this.'

Alan, wolf-greyhound.

Arblast, crossbow.

Ascalon, a town on the Syrian coast, about 90 miles from Acre.

Astrolabe, an astronomical instrument for finding the position of the sun and stars.

Atabals, drums of the Moors.

Azrael, Angel of Death.

Baaren-hauters, bear-flayers.

Bagnio, bathing-house, brothel.

Balsora and Bagdad, formerly great Eastern cities on the River Tigris.

Bandog, literally a bound or chained dog, hence a watch-dog, such as a mastiff.

Barb, a Barbary (Morocco) breed of horse.

Bayard, a famous horse of incredible speed.

Beau-Seant, a term applied to the Templars' black-and-white banner.

Benedictio Domini sit vobiscum (Lat.), 'May the blessing of the Lord be with you.'

Benevent, a city of Southern Italy.

Bezant, byzant, a gold coin of Byzantium, worth about 9s. sterling.

Bickering, tremulous.

Blondel, a famous French troubadour or minstrel who attended King Richard.

Bode, message.

Bolt, arrow of a crossbow.

Borak, the fabulous winged beast, with the face of a man, emeralds for eyes, and jewels on its wings, said to have carried Mahomet to the seventh heaven.

Brewis, broth.

Brigandine, a coat of mail formed of leather covered by thin iron plates.

Buckler, a small shield to ward off blows.

Burgonet, a kind of helmet.

Buskins, a kind of half-boot laced to the ankle.

Ca', call.

Caaba, a temple within the great mosque at Mecca.

Caftan, a Turkish vest or under-coat.

Caitiffs, mean despicable fellows.

Camiscia, a light, loose linen robe.

Cangiar, dagger.

Caracoled, pranced and wheeled about.

Carff, carved.

Casque, helmet.

Certes, certainly, in truth.

Chappe, military watch-cloak.

Charegites, religious enthusiasts.

Coil, disturbance, confusion.

Confiteor (Lat.), 'I confess.'

Copartment, separate portion of an apartment.

Corselet, armour worn on the front of the body.

Costards, heads.

Cote, to pass, outpace.

Couchant, lying down, couching.

Culpa mea (Lat.), '(It is) my fault.'

Curtal-axe, a short sword or cutlass.

Cymar, a woman's loose light garment.

Despardieux, probably a stronger form of 'Par Dieu!' (By God!).

Devoir, duty, act of civility, respect.

Dial-stone, sun-dial.

Divan, a council, an assembly.

Doit, a Dutch coin, worth about half a farthing.

Donative, gift, present.

Doublet, a kind of short coat.

Dromond, dromedary, ship of the largest size.

Dudgeon-dagger, small dagger.

Eldritch, weird, wild, strange.

El Hadgi, the pilgrim.

El Hakim, the physician.

Emir, chieftain, ruling prince.

Engaddi, a place in the wilderness of Judah, near the middle of the western shore of the Dead Sea.

Errant Knight, a knight who sets out in search of adventures for the display of his skill, prowess, and generosity.

Esquires, shield or armour-bearers in attendance on a knight.

Fakir, a Hindu ascetic or mendicant.

Falchion, a short, broad, curved sword.

Febrifuge, a medicine to allay fever.

Fet, fetched.

Flayn, flayed.

For-bar, forbade, interdicted.

Frangistan, the country of the Franks.

Front-stall, the metal covering of a horse's brow.

Fytte, part, section.

Gab, retail incredible stories.

Gear, property, possession.

Genista, broom.

Ghittern, a stringed instrument like a guitar.

Giaour, unbeliever, a Turkish term of contempt for Christians and others who are not Mohammedans.

Gnew, gnawed.

Gorget, piece of armour to defend the neck.

Grace-cup, the toast drunk after grace at the conclusion of a feast.

Gramarye, witchery, devil's work.

Guerdon, reward.

Hadgi, pilgrim, one who has made the pilgrimage to Mecca.

Haick, a mantle or cloak.

Hakim, physician.

Hamako, a madman looked upon as inspired.

Hauberk, shirt of mail composed of steel rings interwoven.

Heathenesse, those parts of the world which do not profess Christianity, heathendom.

Hem, them.

Hoff-narr, Court fool.

Houri, black-eyed beautiful girl, a nymph of paradise.

Imaum, the official who recites the prayers in a mosque and leads in the worship.

Isaack, a famous Arabian musician of the ninth century.

Issa ben Miriam (Arabic), 'Jesus, son of Mary.'

Javelin, a kind of spear, five and a half feet long.

Jean d'Arc, or Acre, a town on the Syrian coast, about 8 miles north of Jerusalem.

Jerkin, a short close-fitting jacket.

Jerrid, a wooden javelin.

Kaisar, the emperor of the Holy Roman Empire.

Kebla, the direction of the Moslem temple at Mecca, toward which the faithful turn when at prayer.

Khirkhah, the torn robe of the Dervishes.

Kurdis·an, the country of the Kurds, a region to the east of Eastern Asiatic Turkey.

Kyrie Eleison, Lord have mercy!

Lance-knechts, spearmen, lancers.

Largesse, gifts of money rudely exacted from a stranger.

Lauds, the earliest hour of prayer among the religious orders.

Leasing, falsehood, lying.

Leech, physician.

Lelies, war-cries of the Mahommedans.

Libbard, old form of leopard.

Liege, lord or vassal, according to the context.

Liegeman, faithful follower.

Lingua franca, the language of the Mediterranean coasts, being a corrupt form of Italian.

Livand, living.

Los, praise, renown.

Lough, laughed.

Louted, bent, inclined.

Lyme-hound, a dog held in a leam or strap, a boar-hound.

Mahound, a corruption of Mahomet.

Mangonel, a large catapult for hurling stones.

Marabout, a religious devotee and fanatic, much given to sorcery, of North Africa.

Maravedi, a copper coin of Spain, worth rather less than a farthing sterling.

March-parts, the Marches on the Borders of Scotland and England.

Maronites, a tribe of Eastern Christians.

Maugis, a famous medieval magician, one of Charlemagne's paladins.

Mazer, a large drinking-bowl.

Melech Ric, King Richard.

Meynie, retinue, household.

Minaret, lofty Mahommedan mosque-turret, from which the people are summoned to prayer.

Minne-singers, German minstrels of the twelfth and fourteenth centuries.

Mollahs, the Mohammedan clergy who interpreted the Koran.

Morion, a kind of open helmet without visor.

Mortier, velvet riding-cap of a knight when far removed from action.

Moussa ben Amram, 'Moses, son of Amram.'

Muezzin, a Mohammedan official who calls the hours of prayer.

Murrain, plague.

Nierenstein, Rhenish wine of Nierstein, in Hesse-Darmstadt.

Nooning, a repast at noon.

Omrah, an officer of the court.

Oo, one.

Oriflamme, the ancient royal banner of France.

Orvietan, antidote for poison.

Palfrey, small horse suitable for a lady; also one for state occasions.

Panoply, complete armour from head to foot.

Partes, divide.

Partisan, a long-handled weapon, combined spear and battle-axe.

Pavesse, buckler of unusual size covered with steel-plating.

Paynim, pagan.

Pennoncelle, a small pennon or flag at the end of a lance.

Periapt, an amulet, a charm.

Pilau, a dish of mutton boiled with rice, butter, and spices.

Planta genista, the broom plant.

Podagra, the gout.

Popinjay, a parrot, a fop.

Pouncet-box, a box to hold perfumes.

Prophet, Mohammed or Mahomet, founder of the Moslem religion.

Propone, propose.

Proveditore, a high officer of state in Venice.

Provost, Scottish mayor, or chief magistrate.

Quhilk (contracted q^{lk}), Scots for 'which.'

Rashid, an observatory.
Rhenish, Rhine wine.
Rote, a kind of guitar.
Rustan, a Persian hero.

Salim olicum, peace be with you!
Samite, a rich medieval silk fabric.
Santon, an Eastern saint.
Sarbacanes, tubes through which to blow small poisoned darts.
Sathanas, Satan.
Scapulary, outer vestment of the Roman Catholic clergy when officiating at Mass.
Secret, coat of linked mail worn under the corslet.
Seraglio, Turkish harem.
Shalm, a kind of clarinet or hautboy.
Sirrahs, a contemptuous corruption of Sirs.
Slee, slay.
Slot, track, footprints.
Soldan, an old form of Sultan.
Soote, sweet.
Spruch-sprecher, speech-maker.
Stradiots, light cavalry recruited by the Venetians in Albania and the Morea.
Styptic, a medicine to check the flow of blood from a wound.
Surcoat, a long, loose, sleeveless robe worn over armour and usually embroidered with the wearer's coat of arms.
Suzerain, a feudal lord or baron.
Swart vis, black face.
Swet a stound, perspired for an hour.
Swilke, such like.
Swyche, such.

Tabard, a long sleeveless upper coat, now worn only by heralds.
Tabour, a kind of kettledrum.
Talisman, some object such as a stone or piece of metal, with or without mystic signs inscribed on it, which through virtue it possesses has power to heal diseases, afford protection, avert misfortune, etc.; an amulet or charm.

Tarriance, delay.
Tecbir, the formula 'Allah akbar,' i.e. 'God is great.'
Techiness, easily-provoked anger.
Tent a wound, to examine or probe a wound.
Thafurs, barefooted zealots who followed the Crusaders to the Holy Land.
Timbrels, drums like tambourines.
Tolpach, astrakhan cap of lamb's wool, worn by the Tartars.
Tophet, a valley near Jerusalem, once the scene of idolatrous worship, later used as a place for incinerating refuse, and hence regarded as symbolical of hell.
Tourney, tournament.
Trained, enticed away by a trick or stratagem.
Tristrem, Sir Tristrem, a knight of King Arthur's Round Table.
Trouveurs, poets and minstrels akin to the troubadours of the Middle Ages.
Trudentes, lawless camp-followers.

Ulemat, a name given to Moslem Church officials.
Uprist, resurrection.

Varlets, followers of a knight.
Venerie, woodcraft, or the rules of the chase, so important during the Middle Ages.
Vera Crux (Lat.), 'True Cross.'
Vert, a game forest.
Vis, the face, visage.
Vizor, the front movable piece of a helmet with holes for seeing and breathing.

Weal, good, welfare.
Wenden, to go.
Wete, knoweth.
Widdersins, from left to right.
Wode, beside himself, insane.
Woodcraft v. Venerie.
Wrest, key for tuning the harp.

Yacoum, a tree of the infernal regions that grows heads of demons instead of fruit.

Yemen, a fertile part of Southern Arabia.

Ysop, Aesop, the fable writer.

Zechin, a Turkish coin, worth about 5s. 6d. sterling.

Zenana, the women's apartments.